KT-210-021

James Hamilton-Paterson's work has been translated into many languages. He is a highly acclaimed author of non-fiction books, including *Seven-Tenths*, *Three Miles Down* and *Playing with Water*, as well as *America's Boy*, a study of Ferdinand Marcos and the Philippines. *Gerontius,* his first novel, won the Whitbread Award, while his most recent, *Loving Monsters* (2001) was praised by the *Sunday Telegraph* as 'tantalising, erudite and ingenious'. He lives in Italy.

Further praise for *Cooking with Fernet Branca*:

'A hilarious farce . . . What is crucial to a piece like this is tone of voice, and with both Gerald and Marta we know that we're in safe hands from the beginning . . . The effect is of a classic Fred and Ginger duet: bitter-sweet and stylish, slightly edgy, expertly choreographed, moving forward at a perfect tempo, and never putting a foot wrong.' Michael Dibdin, *Guardian*

'Refreshingly, the humour of *Cooking with Fernet Branca* rarely derives from the Italian setting. It is not a pastiche of the 'Tuscan sun' genre, and there are no droll olive-picking or goat-milking moments. Instead, as in the *Diary of a Nobody* or *A Confederacy of Dunces*, the effect is achieved almost entirely through the comic magnetism of a single character.'
Times Literary Supplement

'The elegant language, witty asides and vivid observation are memorable, and the recipe for 'Alien Pie' will probably prove unforgettable . . . I have admired other books from this skilful, highly original writer. If ever there were a novelist who does *not* churn out the same book over and over again, or even repeat himself at all, it is James Hamilton-Paterson.' *Literary Review*

JAMES
HAMILTON-PATERSON

Cooking
with Fernet Branca

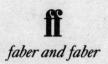

faber and faber

First published in 2004
by Faber and Faber Limited
3 Queen Square London WC1N 3AU
This paperback edition first published in 2005

Typeset by Faber and Faber Limited
Printed in England by Mackays of Chatham plc, Chatham, Kent

All rights reserved

© James Hamilton-Paterson, 2004

The right of James Hamilton-Paterson to be identified as
author of this work has been asserted in accordance with Section 77
of the Copyright, Designs and Patents Act 1988

*This book is sold subject to the condition
that it shall not, by way of trade or otherwise, be lent, resold,
hired out or otherwise circulated without the publisher's prior consent
in any form of binding or cover other than that in which it is
published and without a similar condition including this
condition being imposed on the subsequent purchaser*

A CIP record for this book
is available from the British Library

ISBN 0-571-22091-6

10 9 8 7 6 5 4 3 2 1

To Lyn Rogers and Peter Field

'I'm interested in things that are none of my business,
and I'm bored by things that are important to know.'
    – Calvin (Bill Watterson, *Calvin & Hobbes* strip cartoon, 1994)

Gerald

1

If you will insist on arriving at Pisa airport in the summer you will probably have to fight your way out of the terminal building past incoming sun-reddened Brits, snappish with clinking luggage. They are twenty minutes late for their Ryanair cheapo return to Stansted ('I said *carry* your sister's bloody bag, Crispin, not drag it. If we miss this flight your life won't be worth living . . . '). Ignoring them and once safely outside, you can retrieve your car in leisurely fashion from the long-term park and hit the northbound motorway following the 'Genova' signs. Within a mere twenty minutes you are off again at the Viareggio exit. Don't panic: you are not destined for the beach which stretches its tottering crop of sun umbrellas like poison-hued mushrooms for miles of unexciting coastline. No. You are heading safely inland through the little town of Camaiore.

Abruptly the road starts to climb into the Apuan Alps: great crags and slopes thick with chestnut forest and peaks the colour of weathered marble – which is mostly what they are. After some tortuous hairpins you will come to the village of Casoli, whose apparent surliness is probably owing to its having watched outlying portions of itself disappear into the valley below every few years in winter landslides. Carry on through and up. More forest, broken at the hairpins by spectacular views. Restored stone houses with Alpine fripperies tacked on (shutters with heart-shaped holes) and Bavarian-registered BMWs parked outside. Keep going: the world is still sucking at your heels but you are leaving it behind. Up and up, until even the warbling blue Lazzi buses are deterred and turn round in a specially asphalted area. Not far beyond is what looks like a cart track. Follow this for a hundred metres and you will come upon an area known as Le Roccie

3

and the house I have rashly bought. Even more rashly, I am trying to make it habitable while at the same time attempting to earn a living by writing a commissioned book too ludicrous for further mention. The view, though, is amazing. As we British are so fond of saying, the three most important things about a house are Position, Position and Position. (For some reason Americans call it 'location'.) The British say this with a wise smile, as if imparting an original insight culled from years of experience and reflection rather than repeating a stale piece of businessman's wisdom they have heard in a dozen pubs. Whatever you think of this particular house, you have to admit it's got Position coming out of its ears. Apart from a portion of stone roof barely visible through the trees some way off, there is solitude in every direction.

You're not tired from your journey? Well, *I* am; so I set about preparing a little something suited to what will be the grand panorama from the terrace once the prehistoric privy overhanging the gulf has been removed. Great swathes of mountainside. Between them, lots of blue air with circling buzzards and a distant view of Viareggio and the sea. On a clear day the small island of Gorgona is visible; on a really clear day, I'm told, Corsica. So what shall it be? Something at once marine and disdainful, I fancy, to show how much we care for local *frutti di mare* and how little for rented beach umbrellas and ice creams. Here we are, then:

Mussels in Chocolate
———◆———

You flinch? But that's only because you are gastronomically unadventurous. (Your Saturday evening visits to the Koh-i-Noor Balti House do not count. These days conveyor-belt curry is as safe a taste as Mozart.)

◆

Ingredients

2 dozen fresh mussels, shelled and cleaned
Good quantity olive oil

Rosemary
Soy sauce
100 gm finely grated Valrhona dark chocolate

◆

You will need quite a lot of olive oil because you are going to deep-fry the mussels, and no, that bright green stuff claiming to be Extra-Special First Pressing Verginissimo olive oil with a handwritten parchment label isn't necessary. Anyway, how can there possibly be degrees of virginity? Olive oil snobs are even worse than wine snobs. You're far better off, not least financially, with ordinary local stuff that has been cut in the traditional fashion with maize oil, machine oil, green dye etc. Heat this until small bubbles appear (before it begins to seethe). Toss in a good handful of fresh rosemary. Meanwhile, dunk each mussel in soy sauce and roll it in the bitter chocolate. (Unlike the oil, the chocolate must be of the best possible quality. If it even crosses your mind to use Cadbury's Dairy Milk you should stop reading this book at once and give it to a charity shop. You will learn nothing from it.) Put the mussels in the deep-fryer basket and plunge them into the oil. Exactly one minute and fifty seconds later lift them out, drain them on kitchen paper and shake them into a bowl of pale porcelain to set off their rich mahogany colour. Listen to how agreeably they rustle! Most people are surprised by their sound, which is not unlike that of dead leaves in a gutter. This is because of the interesting action of soy sauce on chocolate at high temperatures. Now pour yourself a cold glass of Nastro Azzurro beer and, mussels to hand, find a seat from which the privy can't be seen. Gaze out over your domain and reflect on the Arrivals queue at Stansted airport where even now the mulish Crispin is taking it out on his sister by treading down the backs of her trainers. Enjoy.

2

The day has dawned bright in every sense and I am making good progress up a ladder painting the kitchen – the most important room in the house – in contrasting shades of mushroom and eau de Nil. Anyone can do the white-walls-and-black-beams bit, but it takes aesthetic confidence and an original mind to make something of a Tuscan mountain farmhouse that isn't merely Frances Mayes. It also takes a complete absence of salt-of-the-earth peasants and their immemorial aesthetic input. It is all rather heartening and as I work I break cheerfully into song. I have been told by friendly cognoscenti that I have a pleasant light tenor, and I am just giving a Rossini aria a good run for its money when suddenly a voice shouts up from near my ankles: 'Excuse, please. I am Marta. Is open your door, see, and I am come.' I break off at 'tutte le norme vigenti' and look down to find a shock of frizzy hair with an upturned sebaceous face at its centre.

This is ominous, but I descend with an exemplary display of patience. Michelangelo, busy with Adam's finger on the Sistine Chapel ceiling, would have been similarly miffed to be told he was wanted on the phone. The stocky lady is apologetic and claims to be my neighbour, feels strongly we should be acquainted, has come bearing an ice-breaking bottle of Fernet Branca. My heart sinks during these explanations and still further as I find myself sitting at the table sniffing cautiously at the Fernet, a drink whose charm is discreeter even than that of the bourgeoisie, being black and bitter. I'd always thought people only ever drank it for hangovers. Seeing no way out I admit to being Gerald Samper while refraining from adding 'One of the Shropshire Sampers', which, while true, would obviously be wasted on her. 'I disturb,' says Marta confidently as I cast my eyes towards the unfinished ceiling. 'No, no,' I lie feebly. 'One can always do with a

6

break.' I am kicking myself for having underestimated the threat posed by that glimpse of stone roof some way off. Months ago my specious little agent, Signor Benedetti, told me it belonged to a house lived in only for a month each year by 'a mouse-quiet foreigner'. Having made sure he didn't mean a fellow Briton I dismissed the whole matter and, indeed, had practically forgotten that my splendid tranquillity might be compromised by a neighbour.

What can I say now about this person who, during most of a long, hot summer and for much of the ensuing long, hot autumn, becomes the principal bane of my life, or *primo pesto*, as I expect they say in Chiantishire? In this role Marta faces formidable competition from Italian bureaucrats and enforcers of building regulations, but she outclasses them easily. I gather she comes from somewhere in that confused area between the Pripet Marshes and the Caucasus. My ignorance of geography, I ought to point out, knows no bounds and hence no frontiers.

'Is that Poland?' I hazard.

Marta looks profoundly shocked.

'Er . . . Belarus?'

She thumps the table. Her bangles jangle.

'Sort of Latvia way?' I try despairingly.

She fixes me with large dark eyes which, I now notice, have fragments of glittery material adhering to their upper lids. 'No,' she says fiercely, 'I am Voyde, puremost of blood. Yes! We of Voynovia are Christians when Slavs and Russians still barbars much more even than today. I tell you history. Many five hundred years . . .'

I tune out at this point, staring sadly at my empty glass and feeling the paint splashes drying on my arms. In a kind of rueful dull rage I curse myself for weakness. Who but an over-mannerly British gent would allow himself to be interrupted in the middle of painting a ceiling in order to be harangued in his own kitchen by a perfect stranger speaking abominable English? Weak, weak, weak. Well, this time the worm is going to turn. I am regrettably going to have to take a very firm hand with Marta, if only she will stop talking. Fragments of her speech snag my attention, like carrier-bags floating down the River Vistula. Apparently Voynovia is one of those enclaves that was on the fringes of the Holy Roman Empire and ruled for centuries by Margraves or Electors or something, clinging to its ethnic identity through thick and thin: thick being represented by the Soviet era and thin by the post-Soviet era. The more Marta talks, the more I can see every excuse for those unsung Margraves' despotism. I wish to acquaint her with knouts.

'So we will becoming close here, you and me,' she is saying. 'I love you British queens and kings tradition. I want to learn. I want to learn you all of Voynovia, the fooding number one of all. Voynovian fooding best in all Europa, best in all of world. Is . . . *mm.*' She kisses her fingertips in a frightful gesture probably copied from a Maurice Chevalier film. 'But you will learn me other things, yes, Gerree?'

For a chill moment I imagine her voice suggests a leer, then reject this as absurd. I am surely not especially good-looking, although discerning people naturally recognize that a certain refinement of manner and mind can more than compensate for a trivial lack of Adonis-like qualities. I scarcely think this frizzy-haired frump slurping Fernet Branca at my kitchen table at ten o'clock in the morning is even on nodding terms with refinement.

'Tonight you will come at dinner.'

'Oh, no, er . . .' I hear myself temporizing. I am thinking of the treat I have promised myself – a dish of poached salmon with wild cherry sauce which I modestly claim is not the least successful of my little inspirations. 'No, perhaps not tonight.'

'OK, tomorrow,' she says with the implacability of a JCB sinking its scoop in a trench. 'You may bringing your wife.' It is her parting shot. This time there can be no doubt about the leer, which lingers on the air behind her like the Cheshire Cat's grin. She obviously doesn't believe I have a wife. And why not, might I ask? I could easily have one. At any moment during the past hour a wholesome creature like Felicity Kendal in *The Good Life* could have wandered down the stairs, spattered with distemper, to counter the Fernet with a bottle of home-made nettle wine. It is entirely presumptuous of Marta to make such an airy assumption.

I wearily pick up the paintbrush which has stiffened into a birch-twig besom. As I climb back up the ladder I notice that quite half the contents of the bottle she brought have gone. Rather disgusting, the way she tucked into her own present. I resume painting. It is hot up here and the ceiling seems to sway a little. I do not at all feel like singing now. The truth is, this neighbourly intrusion has had an upsetting effect on me and I really feel I shall have to go and lie down. This I do; and such is the strain that Marta's visit has produced in me that I fall unconscious for several hours and awake with a headache to find much of the day has vanished. I fully intended to give the recipe for my salmon-in-cherries dish here because like any true creative artist I am eager for a little sliver of immortality. But alas the moment has passed and immortality will have to be postponed.

3

Next morning I awake in a spirit of mischief, more than a little goaded by the thought of having let myself in for dinner with the ghastly Marta while under the influence of Fernet Branca. Being properly brought up, I'm unable to go out even on unwelcome social occasions without bearing a gift of sorts, so I shall have to think of something. Thank goodness I'm going by myself. Sometimes in the company of others I find a disagreeable spirit of competitiveness kicks in and each person is shamed into spending rather more than he would have wished. This is a historically established syndrome, of course. One Magus going to Bethlehem would probably have sprung for a box of After Eights. Three Magi on the same trip found themselves laden with gold, frankincense and myrrh and bitterly contemplating their overdrafts.

So to the mischief. What shall it be? Rossini – come to my aid! And he does, bless him. Only a few bars into 'Vedi la data indicata' I remember he was himself an excellent cook who invented several original dishes (Tournedos Rossini being only one) and had a predilection for ice cream. Ice cream, eh? It being hot in Tuscany in late June, even up here in the mountains, I reason one can't go far wrong bearing home-made ice cream to a dinner. I further reason that Marta requires something punitive to remind her not to make a habit of these neighbourly invitations. So what better than

Garlic and Fernet Branca Ice Cream

————◆————

Ingredients

15 large cloves of garlic
150 gm granulated sugar
4 tablespoons cold double cream
¼ pint Fernet Branca

◆

Put the garlic and the sugar into a blender and empty over them the remains of a bottle of Fernet Branca with paint splashes on its label. This will yield a curious compound the colour of Iodex, which older readers will remember as an embrocation made from seaweed extract that sporty schoolboys used to rub on their little stiffnesses. Whip the cream, but only until it starts to thicken. Then stir in the Iodex mixture. An attractive tawny shade emerges while the garlic note brings tears to the eyes. Excellent. Pot it and leave in the fridge for an hour. Then turn it into your ice cream freezer and proceed as usual. When going out to dinner with someone you would be relieved to learn had died during the course of the day, remove the ice cream as you leave the house. It will have the consistency of a brick but by 10 p.m. will have softened just enough to become the evening's *pièce d'occasion*. If after that she ever invites you round again, you are in very much worse trouble than you thought. Oh, and a spray of fennel embedded in the surface looks well.

By now I am in an ice cream sort of mood so with the fennel right to hand on the chopping board I knock up a batch of Fennel and Strawberry Ice Cream for myself. This particular *glace à la Samper* is definitely one of my entries for the immortality stakes. It is a sensational combo and I urge you to try it out on friends and make them guess what it is. They may think of Pernod because of the aniseedy taste, yet if you do make Pernod and Strawberry Ice Cream it tastes quite different. Fennel and Strawberry actually tastes *green*, while looking puce (use the stalks and foliage rather than the bulb).

All these preparations have made the morning whiz by. Marta's fault, of course. Not only did she cause me to lose most of yesterday but much of today has now vanished on her behalf. A light lunch is called for, with a pause for reflection. This leads to the discovery that the kitchen ceiling is still not finished so at two o'clock I reluctantly pick up my brushes and once more drag myself up the ladder. It is appallingly hot up there among the beams and rafters and it takes all my resolve not to have a little nap and wait for it to cool down. But being made of stern stuff I doggedly paint on until, by around five-thirty, the ceiling is finished and resplendent. The work has also had the effect of making me feel entirely on top of the Marta situation. You know how it is with DIY and circular thought. Either an irritating fragment of tune keeps repeating itself in time with your brush strokes or else you become fixed into long, protesting sorts of argument with absent people. The increasing acerbity of these one-sided conversations is surely due to fury at having to waste yet more hours of one's rapidly dwindling stock of time on a job one would cheerfully pay a menial to do if only one had the money. In any case, by the time the ceiling is finished I have inwardly shown Marta the door out of my life some sixty-three times. Sometimes she went with a set, tense face and at other times she flew out in a storm of tears and hair. In every case, though, she left. Somewhere in the middle of these harangues I remembered another ingredient that I might have included in tonight's ice cream. Bullied cooks, from the grandest hotels to army cookhouses, are tradition-ally rumoured to include various bodily secretions in the food as a way of asserting themselves and having the last laugh. I can quite see that a glimpse through the kitchen door of some sniffy old tyrant in bombazine tucking into a beauti-ful creamy mayonnaise that contains a dash of one's own sperm could well bring satisfaction. However, for the moment Marta is safe. Poor woman – I only wish to discour-age her. Such excesses will be held in abeyance for use only when the situation has degenerated considerably.

At seven-thirty on the dot I present myself at her back door bearing my patent (and uncontaminated) ice cream.

'*Gerree!*' she squeals in welcome. Her abbreviation of my name is something else I am going to have to correct PDQ. Meanwhile she plants Voynovian kisses on both my cheeks and forehead, leaving a dreadful smell. She must have bought her cologne off a barrow in Viareggio. It is the exact female equivalent of Brut aftershave and I have to go and wash it off immediately on the pretext that the ice cream container has made my hands sticky. When I return to her kitchen she presses not a mere glass but a stoup of Fernet Branca into my hands and folds my nerveless fingers around it.

4

Well, all right – I can see I'm going to have to come clean about my source of income. It's pretty humiliating but at least I can console myself with the thought that the Queen makes a living out of cutting ribbons while the Archbishop of Canterbury is paid to address the Supreme Ruler of the Universe publicly in a loud voice as if they were old friends. In comparison with them, being a successful ghost-writer for sporting heroes seems positively intellectual.

How I came to take up this career is not a long story but it's a very sad one, so I shan't tell it. As for the books themselves, things get steadily worse. My present commission is definitely grislier than the previous one, which was the autobiography I wrote for a recent downhill skiing champion. It is grislier even though the procedure remains identical. Their agents fix it up, you see. All I have to do is follow these champions around trying to get them to talk sense for ten minutes at a stretch in between their practice sessions, advertisement shoots, magazine interviews and copulations. The most ironic phrase in this ghosting business is 'in-depth'. In order to talk to the skier I had to hang around the foyers of chalet-style hotels in places like Klosters and somewhere in Colorado whose name slips my memory. That was bad enough, given *Glühwein* and *raclette*, but young Luc turned out to be the sort of person who actually wore the brands he advertised. Can you imagine someone who believes his own endorsements? He was always festooned with chunky action watches and après-ski outfits in nonexistent colours with his own name on them. I kept wanting to tell him that at school even I had been obliged to wear clothes bearing my own name but we had been well-enough bred to have the tags sewn on inside. In addition he wore an aftershave that made me faint, something I had never done before. His manager put it down to the heat in the room.

Anyway, it was grim, although the resultant book sold very well indeed. This was partly because I invented for this skier an aphrodisiac to account for his legendary off-piste (and several times on-piste) behaviour. The recipe is now too well-known for me to repeat here. All I will say is that Luc Bailly eventually came to believe that this potion was indeed the secret of his prowess. Inevitably, he consumed so much it brought on gravel and the end of his career. But at his peak he did have sensational thighs that ballooned out above the silly little knees that skiers have, worn to mere bony hinges with all that flexing.

Yet as I said, my present job has turned out even worse. The subject is the thrice World Champion Formula One racing driver Per Snoilsson, better known as 'The Flying Swede', if you can visualize such a thing. Snoilsson is a vicious young man who unquestionably caused the death of François Bidet at Monaco two years ago when the Flying Frenchman sailed off into the harbour, stopped flying abruptly and drowned in his cockpit right beneath the keel of a standby rescue launch. (Very sad. Charming smile.) All Snoilsson got was a caution and some points knocked off, which didn't matter a jot to him since he had a lead of forty championship points over his nearest rival, who by a strange chance happened to be François Bidet.

Apart from being vicious Per is a consummate cretin. How could it be otherwise when he makes a living out of driving round in circles at breakneck speed? Still, I would rather he didn't kill himself until after my book comes out. Then we can have an updated memorial edition with pictures of the fatal crash. Those *really* sell, probably because the tragic thing about modern motor racing is that fatalities are becoming all too rare. In any case, we have now had six sessions together and I have learned all there is to know about young Per that is printable. No sense in going on milking the same cow in the hope that one day it will fill your pail with champagne. Our sessions included one in a private jet and another in a factory on an industrial estate near Weybridge where he sat in a puddle of chemical foam to make a mould of his hardbitten little bum, surely the first time it had ever made any sort of impression. They said it was for a driving seat. I ask you. Anyway, my job is to turn all our taped sessions into a book, hence my need to buy a remote, quiet house with a view and access to some good delicatessens. I've already written practically all of it; over the next week I just need to come up with a good title. Oh dear, oh dear, these are not ironic people. The more brainless a book's intended readership, the more rib-nudgingly cute the title has to be. Christmas shoppers – the trade my publisher brazenly aims at – prefer 'titles they can relate to', in the words of the editor. 'What you want is a *Life in the Fast Lane* sort of thing,' she suggested with her usual deadpan originality. Obviously, most of these gruelling clichés have long since been used for the autobiographies of previous world champions and one has to hunt around for leftovers. Off the top of my head (as we say in the trade) I proposed *The Absolute Pits* and *Pistons at Dawn* and was a little hurt by how coolly they were received. Maybe they, too, have already been used. Ever since the factory episode when I was able to observe young Per and an even younger mechanic moulding each other's bottoms I have thought of him as 'The Chequered Fag', and this is now my working title.

It's not that I'm snobbish about these sports personalities, you understand. Not in the least. They, too, have a living to make. No, I'm sceptical about the leech industry that clings to them and demands biographies of people who are far too young to have done any real living yet. How can you make someone of twenty-four sound interesting when nothing has happened to him except years of punishing training supervised by a ruthless parent? These kids are just money-spinning automata whom beady people have spent the last decade winding up, and now their sole duty is to go buzzing along their allotted tracks generating headlines and excreting piles of gold for their backers. One feels distantly sympathetic but it does make them less than dazzling company. In fact, my mention of champagne just now reminds me that the only interesting thing I have learned in the last eighteen months of following in the dusty wake of the Flying Swede has nothing to do with him at all. Had you ever wondered why one of those famous houses like Moët et Chandon would permit what looks like a jeroboam of its Premier Cru Brut des Bruts to be shaken up and squirted to waste from a podium by spotty boys who clearly prefer Coke? Well, I have. It's hardly an advertisement for the precious exclusivity of their product. I mean, 'The Champagne Top Drivers Squirt' is not an upmarket selling image, is it? In order to satisfy my curiosity on the point I have now managed to gain entry to several of those hallowed *caves* where cobwebs lie thick and ancient acolytes move slowly through the cool hush with candles, deftly turning the bottles in their productive slumber. My great discovery was that nowadays there is a small concrete bunker near the entrance, an annexe labelled *Dernier Cru Grands Prix Réserve* containing specially large bottles kept exclusively for sporting events. Carefully guarded to ensure that none gets out onto the open market and into the hands of serious champagne drinkers, they contain very sweet Asti *spumante* imported from Piedmont with further addition of carbon dioxide and chemicals to produce the right explosive gush of bubbles for the cameras. I'm glad to have got to the bottom of that little secret.

I beg your pardon? What other little secret? Oh, last night's *dinner*. I had completely forgotten. Of course it went without a hitch. Why shouldn't it? Though I must say Voynovian cuisine is pretty peculiar and I do have a slight headache today.

5

Things are looking good. Two days have now gone by since our dinner and nary a squeak out of Marta. I'm counting this as a culinary triumph: the ingenious use of food as an offensive weapon. Garlic ice cream with Fernet Branca may lack subtlety but it is highly effective and I feel that by giving you the recipe I have placed a pacifist's version of Clint Eastwood's famous .44 Magnum in your hands. 'Make my evening, Marta,' I might have said. And to my amazement she did, taking not one but three massive helpings. If I were a good neighbour I would have dropped in on her by now to make sure she is still alive. But I'm not, so I haven't.

I was somehow unsurprised to discover that she lives in a pigsty. You never did see such a mess. She seems to have bought or rented the house in the condition it was in when its last peasant inhabitants emigrated or else died on the premises. For a start, it has that damp smell of bricks and flagstones laid on bare earth. There are several huge old chests designed for storing bread, blankets and flour. Stuffed in among these is an upright piano with one of those names no one has ever heard of: Petrof, or something. All her living seems to take place in the kitchen, a low cave with a beamed and blackened fireplace big enough to roast a yeti. It is also full of burst chairs with clothes on them. I was glad to notice she appeared to have no cats about the place. I have nothing at all against these animals but in my experience if there's one around, roguish girls like Marta may make compulsive pussy jokes. One is embarrassed for them.

'For you, Gerree, all Voynovia fooding tonight,' she said as we eventually reeled to our seats at the kitchen table, having first pitched off bundles of sheets. By then we had finished most of a bottle of Fernet Branca and even the electric light was beginning to have a brownish tinge. With a flourish she plonked before me a gross sausage the colour of rubberwear and as full of lumps as a prison mattress. It was a little larger than those things in Bavaria that just fit into bowls the size of chamber pots.

'Is *shonka*,' I think she said, resting her breasts on the table on either side of her own plate. Smiling weakly, I made the good guest's obligatory '*mm*' noises and gingerly poked it with the point of my knife. There was the sound of a boil being lanced. A spurt of boiling fat shot across the table and even on that late June evening my spectacles misted over. The contents of the sausage, bright red with paprika, lay there before me like an anatomy lesson. 'My sister Marja she send from Voynovia. We eat like this, Gerree.' Cheekily she speared one of the lumps on my plate with her fork, dipped it into a pot of black treacle and held it playfully to my lips.

Mechanically I opened my mouth and allowed it entry but thereafter there was nothing mechanical about my chewing. It was exactly like trying to cross a hot beach barefoot. When I say black treacle I only mean that was what it looked like, though I'm damned if it really wasn't mainly molasses. What the rest was, I cannot say, but my impressions included saffron, pickled walnuts and lavender, with perhaps a pinch of pluto-nium. The only thing missing, surprisingly, was Fernet Branca.

Once one mouthful of *shonka* and sauce was down a kind of local anaesthesia set in and the next forkful was marginally less lethal. And you know how it is, *l'appetito vien mangiando* and all that, it wasn't long before I had eaten a good two inches of the thing, with a mere yard to go. My attention was nearly monopolized by the food so maybe I was less careful than I'd intended to keep the conversation firmly on small talk. Middle-sized talk (i.e. more than the weather and less than Life) accompanied much of my *shonka* which, as I pro-gressed, increasingly resembled in its effects the hemlock they gave poor Socrates to drink. A curious numbness began in my extremities and slowly converged on the heart. I wanted very much to lie down and found myself musing about famous last words. It was clearly out of the question on all counts to ask Marta to remember to sacrifice a cock for me. Irrelevancies came and went in my mind like brilliant little plankton drift-ing in and out of a tide pool. I suddenly realized *The Bends* would be rather a good title for Snoilsson's autobiography, especially since he'd told me he was going to take up champ-ionship depth-diving when he quit motor racing.

'I'm sorry?' I said through a knobbly mouthful of cysts.

'You are funny man, Gerree,' she replied. I noticed she had hardly touched her own *shonka* which anyway was a fraction the length of mine. 'I am saying I hear you singing from here in your house.'

'Oh? Well, yes, I suppose I do like to sing as I work. Here a bit of Rossini, there a snatch of Bellini, you know how it is.'

'Very loud your voice. I am thinking is strain.'

'Trained? My voice? Oh no. Just as it always was, I'm afraid. Most kind of you, though.' Judging by the general peasant mess of her house, to say nothing of the *shonka*, it was safe to assume she didn't know Italian opera from a hole in the ground. I wondered idly what sort of music she was used to in Voynovia. No doubt wild knees-up stuff with zithers and balalaikas and drunken whoopings when at the end everyone bursts into tears and hugs each other, full of vodka and nameless Slavic melancholy.

'And your work, Gerree, what your work?'

'I'm a writer, Marta.'

'Writer murder?'

'Not murder stories, no, although I *am* getting an idea for one. Biographies mainly.'

'Ah, Gerree, you and me artists.'

'Well . . .'

'But yes. I am songer.'

'A singer?'

'No. I am making songs.'

She shoots me such a look of mischief through the general frizz hanging in front of her face that a plump tumour I was about to dunk in the treacle remained in mid-air, arrested and quivering on my fork. My imagination leaped forward like a pricked hen and I could foresee the loom of *intime* evenings around her Iron Curtain upright. The tumour was jerked off my fork and fell into my glass. A great splash of Fernet Branca drenched the salt, the table, a pile of books, my shirt-front and her frizzy mane. It was like one of those cutaways from Jack Hawkins' face on the bridge as we catch the sea astern of his destroyer erupting in a massive tuft of blasted water as the first depth-charge explodes.

'I'm awfully sorry,' I said, trying to hoik the lump out of the glass. But my manual dexterity had gone haywire, paralysed by *shonka* and drink. I shot a nervous glance at the hair with the gleaming nose poking through it. It was quivering, shaking, suddenly blown apart by a great woof of laughter. She wiped her hair and her face with a blotched napkin and slumped back in her chair, helpless.

'Very funny man,' she repeated when she could speak. 'I want to see more and more of you.'

Oh God.

'And now, Gerree, we try your ice cream. Is very special fooding.'

'Cuisine,' I said curtly. 'We say "cuisine", not "fooding". "Fooding" doesn't exist in English.' For I was reckless now, determined that my natural good manners shouldn't let me in for whatever designs she had on me. Still, those very manners oblige me grudgingly to admit that she not only downed her garlic ice cream like a trooper but promptly called for more. By that stage our taste buds were surely dead and between us we polished it off. Thereafter I remember nothing except an achingly Socratic sensation of coldness which was explained only when I woke myself with a series of awesome farts to find that I was lying on the ground by my front doorstep with dawn breaking all around.

6

There is something radically wrong with Tuscan bread. Frankly, it's a disgrace: the one thing to disfigure an otherwise classic cuisine. Even Italians from other regions make ribald remarks about it – like for instance that it's the only bread in the world to emerge from the oven already stale. This is merely a slight exaggeration. Tuscan bread is non-fattening once it is over three hours old because cutting a slice requires energy equal to the slice's calorific value. (This is henceforth known as Samper's Law.) It is a feature the Italian slimming industry should do more to promote. It now occurs to me that when Robert Graves coined his appallingly sentimental image of 'women good as bread' he may have had Tuscan bread in mind, in which case he meant the far more likely women hard as nails.

The reason I mention this is because in the days following that first dinner with Marta I had a great craving for bland nursery food and found a good use for Tuscan bread in bread-and-milk: little bowls of pap I ate slowly with a spoon that trembled. My complacent simile that had likened Garlic and Fernet Ice Cream to a .44 Magnum had been wrong. One never saw Clint Eastwood incapacitated by his own gun's recoil.

For several days I poke listlessly through the typescript of *The Chequered Fag*, correcting typos and still trying to think up an acceptable title. Like all racing drivers Per Snoilsson is constantly besieged by girls he laconically refers to as 'pit bunnies' or 'screwdrivers': part of the perks of hi-glam living. The readership wants plenty of detail about that, of course, and I have dutifully packed the text with titillating vignettes of post-race celebrations. These include the obligatory showers wearing nothing but the victor's wreath, also the champagne-soaked knickers draped over silver ice buckets. There is even a description of the Pit Stop Game as played by three Ferrari drivers in a Monaco hotel suite. This had involved each driver pretending to be a car coming into the pits and being besieged by a team of girls whose duty was to attend to various parts of his body and have him away (*aliter dictum* 'back in the race') in record time. Pointless to apologize for such unedifying episodes, they're what readers want. But they don't help with the title. I rack my Fernet-damaged frontal lobes. Why couldn't this stupid Swede have had the enterprise to be something unusual, like that American driver who is an evangelical preacher between races and for whom the title *Rev* would have been a natural? Then I remember Per's having once allowed some medical researchers to cover his body with electrodes which transmitted intimate physiological details during a race in Brazil. He informed me proudly that his buttocks had reached a temperature of 41 °C. Bingo! *Hot Seat!*

Oh yes, I like that. It suggests the weight of responsibility, danger, even lethality, as well as gruelling conditions. At a more private level it brings to my mind indentations made in quick-setting foam at a Surrey works. The phrase is so familiar I wonder if it's already in use as a title but then think the editor can worry about that. *Hot Seat!* is good enough for me. Exclamation marks sell books! so I make some copies of the disk and take one down to Camaiore, where I consign it to the post office. Another job jobbed. In the market I find some plump and yearning langoustines and on another stall a refrigerated tray containing pieces of *lontra*. Farmed, of course: you can't get wild *lontra* these days for love or money and I have tried both. Still, irresistible. I buy one and a half kilos for a sum that will appreciably dent my next advance, but what the hell. On the way back I pick up my mail from the bar and by the time I'm home my spirits have soared. Not only have I finished the book and got it out of the house but up here among the trees and crags the summer's day that was sweltering at sea level is cooled by altitude to a pleasant warmth. I also realize my headache has gone, the last traces of *shonka* having been purged from my body.

This calls for some celebratory cooking. The chance proximity in the market of the two major items I have bought prompt my culinary ingenuity to come up with an ideal marriage between river and sea, as it were. I see . . . yes . . . a *cold* dish, a race-day picnic-out-of-the-Bentley's-boot sort of dish, a perfect complement to mood and weather. I come up with an inspired variant of a little something I once pioneered in the water meadows near Oxford:

Otter with Lobster Sauce

------◆------

Before you rush off to try this dish for yourself, a caveat. Otter is a far subtler meat than rabbit (for instance), as no less an authority than Gavin Maxwell attested – and he was referring to sea otter at that. It should be cooked with the greatest care to preserve its uniquely delicate riverine flavour: like that of kingfishers fed on watercress. It is easily ruined by brutal treatment. Banish Clint Eastwood metaphors to another universe. Imagine a dish prepared by the Water Rat in *The Wind in the Willows* in a mood of wistful hyperaesthesia and you will have some idea of the sensitivity you will need to bring off this masterpiece:

◆

Ingredients

1.5 kg otter chunks
8 tablespoons sunflower oil
8 medium nasturtium leaves, chopped
1 sliced shallot
150 ml dry white wine
$\frac{1}{4}$ teaspoon sugar
1 saffron stamen (really and truly: one single thread)
300 gm lobster meat
1 anchovy fillet
1 tablespoon tiny capers
1 teaspoon olive oil
1 teaspoon Fernet Branca
Mayonnaise

◆

Wash the otter well in cold running water and pat dry with paper towels. Ironically, given the animal's natural habitat, otter is a dry meat and to keep it succulent it needs to be cooked in just enough liquid as will cover it. The chunks are put into an iron pot together with the oil, nasturtium leaves (2 medium sprigs of watercress are nearly as good), the sliced shallot, saffron, sugar and white wine. Add as much water as required to cover the meat. *Now remove the meat* and bring the remainder of the ingredients to a boil with the lid on. Add the otter chunks and, when it has all come back to the boil, put the lid back on leaving a crack the thickness of a credit card. Reduce heat to a slow simmer for twenty-six minutes. Remove pot from stove, close lid tight and allow the otter to cool in its own juices until it can be put in the fridge.

Meanwhile prepare and boil the langoustines in the usual way. When cool enough to handle, shell them. Put the shells, claws and legs into a blender together with the anchovy, capers, Fernet and olive oil and reduce to a fine paste. Reserve. Then make about half a pint (300 ml) of mayonnaise. Incidentally, this is the only recipe I know that is associated with a curse. Two acquaintances who tried to make the dish died within the month, one in Buckinghamshire and the other in Somerset. By the quirkiest of mishaps both fell into rivers in spate and vanished into mill-races. The cleric's body was found three weeks later, much disfigured. The drama teacher was never seen again. On enquiring I discovered that each had used commercial mayonnaise purchased in a supermarket for this recipe, so there is some justice in this world after all, even if a bit on the lenient side. Certainly the Bishop should have known better. No decent cook gets to heaven by way of Hellman's. For present purposes you should use half olive oil and half grape seed oil (mix them beforehand) because we don't wish to drown the flavour of the otter. Use the yolks of two eggs – ducks' for preference because they add richness without pungency. Now fold the langoustines' meat together with the paste from the blender carefully but thoroughly into the mayonnaise. You may need to add a smidgin of salt, depending on how salty the capers and anchovy were.

When everything is cold doff the otter's hat and you will find him sitting happily in a little savoury jelly. Bone his meat gently and lay it on your finest serving dish together with the jelly. Around it spread the mayonnaise mixture and garnish in a suitably restrained fashion. Slices of hardboiled thrush eggs, though fiddly to peel and cut, look exquisite arranged in shell patterns. Dedicated foodies with patience, eyesight and steadiness of hand may do the same using kingfisher eggs, as I did in the prototype of this dish. (I here salute my friends in Thames Conservancy, without whose help I should never have established – let alone obtained – the right ingredients). Then pop the dish in the fridge for at least six hours. Serve with reverence, a panoramic view and a crisp white wine.

So cheerful do I become while preparing this wondrous dish that I break into song – Ennio's exhilarating aria 'Non disperdere nell'ambiente, cara' from *Lo stronzolo segreto*. It's when Nedda is threatening to throw away the little flask of tears she has wept for him and he begs her not to. By all means the tears (he sings), for roses will spring up wherever they fall to earth; but not the antique Venetian bottle I bought for you . . . This may, in fact, be the earliest example of environmentalism in opera. As I whip the mayonnaise and sing away in my newly painted kitchen I become aware from time to time of some jarring noises off. Finally, I pause to listen. There is no mistaking that discordant plonking: Marta is taking her piano for a trial gallop. My hand freezes aloft, mayonnaise falling from the fork in disregarded clumps. 'Aha,' I think. 'So that's it, huh?' Grimly I resume beating. The plonking continues too, distant though quite intrusive, as no doubt intended.

That damned house agent, the weaselly Mr Benedetti. My 'quiet foreign neighbour' was to be here just one month a year, eh? It is a situation that calls for immediate investigation.

Marta

7

Dearest Marja

Greetings from your exiled sister, 'who holds precious thoughts of you & the family as it were a wren's egg in her palm . . .' Do you remember? That's how Grandmother Vrilja taught us we should always start our letters, all in that old High Voyde style. There was something else, too, about Mt Sluszic continuing to stand guard over our clan & lands, but I forget it exactly. Perhaps that was the correct formula for ending letters, not starting them?

So here is a progress report on my 'crazy damned career', as our beloved father calls it. I do hope things have become easier now I've left. I dread to hear that he's still going around the castle in a black cloud, kicking the dogs & shouting at poor Mili. Anyway, I shall leave it to your discretion how much of my letters you actually read to him. His not being a reading man is rather fortunate in some ways, ek ni? (as the woodcutters say.) Our menfolk hold our clan's fortunes in their hands, not flimsy pieces of paper – it's true! But it's also true we women can write things among ourselves that the men have no need to know.

I have settled in perfectly well here, as I knew I should – thanks in no small part to the bank account dear Ljuka arranged for me in Viareggio. How is he, by the way? Are his clothes still full of Makarov pistols when you hug him? Our little brother! And he used to be so delicate, too. He certainly came back from the army a changed boy. I think this place would please you, although Ljuka pretends to find it peasant-like & infra dig in order to give himself the airs befitting someone of his rising eminence in the clan. Secretly, though, I know he's charmed: it reminds us of that house at Bolk we loved so much on those fishing holidays, even though there's no river here. But there are great crags & views as well as silences patrolled by eagles. I feel sure I shall fulfil my ambition here & do some commendable work &, despite Father's misgivings, will bring honour to our family name. I've already had such a nice letter from Piero Pacini welcoming me to Italy & saying he can't wait to get started. That's the sort of encouragement a girl needs! He's terribly famous here – the film director of the moment.

Despite that, I'm afraid I've allowed myself to become a bit distracted – no, diverted would be more accurate – by the oddest neighbour imaginable. Yes, I know what you're going to say: that plausible little house agent Signor Benedetti told Ljuka & me the other house was owned by a foreigner who was only ever here one month in the year. Well, we may yet need to have recourse to some lesson-teaching where that rogue is concerned. Anyway, this neighbour is an Englishman with a little paunch & one of those strange empty trouser-seats that always suggest an amputated bottom. They may be an English speciality. His name is Gerald Samper & he's truly comic. I thought it would be neighbourly to pay him a visit & introduce myself, so I picked up a bottle & went over. I found him up a ladder, very pink and sweaty. He was obviously put out by the interruption, quite enough to make me want to stay for a bit. Late thirties, at a guess, but there's something elderly about him so I could believe ten years older. Almost certainly dudi, I should say, as well as alcoholic, for he seized the bottle (it was an aperitif called Fernet Branca – a rather insipid version of that galasiya our hunters drink) with the offhand alacrity of the seasoned toper & started pouring. You know how it is with real drinkers – that way they have of always pouring about an inch more into their own glass than into everyone else's as if by accident? It's a dead giveaway.

Well, I mustn't be unfair to poor Gerald – though don't ask me why. I must admit things aren't helped by my inadequate English but something about him makes it even worse than usual & I can hear myself sounding like a caricature foreigner. Too infuriating but I suppose it's not his fault. Really, though, I suspect he's the sort of person you can fathom without words. I mean to say, he's just the complete dudi, like that sad teacher who tried to follow

Ljuka around until Father had Captain Panic pay him a visit. Gerald sings as he does his housework: squally arias from, I should think, wholly imaginary Italian operas. At any rate I don't recognize them. But even without understanding everything he says I'm sure I get his gist: petty & snobbish with a kind of dandyish disdain. Dandyish! With that bottom & the thinning hair! Poor love! He was sitting there pretending he'd never heard of Voynovia to try & make me feel like a nobody from Central Europe, can you imagine? I've no idea what he does for a living, although he claims to write a bit. I've got him down as one of those dilettante types who dabble in this & that.

I do wish you could have seen us, Mari. There I was at his kitchen table, taking the occasional sip & trying to make bright, cheerful conversation. And there he was, knocking back this Fernet stuff which, after half a bottle, began to have a noticeable effect. Funniest of all, every time I reached over to refill his glass or our hands touched by accident he shied away as though I might launch myself at him, pin him to the floor & ravish him. It made me laugh a lot & I was tempted to try it just to see his horror. I'm sure it would have blown all his fuses.

I can hear you chiding me. But you know me, Mari: I'm more mischievous than cruel. All the same, these are passages you'd do well to spare Father if ever you read him bits of this letter. So what else about the estimable Mr Samper? Inevitably, he's a cookery queen as well as an opera queen and a DIY queen. In keeping with that grand old maxim of ours, 'Beneath kindness a fortress will crumble', I invited him to dinner. He put up some token resistance but dutifully turned up with a huge bowl of ice cream he'd made for the occasion. Rather sweet of him. He'd put himself out so I felt well disposed towards him, even a bit touched, & resolved to be on my best behaviour throughout the evening, not to scare him with sudden provocative gestures etc. My one oversight was to have forgotten that I'd run out of wine & hastily had to open some more Fernet Branca. Luckily I'd been given an entire case by the bank manager who came up to give me my cheque book, did I tell you? I now wonder if Ljuka had a

hand in that. Anyway, what could I give my visitor to eat but
your shonka & pavlu? An authentically Voyde meal, a little
European gastronomy lesson. But oh, it so reminded me of home
I had tears in my eyes – dear Mari, I'd have known that shonka
anywhere in the world, it was so unmistakably from our estate.

Poor Gerald started by being nervous & I suppose that's why he
ate & drank too much. I haven't met enough Englishmen to know
whether this is a national trait or not, their being unable to leave
half-filled plates and bottles on a dinner table without feeling com-
pelled to empty them as though they were a reproach to their manhood. Gerald's manhood became steadily more & more like those
Potemkin suburbs the Soviets put up in Voynograd: a rickety
façade against which a dog dared not lift its leg for fear of collapse.
He giggled. He became shrill. Eventually he ceremoniously
brought on his bowl of ice cream & burst into song. As a matter of
fact the ice cream wasn't at all bad, though a bit bland. A sort of
mild herbal flavour. But by then he was so drunk he simply went on
eating it until he'd finished that, too.

At length I became alarmed he might pass out in my kitchen so I
took him for a walk ostensibly to look at the night sky (which was
indeed magnificent & rimmed on all sides with mountain outlines).
I craftily edged him back towards his own house where he stared at
the sky, winced, belched, apologized, laughed uproariously & said
'Next time you're my guest.' Then he added in a puzzled voice: 'I
didn't really say "breast", did I?' & fell to the ground like a
stunned peewit (as the Bunki say). So I left him there. But I know
he survived because I've since heard him bawling arias in his
kitchen. Really, he's so awful I'm growing quite fond of him
except that it may be difficult to work against the noise.

Now I shall stop, Marja dearest, with all sorts of messages to the
family & a fervent prayer that Mt Sluszic will indeed continue to
stand guard over our clan & lands.

Much love
Marta

32

8

This morning I go down to Viareggio to meet Sasi Vlas, who has come over from Florence for the day to act as interpreter for me. She's married to a local lawyer and acts as consul, cultural attaché and general representative of Voyde affairs in that city. A handsome lady with the narrow forehead so characteristic of the Bun region – a first impression confirmed as soon as she opens her mouth (a showcase of Soviet-era dentistry). Oh, that Bunki accent we Voyde mock so much at home! Yet on the concourse of an Italian station it's a welcome and nostalgic sound. Here we are, all alone in a foreign world, allies under the skin, holders of the same shit-brown Voynovian passports as well as of *permessi di soggiorno* . . . Actually that is not quite how Sasi sees it, as soon becomes clear. Married to an Italian, fully fluent and acculturated with two small children, she probably has to overcome an instant's irritation – even *embarrassment* – at this hick from her home-land before remembering who Father is and that I'm doing the music for a Piero Pacini film. She better had remember, too; so she's pleasant and helpful. In due course we meet up with a couple of Pacini's step'n'fetchits and drive out as arranged to view the prospective set.

The coast road from Viareggio heading south towards Tirre-nia and Livorno is scrubby and piney and agri to the left. On the right, once the estuary's boatyards and marinas have thinned out, are beach resorts. These are faintly hysterical in their down-market but pretentious rivalry, their walls of shrubbery and grandiose gateways and names in lightbulbs reading 'Eden' and 'Nirvana'. It is the first time this landlocked girl from middle Europe has actually set foot on one of these golden rivieras, but I can't say it's much different from the beaches near Danzig where Marja and I were once taken. I suppose the sun's hotter here but the dockyard cranes in the distance look the same. However, I'm expected to gaze seaward with due awe.

According to Sasi we have only stopped 'to give me my bearings', but I suspect it was more to teach me my place.

On we go for several more kilometres of resort architecture. It must be bleak here in winter. The shops and restaurants and awnings – even the very pavements – seem designed to echo to the slip-slopping of beach sandals and the inanities of holiday conversation. The signposts suggest we are nearly in Tirrenia when the contemporary beach lots suddenly stop and semi-jungle takes their place behind chain-link fencing. This is dotted with decaying white fascist villas: immense concrete ruins through whose drunken shutters and windowless embrasures come glimpses of sweeping Hollywoodian staircases. It is at one of these villas that we fetch up. The rusty padlocked gates are already open and inside, among the rioting shrubs that have taken over the driveway, is parked a bright red racing car. Beside this stands a handsome young man wearing dark glasses on the top of his head, every inch a *fils à papa*. He is introduced to me as Filippo, Pacini's son. He is courteous and apologizes with plausible sincerity for his father's absence. The great Piero is in America, receiving a prize. One of those unavoidable things in the life of a film director. Fame has its tiresome obligations.

So there we all stand in the shade of a holm oak like time-travellers dumped in the nineteen thirties while Filippo explains in English far better than mine something of the history of this jungled lot. Apparently these shattered villas once formed part of Pisorno Studios (the mixture of Pisa and Livorno was probably always a bad omen, he adds with a smile that implies a famous historic rivalry). Pisorno was an earlier, Tuscan version of Rome's Cinecittà where in the days of Mussolini a good many films were shot. Most of these fell into the category known as 'white telephone' films, so called because they inhabited a fascist fantasy world of good living peopled by haut-bourgeois layabouts. After the war Cinecittà pretty much took over the Italian film industry and since the sixties no one has been able to agree what to do with

Pisorno's remains. The hundreds of acres of abandoned real estate by the sea are periodically earmarked for a projected cultural centre, a commercial centre, a theme park, even a nature reserve, but the plans have always fallen through. Maybe only fascism ever had the power to make Pisans and Livornese agree to anything and in its absence there is only indecision, stalemate and a golf course. Now where the white telephones once stood on gold-trimmed tables beside canopied double beds are the discarded condoms, cracked syringes, cigarette butts and other leavings of intruders.

'But see for yourself,' Filippo ends, taking my arm and leading us through vertical glare across a terrace rumpled with rotting concrete. The salt air of seventy years has penetrated to its reinforcing rods, puffing them up with rust.

Oh, perfect! Scabrous! Fabulously derelict! 'What a place to shoot a film in,' I say appreciatively to Filippo. 'All those decadent fascist ghosts undermined by real decay.' At least that's what I try to say and I think he gets the gist. Sasi has a disapproving air, perhaps at being linguistically sidestepped or to make it clear that these ballroom and dining room floors crunching with broken glass and dried turds (animal? human?) are very far from her own natural habitat. I'm taking bets that the phones in her Florence apartment are white. Filippo meanwhile is clearly pleased I'm responsive to the place. It all feels like a good omen and the almost undreamable dream of writing the score for a Piero Pacini film suddenly begins to be a practical proposition. We wander about the house, each in her or his own world, pleased by the generations of graffiti and prompted to speculation by incongruities. Why would anyone ever have used one of these rooms for storing bales of cardboard egg racks, hundredweights of them, soggy and rotting?

When by sheer fortune Piero Pacini had seen *Vauli Mitronovsk* after it won Voynovia's Gold Stoat in 1999, he had liked my score enough to write asking if I would care to do the music for a film he was going to make. I stared unbelievingly at the letter, then ran from room to room of the castle showing it to everyone I met, except of course to Mili who is illiterate. Father had never heard of Piero Pacini, predictably. Bringing him around took weeks of cajoling and careful work by both Marja and myself. He said the modern Western cinema is notoriously decadent, full of bad language and gross indecency and run by drug-addict *dudis*. It would be a completely unacceptable occupation for one of his stable-boys, let alone for his own daughter. Meanwhile Pacini wrote me more letters outlining a proposed plot I made sure Father never got wind of. It was about a group of left-wing liberals full of Green zeal who start a fishing commune. They are united by their loathing for the corruption of Italy's Christian Democrats and a determination not to let the environmentally friendly way of life they are pioneering become contaminated by deep-frozen convenience foods and high-tech fishing practices. This struggle is made the more piquant because the father of one of them is a fervent *democristiano*, a great friend of the former prime minister, Giulio Andreotti. He owns fleets of trawlers and factory ships which have made him a multi-millionaire as well as notorious for having wiped out a particular pod of dolphins that were being observed by a nearby oceanographical institute. Gradually the communards entice back to the sea some of the local fishermen who have been driven by industrial competition to hang up their crude little nets and hand lines . . . It all goes wrong, of course. Industrialization and city life lurk nearby. Something spoiling seems to leach out of the very sand on which the commune is founded (and here I see Pisorno's ruined lots with the utmost clarity). Some virulent fascist germ that has been lying dormant in the damp concrete and blown plaster infects the commune. Bit by bit the Greenery turns nasty. In one character it becomes outright racism directed at an Albanian fisherman, fuelled by bitter assertions that no immigrant ever has the least respect for the environment in his adopted country because he never really believes it's his . . . There are meetings, struttings, fights. Couples break apart. Later there are orgies in the abandoned villas. I got the idea. The only important thing was to stop Father also getting it.

Well, the simple fact of my now living in my own house high above Casoli hides the incredible effort and upheaval – not to say downright lies – it took to achieve my autonomy and independence. For the moment Father thinks Pacini makes documentary films for the Italian tourist industry, full of jaunty footloose music and heartwarming images of Benetton-clad toddlers trying to catch pigeons in the Piazza San Marco. May God help this famous director if he ever discovers otherwise. After all, Pasolini was stabbed to death by a seventeen-year-old. I dread to think what might happen to Piero Pacini if Father calls out the clan to avenge his elder daughter's lost innocence.

Anyway, standing here in late-June heat in the overgrown garden of the villa Pacini has apparently chosen as his main set, the whole project becomes very vivid to me. Between the acacia branches the blue sea twinkles noisily. Behind me the house glowers as if waiting for redress from the awful wrongs of history. It wants its white telephones back. The place is perfect and sinister and I can feel all sorts of suitable music elbowing out a space for itself inside me. I take some Polaroid snapshots as atmospheric aides-memoire so that when I'm back up the mountain in my kitchen trying not to be distracted by my neighbour's singing I shall be sure to hear once again what I can hear now. That's how it works with me. First impressions always bring music with them. Unreadable credits and titles flow upwards in my mind's eye while my mind's ear fills with an appropriate score.

At last Filippo insists on driving me back to Viareggio station where I've left my own car. Sasi is now quite grumpy and mutters a Voyde saying about stoats of the non-golden sort. I make an attempt to take my place nonchalantly in the scarlet car but this boy-racer's toy is not designed for nonchalance. It is like inserting oneself into a shoebox lined with

37

cream leather. The car is called a De Tomaso Panther and is so low my bottom puckers each time we go over a bump, expecting to be abraded raw by hot tarmac. We arrive at the station with a bellow and everyone stares so hard at the car and its driver they hardly notice my struggle to get out, still less my anonymous but cheerful trudge through the heat towards my own nondescript vehicle.

9

Next day I clear a space on the kitchen table (I can't quite get used to doing my own washing up. It feels far stranger than preparing one's own food. I wish dear Mili were here) and lay out my new 16-stave score paper. Also lots of different coloured pens. My task is to renounce my songs temporarily and concentrate on this film score. I realize this is premature since I still know nothing about exactly what Pacini wants. But I'm determined at least to get down the germs of what I began to hear yesterday while crunching through those empty cement rooms at Pisorno Studios. Get it down, that's the thing, otherwise it goes. Anyway, Pacini's sure to need some atmospheric passages. What I have to do is invent the film's characteristic *sound*. I want to do what Ennio Morricone did for Sergio Leone's spaghetti westerns. One can't even see Clint Eastwood's face without hearing a single bell in the orchestra, that portentous funereal sound as from a sunblasted and crumbling Mexican church. And as for whistling . . .

I'm thinking vaguely of tangos (very white-telephone, those!) and am beginning to put notes on paper when my neighbour sets up his dreadful howling. True, the sound is muffled by distance – our houses are quite fifty metres apart and screened by trees – but his voice has a plangent, intrusive quality. It insists on being heard. I suppose it doesn't help that it's almost July and all his doors and windows are open, as are mine. I'm about to reach for the phone and speak my mind to that silky little house agent when I suddenly realize that what I'm hearing is *the* sound for the film. Always, somewhere in the distance, some *dudi* massacring Italian opera, or else making it up as he goes along. It's incompetent, unconscious, egotistical, yearning. Perfect ironic backing for the idealism of a failing Green commune in Italy. There's one particular florid phrase Gerry keeps repeating that somehow manages to encapsulate the essential saccharine vapidity of Puccini without being identifiably by anyone. I can't make out the words but the rhythm uncannily suggests the phrase 'Telecom Italia'. Maybe I'm too influenced by the frustrations of phoning home recently. Come to that, maybe Gerry is too influenced by being able to stand on his terrace (next to that object which in Voynovia would be a peasant's privy) and see, far away down the coast, the very lake beside which Puccini once lived. Oh dear, I wish I were fonder of Italian opera. My favourite of all Verdi's works is his string quartet. I know that's perverse. I *know*.

In any case the florid phrase goes well with some wry tango rhythms behind it and I'm getting on like a house on fire (as we Voyde picturesquely say) when there is a knock at the open door and Gerry is outlined against the brightness.

'Not disturbing, I hope, am I?' he asks, advancing and peering. I realize he probably can't see much after the sunlight outside, and of course his eyes won't be adjusting as readily as they would have even ten years ago. 'Thought I'd drop by with a little something . . . Ooh! You're busy,' for he can now make out the MS paper on the table. 'I say, that looks awfully . . . Your songs, I suppose? Anyway, seeing as how you're so fond of this stuff I just thought I'd run across and drop you off a bott.'

It is, of course, Fernet Branca he has brought. Bemused by this sudden intrusion, I gaze dumbly at its yellowish label with the picture of an eagle clutching a bottle in its claws while teetering atop a blue globe.

'I know just how you feel,' he goes on sympathetically. 'Sort of edging towards lunch-time and wondering whether a little snorterino mightn't hit the spot.'

I don't believe I shall ever master English. I'm still trying to work out his meaning while dragging myself back from an inner soundscape. Obviously I'm too slow for he takes the initiative, finding a couple of glasses by the sink and pouring slugs of liquor that would gag a Bunki huntsman. 'There,' he says, downing his at a draught with only the smallest shudder. 'Grows on you, this stuff, don't you think? Anyway, I didn't want to disturb you.'

'But you have, all the same.'

'I'm afraid I couldn't resist a discreet celebration. Fact is, I've just heard that my new book is going down uncommonly well with the publishers. Even its anti-hero, the appalling Mr Snoilsson, apparently thinks it's "ace". They foolishly sent him a copy of the typescript but it turns out he can read after all. It's going to be previewed simply everywhere, as far as I can gather. International paperback rights about to be snapped up like hot – Good God! How could I have forgotten? Got a cake in the oven. Be right back.'

Now that I can see him from the inside out, as it were, instead of as a black blob outlined against the glare, I notice as he trots away that he's wearing a horizontally-striped matelot T-shirt, white shorts that beautifully emphasize the bum he doesn't have, with a pair of those Deckers or Dockers or Dickers on his sockless feet. I reach resignedly for my glass. If there's anything more enraging than having one's work interrupted by news of how well a neighbour's work is going, I can't offhand think what it might be. Who *is* this importunate fellow, anyway? No doubt it will be painful but it's high time to bring this burgeoning mateyness to a halt. Very likely he's quite sweet really but he more and more strikes me as one of those lonely bachelors who, before you know it, start dropping in for a cup of sugar or rice on a regular basis and then stay until you can't avoid inviting them for lunch, and there's another day's work down the drain. Just like poor Pavel at Moscow Conservatory. Another *dudi*, of course. Why do I attract them, dammit? But here he is, back again.

'Saved by the bell,' he announces, fanning himself with one hand. 'Phew – just in time. Another minute and that skewer would have been emerging cleanly from a cinder. Ooh, our glasses are empty, look. Can't have that on a torrid summer's day in Toscana.' The sound of much Fernet fills the room. 'By and by, when it's cooled, I'll bring it over and we can have a naughty tea. Terribly decadent, cake and fizz in the afternoon, don't you think? Sorry to be babbling but I can't tell you what a relief it is when people approve of what you've done. Books are hellish. You can spend a year fiddling away and then at the end they say you struck the wrong note, meaning that in their view you've wasted twelve months of your life. Really, I envy you, Marta. At least you can dash off one of your little songs and if it turns out a dud, well, that's only an hour or two down the drain, chalk it up to experience sort of thing. Whereas a *biography* . . .'

Here Gerald downs another glass of Fernet with a man-of-the-world gesture. 'Trouble is, I simply can't make up my mind what to do next. My editor and my agent just want more of the same, of course. But I'm fed up with these sports personalities. Can you believe they're now trying to team me up with some zonked-out South American footballer with a paunch and a cocaine habit? I suppose since he's older he might be marginally more interesting. I'll tell you a secret: I feel like branching out. I'm sick of people setting themselves challenges and bursting through pain barriers. I want a subject worthy of my talents.'

'Someone like Luciano Pavarotti?' I ask mischievously. 'Your voice is remarkably similar.'

'You're joking, of course,' he says unconvincingly. 'Besides, Marta, he's been done already. Dozens of times, probably. No, I was thinking more of a film director. Take Piero Pacini, for example. All those wonderful decadent films. *Nero's Birthday* –

I mean, anyone who could dream up some of the scenes in that film gets my vote. And did you see *Mille Piselli*? I shouldn't mind investigating an imagination like that, would you?'

I am momentarily speechless with horror. What atrocious piece of fate is this? How can this absurd creature be encroaching on my life in this way?

'No!' I hear myself say firmly. 'Really not, Gerry. I don't think this Pacini fellow is you at all. I don't know you that well, of course, and it's certainly none of my business, but I'd say it's obvious that your talents lie more in the musical field. Not necessarily with a singer, though. Perhaps a conductor or an instrumentalist? Someone like Pavel Taneyev, maybe. Have you heard of him?'

He looks at me pityingly. 'Of course I have, Marta. Everyone's heard of Pavel Taneyev. He's world-famous. Won the Tchaikovsky Prize.'

'Well, he's had a most interesting life. His father was an aircraft designer for the Soviet air force who always kept a suitcase packed and ready in the house in case he was suddenly sent to the Gulag. If one of his aircraft crashed during testing and he had previously signed it out as airworthy he knew he should go straight home, collect the suitcase and present himself. No excuses, especially if the pilot was killed. That was the precariousness of the family in which Pavel grew up. He scarcely ever saw his father. He was always in the Gulag.'

'His planes kept crashing?'

'Like shot pheasants. But it was never his fault. Always some jealous engineer had made an alteration.'

'Goodness, how melodramatic. How do you know this?'

'Pavel told me himself.'

'You mean you've actually met Pavel Taneyev?'

'We were at Moscow Conservatory together.'

'Moscow? But I thought you were from Volodiya or somewhere.'

'Voynovia,' I say with weary patience for this buffoon. 'But in those days Voynograd Academy of Music, though excellent,

42

taught very little composition. So I went on to Moscow. I haven't seen Pavel for several years but we were quite close once.'

'Quite close, eh?' and I swear this idiot tries a leer, although it may be that he is losing control of his facial muscles as people do with three-quarters of a bottle of Fernet Branca inside them.

'Quite close. And now, Gerry, if you will excuse me, I simply must do a bit more work. My little songs, you know.'

'Oh yes, of course. Frightfully sorry, taking up your time with my problems. But it's been nice chatting to you, I must say. Pavel Taneyev? Yes, I can see distinct possibilities. Wonderful pianist, exotic – not to say dramatic – background. Er, wife and family? Would they be tricky to work with, do you think?'

'No wife, Gerry,' I say, looking him straight in the eye. 'Pavel's not married, you can be quite confident of that. You'll have no problems there. You may even have much in common.'

'I see. H'm. *I see.* Something to think about, all right. Thanks for the drink. Must be getting back.'

And off he goes again through the trees, lurching a bit. Well, Pavel dear, I think grimly as I pick up my pen again, sorry to throw you to the wolves like that. But you're a big boy now and you can easily refuse the Geralds of this world. And if you can't, then it just serves you right for spending so much time crying on my shoulder back in Sverdlovskaya Street. The main point is, I will do anything to ensure that Gerry forgets all about Piero Pacini.

10

Thanks to working through lunchtime, pausing only for a cup of strong coffee to counteract that involuntary glass of Fernet, I manage to get most of my Pisorno Studios ideas down in short score. If I fall under a bus tomorrow nobody will be able to decipher my squiggles, no doubt, but then it will no longer matter. A blessed silence has fallen from the direction of Gerry's house and I imagine him sprawled across a double bed poleaxed by drink: eyes shut, mouth open and the matelot shirt plastered with sweat to his unmuscular chest. There is a certain pathos about this neighbour of mine but I refuse to dwell on it.

In mid-afternoon, not thirty seconds after I have put a double bar-line at the end of my sketch, Piero Pacini himself rings from Rome, newly returned from America. Filippo has told him that the proposed set meets with my approval and he hopes this is true. They are due to start shooting there in six weeks' time and am I feeling inspired? I tell him that not only am I feeling inspired but I have already written something that I hope captures the place's sinister, derelict atmosphere. Piero is – or affects to be – ecstatic and promises to despatch by courier a copy of the script as it stands so far with the music requirements marked and roughly timed. I ought to get it tomorrow and should begin to think in terms of an overall leitmotif, the same technique I used so effectively in *Vauli Mitronovsk*.

'But I don't have to tell *you*, Marta darling,' he says. 'You know I can't bear those scores that make films sound like an American TV series. Those style-less bridge passages to stuff up the cracks between the scenes are anguish to me. My films never subordinate the aural to the visual. Now, when can I hear what you've written?'

'Well,' I say, a little flustered, 'I've only sketched out some pages to establish the film's characteristic sound. It's just in short score at present.'

'Fine. Send me the disc.'

'I'm sorry . . .? Er, disc? It's written on paper – you know, music manuscript. Score paper?'

'You mean you write in *ink*?'

'It's the only way I know,' I say stiffly, managing to stop myself adding that it was a method that had served both Beethoven and Stravinsky quite well. 'What did you think?'

'Oh my,' says Pacini. 'I naturally assumed you work on a

keyboard with a computer. I thought everyone did these days. You play something, it automatically notates it, and then you fiddle around with the instrumentation until you get the sounds you want. Then you put it on a disc and send it off.'

'I'm afraid I've never used a system like that,' I tell him, feeling a hick. 'I just do it the old-fashioned way. I know the sounds I want and write them like that from the start. I don't need to "fiddle around".'

'Of course you must stick to the method you know,' says Pacini encouragingly, managing to imply that I pluck my quill pens from the nearest goose, 'although it's inconvenient if I can't hear it immediately. I like to shoot with the music ready. I am not like other directors,' he adds disdainfully, 'who shoot a film and then bolt some music onto it. For me the aural and the visual are concurrent and influence each other at the moment the film is made.'

Clearly he has used these words hundreds of times in as many interviews. All of a sudden I'm conscious of standing in a centuries-old kitchen filled with my own private disorder, an ex-Soviet-bloc composer who was trained in a traditional way in threadbare circumstances. I feel shame at being so far behind the times. I even begin to panic lest the great Piero Pacini loses faith in me as too untechnological to work with.

'I'm sure I could learn,' I offer gamely.

'Of course you could. I may courier a system up to you with the script. I'll get my people onto it. Now I must leave you. Even this late we're still having casting difficulties with one of the minor roles, can you imagine that?'

He rings off, leaving me obscurely chastened like a student who has unaccountably disappointed her favourite teacher. Still, I tell myself, he's not going to change his composer at this stage, not the way the great Pacini works, not unless he reschedules the shoot and everything. And besides, my music is going to *make* his film . . . But now I've caught a little of his fretfulness and am anxious he should hear what I'm doing as soon as possible to give us both confidence. Maybe after all I need to become computer literate. How horrid! Surely these electronic crutches are for people who don't know what they're about, for amateurs and the musically illiterate? They are not for proper composers who have been brought up to be able to sit in a corner like Mozart or any other professional, scribbling down the full score of the overture even as the dress rehearsal is proceeding onstage.

At that moment, right on cue, Gerry starts up again in the distance. Not so much *nessun dorma* as *nessun lavora*, frankly. He is repeating the same florid little passage I was notating earlier. Because his voice sounds louder I resignedly go to the door to see if I am about to be honoured with yet another visit. It seems not, however. I catch glimpses of him between the trees in full DIY mode carrying a hefty-looking crowbar. He is wearing boots and one of those thick belts that telephone linesmen wear from which dangle various steel implements. He also has on a yellow hard hat to complete the picture of construction-site chic. He neither looks nor sounds like someone who only a few hours ago drank three-quarters of a bottle rated at forty-five per cent alcohol, which is the same as the *grappa* on my mantelpiece. This is evidently the butch Gerry, the effect spoiled only by the high tenor singing which sounds like a pinched puppy. The words seem to approach the edge of decipherability but stop short, reaching my ears as a most unlikely entreaty for a despairing lover: 'Vedi, vedi, vedi il fondo del barattolo!' *See the base of the container?* Whatever else he set, Puccini never set those words.

But where can this jaunty workman be headed? I lose sight of him but can still track him by an upward scale ending on a high F sharp. Then there is an ominous creaking, topped by a wailing E flat in alt. to which Maria Callas herself could only vainly have aspired. This fades and is followed by a far-off sound like that a wooden Potemkin suburb makes when enthusiastically flattened by many pairs of feet. Then silence. Intrigued despite myself, I hurry over.

Gerald

11

The good thing about the commercial trash I write is that because there's seldom much lead-time my submitted text always gets speedy feedback in case they want to make changes. I admit to having been cheered by *Hot Seat!*'s initial reception. At least they liked it. Mind you, editors and agents and publishing folk hardly constitute a representative slice of the reading public. For a start, few people in publishing these days are able to read at all, it being a largely superfluous skill in a business that depends more on feel and image and marketing.

So it was good that Per Snoilsson's dreary life story had been well received by those who commissioned it, though naturally my pleasure was short lived. Who cares to have written a non-book? Not that I have the slightest desire to leave any lasting mark, of course. One barely casts a shadow even while the sun's out. But I shouldn't mind doing something that temporarily engages me. Actually, I should like to lose myself totally in a piece of work, but I can't imagine what it would be. And whatever it is I'm damned sure nobody would pay me to do it. In the meantime, then, is one to go on tossing fanciful recipes and fanciful arias into the face of despair? Is one to go on writing asinine books about asinine people with a few felicities thrown in to relieve the private torment? Answer: *Yes*. Keep bearing in mind that tunnel at the end of the light, Samper, the one that goes on for ever. How I wish I'd been born in 1865 instead of 1965. I also wish I'd been born with a clearly defined talent for something, or else stupid. Come to that, I wish my mother and elder brother hadn't walked to the end of the Cobb in Lyme Regis on that early September afternoon while my father and I went to buy another film for my camera. I wish that we hadn't seen them turn to stroll back and then be swept off the face of the earth by a freak wave that spared some children trying out the Cobb's whispering-gallery effect, a watercolourist sitting on a canvas stool, three couples, a dog and a man selling Jane Austen souvenirs. They all got a fright and a good soaking, whereas Mama and Nicky vanished utterly, leaving behind a vast and empty expanse of salt air that has surrounded me ever since. It's easy to see why it would always have been necessary to invent a God, if only to account for the sardonic humour of these playful and arbitrary acts. On with the farce. I wish . . . I wish I could stop drinking Fernet Branca in the middle of the day.

Truthfulness leads me to blame the ghastly Marta for starting and fostering this Fernet habit. I merely describe what happens. The writer's eye, like the surgeon's, is indifferent to what it sees. It has an insatiable accuracy while aiming to serve up a dish consisting of plain ingredients perfectly in balance. It is for the diners themselves to add their moral garnish, salt it with tears, pepper it with outrage etc. Still, I will editorialize as far as to say Marta is a fat slattern from the Pripet Marshes and I dislike nearly all of her and fear the rest, 'the rest' being made up of her bottles of Fernet Branca and her clumping seductiveness. I fear her seductiveness not because I feel threatened by it but because sooner or later it will force me into the corner of having to say NO!, and I was brought up among civilized people who make a point of never cornering anyone. I fear her Fernet because it forces me into a corner where I hear myself saying YES! *Faiblesse oblige*.

It is true that the other day I took her a bottle as a social lubricant. I went over to her dingy dwelling with the idea of delicately broaching the matter of her piano playing, which quite frankly is driving me mad. But somehow she managed to sidetrack things in a way Stephen Potter could hardly have bettered had he written a book on musical one-upmanship. She must have guessed I was coming since she had cleared the kitchen table of its usual bundles of dank laundry and crusted plates and spread it instead with music manuscript paper. Brilliant! Having heard enough of her piano playing to know she is about as musical as Beethoven's ear-trumpet, I had to be impressed by her ostensible 'score': several sheets of paper liberally covered in scrawls. Of course she was eager enough to abandon this piece of humbug once I'd drawn the Branca brothers' cork – or rather, had induced liquor to flow through their patented plastic pourer. Personally, I hate drinking in the middle of the day, especially in a hot climate. One simply gets nothing done thereafter. I did manage to slip away on the truthful pretext of having left a cake in the oven: an oversight that will give you some idea of how thrown I'd been by her sonic pollution. I'm really quite a spur-of-the-moment sort, despite my mild-mannered Clark Kent exterior, and had gone across to her house fully prepared to read her the riot act, only to be distracted by the princely cake whose muffled cries in my oven I suddenly heard all the way from her kitchen. And just as well, too, because by the time I had got back I could detect the beginnings of that bitter, caramelized smell of exposed sultanas turning to carbon. I will give you the recipe shortly.

When I returned to her hovel Marta had already passed the point where I might usefully have broached any topic, let alone a delicate one like complaining about her piano play-ing. None of my business, of course, but I swear she had drunk half the bottle: a quantity that would have put me in line for *pronto soccorso*, stomach pumps and a night in Viareg-gio Hospital but which merely left her leering wetly behind her hair. She is evidently one of those whom drink makes cunning, because she shamelessly pre-empted any airing of my grievance about her piano by introducing the musical motif herself and then *flattering* me. When one's voice is com-pared to Pavarotti's and one is urged, as a like mind, to write his biography, there is not much a gentleman can do but blush prettily and make ritual protestations of general unworthiness. Marta then had the brass face to claim intimacy with none other than Pavel Taneyev, with whom she implied she had been a fellow student at Moscow Conservatory. Oh, sure. And Mrs Beeton was my aunt. I mean, do us a favour. High time for that recipe:

Fish Cake

No – we are not talking about exquisite fish and potato patties rolled in breadcrumbs and fried, that classic of English cuisine. This is a good deal more exotic, a Gerald Samper creation designed, as any work of art must be, to remind us that the world is an unexpected place full of unfamiliar challenges. I perfected it while compiling a small volume provisionally entitled *The Boys' Reformatory Cookbook* whose witty asides proved too much for the fifteen hidebound UK publishers I tried to interest before I lost faith in the project. (The typescript joined many others in my bottom drawer that together constitute the graveyard of my literary hopes. These include the libretto for a delightful and lubricious operetta, *Vietato ai Minori*, that I now despair of ever seeing set to music, ditto my ballet *Jizzelle*.)

◆

Ingredients

377 gm self-raising flour
151 gm semolina
62 gm cornmeal
149 gm granulated sugar
83 gm unsalted butter
1½ eggs
1 tinned mackerel (about 74 gm)
Grated peel of 1 lemon
99 gm freshly ground almonds
26 gm sultanas
Pinch of black pepper
2 tablespoons plain yoghurt (optional)

◆

Stir the flour, semolina, cornmeal, sugar, eggs and almonds together. The mixture will be severely crumbly. Now use your fingers and work in the butter and the fish. Don't despair: after five minutes or so it will confound you by taking on the correct fatty consistency. Add the sultanas, pepper and grated lemon. Still on the stodgy side? The optional yoghurt will cure that. Go on working until the dough is uniform, with no individual flecks of mackerel. Your fingers may ache but you can console yourself with the thought that your nails will be all the cleaner (also one of the hidden benefits of making one's own bread). Set the mixture aside to rest for an hour. Meanwhile pre-heat the oven to 190 °C – what used to be Regulo 5 in the dear dead days of the Radiation Cookbook – and oil a baking tin. When the hour is up transfer the dough to the tin and bake for forty minutes, or forty-four minutes if you become distracted by a drunken slut in a neighbouring cottage.

To taste GS's Fish Cake at its best it should be left to stand for twenty-four hours. This enhances both texture and flavour, though don't ask me how. On the grounds that lilies are much improved by gilding, this cake benefits from an austere icing: 226 gm icing sugar mixed with 2 tablespoons Fernet Branca. This will top off your masterpiece with a toothsome cap of an interesting ginger shade.

For incurable R&D types, a word of warning. You would be amazed by how few varieties of fish are really suitable for this recipe. I have found by far the best to be 'Pinocchio' brand tinned *sgombri al naturale*, readily available in most Italian supermarkets. Flaked salmon runs them a close second. In the past I have also tried eel, baked halibut and kippers. This last was not a success and I gave it to the birds. There was something a little too fantastic about fish bones in an iced cake, though it may be just that I'm getting old. Once upon a time my bird table in the Home Counties was an oasis of *cuisine expérimentale* in a desert of dull fare. Birds must surely be bored by an unrelieved diet of worms, bacon rind and burnt toast. My slow path to culinary mastery was

marked by offerings that became the height of avian fashion –
the *dernier cri*, one might say, which occasionally they proved
to be. One of the victims, a green woodpecker, was in turn
converted into a tasty mouthful by glazing and truffling.

12

The more I see of Marta's place, the more I'm reassured she
can't have bought it and will just be renting it. That little
rogue Benedetti must have split his sides at finding an idiot
foreigner actually willing to pay hard cash to take the place
off his hands. I suspect her of having an acute lack of funds so
it can't be very much, but the house's lack of Position is the
clincher. Those fifty-odd metres make all the difference and
render it very much less advantageously placed than mine.
No doubt there's less incentive for her to get out there and
create a garden to make the most of what view there is,
although I notice she or someone has laid waste to a football-
pitch sized area at the back with a brush-cutter. Meanwhile, I
can only assume it was written into the terms of the lease that
she should leave the interior looking like a Beatrix Potter
illustration: damp brick floors, rusty iron range, cobwebby
windows. One expects to see Mr Tod sidling down the
flagged passage to the back door, glancing over one shoulder
with a cocky grin of bared teeth.

I was enjoying such reflections having returned to my
own bright kitchen, now smelling so agreeably of newly
baked Fish Cake. Although the way she lives is none of my
business, I still find there's nothing like a visit to Marta's to
inspire me to fresh zeal. The view from the window of my
own terrace is enough to remind me that the only thing
standing in the way of a perfect panorama is that veteran
privy: unreconstructed relic of a peasant past. Suddenly I
can bear it no longer. I don suitable gear, collect a few stout
tools and set off to deconstruct it.

Years ago in the feckless wanderings of a gap year I found myself travelling by bus in Bolivia. Or was it Ecuador? Somewhere, at any rate, with that standard Latin American mix of vertiginous mountain roads, a bus with no glass in its windows and bald tyres, impassive Indian women passengers in bowler hats, and a matinée desperado at the wheel who periodically removed both hands from it in order to groom his heroic coiffure in the driving mirror. My internal voice was long since hoarse with shrieking and I had lapsed into the numb fatalism that can only be interrupted by a very few major urgencies. One of these was now making it imperative that we stop in the next five minutes. I had already checked the reassuring wad of tissues in the pocket of my rucksack and was going forward to order the driver to pull up when we swung into a mountain village over a hen or two and stopped by a rambling shack calling itself a bar. I was out of the bus and through that bar like Road Runner, leaving twisters of dust behind me. My face was probably more communicative than my Spanish; at any rate I was directed straight to the back of the building where a privy stood with its door hospitably ajar. Springing inside and banging the door to I found the only light came from a hole in the floor: a crusted circle about a foot across. I was in no state to argue. Mere seconds later I was panting in that squatting position so familiar to desperate travellers, sweaty face on knees, in a blissful state of release. I was able only to take in that disaster had been averted by a whisker, that life would go on and for all I cared the bus could too, without me. Gradually my senses returned even as I fumbled for the tissues and began to take in for the first time the unsteady planks of the floor, the drone of blue-bottles and – most interesting of all – the view beneath me. The hole of this jakes afforded the sight of a stupendous gulf of blue air: a vertical drop over a chasm so deep I might have been in a helicopter. A thousand feet below my dripping rump lay stained and wicked crags above which my eye caught the slow wheeling specks of vultures sizing up my offerings. It was the first time I had experienced vertigo in a lavatory. I left the hut a good deal more gingerly than I had entered it, now having the leisure to note its true nature as a place of easement cantilevered out on bleached poles over an abyss.

What days! And what I wouldn't give to be able to return to them, though less for the conventional reason of erotic adventuring when sap was high than because even fifteen years ago the prospects still seemed good for living a reasonably serious life in my native land. I looked forward to becoming neither a wage slave nor a tycoon. But that was before British culture slumped to an infantile consensus obsessed with cash and fashion. New Labour and wall-to-wall football have left only exile, the stoic's way out. If one is not allowed to be serious one may as well emigrate. Even mockery is an art form requiring discipline and sacrifice.

So now I sally forth from my pointless house above pointless Casoli with a song on my lips to do away with a privy I have just recognized as a spectre from my own, as much as from the house's, past. Obviously the Ecuadorean and Italian peasantry had thought along the same lines when viewing a handy precipice. Why dig when the hand of nature has already dug for you? However, the gulf in this case is nowhere near as deep or as steep, and as I run a practised eye over the job I realize for the first time that this privy was never built out over anything but was merely an earth closet at the edge of a hillside terraced for vines and vegetables. Gradually the hillside has been eroded by winter rains and a minor earthslip some time ago has left the hut's outer wall dangling and sagging over thin air. Good: it shouldn't take long to complete the job and send the remains down into the cleared patch below, where I've made a start on reclaiming the terraces from the jungle that has buried them over the years of abandonment.

Do you find that certain pieces of music automatically suggest themselves as the only possible accompaniment to particular tasks? Well, *I* do, although I can't always say why. As I contemplate the murder of this hut I find myself locked into that dramatic scene where Massaro confronts the terrifying Brasi who has sold him poison to kill Don Antonio, Erminia's guardian, who refuses to countenance Massaro's courting her. But the poison hasn't worked although Don Antonio's hair has fallen out and his skin has acquired a curious metallic sheen. Being a man of lively intelligence he has become suspicious. In terror and fury Massaro returns to Brasi to protest that the poison he sold him has itself expired. 'Vedi!' he sings with a passion provoked by his impending arrest and Erminia's taking the veil, 'vedi la data indicata sul fondo del barattolo! Perfido! Oimè!'

Decisively I insert the end of the crowbar between the hut's floor and the ground and lever upwards with a fine gesture imitative of Massaro's rage and passion. Unfortunately the floorboards are rotten and spongelike. Since I am standing a little higher than the hut I am flung forward by the unexpected lack of resistance and go crashing through the doorway itself, thudding against the far wall. There is a sudden lurch, a lot of noise and a confused tumbling, shot through with streaks of sunlight and bright pain. Silence. The world recedes and reapproaches, lulling like waves in tropical shallows. For a timeless period I am suspended, then unceremoniously cast up on dry land. When I open my eyes something terrible has happened and I am blind. I try some weak screaming but it hurts my side so I stop. I'm blind and going to die and the melodramatic effusions of halfwits like Massaro are not in the slightest bit consoling, any more than are the prospects of *Hot Seat!* selling a million. What do such trivia matter when I'm pinned to the earth and about to be pecked to death by the circling vultures? More time passes while I miserably drift, then without warning there is a neck-ricking wrench and the sensation of a lid being lifted. Light floods me. I can see again! It's a miracle. *'Un miracolo,'* I murmur weakly, like Erminia in Act 3 on discovering that her confessor

57

is Fr Brasi, the ex-venefice who has now repented and taken holy orders. (They, I'm glad to say, are soon destined to elope, the *nouveaux* Héloïse and Abelard of pulp opera.)

'No, Gerree, is no miracle.' And there, with grisly inevitability, is Marta holding my hard hat which I suppose must have become jammed over my eyes by the fall. I notice – because in such moments of revelatory clarity one notices everything – she is also holding a bottle of Fernet Branca in the other hand. Poor dear, she simply can't be parted from it. Awfully sad, really, what with her bogus musicianship as well. Still, in my present shocked and dishevelled state I experience an almost affectionate pang of neighbourliness towards her. Pretty lucky she was around, frankly. We're a long way from civilization up here. I reach to pat her hand reassuringly but she misinterprets the gesture and holds the bottle to my lips with a murmured 'Just a little, Gerree, if you must. Very bad for hospital.'

I stop sucking at the pourer. 'I'm not going to hospital,' I protest. A dribble of Fernet runs down my chin. 'I'm perfectly all right. Just a bit dazed, you know. Took a bit of a tumble.'

'You asleep ten minutes.'

'Oh nonsense. Just help me get – *Ow!*' For as I sit up an interesting pain shoots through me. The phrase 'cracked rib' leaps into my mind. Thanks a million, God: that's all I needed.

'Maybe you break inside.'

To the ironic the world is boilerplated with irony and I notice far overhead a pair of vultures twirling: buzzards, actually, but close relatives all the same. Their thin mewing drifts downwards, a feeble noise like kittens being wrung out which is so at variance with their supposed raptorial majesty. With some anguish and Marta's brawny assistance I get to my feet. Already her alcohol is making my knees weak. I must have fallen a good half mile, to judge by how far overhead the plateau seems on which my house stands and which somehow has to be reached. Slowly and painfully we climb the path up the terraces. The pain eases somewhat, probably the effect of the Fernet, creating the illusion of my head floating upwards while a numb body plods below. At long last I slump into a chair in my kitchen.

'Now I call ambulance,' says Marta, looking around for the telephone.

'You will do no such thing,' I tell her in my most commanding tone, which even to my ears sounds feebly buzzardish; Clark Kent emboldened by sherry. 'As you can see, I'm perfectly fine, just a bit shaken and bruised. I shall retire to bed. Maybe you ought to do the same after your heroism. If tomorrow morning I'm at death's door we may have to call in the sawbones, but not until then. I'm most grateful to you for your help, Marta, dear. That was a very neighbourly act. Thank you.'

My quiet sincerity has its effect and she dimples at me.

'Now I help you upstairs, Gerree.'

'No,' I say firmly, 'that won't be necessary at all.' There are limits. I mean, where will it end? With her tugging off my *intimi*, as the Italians primly call underwear? She should be so lucky. Being helped out of one's clothes by strangers is something the discriminating person reserves for Emergency Room staff, mortuary attendants and casual lovers. Ex-Soviet-bloc neighbours who try to get one drunk do not hack it. 'Thank you all the same.'

At last I persuade her to leave, which she does reluctantly after swapping phone numbers. It is agreed I shall call her if I need assistance and she will anyway come over in the morning to see if I've survived the night. We part with expressions of goodwill. When I discover that she has forgetfully left behind her bottle of Fernet I almost call her back. Having collected a few necessities I climb the stairs stiffly, but not before I've noticed through the window the grand new panorama left by the privy's demise. This sends me quite cheerfully to my bed of convalescence. My methods may have been a little crude but the end has been achieved – a thought that enabled even the Creator to take a day off.

13

By the time Marta calls round next morning at ten I have long since been up and about. We Sampers bounce back. I have the piratical makings of a black eye, presumably where the edge of the hard hat caught me, and I am covered with raw scrapes and contusions as well as having a large purplish bruise beneath one armpit. But the damage is all superficial and I don't believe any ribs are cracked after all. I also have a light headache as a reminder that I was knocked silly in the fall. Otherwise I am in fine if stiff fettle.

'Gerree!' she cries, and certainly her voice has no connection whatever with music. It goes right through your head like a bullet, leaving a track of gross tissue damage. 'You are not bedding! Is very good. Look, I bring a break-fast. Yes. Is Voynovian food for dying.' She produces what looks like a ball of putty wrapped in a sock. 'Is *kasha*.'

Kasha, I remember, is Russian buckwheat or bulgur or something. I associate it with that vegetarian restaurant chain in London where the bread is dark and dense, the flans look like coconut matting and flapjacks fall like paving stones to the pit of the stomach where they lie for a week fermenting. For days afterwards one's underwear smells of silage. I raise the ball gingerly to my nose. It is covered in her fingerprints. Molasses again. And . . . can that be linseed oil? Maybe it really *is* putty.

'Is very good with cream. We boil like that.'

Ah. A sort of Voynovian haggis for terminal invalids. Just what I need.

'It gives very strength to stiff body.'

Once again I would swear there was a leer. Surely she can't mean . . .? Even in Voynovia could there be such a thing as an aphrodisiac for convalescents? This woman is terrifying. I am below par this morning and before I can utter a squeak of protest she has barged to the cooker, plonked the ball in a pan of cold water and lit a burner under it. Then she opens the fridge and appears to make a scornful inventory. Eventually she picks out a pot of cream which she sniffs suspiciously. I admit that its pretty buff colour is deceptive. She is not to know that I have doctored it with cinnamon for a fabulous baked pears in cheese sauce recipe I'm perfecting.

'You have no good food, Gerree,' she says, slamming my fridge door shut. 'Of course you are weak. You not eating food to make you strong with good meats. Is everything delicatessen food.' This comes with real contempt.

'Not enough *kasha* and *shonka*?' I suggest satirically.

'Is right.'

She nods vigorously and particles of this and that fall from her mop of hair. Insects? Really, it's all too much. It isn't right for the survivors of crashed privies to be bullied in their own kitchen. She'll pay for this, I swear. It's obvious that to a person with her peasant's interior a mere gallon of garlic ice cream is like a mouthful of bread or a coffee bean: something with which to clear the palate before going on to the next dish. I shall have to devise an offering that even she will interpret as the cuisine of contempt. *Cuisine mépriseur.* How can we have managed without this category for so long? But for the moment I'm saved by the bell ('below par', 'saved by the bell': you can see what writing about sport heroes does to one's style). I mean the phone rings and it is Frankie, my agent in London. Given they're an hour behind over there it's bright and early for him and suggests urgency.

'Do you know Nanty Riah, Gerry?'

'It's an Indonesian scuba resort?' I hazard. 'A disease? A dish?'

'He's the founder and lead singer of Britain's number one boy band. Freewayz. Even you must have heard of them. You probably know him as Brill.'

'I don't.'

'Well, he's a fan of yours.'

'Surely not.'

'Apparently so. His agent rang last night to say that Brill has just been reading *Downhill all the Way!* and is, quote, "slammed" by it.' *Downhill*, of course, was the book I wrote for Luc Bailly, the skier with the pop-up flag in his pants.

'Ah. He wants the recipe for another love potion?'

'That wasn't what he said. According to his agent Brill has reached the difficult age, the pop star's grand climacteric.'

'Twenty-three?'

'No, he's actually just over thirty but keeps it secret. The point is, he's extremely impressed by the way you made Luc seem a substantial figure even off-piste. A man of stature.'

Twenty-five centimetres, by all accounts, although I do not mention this. I am trying to work out what Brill and Luc Bailly could possibly have in common apart from mountains of money.

'Basically he's got an early attack of McCartney's Syndrome,' explains Frankie. 'You know: unlimited fame, unlimited cash, unlimited adulation, but wants to be taken seriously into the bargain.'

'Don't tell me: he's going to write a Requiem for the Human Race to be premièred in St Peter's, Rome. It will include recordings of whale song. Or else he's working on a collection of rock sonnets called *Roll Over, Shakespeare*. Or could there be a forthcoming exhibition of artworks made from his body fluids at the Saatchi Gallery?'

'At this stage I think he wants help with an autobiography as part of a campaign to invest the name of Nanty Riah with all-round artistic gravitas . . . I know, I know, but there we are. We ordinary mortals can only let our jaws drop at these people's monumental chutzpah. Meanwhile, remember they've also got monumental quantities of dosh, which is why I think you ought to take it seriously that a pop idol wants you personally to help him towards his Nobel prize.'

'Look, Frankie,' I say. 'I nearly fell to my death in a lavatory yesterday, but I don't want to explain now beyond saying that I'm feeling a little delicate. I know nothing about the pop world and care less.'

'That's why Brill wants you. He was hoping you'd known nothing about downhill skiing, too, and his agent was partly ringing me to check. That's the whole point. He expressly doesn't want a pop biography done by one of those authors in Armani leather who come complete with baize scalps and closely-observed mockney vowels. He already has a brace of those, anyway; they go with the territory. No, he wants real writing. You're very good at the wider picture, Gerry. Which you've just done for Per Snoilsson, by the way. I don't know how you do it but you manage to make these one-dimensional people seem positively Renaissance figures. That's exactly what Brill's after. He's determined to hit middle age as the twenty-first century's Leonardo, though my guess is he'll settle for an Order of Merit or even a humble K.'

God's piles. 'Will I have to start from scratch? I mean, would I be his ghost writer or his editor?'

'He told his agent he's already written something but no one has seen it. It may be five hundred pages of dazzling prose or it may be some stertorous jottings on the back of an envelope. No prizes.'

'Well, Frankie, if you insist, I suppose I'd better see him. I'll call you back a bit later when I've got my mind properly around it.'

I hang up to find Marta prodding the putty-ball in the pan. It has swollen horribly and now looks like an enormous fibroid trapped in stockingette. For a while I had forgotten about both it and her. The thought that I'm about to move in the grand international ambit of a pop icon worried about middle age somehow makes Marta's bossy importunings less threatening, even slightly touching.

'You really think I should eat this?' I ask her, playing cowed patient to strapping nurse (Hattie Jacques in a starched cap).

'Yes, Gerree, you eat. Very good and stronging, you will see. So – we cut bag.' She lances the stockingette and, unconfined, the monstrous dumpling bursts forth. She puts it on a board and bisects it with the bread knife. With a gasp of steam the two halves flop apart revealing a dense, greyish interior with what looks like an engorged prostate at its centre. 'Very good,' says Marta judiciously. 'I make last night.'

Numbly I watch her hack off a sturdy portion and pour sugar and cinnamon cream over it. After that there seems to be nothing for it but to sit at the kitchen table and address myself to this colossal duff.

'Eat,' she orders, joining that huge historic chorus of mothers with hairy forearms who stand over small men bellowing *'Mangia, mangia!'* and *'Don't be shy!'*

Strangely enough it turns out to be edible, though hardly palatable, its major challenge residing as much in the texture as in the taste. I remember as a child reading the Amazing Facts column of a boys' magazine that told of the discovery of a star so dense that as much of it as could fit in a matchbox would weigh 32,000 tons. I used to while away boring lessons by imagining winning endless bets ('Ten quid says you can't lift that matchbox, Thompson') and devising ways of preventing it simply falling through the ground towards Earth's centre. It was intriguing to think of something that was both easily possessible in terms of size and utterly unownable because of its weight. And here I am, a quarter of a century on, eating a similar substance that I can feel falling in a straight line inside me between gullet and rectum. Surely when I stand up there will be a tearing sound and I shall find my trouser seam in tatters and a smoking pile of undigested *kasha* on the chair? Until that happens the stuff is massively filling. If you can imagine a planet-sized marron glacé that has begun to collapse under its own gravity – a sweet chestnut on its way to becoming a Black Hole – you will have an idea of quite how filling this syrupy, mealy, oiled substance is. There are serious calories in every crumb.

'You must finish, Gerree,' says Marta, standing over me in her parody of the maternal tyrant. I blame it on *glasnost*, or was it *perestroika*? Whatever it was, anyway, that allowed *kasha* and Martas to escape from behind the Iron Curtain . . . Such are the dishevelled mental babblings that accompany the cracking of my maxillary muscles as I chew on and on. The prostate in the middle turns out to be a toffee-like filling based apparently on horse liniment. The linseed oil is loud and clear. 'Very good,' she says approvingly as I get the last spoonful down and sag back in my chair. Evidently I now have permission to get down and go out to play. Oh, that 'twere possible. I debate what to do about Marta but no idea comes. In the face of this *kasha* offensive I now realize how puny my Garlic and Fernet Ice Cream was. I recall the interesting but not well-known fact that several honeys are actually poisonous, in particular – and I shall need to check this – rhododendron and laurel honey. I envisage the gift to Marta of a *bombe surprise* based largely on meringues and ice cream held together by rhododendron honey. Nice idea, and probably immune from suspicion, let alone criminal conviction ('"A tragic error on the part of 62,000 bees," the judge began his summing up'), but too leisurely and roundabout a way of solving the immediate problem of an irritating neighbour. Planting rhododendrons or laurel, waiting for them to flower, learning to keep bees . . . Hopeless.

Long after my tormentress has left I can do little but loll, sipping weak tea made from some much-touted South African bush that tastes like stewed hay. Slowly the bolus in my stomach dissolves and with it my lassitude. It will do no harm to make a date to see this Brill fellow, or Nancy or whatever he calls himself. It feels neither like advance nor retreat, more of a sideways shift away from the world of the starting pistol and the stopwatch. Oh well, why not? Same old despair but at least a different scene. My bruises ache. Great putty-flavoured farts follow me from room to room.

Days have gone by. I am back on form. Marta has been strangely and agreeably quiet over in her warren, except for a mysterious episode a few nights ago when it briefly sounded as though she were motor racing. It woke me up but faded almost immediately so I gave up thinking about it. None of my business. Maybe one day I shall discover that in addition to everything else she is an expert mechanic and has a secret workshop hidden away at the back. She may even turn out to be a Per Snoilsson fan. Nothing about that woman would surprise me.

I am bustling about my own house, generally straightening it up and getting things into some sort of order for a famous visitor. I have even been creakily down the terraces to inspect the crash site and put a match to the remains of the privy. A faint smell of dry rot and creosote hung over them and they burned briskly, sending up gratifying clouds of fatal tars and dioxins into the Tuscan sky. In a day or two I am supposed to drive down to Pisa airport and collect the great Brill, who will be flying out Ryanair in horn rims and a wig, as I myself have often thought of doing. It seems he is so keen to get this project of his under way he is prepared to take time off in order to see whether we like each other enough to work together. His agent insisted he would do better tucked away in the anonymity of my mountain retreat for a day or two than heavily disguised in a hotel suite in Pisa. Naturally I'm uneasy. I have no idea what it takes to get on with the lead singer of a boy band. Cocaine, possibly, and I seem to be temporarily out of that.

What I can supply, however, is culinary creative genius. I am planning menus in my guest's honour while ignoring the advice of a streetwise interior know-all who urges me not to bother but just to lay in oven-ready chips and deep frozen pizza. Well, Brill can get that sort of stuff anywhere. I shall make it clear that if he wants to do a deal with eternity he'll have to do a deal with Gerald Samper first, and that includes expanding his dietary horizons. I debate making my celebrated otter dish but one can never be sure what will be in the market. Tuna stuffed with prunes in Marmite batter? A good old standby but maybe unsuited to a Tuscan summer lunch table on a terrace beneath vines. Deep-fried mice? I sometimes wonder if one is not more seduced by the mellifluous *sound* of a dish than by how it would actually taste. You might think the same went for pears in lavender, but I have discovered that poaching pears in water with a double handful of fresh lavender heads, honey and a cup of Strega makes a striking change from the usual wine-and-cinnamon routine of suburban dinner parties. Don't be tempted to use Fernet Branca in place of Strega, however. It will taste revolting.

Meanwhile, I have gone right off my beautiful idea of pears in Gorgonzola with cinnamon cream. It's all Marta's fault. Had she not drenched that putty ball of hers in the cinnamon cream I was experimenting with the other day it might still be a possibility. But the whole idea now reeks of linseed oil and bullying and has been ruined for me. Imagine Bach busy writing a soulful aria for the St Matthew Passion when in the street outside a butcher's boy goes past whistling a popular ditty about three jolly swineherds. Suddenly poor old JSB realizes it's the very tune he's now writing, only much faster and in a major key. 'God *damn*,' he mutters softly to himself as he slowly tears up his manuscript, having unwittingly had a preview of what in a hundred and fifty years will be known as the unconscious. That's pretty much how I feel about the irreparable damage Marta has done my cinnamon cream.

Since the purging of the privy I have been more attentive to the terrace and the now unobstructed panorama it affords. I sit out there a good deal these days. The funny thing about a coastline when seen from this distance and altitude is that the sea doesn't look like water at all but, depending on the weather, more like concrete or blue lino or occasionally smirched tinfoil. It's much too far away for actual waves to be visible, which is one of the things that recommended this place to me. Instead at evening, as Viareggio leans wearily away from the sun, one can sometimes see frozen frown-lines in opposition to the prevailing breeze. That is all. The quick white scars left by ships and pleasure craft are obviously some kind of sap or latex that the ocean briefly bleeds when its skin is broken and which hardens almost immediately on exposure to air. This is the view from a terrace I have always wanted.

How have I allowed myself to engage for a living with that world down there? ('That world' of course refers not to the specific gridded quilt of Viareggio's sprawl and greenhouses but to the cancerous showbiz ethos that today extends over all horizons.) Ghosting the little lives of famous nobodies – was it for this I passed so many A-levels? Maybe it is not too late to become Nietzsche, a cantankerous visionary or secular monk with a kitchen garden full of exotic international pods and legumes. The man with his finger on the pulses of the world . . . And there you go again: everything has to degenerate into a joke. But of all things, to be making your living – and not a bad one, either – as amanuensis to knuckleheads! And doing it well, what's more. Doing it so brilliantly these idiots recognize the persona I've invented for them, even to the extent that I'm told that ghastly sprinter who now runs for Parliament in elections firmly believes he wrote his book himself (*Alone Out There* – don't bother to read it) while I merely sat taking dictation like one of Barbara Cartland's stenographers. I suppose I should be flattered. As he's planning his new political career on the basis of an entirely spurious personality I ought, if there were any justice in the world, to have the last laugh. But of course there isn't and I shan't. In politics as in showbiz, bogus *wins*.

The worst thing is that when I'm working with them – the awful Luc, the unspeakable Per – I occasionally experience the fleeting conviction that I'm related to them, or at any rate have known them a very long time. This must be the direst legacy of that distant, ever-present day on the Cobb when I grimly saw ('grimly see' being only one of Lyme Regis's anagrams) my adored elder brother gulped like a tidbit by the Atlantic. Oh, poor Nicky, how I worshipped you! You were, at eleven, everything I aspired to be: big and brave and heroically athletic. Nothing my nine-year-old self could do came anywhere close to measuring up to your daunting example. I even failed to learn your trick of tossing the hair out of your eyes with a gesture that looked so wonderfully casual: a jerk of your neat head punctuating your passage through the world as though dismissing the moment and its achievement. On to the next effortless triumph.

Of course the trouble with hero-worshipping an elder brother who dies is that you catch him up and overtake him and leave him there, forever eleven and stranded in a golden pool of promise. And when some of your absurder myths about him have likewise been outstripped by sober accuracy and family photos, you recognize what you probably knew all along: that he was actually quite an ordinary little boy, even a bit timorous and weedy, for whom his teachers were predicting an auspicious academic career. Smile, Gerry (another Lyme Regis anagram, lacking only an 'r').

So maybe, by reminding me of a physical prowess I once looked up to, these hellish athletes are a legacy of that rotten day which marked the beginning of a new family regime that looked to me like blackest treason even as my father embraced it with obvious relief. Hardly had the coffinless double funeral been held (I suppose it was more of a memorial service) than my father married my new 'auntie', a heavy woman with a spotty bottom. Laura, she was – and is – and from the first her name and very being became confused in my mind with *laurel*: dark, funereal and poisonous, entangling one in its shrubbery. I still have no idea what my father saw in her except perhaps that she was a good ten years younger than Mama. Laura was from the first a woman of dazzling stupidity who made the awesome mistake of trying to step into her predecessor's shoes, reading me the same books that Mama had read me, even insisting on finishing a Roald Dahl story Mama had started that fateful day. 'Continuity,' I could imagine her saying to my father, 'that's what kids need.' Never the world's most astute man and anyway at a loss over the tragedy that had overtaken his little family, he must have gone along with her, no doubt bewitched by the shrubbery. Anyway, she soon learned to hate me, which was clearly my intention all along. And it is only now, as I sip Campari and orange juice (try using those resinous Sicilian blood oranges instead of ordinary navels) at dusk on my terrace that I realize how very much Marta's hair reminds me of Laura's. Both have the same detestable thick frizziness. I am sorry my carelessness the other day gave Marta an excuse to be neighbourly. A single ill-judged thrust with my crowbar and there she was, invading my kitchen full of demonic virtue, force-feeding me gigantic balls of ex-Soviet putty.

And now this Brill person. Was it going to be worse, going from proto-showbiz sports personalities to the real thing? I know nothing about these people, only the clichés the media purvey. Naïvely I assume superstars either spend most of their time lying in pools of vomit in very expensive hotel suites they've just trashed or else flying to Zürich for long, serious meetings with the gnomes in suits who manage their millions . . . Gnomes. Toadstools. *Mushrooms*. That's it! Got it at last!

Rabbit in Cep Custard

————◆————

Ingredients

1 kg fresh rabbit chunks
1 clove garlic
6 tablespoons humdrum olive oil
No rosemary whatever
16 gm dried ceps/porcini

Fernet Branca
3 egg yolks
125 gm icing sugar
48 gm flour
451 ml milk
Grated rind of $^1/_2$ lemon
Hundreds-and-thousands

◆

If it's nearly lunchtime and you're a housewife who has just had this brainwave that rabbit in mushroom custard is exactly what's wanted for tonight's dinner, forget it. You're already too late. The first job is to soak the mushrooms in the milk overnight in the fridge, and they need at least eight hours' steeping. In any case, your husband's gormless business partner who keeps trying to see down your cleavage will be much better off with Kippers 'n' Kimchi, a nifty little number that will strain his manners until they creak even as you describe it brightly as 'a Korean speciality in your honour, Rupert'.

Anyway, soak those ceps. At the same time steep the rabbit overnight in abundant cold water to which you have added a generous dash of the Branca brothers' nectar. In the morning retain the soaking water and rinse the rabbit under the tap, then pat the chunks dry and roll them in icing sugar. Into your iron Le Creuset frying pan that you need both hands to lift put the oil, crushed garlic, rabbit chunks and the now flabby and expanded ceps that you have meanwhile strained out of the milk. Cover tightly and cook for two hours on a low heat, turning now and then. Uncover the pan, increase the heat and boil off the liquid that has surprised you by seeping out of the rabbit in such quantity. Over the resulting succulent brown nodules pour half a cup of the Fernet-tainted overnight soaking water and boil that off, too.

While the rabbit was slowly seething for two hours you will have busied yourself with the custard, which is more or less a mushroom-flavoured *crema pasticcera*, although that is far too offhand a way of describing this grand culinary break-through. Beat the egg yolks and remaining icing sugar in a heavy saucepan, adding the flour gradually. Meanwhile the milk in which the ceps were soaked should have been brought to just below the boil. Amalgamate the contents of both pans gradually, using every sauce-maker's trick at your disposal to prevent lumps forming, cook for five minutes, stir in the grated lemon zest and *voilà!* Mushroom custard. Test for exaggerated sweetness. A drop or two more Fernet to off-set it? You have failed completely if you are remotely reminded of Bird's custard in either texture or taste, even allowing for the absence of vanilla.

When the custard is ready pour it over the rabbit, cover, and finish off over low heat for fourteen minutes or there-abouts. Do not uncover the pan again but let it cool, allowing the flavours to mingle and develop. Serve tepid on an oval dish, preferably one with a deft pattern of hellebores around the edge. A light dusting of hundreds-and-thousands will intrigue. The aim, as always, is to provoke in your diners the aesthetic reconsideration that is such a vital part of all new experience. The perfect offering for visiting boy-band leaders, madly conservative as they probably are in all their tastes that fall within the law.

Marta

15

Dearest Marja

Many thanks for your amusing letter. Father doesn't change, does he? Talk about Mt Sluszic! Your story of the policemen reminds me of that night we were sent to bed early & Mili was ordered to close our shutters, remember? Heavy engines, a burst of shooting & that horrid screaming. Then next morning a landscape innocent as dawn. The estate clean as a pin, not a tyre mark anywhere, looking as though nothing had changed for 200 years. The only way you could tell something had happened was by Father's black rage that they should have behaved like that on our ancestral property. Well, by all accounts they paid for it later in Marseilles & Trieste, although I definitely do not wish to know the details.

But darling Marja, for heaven's sake don't imagine that just because I've gone away for a bit & am trying to make my own life I'm forgetting my own sister or else repudiating the family. You're constantly in my thoughts, my love, especially now Father's sounding so heavy handed about you & Timi. We've known Timi since we were all kids. Remember what the huntsmen say about wild piglets not growing up into stags? Once a boar, always a boar. Yes, we know his attractions – God knows he showed us them often enough up at Bolk – but we've grown up since then & your feelings about him tally exactly with mine, I assure you. Go along with Father's plan & marry the man & you'll be waking up with a snout & bristles on the pillow beside you. You worry me when you say you think Father's holding you hostage there against my return. Surely not? I'm certain his reason for not wanting you to go abroad yet is partly because you're so young (by his old-fashioned standards, I mean. In some ways 22 is young . . . although it's sure as hell old enough not to get hitched to Timi).

This new boy you met in Voynograd, Mekmek, sounds fun. Let's see how things go in the next few weeks. Maybe with our baby brother's help we can smuggle you out of purdah, assuming Ljuka hasn't lost his independence too. He's becoming awfully like Father in some ways.

Things are moving along excitingly here. A few days ago I had a call from the boy racer, Filippo Pacini, to say he wanted to come up & see me. An hour later with a sudden roaring there was his exotic car with him at the wheel & . . . his father climbing out! The great Piero Pacini himself had come to see how his little Voyde composer was getting on. We drank iced slivovitz in the kitchen while he reminisced at length about cutting his filmic teeth on location in Spain with Sergio Leone in the sixties. I hadn't realized what shoestring budgets those first spaghetti westerns were made on. Peanuts, really. Pacini was very lowly then, of course, just starting out, but working on A Fistful of Dollars was a pretty good way to learn the trade because everything was improvised & you might find yourself having to play an extra in the morning & in the afternoon looking for a suitable tree in the desert from which to hang someone. Pacini periodically broke off to pay me small compliments with that Italian male gallantry that to us often looks a bit smarmy but in his case really isn't. They'd brought me all sorts of little gifts including, curiously enough, a bottle of Fernet Branca & kilos of the most fabulous florentines that must have cost – but what the hell does it matter what they cost? I'm now moving in circles where people fly to New York for a haircut & drive De Tomaso Panteras.

'I love the way you live, Marta,' Piero said loyally, looking around at the cobwebs & laundry (well, I'm not about to clean the house & mend my sluttish ways just because a world-famous film director might drop in). 'I really like it that you foreigners come here & rescue our old houses by leaving them as they are. Well, sometimes you do. But an Italian would have ripped out everything & put in marble bathrooms with gold taps. That's the way we are. Bella figura. But this is exactly how I remember my grandparents' house. They were just peasants, you know. I love it: the same smell, the shallow sink hacked out of a block of stone, that rough old chest to keep the bread in. And I notice you've kept the original stone roof, too. Almost nobody these days knows how to repair them so they get replaced with conventional tiles. And – you must excuse a film director talking – dare I guess at one of those old iron matrimoniale bedsteads upstairs with a painted tin headboard probably figuring the Virgin?'

He was so enthusiastic – how could I have not led the way upstairs to show them my delightfully natural unmade bed strewn with the usual books & hairbrushes & knickers which has exactly the tin head-board he meant except mine has hearts & roses all over it, which I suppose stand in for the Virgin iconographically.

'Perfect,' he said as we all trooped downstairs again. 'It would cost a fortune to build a set as faithful as this. Faithful to the old Italy, I mean. It's hard these days to find a casa colonica up here in the north that isn't a shell or hasn't been tarted up. The first thing they always do is enlarge the windows because peasants didn't need a view or fresh air. They were out working in those all day. Nor did they read at night, so interior gloom was traded for making the place warmer in winter. What I'm wondering is whether we mightn't write in a scene set in this house – with your permission, of course. It's a crime to waste the place & it would certainly contrast well with the ghosts of all those telefoni bianchi . . . Perfect for the scene with Franco the fisherman and his wife. Make a note of that would you, Filo?'

We talked in that mixture of English & Italian I'm beginning to get the hang of – those lessons in Voynograd with Signora Santoliquido were really useful. Then Pacini asked me to play what music I'd written so far for the film, which was mostly the atmospheric stuff inspired by my visit to Pisorno Studios. So I obliged on the piano & I must say he was very flattering, said it was absolutely right for what he'd got in mind, & could I think about inventing a suitable 'sound' for each of the main characters? It's the Peter & the Wolf approach to film scoring. Apparently Italian directors of his generation are famous for doing everything post-production. They shoot a zillion metres of film & then spend

77

months in editing suites & dubbing sessions because they don't like doing voices live. That's when the music usually gets written, to fit the cuts. But Pacini's different. He's like Leone: he likes to get the music written upfront & recorded so he can play it while they're shooting to establish the mood of each scene for the actors. I think it's a brilliant approach & I wish Vasily had done that with Vauli M. & made an even better film.

Now I've got a script to work from & Pacini has sent all sorts of computer gear to help me record it as soon as I write it & send it off to him for his reaction. I told him I couldn't understand the equipment so he's promised to send me a tame geek or nerd to teach me. I can't remember if I've already told you that Gerry, my dudi neighbour, has unwittingly provided me with one of the film's defining sounds? He compulsively – & repulsively – sings as he works – sort of pastichey, bogus, all-purpose sub-Rossini ramblings with a characteristic yodelling effect that is absolutely perfect for my score. Pretentious, vapid & amateurishly earnest. Piero said it was a brilliant inspiration. Unfortunately I couldn't tell him I'd stolen it from the Englishman next door: I want to keep Gerry very much at arm's length & certainly well away from Pacini. I just know he's one of those showbiz groupies who, once he gets wind of what I'm working on, will never leave me alone for a minute. Just let him learn that Piero Pacini has dropped by & he'll be over here every other hour trying to borrow a cup of Fernet Branca (his preferred tipple) or else bringing me some inedible example of British cuisine. Story follows, incidentally, after I've had a shower & a break.

But to round off, the Pacinis stayed late & were excellent company. As I said, Filippo may be a bit figlio di papà but he's growing on me. He's certainly a very handsome creature even if the dash he cuts in that ludicrous car is over the top. He really does look like a celebrated film director's spoiled brat, but there's more to him than that, I think. He has nice manners & pretty ears. He & Dad roared off together in the small hours leaving a strange silence behind them in the house, although less so outside. Long after they'd gone I could hear that burping snarly

noise Filippo likes to make on the corners dying away further &
further below. I bet they woke everyone in Casoli as they passed
through.

Later

*I now smell of rosemary, having used that shower gel you gave me.
It made me all nostalgic. I really do miss you & am determined you
shall come here as soon as possible.*

*Apart from anything else you would get a big laugh from Gerry,
who nearly came to grief terminally the other day. It was lucky for
him I happened to catch sight of him in 'off to work' mode,
yodelling away in the campest outfit you ever saw: yellow construction worker's hat, thick leather toolbelt holding up his shorts
& toting a crowbar he could barely lift. He could have strolled
unnoticed onto the set of any gay porno movie. I happened to know
he also had most of a bottle of Fernet Branca inside him. So there
he is in the distance warbling & striding off to work like Disney's
eighth dwarf – call him Doody, what else? – & he disappears
around the corner of his house. Stage wait. Then a wail like Callas
being goosed followed by a distant crash. Well, you know me:
we're none of us exactly neighbourly by instinct but I can't resist a
laugh, so I grabbed a bottle of medicinal brandy & hurried over. At
first I couldn't see anyone but then I made out his yellow hat. He
was lying right down below on an overgrown terrace in a heap of
mouldy planking. He looked quite dead, actually, & I wasn't too
keen to go down, but then I saw him twitching so felt obliged. When
I got there he had his hat over his face & seemed to be knocked out
but when I removed the hat he came to. I knew he'd be all right
then because the first thing he did was blaspheme quite inventively
(I think) & reach for the bottle I'd brought – not good Voynovian
slivovitz, I'm afraid, but more to his taste.*

*Eventually I got him back up to his house & into bed. Remind
me to tell you some day about this house of his. For the moment
it's enough to say that I glimpsed a teddy bear wearing a blue
waistcoat sitting on the cistern in the downstairs lavatory. That*

will tell you all you need to know. The next morning I called around with home-made kasha to aid recovery. You can't say I shan't be going to heaven. He was a bit stiff but there was nothing wrong with his appetite. He said he'd been demolishing an old lavatory that had collapsed with him inside it. 'Of course, Gerry,' I said soothingly. A likely tale. You don't wear a tool belt to knock down a flimsy old hut. No, I think he was going to mess about with the fussy little balustrade he's put up along the edge of his terrace, lost his footing in his alcoholic stupor, crashed down onto the hut & took the whole lot with him to the bottom. He's lucky to be alive. One of his eyes was slightly black & he looked so pathetic sitting there woozily eating kasha like an obedient small boy in a nursery I suddenly couldn't help feeling sorry for him. Stranded up here in mid-life, blundering around in DIY outfits in a daze of alcohol while singing fake arias, I mean excuse me. He really is none of my business and quite awful. As a matter of fact his singing was so obtrusive the other day my lineage asserted itself & I wrote that little rodent Benedetti a good strong letter. I told him bluntly he had shamelessly lied & that the neighbour who was 'only ever here one month of the year' was in fact a permanent & highly irritating fixture. Still, after Gerry's accident I've repented somewhat & now feel sorry I sent the letter. I think Gerry is disturbed in some way. Perhaps it's this that manages to press a maternal button deeply hidden inside me. But it's a very small button & only connected to some extremely basic circuitry.

On that note I shall stop. Keep me in touch, Mari darling. I want to know about Timi & how you're going to induce Father to let you come here soonest.

Heaps of love
Marta

16

I can at least admit to myself what I can't even to Marja – *viz.*, that the script for Piero's film has come as quite a shock. The basic story as he originally gave it me in his letters is still there after a fashion, I suppose; but what in my naïve former socialist way I had taken for a biting political satire on the eco-cant of the times seems to have slewed off sideways into something altogether more urban and an excuse for orgies and violence. The working title has changed significantly, too. Originally it was something harmless – *Mare Verde*, I think Filippo said. Now, though, it is *Arrazzato*. That meant nothing until I asked Simone, the boy they sent up to help me install and use the computer equipment. He blushed prettily and prevaricated but I persevered until he explained it was dialect or slang for sexually aroused, apparently formed from *razzo*, which means rocket. You live and learn. It's true the film is going to end with a huge display of distress rockets sent up by some Albanians trapped on a beach by crazed racist Greens, but even so, Simone said it's not a commonly used expression and not everyone knows it, so perhaps the film will intentionally sound enigmatic.

That I should feel obscurely let down is an unwelcome reminder of the earnest bore I suppose I am at heart: the middle-European hayseed whom no doubt Gerry spotted at once and has been laughing at ever since. Still, I cling to my confidence in Piero Pacini that he knows what he's doing. I believe he has yet to direct a bad film, although they have not necessarily all been winners at the box office. Given that in the last twenty years the Italian cinema has become more and more dependent on American money it may be that even Piero is obliged to compromise his artistic scruples in order to earn his crust. As I said before, we'll see, even as I dread anew to think what would happen if Father could see too. A glance at virtually any page of this script would confirm his worst suspicions. Opening it at random to prove to myself that I'm not just being rhetorical I find on page 63 that Carla, one of the young girls in the Green commune, is victimized by the others for being 'saintly'. They force her – good God! I must have missed this the first time around – to put a cigarette in her, well, private part and learn muscular control in order to smoke it. Such are the bored games of spoiled youth in post-modern Europe, apparently. Father would simply not believe his own precious elder daughter was setting *that* little scene to music for a living.

Despite all this, I'm working well. Evidently my creative unconscious is relatively unaffected by my innate moralism. I have composed little tunes for three of the main characters and special sounds for the other two. I still hear it all in my head, of course, and write it down as a score in the traditional way. How else is an orchestra to perform it? But now I can play it on a keyboard connected to this computer they've sent me, thanks to something called MIDI. Simone tells me in heavily accented English that this stands for 'Musical Instrument Digital Interface'. The information leaves me strangely unmoved, as do the various opaque phrases that litter the immense and unreadable user's manual: 'layer mode', 'split mode', 'voice selector', 'velocity curve', 'panel voice' and the rest. They haunt the pages but not me. I simply told Simone I wanted to produce a disc of synthesized sounds that I could e-mail to Piero from time to time. But what about playback? he asked. What about experimenting with various combina-tions of sound, bringing out particular instruments, etc? I said I could do all that in my head, but I don't think he believed me and loaded a computer program called Sibelius which he claims is what most professionals use. I learned what to press and wrote it all down so even I can understand it. This method has worked fine so far but I'm under strict orders to call him day or night if I get stuck. We're both servants of the great Pacini and must allow nothing to stand in the way of my drafting the bulk of the score in the next three weeks. If

Schumann could compose and short-score his substantial Mass in C minor in only nine days, I think I can manage some repetitious film music in twenty-one.

The kitchen now presents an odd sight. It offers a bizarre juxtaposition of ancient and modern – or poet and peasant, come to that. I had to buy another table for the new electronic keyboard, which incidentally has a horrid spongy feel not a bit like the positive, alive feel of a real piano like my beloved Petrof. The two massive speakers have gradually concealed themselves shyly beneath laundry like hunted fauns trying to blend into a landscape. One can listen to this system through headphones, of course, but now and then I take pleasure in playing things aloud and must admit it's quite fun experimenting with combinations of sound. The imagination is not infallible and welcomes an occasional rest, and even I was unprepared for the effect of playing the gigue from Bach's G major French Suite on bagpipes and bongos. It's a tribute to the world's greatest composer that although it sounded frightful it still made musical sense. In some ways it's a remarkable machine; and while I can see it will never supplant the way I have always worked, I should be sad never again to have one in the house. In the meantime poor Petrof is getting less of my attention. I've had him since childhood and he's the only stick of furniture I bothered to bring with me from home, so I can't believe he's feeling seriously upstaged. He's the sweetest-toned little instrument I've ever played and I swear he and I shall never be parted. I don't know if all Czech pianos of his vintage were as good but I feel sure my Petrof is unique.

I've certainly had huge pleasure working on Gerry's bogus Italian opera motif with the electronic keyboard. I spent most of a happy morning trying to reproduce the plangent querulousness of his voice, the yodelling effect he gets when he crosses registers into falsetto. (I had never really taken in before that this word is simply the diminutive of 'false'. 'The little fake' or 'Il Falsetto' is how I shall think of him from now on.) I'm afraid I reduced myself to helpless giggles the more nearly I approached the sound I wanted. Two can play the pastiche game and I'm a rather better musician than poor Gerry, so I soon had some most convincing *faux* Rossini-Bellini roulades laid down. I then monkeyed about with the scales, putting in split notes, missing out others, sharpening gruesomely here and flattening horribly there, until I was left with a short parody of an untalented amateur singing Rossi-, Belli- and all the other -inis of nineteenth-century Italian opera. As yet I had no words but found I could make this spoof voice sing it all on a single vowel or else with any vowel combination in turn. This was hilarious. I'm pretty sure a talented geek like Simone knows how to synthesize the sound of real words to go with the voice but it's way beyond me. In any case, as far as I can tell Il Falsetto mostly pulls his fragments of text off tins and cartons and notice boards for some mad reason of his own, so textual fidelity is no problem. But for the film we won't need any more than a wordless braying somewhere in the distance from time to time. A shame, really.

Undoubtedly this computer setup does offer some fine satirical possibilities. Perhaps when I've finished Piero's score and have some spare time on my hands I may try writing a *scena* from an imaginary Italian opera with several strident voices and a thoroughly overwrought orchestra. One of those obligatory mad scenes, perhaps, but one in which *everybody* is barking, not just the prima donna. We're deep in Ossian territory in a gloomy Scottish castle belonging to a mad baron, a near neighbour of Macbeth's. He's a bass. For a year now he has been keeping his younger brother – whom he suspects of trying to kill him in order to succeed to the barony – locked in the dungeons, a vile confinement that has driven the boy insane. That one's a cracked tenor. Then there's a demented soprano, the younger brother's erstwhile lover, who is beside herself with anguish and is visiting the castle with her mother (contralto) to demand yet again what has become of her boyfriend. The *scena* takes place at midnight in the hall of the castle. Gothic traceries, oak panelling, a fireplace the size of a garage, guttering candles. The baron can't sleep because of his conscience and has had the gaoler, McTavish, bring his brother to him. Their demented duet wakes the household. The visiting mother comes down in her nightdress, crazed with worry about her daughter and her own lack of sleep and the duet becomes a trio. Finally the daughter herself appears and loses it completely when she realizes the decrepit creature hunched in gyves and shackles is her once-handsome lover . . . I see (and hear) it all, and am confident that with this malevolently star-crossed tartan quartet I shall be able to shatter all existing Italian records for over-the-top opera.

And yet . . . I'm now beginning to wonder whether, in the way its characters degenerate so spectacularly, Piero's *Arrazzato* may not easily eclipse anything I could do by way of a spoof. That's the trouble with Italian *verismo*: it always goes just that little bit further.

17

A slightly worrying phone call from Marja last night. Apparently Father has been saying it's 'time to check on Marta' to 'make sure she's all right'. Cannily, she offered to come out and report back to him but dear Father was wise to that. He said he wasn't prepared to lose both daughters and quoted some hoary old Bunki hunting song about how, if you've lost a favourite hound, you don't send out your next favourite dog to look for it. Charming. Father's ability to be insulting in about ten different ways while wearing the disguise of a concerned parent is unique – or would be if it weren't shared by practically all Voyde males of his generation. I keep thinking what a mercy it is for me that Father has this crippling phobia about telephoning. I think it may have to do with horrors in the past involving death sentences or something ghastly like that, but I don't ever remember him making a call. In very exceptional circumstances, though, he can be induced to receive one. So today I gritted my teeth and did what I ought to have done weeks ago, which was to call him myself and reassure him that I'm still his dutiful baby daughter.

'And this Pacini fellow, is he courteous to you?'

'What an odd question, Father. Yes, of course he is. After all, he wants good work out of me. Besides, he has perfect Italian manners.'

'You mean he asks before pinching your bottom?'

'For heaven's sake! You've spent too much time cooped up there in the backwoods. Not every man behaves like that one-eyed henchman of yours, Kyril Whatsisname. Or Captain Panic.'

'*Hmpf.*'

'It's true. All the men I've met here have been most polite and helpful.'

'They'd better be. So what about this film of his? Pigeons in Venice, I think you said.'

'Well, they still haven't *absolutely* finalized the script yet. Still early days, you know. Things move quite slowly in the film world. It's changed a little from the original, um, pigeons concept. It's shaping up to being a pretty interesting sort of docudrama about a fishing commune and Green politics. What he's tryi–'

'*Politics?*'

'No, no, not that sort of politics. More, you know, environmental concerns. They're very big here in Western Europe.'

'A fishing commune? That's not political? What, pray, is a member of a commune if not a communist? Tell me that, Marta. Indulge your stupid old father living in the backwoods of Voynovia.'

'Now you know I didn't mean that, darling. You just goaded me with that joke about bottom-pinching.'

'That was no joke, Marta.'

'OK, but neither is this film. These are not *communists*. They're just students – kids, really – who don't like the way

86

commercial interests always override the well-being of the environment and who want to reinstate traditional, less harmful methods of fishing.'

'Oh, you mean sentimentalists.'

'If you like. Just so long as you don't imagine Lenin appears at the end of the film, walking on the water.'

'Are you able to get paprika there? And *pavlu*?'

These abrupt shifts of attention are entirely characteristic of Father and mean nothing other than that he's bored with the previous topic. I was able to assure him that paprika is available, that Italians eat quite well really, despite a chronic absence of *pavlu* in every delicatessen I've tried so far, but that Marja is sending me regular Red Cross parcels of goodies to keep my Voyde body and soul together. Furthermore, I am working well and Pacini is pleased. There being no polite way of saying to one's father 'and would you for Christ's sake calm down and leave me alone to make a life for myself', I didn't try, but anyway he had seized on Pacini's name again.

'Didn't he do a film called *Nero's Birthday*?'

'Er, I'm not absolutely –'

'Take my word for it, Marta, he did. And I take Professor Varelius's word for it – he's at Voynograd University, in case you've forgotten. You do realize that until recently if a Voyde had made so much as a single metre of a film like that he would have been arrested, taken down to the basement at Stepanky Square, and shot. Not sent to Siberia, Marta. Not even tried. Just shot with a single nine-millimetre round his next of kin would have to pay for.'

'Well, thank goodness those bad old days are dead,' I heard myself saying cheerily.

'I sometimes wonder if they really were so bad after all,' came that familiar gravelly tone. 'And don't give me one of your impertinent little lectures about freedom and licence, Marta.'

'No, Father.'

'I've got my eye on Mr Pacini.'

'Yes, Father.'

Eventually I managed to ring off; and it is a measure of how wrung-out I felt that I actually poured myself a small glass of Fernet Branca for medicinal purposes. I think by the end of our conversation I'd more or less managed to convince him that I was not in immediate moral or nutritional danger, but it wasn't easy. Poor Father. The trouble about our mother having died when I was fourteen was that all the burden of bringing up two rather independent daughters fell on him. Of course various female retainers like old Mili did the day-to-day domestic stuff but he had immediately seen himself as responsible for our honour, which in turn is so inextricably mixed up with his own and that of the family. Ljuka has often told us how much worse it was for him as the only son, with all that pressure to become worthy of taking over the clan and its affairs one day, whereas all Marja and I need to do is make sure we're both virgins when we become officially engaged.

'You think that's *easy?*' I cried, pleased to make my brother blush and protest that I ought to watch it, that one shouldn't make such jokes. 'I don't see why not,' I countered. 'It's a funny business, sex. It was certainly very comic watching you trying to protect *your* virginity from that *dudi* schoolteacher until Captain Panic got on the case and he disappeared.' Whereupon Ljuka chased me all over the house. Voyde society is no place for free thinkers, least of all for free-thinking girls.

Ordinarily speaking, you might think such a phone conversation with Father is drama enough for one day, but the surprises are not yet over. A minor one occurs at lunch-time when distant voices indicate that Gerry is not alone. Nothing of his private life is remotely my business, of course, and being the very reverse of a nosy neighbour I am indifferent as to whether it is a guest in the singular or guests in the plural. Still, I have discovered that from the window of the end room upstairs one can just glimpse a tiny bit of Gerry's terrace between the leaves of the trees, and through binoculars it looks as though 'singular' is exactly the right word: a scrawny creature with a polished head. Quite a knowing young man, I'd say, from that worldly little face. They seem to be laughing a lot but then I'm hardly surprised to see more than one bottle on the table. Some connection with work? Or a lover, perhaps? It does seem that Gerry's been quieter recently, come to think of it. It's some time since I consciously heard his singing but maybe I'm so used to it by now that I scarcely notice any longer. Well, well. No doubt all will be revealed in due course. Unless I've got him very wrong, Il Falsetto can keep a secret about as well as a wet paper bag can hold a carton of ice cream. I do hope it's a lover: the poor dear badly needs someone to look after him and it'll get him out of my hair.

But the real surprise comes much later this evening after I've had supper and am playing to myself at the electronic keyboard with headphones on. I'm trying out various combinations of sound and am quite pleased with the effect the opening of Beethoven's 'Moonlight' sonata makes when played on trombones. It's stately and mournful and I'm just trying out the left-hand octaves with tubas when an alien sonority begins to creep in. Puzzled, I punch some buttons but it goes on becoming more obtrusive. On impulse I raise one earphone and realize it's an external sound: a deep clattering hum getting louder and louder and then swirling deafeningly over the house. Obviously a helicopter. I leave the headphones around my neck and jerk out the jack plug. I'm quite distracted. By the time I've found a torch and gone outside it has landed at the back and is standing in a winking pool of its own lights, rotors freewheeling with the winding-down sound a switched-off turbine makes.

Even though I'm fairly sure who this is, I'm still gripped by alarm. The sudden noise and drama, as well as the torn-off leaves still floating to earth everywhere, seem aimed entirely at me. In our part of the world helicopters have always meant trouble. This one is particularly sinister, being of racy and futuristic design as well as finished in matt black without identification that I can see. The navigation and landing lights go off. The door flips upwards and the pilot steps out, also black-clad and removing a silver helmet with night-vision visor. He reaches back into the cockpit for a flashlight, ducks perfunctorily beneath the slowly revolving blades and comes towards me in the starlight. Behind him a few green and red panel lights continue to twinkle eerily on the rakish canopy. I flash my own torch uncertainly.

'Marta!' he calls.

'Ljuka!' I reply in relief. 'My God, you gave me a shock! I mean, how could you find this place in the dark?'

'GPS,' he says. 'I set the co-ordinates when we bought the house, remember? When I waded out into this paddock and asked you to mow it?'

And my baby brother folds me in his flying suit, which smells sexily of kerosene, as the rotor blades of his magic chariot finally halt with a sigh. My forgotten headphones dig into my collarbone, the dangling jack plug knocks softly against my shins.

18

'God, this place is a tip,' observes Ljuka, blinking in the electric light and taking stock of my charming kitchen. 'Why do you always have to live like this, Matti? What point are you trying to make? It reminds me –'

'I know,' I say. 'It reminds you of that house up at Bolk where we used to spend those holidays. Perhaps that's why. Happy times. So why the Men-in-Black, stealth-chopper visit on this moonless midnight?'

'Father, mainly, though I wanted to see for myself how you're getting on. I don't know what you said to him over the phone today but he told me that as I'm on business for him in Torino tomorrow I'd better drop in to find out what's going on.'

'Nothing, obviously,' I say, my natural asperity a little submerged beneath the pleasure of seeing him. 'Can you spot the evidence of debauchery? The floor littered with syringes and crystalline white powder? Can you feel the squelchy squeak of used condoms beneath your feet? Ought you to check the bedroom for unconscious lovers, exhausted in torn rubber-wear?'

'*Marta!*' He sounded genuinely shocked. 'How can you be so flippant about such things? Of course I don't expect my elder sister to have, well . . .'

'A life of her own? Have you eaten, by the way?'

'Sort of. That reminds me, I've brought you a box of goodies from home. Father was most insistent about your having enough *kasha*.'

'He's a complete peasant in some ways, isn't he?'

'You do say the most awful things, Matti. If he could hear you . . .'

'Oh, I know. But you also know what I mean. A clan chieftain presiding over a multi-million-dollar business empire' (and my voice puts expressive inverted commas around the phrase) 'who could buy any pharmaceutical or dietary product by the ton. And what does he send his favourite erring daughter? A peasant staple that can be eaten or turned into a poultice. Or smoked and inhaled, too, probably, in times of severe hardship.'

'I'll get the box,' says Ljuka, disappearing with the torch. Boys can't handle theory, I've noticed. He is soon back with an immense carton that obviously weighs half a hundred-weight.

'Just like Christmas,' I say, unpacking *shonka* and *kasha* and slivovitz made from our own plums. Also many murky jars.

'Mili sent you *kompot*. She made it herself.'

'Darling Mili. How is she?'

'Worried about you. Her little girl exiled in a land of foreigners. The same as ever. Ageless. She doesn't seem a day older than when we were in the nursery. I think she was always seventy-nine even when she was a little girl herself. That wooden tub there's from her, too.'

'It's not –?'

'Oh yes it is. She's very concerned that you're not brushing your hair with goose grease first thing in the morning and last thing at night. You remember, two hundred strokes –'

'– and fifty extra when there's a "z" in the month. In other words every month except February. Oh Uki, it's as though we were still eight years old.'

'Sure. But if *she's* not getting any older, why should we?'

I make coffee. Ljuka sits at the table and runs his fingers over the electronic keyboard. He can't play a note of music on any instrument. Indeed, the more successful I become as a composer, the more disdain he affects for music in general.

'Go on – what else?' I prompt.

'What?'

'I know you too well, Uki. And I've only been away just over two months. You're Father's boy to the hilt.'

'He's really unhappy about this career of yours, Marta, but I guess you know that. He wants me to talk you into giving up and coming home. Money no object, of course. I know you won't, but I did promise I'd try.'

'And this is you trying?'

'What do you expect me to say? What does *he* expect me to say? I think he's most of all bothered about the company you're keeping.'

'Which company is that?'

'Well, what about this neighbour of yours? Marja said he was being a nuisance. We don't like the sound of that at all.'

'Gerry? Oh, he's just a harmless *dudi*. A bit pathetic. He has this habit of singing rather loudly and now and then he comes over with a bottle of something. I think he has a problem with bottles.'

'Not just with bottles, if he carries on. I'll be over there to break his legs.'

'*Ljuka!* You'll do no such thing. You can leave that sort of behaviour for your business activities' (again the inverted commas). 'I don't know how you can talk so casually about going around the world breaking people's legs as if it were a perfectly normal thing to do.'

'You're a girl, Marta. I guess you're also an artist. You don't understand the first thing about how the world runs.'

The coffee is ready at exactly the right moment to accompany some home truths.

'Listen, Uki,' I say to him earnestly, 'I love you. You're my little brother and you always will be. But it's time for you to grow up. You know I've never asked questions of you menfolk but that doesn't mean my brain isn't fully functioning. One of the reasons I'm here is because I *had* to get out, and you do know what I mean so you can wipe that pretend frown off your face. I'm as devoted to Father and the family as you are, but I also know he's a lost cause. He can't change. All that time Voynovia was under the Russians, all those years he was in the OKU, what do you expect? Of course he professes himself to be passionately anti-Russian, like any good Voyde, and obviously he is. But underneath you know as well as I do that he misses something: all that secure power structure, all that state bureaucracy tilted always in his favour. You don't have KGB officers as your colleagues without coming to believe that you, too, are above the law.'

'Dangerous thinking, Marta,' says my brother, pouring slivovitz into his coffee. Who breathalyses pilots?

'Listen to you! Even you sound as if nothing had changed since 1989 when you were barely ten years old, for God's sake. As if we weren't sitting here in a free, democratic Europe where the one real danger is not thoughts but *lack* of them. I'm not stupid, Uki. Without Father's contacts do you think I should ever have gone to Moscow Conservatory? But I've made my own way by my own contacts ever since. Pacini saw *Vauli Mitronovsk* and here I am in Italy at his request. Nothing to do with Father. Not a string pulled anywhere. Agreed, our money bought this house, and this dubious family business of ours now brings me my little brother bearing gifts. But I'm making my own way, Ljuka.'

He looks up from his empty cup and smiles that smile which makes him look about ten again and melts my heart. 'I had to try,' he says. 'At least I can tell Father I tried.'

'Oh Uki, Uki, move on. Now you've got to get out, too. You know you have.'

'Easier said than done.' His voice is sad.

'Sooner or later it'll go wrong, Ljuka, you know it will. You'll notice I'm not making a moralistic point about it *being* wrong, only that it will *go* wrong. As far as I'm concerned it already has, because my little brother now talks casually about breaking legs and he's obviously up to things I don't want to know about and which he also doesn't want me to know about. I just ask myself what sort of a deal needs to be done, and at what level, in order to square the Italian authorities so you can buzz around their airspace at night in an unmarked and presumably unarmed Russian-built attack helicopter. It's one of the new MILs, isn't it? There, you see: you think I'm just some dumb bunny with her head in a pile of music. But we've all read these stories about ex-Eastern-bloc mafias forging links everywhere. *Uki!* Sooner or later it's going to blow up in that handsome face of yours. It's no way of life for an intelligent person. We don't need the goddamn money.'

'Oh, Matti, you really don't understand. Of course you understand some of it: we're none of us stupid, we grew up with the system, we sense how it works even if we don't know the details. But when you talk of the father who wound up a full colonel in the OKU, you're forgetting the father who's also the head of an old Voyde landowning family. We four – we're living proof of a *miracle*. There's no other word for it: that bureaucratic oversight or freakish chance that meant our family was never purged or sent to Siberia or eliminated altogether. However it was, we survived and now incredibly our ancestral lands are ours again. That means everything to me, Matti. It's my blood. I'm the son.'

This discussion goes on in much the same declamatory and pointless fashion for another hour, with each of us telling the other things we both already know, which seems to describe ninety-five per cent of all human discourse and especially that between family members or lovers. Finally Ljuka looks at his watch and yawns and says he must go. He's locked into it all in a way I can do nothing about. My little brother, so handsome (and my God he *is* a handsome kid, everything his elder sister isn't) is unreachable and alone as he walks out into the night in his black jumpsuit. When I embrace him I leave my stupid tears on the flap of his breast pocket as I grip his shoulder blades, pulling us together and determined not to allow my hands to stray in order to satisfy a bleak curiosity that wants to know if he is armed. Those Makarov pistols, whatever became of them? If you fly mysterious unmarked aircraft in a NATO country things will go hard with you if you're also found to be carrying concealed weapons, unless . . . unless . . . Oh, I don't want to know.

'I'll be back in a bit,' he says. 'You only need call and I'll come, Matti.'

These childhood names. We're still the kids we've always been. What on earth would Mili think if she were standing here in the dead of night watching the children she had nursed waving to each other through perspex as the turbine groans, whines, and the sagging blades overhead whirl and stiffen? But she's a survivor, too, and has seen far worse. In a calamitous typhoon of downdraught and hot kerosene gas the winking machine lifts, tilts out over the gulf and sinks, its *whup-whup-whup* banging back from the cliff face opposite as it flogs the night air below where I stand. Long afterwards I glimpse his lights as he curls away towards the northeast, gaining height to clear the Apuan Alps. Far below, the quilt of lights that is Viareggio and the coastal strip ends abruptly at the black invisible Mediterranean Sea. If I follow that coastline down far enough I might just see the lights of Pisa. I wonder if even at this moment some

American at Camp Darby is watching the blip of my brother's helicopter on a radar screen with a puzzled frown, reaching for a telephone. A sister's paranoia? (But pride, too, that our family should have such power.) I shiver and stare long at the now silent sky and its pricklings of ancient starlight over Mt Matanna.

Gerald

19

Off to a famous start down at Pisa airport, having with some difficulty spotted my man coming out of the Arrivals hall with the bemused look common to air travellers. This, together with his gamin figure, gave him an air of youthful vulnerability I wasn't quite prepared for. I was expecting something rather more raddled.

'Mr Riah? I'm Gerald Samper. Welcome to sunny Tuscany. May I call you Nanty?'

'Nanty's fine.'

'Right.' I lowered my voice as his fellow passengers elbowed their way past in order to beat each other to the car rental windows. 'I recognized you at once, thanks to having been warned. I must say that's far and away the best bald wig I've ever seen. Congratulations.'

He removed his dark glasses and revealed cold blue eyes. 'It's not a wig.'

Oh well done, Samper. 'Ah. Sorry. I was told you'd be wearing a disguise. Wig and shades, they said.'

'This *is* a disguise.' The blue eyes blinked once as though taking a snapshot. 'You didn't recognize me, did you? You just guessed.' His voice is triumphant, bright boy catching out teacher.

We Sampers are not often at a loss for words but I led the way to the car in what I hoped was a conciliatory silence. Only when we were on the Genova motorway did he say: 'You really don't recognize me, do you? Not even enough to know that when I'm Brill I wear a blond wig, which is too much of the time. That's fine.' He smiled at a passing truckload of soiled pigs speeding towards their Golgotha. 'That's just what I wanted. Someone who can see me for what I really am.'

Bald, he means? My fingers tightened grimly on the steering wheel, like Per Snoilsson's in chapter three. How many days of this would I have to endure? My mind started flitting, for some reason touching on roasts and fricassées. What would make the best stuffing for Marta if I survived an Andean plane crash and she didn't? We could hardly be a planeload of rugby players, though. Hang on – a planeload of *chefs*, of course, flying to Valparaiso to take part in a televised cookery contest. Each is bringing his own supplies and equipment with him so the aircraft's hold is stuffed with exotic spices and personal kitchenware. That's why the glacier outside the shattered cabin windows is strewn with brightly polished copper chafing pans flashing in the high-altitude sunlight . . . 'I'm sorry?'

'I said, I've never been to Italy before.'

Izzat so, buster? 'That's quite an achievement, Nanty. Not easy, these days. I thought all the British nobs came here now. You know, Tony Blair and the rest. Tuscminster.'

'I must have been avoiding it.'

I catch the blue glance sideways. Maybe he does have a sense of humour? Like a lot of showbiz stars young Brill is surprisingly small. The baldness is distracting but underneath is a professional youthfulness that makes his actual age hard to guess. This little number, I think, may even do a Cliff Richard if he can keep it up and shun evil. I go on mentally fitting him with a succession of wigs to see if I recognize him. Nope. I'm afraid that like many people with rather a good head of hair I'm quick to notice the follicularly challenged. I wonder what happened to his? A fashion statement, perhaps. One of those clones with high-gloss scalps. Or maybe he was staying in the Chernobyl Holiday Inn when . . . *Not AIDS??* The thought is disquieting. Naturally I know all that stuff about loving the patient and not the disease, easier said than done, and no doubt it's difficult to catch in the normal course of non-erotic domesticity. We all saw those pictures of Lady Di fearlessly pressing terminal flesh in hospices around the globe. But we were never shown the next shot, when she was whisked away to gargle with bleach and plunge into a bath of boiling Dettol. After Nanty's gone am I going to have to smash all the crockery like a Romany who's discovered that his daughter was menstruating when she did the washing-up? Make a funeral pyre of my choice oak lavatory seats? Am I being a little hysterical?

'Alopecia,' he says.

'Sorry?'

'You're wondering why I went bald. Everyone who sees me like this does. How can the leader of a boy band be bald? It's simple. I got alopecia and they don't think it's reversible. It mostly all fell out except my eyebrows and, if you're interested, what the specialists call "scanty body hair".'

The funny thing about hearing a phrase like 'scanty body hair' (or even 'Nanty body hair') is that you can't stop yourself trying to visualize it. Young Mr Riah has been there, too.

'Not enough to fill a contact lens,' he said briefly.

We had long since left the motorway and were just winding uphill to Casoli. 'You must be wondering where on earth I'm taking you.'

'Not really. Your bloke said it's secluded. That's good enough for me, unless you're a mad axe-murderer.'

Not yet, I thought to myself. Just don't push it. Ten minutes later my megastar guest was clearly taken by the house. He admired it, he admired its position, he admired my downstairs lavatory.

'He's kick, your teddy-bear,' he said when he returned to the kitchen.

'He's called "Gazzbear".'

'That right? I saw he's wearing a waistcoat saying "Squeeze me – I'm a gas." So I did. Seriously unbad.'

'He's advertised as "The World's First Farting Teddy Bear." He comes from Pennsylvania. I discovered you can modify the fart with KY Jelly, depending on how wet you want it to sound. You feel a bit of an idiot with your little finger inserted in the pink rubber anus of a stuffed toy, but you get over it.'

'I've seen worse at parties.'

'Oh, good. We're going to need a lot of baroque detail for this book of yours. That's what the punters come for.'

'You reckon?'

'Trust me. It's always been like that. Whoever wanted to read a biography of Nero without the orgies and tortures?'

'Did you catch that movie, *Nero's Birthday*? Hey – unbeliev-able stuff. I've got the director's cut on DVD.'

'Exactly. We're voyeurs at heart. After half a century of TV we all want to *see* without actually having to risk anything. Heroin overdoses are really only fun to read about. True of many things. Even sex, quite often.'

Nanty glanced at me sharply. 'The voice of experience?'

'Maybe it's not as uncommon as people like to pretend,' I said evasively. 'You may remember a predecessor of yours, John Lydon, a.k.a. Johnny Rotten? He memorably said "Love is just two minutes fifty-three seconds of squishing noises." I think he went on to remark that only someone who needed his head examining would bother with it, but I can't remem-ber the exact quotation. And that was love, mind.'

'John's not wrong,' said the lead singer of Freewayz with conviction.

We ate lunch on the terrace. I had deliberately prepared nothing exotic for my guest, after all. My Rabbit in Cep Custard could wait as I already had a good cold bird in the fridge. I thought I'd try him with a perfectly standard scratch luncheon: home-made bread, salami, prosciutto crudo, a salad of tomatoes, mozzarella and basil, with three different cheeses and fruit to follow. He blenched at nothing, didn't call for Branston pickle, and addressed himself like a trooper to the wine – a quite passable chilled Greco di Tufo. Indeed, he became merry as the afternoon slipped by and positively flattering about *Downhill all the Way!*

'Great book,' he summed up, pouring himself another glass from the third bottle I had opened. 'Great title, too.'

'I don't know how on earth I got it past them. I really don't think they noticed. They just registered the word "downhill" and because Luc was the world's most famous downhill skier they didn't see beyond it. Even stranger because he was clearly past his peak at the time I wrote it, although he didn't do his spectacular collapse until after the book was out.'

'Burnout?'

'Oh, everything. Knees had gone, hips were going, bladder problems. Plus he'd snorted more snow in ten years than he'd skied over. Couldn't get it up, but not for want of trying. And all this at twenty-eight. I'd call that downhill, wouldn't you?'

'But, like, you were sympathetic, you know? You made him a real person. I mean, not just an icon in snow goggles.'

'Luc *was* a real person. Still is, I suppose, in that Swiss clinic of his. These days he's a prematurely aged businessman who totters from chair to chair discussing sportswear franchises and authorizing his signature to be put on a line of skis he'll never wear. He's surrounded by nurses who look like Playboy bunnies and who, when he's in wistful mood, give him vigorous enemas. But it does no good.'

Shortly after this we both had to go and lie down, Nanty describing his condition as 'totally stocious'. I wouldn't have said he was a fellow I yearned to work with, exactly, but compared to Per Snoilsson he was practically a kindred spirit despite his occasional Buffyisms and mockney vowels (he's actually from Harpenden). As far as I was concerned he'd passed the first test by not being faddist about food. The second test, too, by not being especially boring and for having some sense of irony. The third test . . .

The third test he flunked – and retroactively the second one after all – when we were sitting on the terrace later that evening having eaten a resplendent bird stuffed with some of the precious smoked cat I get from a little alpine village in the Alto Adige and which I must learn to make for myself. You hang the cat in a chimney for some weeks. If you mince the meat fine, mix it with porridge oats soaked in Fernet, pack it into the hollowed skin of a pomegranate pierced with holes and stuff a bird with it, a delicious smoky-sweet scent pervades the flesh of the stuffee – in this instance a guinea-fowl. I didn't tell Nanty exactly what the stuffing was made from, saying only that it was a chef's secret. I don't yet know him well enough. Still, he ate a good two-thirds of the bird.

But it was after this, when we were toasting each other in *vin' santo* and gazing out past the dark crags of our eyrie at the twinkling panorama below, that he asked the dreaded question that failed him the third test: 'Gerry, do you believe in UFOs?'

There was a pause.

'No, Nanty.'

'I guess that means you've never seen one? You will when you do.'

'No doubt. The same goes for ghosts and visions of the Virgin Mary. Until then I remain a profound unbeliever.'

'*I've* never seen one,' he admitted to my surprise. 'But I've read enough to know they exist. You ought to read Timothy Good – he'd convince you. It's completely impossible that all those people are either liars or nutcases. I do wish I could see one,' he said. 'This is just the sort of place. Nice and dark up here. Panoramic field of view.' He stared wistfully upwards. 'I *know* they're up there somewhere. The question is, would I definitely recognize one if I saw it?'

'I should imagine so. Aren't they usually like whatever it was they think landed at that US air base in Suffolk in the early eighties? Revolving lights, tripod feet, the little turret on top, the classic saucepan-lid profile?'

'That's the whole point,' he cried, spilling his drink for emphasis. 'You can never tell. A UFO doesn't necessarily have to *look* like a UFO. You can't ever tell about aliens, either. They don't always look like Greys in *Close Encounters* any more than they've always got green antennae. They can look however they choose. They might look like you or me.' There was a pause. 'They might *be* you or me.'

Just for a scooting instant as I looked into those mildly insane blue eyes beneath the hairless dome I felt a chill pass over my bare arms and saw the hair on them rise. Long ago as early teenagers a friend and I had played that game of scaring each other shitless while walking home in the dark. It was an unlit country lane on a moonless night. We both knew the lane blindfold and in any case there was enough starlight in the sky for the hedgerows to be clearly visible. But we both saw the menacing figure at the same instant, its claw upraised. It was unquestionably keeping pace with us. We stopped in terror.

'It's just that dead tree the cows scratch on.'

'No it's not. That's further on.'

Bit by bit we talked ourselves into sidling close enough to see that it was the tree. 'But supposing it *hadn't* been?'

'Yes. And supposing . . . just suppose *you're* not the person I think you are? Suppose I turn my head suddenly and it's not you at all? It sounds like you, but that's because it's taken over your body.'

The tremble in his reasonable voice scared me too. 'I could say the same about you,' I said. 'You might have been taken over ten minutes ago, and whatever you are now is just saying these things in your voice to lull my suspicions. If I dared look at you I might see you had a scaly tail dragging silently behind.'

'Well, I haven't. I promise you I haven't.'

'But you may be only *saying* that . . .'

Together we worked ourselves into a state of barely suppressed panic, rigidly walking the last half mile not daring to look at each other, staring straight ahead and promising on everything we held sacred (suddenly quite a lot) that we really were the old friends we said we were and not monsters who might suddenly give a triumphant scream and turn with glowing eyes and rending claws. We tested each other on intimacies surely no monster could know about, listening intently for any uncharacteristic tone or word that would reveal the lurking impostor, even as we silently knew that the fiend could inhabit every last cell in our brains.

And here on my terrace in Italy, maybe a little 'stocious' with wine, I felt the same momentary chill at the resurfacing of this half-forgotten childhood game, now played not in terms of monsters, which were kids' stuff, but in terms of aliens, in which millions of adults worldwide fervently believed.

'You think about these things a lot, do you?' My tone was one of sympathetic detachment, the cool old analyst noting down a young patient's wacky fantasies.

But Nanty wasn't listening. He was staring out across the dark bowl of panorama whose craggy edges were formed by mountain outlines and whose bottom was stuck with myriad crumbs of light. 'What's that?' he asked, pointing.

'What's what?'

'There – that flashing red light. It's coming towards us.'

'God knows. Some sort of aircraft. Pisa airport's only just down the coast and there's an Italian air force base attached to it, to say nothing of a US base near there. I agree, it does seem to be coming in this direction. Yes – it's a helicopter. You can hear the rotors.'

My guest remained silent. I reflected again on what a lot he'd drunk tonight in a quiet sort of way.

'I can see a blue light,' he said. 'And a white light. *And* a green one.'

The helicopter, which had at first been rather lower than us, had gained height and was still holding steadily in our direction, much to my surprise. To the best of my knowledge there was nothing above us on this mountainside except steep forest and some nasty vertical cliff faces. At his present rate of climb the pilot would never clear the summit. Now the nearby crags were throwing back the sound of the engine as well as of the rotors themselves.

'Perhaps he's playing chicken,' I said uncertainly. 'Proba-bly some air force trainee pilot trying to give his instructor a heart attack. At least you can be sure it's a helicopter and not a UFO.'

'Yeah? Maybe not. There's no reason why a UFO mightn't look like a helicopter.'

The poor kid's quite off his head, I thought. It's going to be heaps of fun working together. 'Nanty, there's nothing on this mountain besides us, not at this level or above. I promise you, it's just forest and ravines up there. If he tries to land anywhere up here it'll be suicide, so in a second or two he'll go away.' But even as I spoke the machine was suddenly close enough to acquire bulk against the darkness, a huge shape lit from within by a pale glow. Before either of us could say anything more it was arriving slowly above the terrace a hundred feet up, the scream of its turbine deafening. Our paper napkins whirled away in the downwash and bits of twig and leaf rained from my carefully tended pergola. The damned thing obviously *was* going to land, but where? It passed over us and seemed to drift down behind Marta's house and I suddenly remembered the patch of semi-jungle she'd cleared at the back. Even so, I saw no significance in this. To me, the helicopter was evidently in some sort of difficulty and was heading for her backyard as the only available landing space up here. Giving a small inward groan, the finely honed Samper conscience reminded me I owed Marta a debt after my accident with the jakes. Quite a small debt, it was true, but the redundant English gent in me was going to have to go over and see if the fat slag needed assistance at this moment of high drama. As my Norman ancestors would have reminded me, Samper derives from 'Sans Peur'. Fearlessly I nipped into the kitchen and snatched up my torch. 'Come on!' I called. 'Let's go and see.'

Nanty appeared paralysed, pieces of vine leaf resting on his bald head. He looked like a boy Bacchus whose wreath had failed. His face was china white.

'Well, I'm going anyway,' I told him impatiently, turning away.

'Wait for me! Don't leave me here!'

'It's not aliens, you idiot. It's a helicopter that's just landed at the back of my neighbour's house, and I want to know why. She's a Voynovian,' I added as we hurried off together through the trees. He gave a small squeak as though I had mentioned a planet with which he was horribly familiar.

'Turn that bloody torch off or they'll see us,' he said urgently as we skirted Marta's house and approached her clearing. 'Oh, Jesus H.'

The matt black helicopter was crouched like a space age beast, hissing slightly as its blades twirled to a standstill. Nanty clutched my arm as the black-clad pilot removed his silver dome and walked towards Marta. It was she who held my attention. She was walking forward with her arms held stiffly out, easily recognizable by her frizzy mop of hair but tonight looking different in some way. Mesmerized? Drugged? Sleepwalking? She was wearing a long robe and something lumpy and unidentifiable around her neck from which dangled a long string ending in a plummet that sparkled in the machine's coloured lights. I could make nothing of this. And I could make still less of the fact that she walked straight into this sinister black figure's close embrace.

This was a Marta I hadn't suspected. *My* Marta was a dumpy peasant from Mitteleuropa who lived in Beatrix Potter rural squalor and pretended to write music in order to annoy me. Now here she was, wearing strange kit and greeting helicopter pilots at midnight like one of Frankenstein's brides. A demon lover? *Marta??* Something didn't add up. They disappeared into the house together and I managed to pull Nanty up by the roots his feet had apparently put down. His hand trembled violently on my arm.

20

Getting my guest to bed that night was no easy matter. As Brill, surrounded by fixers and bodyguards and able to deploy untold millions to get his own way, he was probably quite a little tyrant. But as Nanty Riah, shorn of his wig as well as his recreational substances in order to fly Ryanair undetected, he was a baby. Without asking, he threw the bolts on front and back doors, turned on every light in the house and sat at the kitchen table shaking and knocking back Fernet Branca.

'There's *really* no coke in this place?' he asked plaintively. 'No hash? Not even a disco biscuit?'

'Sorry. Plenty of booze, though, plus my calm and reassuring presence to remind you that what we've just witnessed has no connection whatever with outer space. What it's all about I don't know, but it's obvious my dumpy neighbour isn't quite the person I've been taking her for. Or at least she's got herself mixed up in something I probably don't want to know about.'

'She was wearing cans, did you see? Headphones, right? Like, round her neck? She talked that *thing* down, whatever it was, disguised as a paraffin budgie.'

'Oh, right, on her sub-ethernet communicator, you mean? And his disguise was so realistic he even made his down-draught stink of kerosene . . . Come *on*, Nanty, that was no wily space alien we saw. That was a demon lover or a co-conspirator or maybe a DHL courier. I shall certainly go and see the old slag tomorrow morning and ask if we can expect late-night air activity on a regular basis because it's playing havoc with our sleep pattern, not to mention my pergola. I expect her to say something like "Ooh, Gerree, is very apologies. Was flying doctor urgent for my parts", but I suppose I might learn something.'

I thought he looked faintly reassured that I was taking it all so lightly. Perhaps my manner also did something to allay his suspicions that beneath my natty leisurewear (from Homo Erectus, thank you very much, and not cheap) I was really one of the six-foot extraterrestrial lizards that David Icke knows to be the true progenitors of the House of Windsor. But I realized it was probably not enough to change his terrified townie's perception that we were a long way up a mountain with the lights of civilization twinkling unreachably far below. I could imagine that if we ever did work together he might insist on doing it in a guarded hotel suite in downtown LA. At that moment the helicopter burst into distant life again and took off in a crescendo of sound that peaked and dwindled rapidly as it went behind a mountain ridge. Nanty's bulging eyes followed its course as though the walls of my house were transparent.

'For my money that's a helicopter,' I said. 'But whatever it was, it's gone.'

'You *think*,' he said. I noticed his fingers were trembling. 'And who knows what it might've left behind? Her intergalactic cuddle-monkey, perhaps.'

As he went upstairs at last I pressed Gazzbear on him for company. Its reassuring little *blutt!* of flatulence provoked a brave smile and the bald kid megastar gratefully took my teddy off to bed with him. That's what years of recreational drugs and vampire-slaying do to you, I thought. Rampant paranoia.

What lousy company we keep to earn our living.

Sometime during the night I heard his voice distantly from his room. Its tone was raised and anxious, though I couldn't make out any individual words. My first thought was that he might be praying, but then thought no – *of course*: he's on his mobile. I'd not seen it, but it was hardly likely a zillion-dollar property like young Brill would take off into the unknown without one. His managers and lawyers had probably got this house on a satellite fix. I'd no doubt he was lying in bed clutching Gazzbear and hysterically spilling UFO stories into the ears of agents, band members, his psychiatrist – anyone who'd listen – while outside his hermetically closed windows owls went about their bloody business making noises like extraterrestrials homing in on him. *Poverino*.

The brilliant Tuscan light of a new morning restored a good deal of perspective to the events of the previous night. They had already acquired an unreal air, almost as though they had come out of a bottle along with the fermented juice of many grapes. My guest's lunacy also appeared to have passed its acute phase. He came downstairs wearing a gold chain around his neck and a light blue T-shirt emblazoned with the word 'Fothermuckers' in dripping yellow letters. Odd lumps could be seen on his thin chest beneath the T-shirt as he sat down. His face had the crushed look of a newly awakened child.

'Don't want to talk about last night,' he said illogically. 'Freaking maxi-wig.'

Without asking I placed before him a plate of grilled bacon – real English bacon from Waitrose out of the freezer, not *pancetta*. It's sad, but the Italians don't do proper bacon.

'My guru says bacon and speed are the two greatest evils in the world.'

'Speed? Worse than, oh, crack cocaine?'

'No, no, *speed*. You know – the hectic pace of modern life. Too much speed, too much rush, too much communication. That's what she says.'

'I see. And bacon, too.'

'Yah, bacon's the worst. I'm becoming a vegetarian in two weeks, maybe a vegan if all goes well. My karma needs rebalancing.'

'I can hardly believe it, Nanty.'

'Really. Probably yours does, too. Beetroot croquettes are the thing.'

'Beetroot croquettes, eh? Let me tell you something. After careful observation and much meditation I've no longer any doubt that beetroot are capable of experiencing pain. That has to be bad for one's karma, surely.'

'Beetroot can feel pain?'

'Definitely. Not pain like ours, maybe, at a death in the family or on hearing bagpipes, but certainly anguish of a kind. You must have seen that famous Kirlian photo of half a beetroot? You can clearly see the outline of its phantom other half, its missing limb. I ask you, what could be better evidence of lack – the absent twin or brother without whom the amputee beet can never again feel whole?'

'You're shitting me.' Bacon dangled momentarily from his lower lip.

'Absolutely not, Nanty. Such are the cruelties committed in the name of vegetarianism even as they're concealed by a cloak of virtue. Come to that, imagine dropping a live potato into boiling water.'

'Nah, you're shitting me, man,' said Nanty again. 'Spuds don't have nerves. Someone's been having you on.'

'On the contrary. Did you never see that programme about scientists recording the sounds made by individual cells? It's a new technique called CS, or coherent sonagrammetry. They actually took this potato, hooked it up to electrodes and dropped it into boiling water. Unbelievable. Horrible. As it died each cell gave out this awful squeak. Millions and millions of them, rising in a crescendo and then fading into silence. Even the scientists doing the experiment looked shaken. It really made you think about the everyday vegetable agonies that take place below our crude sensory thresholds. We're not aware of even a fraction of the pain we cause each day.'

Nanty was listening with the remnants of a sceptical expression on his face, a last morsel of cold bacon impaled on his arrested fork, but his eyes were round.

'So how can you even make french fries humanely?' he asked.

'My very question when I was scripting a video recently for the London Institute of Ethical Culinary Practice. They told me the kindest way to dispatch a potato is to plunge a

Sabatier knife cleanly between its eyes. Or else it may be placed gently in cold water and brought slowly and mercifully to the boil. Peeling is agony, of course, so you need to soak the potato first for half an hour in a solution of local anaesthetic. They were using xylocaine.'

'Nah . . . Are you having me on?'

'I wouldn't dream of it. Now the trouble with vegans is they're even crueller than ordinary vegetarians because they don't stop at the usual tortures. It's a good thing there aren't more vegans because if there were their beliefs would cause massive environmental damage as well, by helping to drain the gene pool. How? Think about it. By outlawing all animal husbandry, as vegans would like to do, you'd bring to an end domesticated species such as the humble cow and the humble hen, to say nothing of the humble pig. If at the same time you also outlawed their slaughter, the only ethical thing would be to turn farm animals loose to live out their natural lives. But they've been selectively bred for centuries – genetically engineered, if you like – so they're not proper wild animals and anyway there aren't any wilds left for them to return to. Whoever saw a feral cow wandering the pedestrian precincts of Milton Keynes? I mean, it's not New Delhi. As for chickens, are we to believe this ex-tropical jungle fowl would happily revert to its natural state in Epping Forest? I know some parakeets have found niches in the London suburbs, but can we really imagine vast flocks of rehabilitated chickens darkening the sun as they migrate over the South Downs? And consider pigs. What is the pig's natural predator, other than man? Nothing. Or nothing in Europe, at any rate. After five years of the vegans' benign sway the whole of the EU would be knee-deep in famished porkers, grubbing up and devouring innocent potatoes and beetroot all oblivious to the vegetables' anguished screams. What does your guru have to say to that, Nanty?'

'Er, well, I'd have to ask her.' My guest was looking a little abashed. Unconsciously he had pulled from his T-shirt a bunch of amulets, pendants and stones he wore around his neck on a gold chain and was fondling them like worry beads. 'I've never thought of it in quite that way. It's sort of muddling, what you're saying. It's not what you usually hear about vegetarians and vegans, is it?'

'No indeed,' I said gravely. 'It wouldn't suit their conspiracy.'

'Conspiracy? Are you working on an exposé or something? I mean, where are you coming from?'

'The kitchen, mainly,' I said. 'I'm a cook. Incidentally,' I changed the subject, 'what does your T-shirt mean?'

'"Fothermuckers"?' He laughed. 'That was the band I started back in uni. Down-and-dirty heavy metal sort of thing. There's a lot of Jaggerage in me, I guess. But these days there's more dosh in being a nice boy, so for as long as I can stand it I'll wear my wig and do the clean teen. Goes against my true nature, though. That'll be majorly themey in your book, I reckon, this business of me being musically compromised. That's why Freewayz is different from other boy bands: we all play instruments as well as sing. It's the legacy of my true self.' He heaved a sigh. 'Fothermuckers was a great band, specially for uni.'

'Which university was that?'

'Well, it was a poly when I went. Molesey Polytechnic. On the Thames? It became Hampton University my second year. I took Counter-cultural Studies and majored in Neo-Paganism. But of course,' said Nanty hurriedly, 'I've moved on since then. Light years. I was abused by Druids and that opened my eyes, you bet.'

'Abused by Druids?' Stone altars? The ruthless insertion of willow wands?

'Verbally as well as physically. In the canteen one day. I made a joke about Isaac Bonewits. The Archdruid of Ár nDraíocht Féin? "Our own Druidism". Well, a name like his is just asking for it, right? Before I knew it there's this spotty geezer tips a bowl of mulligatawny over my head. Can't take a joke. Celtic arsehole . . . You're not Welsh or anything?'

'No,' I said faintly.

'You don't get off on oak groves and mistletoe?'

'No.'

'Yah, well, I could see they weren't very serious,' said Nanty. 'Imagine trying to reconstitute a religion that was completely wiped out by the Romans. Daft buggers. One of their course projects was to compose a Druidic ritual, kinda tricky given there's exactly one classical account of a ritual and *that's* about how to harvest mistletoe. Oh, and there's one sacrificial victim, that guy they found in a bog near Manchester, Lindow Man or whatever he was called. Great basis for a liturgy, right? A complete con, Druidism.'

'Unlike UFOs.'

'Sure, you can laugh now but it wasn't so funny last night, was it? You can't just dismiss ufology. Ever since Roswell it's been more thoroughly studied in more countries of the world than just about anything. Your explanations were all very rational but you gotta admit there's things you can't explain. Like how was it that thing turned up just at the moment we were talking about UFOs? You're not going to tell me it was pure bloody coincidence, I hope? My mistake was, I wasn't wearing my crystals last night. I shan't be taking them off from now on, want to bet? Plus –'

But at that moment he was interrupted by sleigh bells playing 'Für Elise' with increasing urgency. He hauled a mobile out of his pocket, all a-twinkle with violet lights, and killed the tune in mid-chime. Score one for Samper, I thought, as the founder of Fothermuckers took his call and left me to clear the breakfast table and sourly contemplate the prospect of writing this idiot's life-story. It was odd to overhear a phrase in that boyish voice that sounded like 'offshore negotiables'. Nanty's New Age blarney had smoothly given way to hardnosed finance. I thought I'd better trot across and hear what bizarre explanation Marta could provide for last night's events. Outside among the trees and sunlight I reflected bitterly on how little time it had taken to turn a quiet rural retreat into bedlam. Counter-cultural Studies, forsooth. Offshore negotiables, my eye. *Crystals* . . . !

21

As I neared Marta's house I could hear peculiar noises from within. It was as though a really awful Italian tenor were practising high notes and always failing to reach them. It seemed to be a recorded performance, too, since there was an orchestra in the background. '*Uffa . . . buffa . . .*' At the back of my mind the impression formed that somewhere, sometime, I had heard this incompetent before. Maybe he was the male equivalent of Florence Foster Jenkins, a self-deluded amateur rich enough to hire his own orchestra and Carnegie Hall? With difficulty I made my knocking on the kitchen door audible above the demented squalling and peeped in.

The Voynovian vamp was seated at the table wearing a rumpled beige night dress with embroidery over its mountainous regions, no doubt a galumphing peasant attempt at the baby-doll effect. She was also wearing the headphones we had seen the previous night. Before her on the table was a keyboard, a screen and a computer. The music was coming from beneath the usual pile of old bedsheets, scarcely muffled. Marta was just then leaning forward intently to correct something on the tall sheaf of music paper propped on the keyboard's stand. Her awesome bosom, barely contained by the *babushka* chic, depressed several keys at once, not to mention her distracted visitor. There was a gigantic yelp of sound. She glanced up, saw me, and with what looked like a guilty start killed the music and snatched off the headphones. Silence fell.

'Good morning, Marta,' I said with my customary civility. 'You must excuse my barging in like this and interrupting your, er, work, but my guest and I were just wondering if you had noticed a helicopter around these parts last night? Not that it's any of our business, of course. Round about eleven o'clock? Very low, it was. We were sitting out on the terrace and we thought it was going to hit us but then it seemed to come over in this direction. Did my vine no good, I'm afraid. Rather a pity, considering the effort I've made to train it the way I wanted it.'

If I had hoped this horticultural mishap would jar loose some vestigial sense of responsibility in her, I was mistaken. With a brazenness one had to admire she merely shook her head, her rank frizzy mop oscillating like those slo-mo sequences of wet retrievers shaking themselves on emerging from a river.

'No, Gerree. Helicopter? But no, I hear nothing. Last night, you say? No, very quiet night so I am bedding early. I see far off your lights and thinking, "Lucky Gerree, he have companion and they make fooding together." It is true, Gerree, it is not good always to be alone. Sometimes we all are needing what we say in Voynovia, *close muscle*.'

Even the meaningful simper which accompanied this bizarre vulgarism was eclipsed by the aplomb with which she had delivered her monstrous lie. I could quite see that if she were in the habit of quietly opening her midnight door to some gamy peasant youth – a charcoal-burner's son, as it might be, strayed in from the forest in stout denim with twigs in his hair – Marta could reasonably deny it. But a helicopter landing in one's back garden is a difficult thing to keep hidden from a neighbour, especially one as alert as the last of the Sampers. Yet so thoroughly was she simulating wide-eyed innocence that just for a split second I did wonder if after all the whole episode had been a dream or even a sort of hypnotic illusion to which Nanty and I had fallen victim as a result of too much wine and UFO talk. Then I thought again of having watched Marta embrace the black-clad pilot while wearing the very headphones even now around her neck. That was not something I could ever have invented.

'I see,' I said. 'No helicopter, then?'

'I am hear nothing,' she repeated, looking me straight in the eyes.

Another, lamer, silence fell and suddenly I could think of nothing to say.

'Well, I'll be off then. Sorry to have troubled you. You can get back to your, er, music.' I eased the door open. 'Curious stuff, incidentally, if I might say so. I mean, what you were playing as I came in just now. Though actually I could hear it *some way* before I came in.'

'Ah, is *satjriski*,' said Marta. 'For a filming.'

'Satirical, eh?' I withdrew, thinking it sounded no more improbable than anything else Marta did or was. Next time I was on the internet I would have to find out if Voynovia really existed. As I think I mentioned before, geography has never been my strong point, and if she had told me she came from Szlutvya I would have had no reason to doubt her. 'I am Szlut, Gerree, puremost of blood' sounded quite as plausible. Behind me as I walked back through the trees the awful, strained tenor began again. '*Uffa . . . buffa . . .*' I wished I could put my finger on why it sounded familiar, a conundrum I still had not solved when I reached home to find my guest had finished his offshore negotiating.

'We didn't dream that helicopter last night, did we, Nanty?'

'Dream it? It wigged the willies out of me.'

'Well, mad Marta across the way denies all knowledge of it.'

'She was the slut-o-rama snogging the pilot?'

'Exactly. Either she's a liar or we're both nuts.'

'She's a liar. She's one of them.'

For the rest of the morning a withdrawn mood settled on my guest that even a mid-morning slice of my iced fish cake failed to relieve. In an effort to be businesslike I tried sounding him out about the autobiography he wanted me to ghost but he was less forthcoming than I had banked on. His burst of confidence over breakfast about Druid abuse at Hampton University seemed to have been an aberration. As I started to lay the table for lunch on the terrace he suddenly stood up and announced his departure.

'Going? Where?'

'Home. Sorry, Gerry, yeah? Tell you the honest truth, there's no way I'm spending another night up here. I mean, don't get me wrong, mate, great place, ace host and that. But last night, that was something else. I nearly shat myself. That neighbour of yours, *she*'s something else, and I'm not kidding.'

'You still think she's from Betelgeuse, Nanty?'

'All I know is she's not from this planet.'

'She's from Eastern Europe.'

'Europe, shmeurope. Those were not human beings we saw last night, Gerry. No way. And it was no more a helicopter than it was a Volvo estate. Until you went over to see her this morning I was sort of going along with your version, demon lover or whatever you said. But when you said she denied the helicopter, man, that was it for me. Then I suddenly remembered what they'd stopped me from remembering last night.'

'Nanty, listen to me: this is loopy. The only thing that would have impaired our memories last night came in bottles, not helicopters.'

But he was clearly too frightened by his own story to be reasonable any longer. His face took on an adolescent petulance.

'OK then, smartass. When that pilot took his helmet off, what did his face look like?'

I was about to give a patient description when I realized I didn't have one to give. I had been so stunned to see Marta in headphones and night dress walking into his arms like a somnambulist I'd paid him little attention, whereas I could remember her exact expression – one that mingled fright, relief and familiarity.

'You see?' said Nanty triumphantly. 'You can't describe him. And you know why?' He stopped and I was flummoxed to see his eyes suddenly fill with tears. 'Because he hadn't *got* a face, that's why. *No fucking face!* When he took off his helmet his head was blank, like one of those shop window mannequin things. Just a smooth knob on top of his body . . . I'm sorry,' he sat down abruptly and mopped his eyes. 'Just a reaction I have. Whenever I start talking about scary supernatural or other-world stuff my eyes start watering, I don't know why. Do yours?'

But I was still trying to remember the impression I'd had of the pilot's face. A young man, definitely. Dark hair pressed flat by the helmet, vaguely handsome if you were Barbie and happened to fancy Ken dressed for hi-tech action. It was true I couldn't recall his features, but then it had been the middle of a dark night with only intermittent flashes of light from his helicopter and Marta's torch. It came to me that I was now standing in my kitchen with a madman, and nothing between us but a table and the rather pretty Deruta bowl in which I was hoping to create a nifty salad when I was allowed to get back to important matters. If ever I had been prepared to manufacture an interest in this bald dolt, the mood had definitely passed. It was one thing to be bored by singleminded and humourless sports personalities who were still too young to have become interesting, but I could see no excuse for Nanty Riah, ex-heavy metal wannabe turned teen idol. Not only was he older and a graduate of a university of sorts, he was making a flamboyantly successful career in what nowadays passes for mainstream British culture. All I could see in him was yet another juvenile, vapid and lost. Even the language he spoke had no – what would they call it these days? – core identity? It was an aleatory mess: dated hip, mockney, midatlantic, Southern Californian, all over the place. 'Paraffin budgie', I ask you. Royal Navy slang dating from at least the seventies, I'd think, later migrating with the pilots to North Sea oil platform roustabouts. Less than trend-setting in 2003 and anyway, what was it meant to prove? That this bewigged craven who took farting teddy bears to bed with him for comfort was on can-do terms with the rufty-tufty world of the armed forces?

But the real clincher was Nanty the Counter-culture student – even, God knew, *graduate* – who was so hysterical or paranoid with drug residues he was about to be driven out of my house by the conviction that my fat-arsed neighbour was an alien. Apart from which, anyone who could be talked into believing in screaming potatoes was hardly fit company for a single breakfast, let alone for the duration required to write his biography.

22

So I drove my kid guest back down the mountain. His spirits visibly lifted the further we descended until he became apologetic with relief on the motorway to Pisa. I don't do cliché so I didn't actually grind my teeth but I was aware of a private, clenched sensation familiar from a lifetime's social disasters.

'I mean, sorry,' Nanty was blithering on, 'but, like, that was my very first UFO. What a *blast*! I knew Timothy Good was right all along. They really are among us. *Really*.' (And on and on.) He was gazing happily towards the range of hills now safely away to our left. 'This changes everything.'

'Too right,' I thought to myself.

'From now on the group's re-born. Bye-bye Freewayz, hello . . . What?'

'I didn't speak.'

'No, I mean what are we going to call the group? We're going to have a makeover.'

I winced. 'I'm not sorry you're getting rid of that awful name.'

He glanced at me. 'You're not fifteen,' he said sagely.

'Bits of me are, but obviously not the right bits. Anyway, when you're choosing your new name, nothing with the word "encounter" in it is my advice, Nanty.'

'What about "meeting" then? "Strange meeting", that's kinda . . . Yeah, "Strange Meeting".'

'It's the title of a poem by Wilfred Owen.'

'Who? No copyright on titles, is there? And anyway, *Wilfred*? Can't be serious.'

How long, O Lord? I thought to myself and was answered by a sign for Pisa airport saying 11 km. Certainly the whole gruesome episode demanded to be commemorated in a special culinary creation, something that would capture last night's flavours and associations. Alien pie, perhaps. There would have to be a place in it for smoked cat as well as for potatoes and beetroot in memory of Nanty's vegan guru. Maybe if –

'Go on, what are you thinking?'

'I was thinking about alien pie, actually.'

'That's a *great* name, Gerry.'

'I meant as a dish.'

'*Great* name for a group. "Alien Pie". Oh yeah, I can see that. I'll try it on the boys first but maybe we'll go with that. You'll get an acknowledgement, promise. You can do the liner notes for our next album. So what about this project of ours?'

'The book, you mean?' I was hoping he'd forgotten about that. How awkward. On the other hand, turning down work can be less embarrassing in the long run than taking it on. As far as I was concerned this spurious juvenile fidgeting in the passenger seat wasn't mildly dotty, he was moon-baying crazed. 'You know, Nanty, on second thoughts I don't think it's going to work.' Ah, that British diffidence! It was exactly the tone one uses for fending off unwelcome sexual liaisons. Or would use.

'What do you mean, "not going to work"? I told you, I really dig the way you write.'

'I think the world you move in is too different from my own,' I heard myself say primly.

'Nah, nothing but the odd detail. Fix that, easy.'

'You do want the airport, I assume?' I changed the topic with my tone. 'You were in such a hurry to leave you haven't got a flight booked today, have you? Point being, there's a motorway exit coming up and I shall have to commit. If you want a hotel in Pisa proper for the night instead of the airport, now's the time to say.'

'Make it the airport,' said Nanty, adding confidently 'I never have problems getting a flight.' *Also sprach Brill.*

As we swung down towards the terminal I told him I would talk it over with Frankie. 'My agent, you'll remember. And I'll give it some thought of my own in the next day or two.'

'You're not narked that I shan't be staying, are you? A UFO, man, I mean, for Chrissake, who could ever have foreseen that?' Somewhere between the buildings on our right the joc-ularly painted tail fin of a newly landed BA aircraft was slicing towards its allotted stand. 'Not to worry. Next time we'll go somewhere more . . . You know what I mean: less . . .'

'Remote? Scary?'

'In town, anyway. London. Amsterdam. New York. LA. Who knows? But soon. I'll be in touch, don't worry. Been great. And thanks again for "Alien Pie". Well random.'

He retrieved his bag from the back seat, settled his dark glasses on his nose by way of disguise and disappeared into Departures, blending without difficulty into that afternoon's collection of British mums and dads and Crispins. I had a feeling he was about to forgo the anonymity of the Ryanair common herd, and with it the inconvenience of Stansted, and instead would produce a platinum credit card and ensure himself a First Class seat to Heathrow on BA. But then I real-ized he'd most likely given one of his gofers a call and told him to fix a flight. That was probably what he'd been doing in his bedroom in the middle of the night. Beam me up, Scotty. I drove away, subdued. No question, my instinct was to blame

Marta. None of this could have happened had her house either been empty (as that shifty little agent Benedetti had led me to believe) or lived in by a normal member of the human race. Who but a Fernet-swigging sloven – or maybe Slovene? – would have a late-night rendezvous with a helicopter? And then, mark you, lie in her teeth and deny it even though the machine had practically stripped the leaves from an entire hillside and made a noise like Farnborough air show.

On the way back along the motorway I admit I allowed rising antipathy to displace onto Marta's dandruff-speckled shoulders the responsibility for what I secretly recognized as a narrow escape. Really, I ought to have been feeling grateful that her amorous midnight liaison with a parcels courier had revealed my guest's true self before it was too late. Instead, I began indulging in luxurious indignation that she had finally crossed the line of mere colourful eccentricity and was now actively jeopardizing my professional life. By frightening off a prospective client she was making it impossible for me to earn a living . . . It was too much. Drastic steps would have to be taken.

But what steps, exactly? That's the worst of having the Samper imagination. The mind comes up with various scenarios for dealing with impossible neighbours but races ahead all too easily to see the inevitable outcome: escalating warfare with both parties becoming steadily more entrenched in the conviction of their own righteousness and with ever more aggro and distraction. Ought I to do some pre-emptive fence mending – even though I was manifestly the wronged party – and confess that I and my house guest had actually watched her greet the helicopter pilot? True, this would expose her as a liar; but if it were done with the right degree of manly openness and with apologies for what might seem to have been our snooping, surely Marta would come clean (an outstandingly inappropriate image)? I saw her suddenly opening up . . . Well, no. To be frank, what I saw her opening up was a bottle from her bottomless Fernet Branca cellar, albeit in a convivial spirit of neighbourliness. 'Ah, Gerree, I cannot 'ide it from you, you wicked boy! Zat was my lovaire!' No: wrong accent. Far too Brigitte Bardot. What she really does is lapse shockingly into fluent American. 'OK Gerry, let's cut the crap. I work for the CIA. Right – that composer act was just a cover. Trust my luck to get someone for a neighbour who really knows about music, but it was a risk we had to take. There wasn't time. I'm gonna have to trust you. I guess you've heard of Al Qaeda . . .?'

With a start I realized I was even then overshooting the Viareggio exit. Goddamn it! Not being Italian I unfortunately lacked the nerve to stop and back up along the hard shoulder and have another go. Now I should have to go all the way to Forti dei Marmi and come off at the Pietrasanta exit and it was *all Marta's fault*. Only she had the power to cause me such upset and distraction. Did I mention fence mending? Can this be the last of the Sampers talking? Fence *building* is what I needed to be doing. That had to be the answer: ten-foot high beech panels topped with razor wire. Actual electrification would be going too far as yet, but a good solid fence between us would solve a lot of problems. A pity to inject precisely the suburban note one had moved to the mountains to avoid, but there seemed to be little choice. Where was the nearest garden centre or DIY place? I could order the fence right away and have them deliver the panels and posts the following day. Plus some gravel and cement to bed them in. Question: would it be worth hiring one of those two-stroke hole borers that look like motorized corkscrews? A lot easier than –

That *can't* have . . . That *was* the sodding exit! God's buttocks and earlobes, at this rate I would be in Monaco for dinner. I couldn't believe what that woman was doing to me. Now I would have to come off at Massa. But that did it. My mind was made up. One good stout fence, and a phone call next morning to Frankie to tell him the Nanty Riah project was a non-starter. He could call the kid celebrity and tell him so in person. That was what one paid an agent for.

Marta

Dearest Marja

It seems an age since I last wrote but it isn't really. It's just that enough domestic trivia have been going on here to make the exact sequence of things hard to remember. Have you noticed how just trying to impose any sort of chronology on events makes it seem as though a lot of time has been occupied?

By now Ljuka will have told you of his flying (literally) visit here. Really, he gave me the shock of my life. Can you imagine, a helicopter landing in your back yard in the middle of the night & you go out to find someone looking like Special Agent Z-57 standing there all in black? I nearly had kittens. I was more scared, & consequently crosser, than I let on. I don't believe it ever occurred to him that he might have given me a shock. Boys: they have no imagination whatever. They just star in their own private film & that's enough for them.

I must say the Red Cross parcel he brought from home did make me homesick. Mili sent me some jars of her blackberry kompot & a box of goose grease just as if I were still 10.

I'm working well & all that film stuff's coming along brilliantly. The only cloud on the horizon (and it's a very small one, and passing) concerns my dudi neighbour. That's my only real news, to be honest – just to tell you that a sort of temporary war has broken out between us.

How on earth? you're wondering. Well, the night Ljuka turned up Gerry had a guest staying with him (& although it's hardly my business I can't say I think much of his taste. Bald as a goose egg). Apparently they were sitting out when Uki flew in directly over their heads! I must tell him to land from a different direction next time because Gerry came across in the morning after breakfast, ratty & moaning about damage to his precious pergola. That weird roundabout way he has of saying things: had I by any chance noticed a helicopter around these parts last night? Well, Mari, you know me: Ms Mischief herself. What could I possibly do but feign complete ignorance? I mean, our little brother had practically landed several tons of howling machinery on his roof, but instead of laughing & telling me what a dreadful liar I am Gerry was completely thrown. He went all baffled and sulky. I still don't know if it's just him or whether all Englishmen avoid being direct (lack of courage?) and are forced instead to become tetchy. It was also unfortunate that when he came in I'd happened to be playing my pastiche of his singing. I couldn't tell if Il Falsetto recognized it with thirty-six tracks of synthesized orchestral backing & I now suspect he can't have: he would surely have been much angrier if he'd realized what I've been up to at his expense. Poor Gerry! Memo to self: in future only play those bits of the score through headphones.

He went away still nonplussed by my literally incredible lying but came back again the following morning, slightly strutty like a cock mounting its dunghill to make an announcement to the farm-yard. 'I've been thinking, Marta,' he said, 'and it seems to me it would make sense if we established some sort of visible boundary between our two properties. Those little red pegs the geometra put in the ground when I bought my house are obviously a short-term way of marking our confini. As it cost me money to have the survey done I'm suggesting we put up a fence by way of some-thing more permanent.'

'Like the Berlin Wall?' I couldn't help asking.

'Obviously not, Marta. No – just something rather more tangible than a few sticks of wood that any passing helicopter could blow out of the ground.'

This showed spirit, and I mentally awarded him a point. To make things still easier for him I poured a glass of his favourite tipple which he accepted with an admirable show of reluctance. I remarked that a fence would probably be even more susceptible to helicopters than pegs.

'Certainly it would if the helicopters became a habit & if they were flying low enough to contravene every possible air safety regulation, like the one the other night,' he said with what he probably thought was witty aplomb but which just sounded petulant. 'But at least if our fence were blown flat we would have tangible evidence. Certainly enough to show to the carabinieri. A valuable fence destroyed. So might I ask, Marta: would you be willing to share the cost of this fence?'

'No,' I said – & I suddenly heard Father's intransigent voice in my own. Breeding will out, ek ni? 'No, Gerry, I wouldn't.'

'I thought not,' he said. (I then topped up his glass with Fernet & the poor addict, powerless to resist, was reduced to a social blithering: 'Really oughtn't . . . Barely ten a.m . . . Frightfully naughty'.) Then obviously emboldened by the stuff he went back to being 'the coward who kills tigers in his sleep', as our huntsmen say. 'Marta!' he said with an attempt at sternness that made me turn away to hide my smile, 'This is all terribly silly! I may as well come out with it and tell you that my guest and I saw that heli-copter land here. Not only that, but we came over to see if you needed help and watched you greet the pilot and bring him into this very house. So it's useless your going on with this pretence of not knowing anything about it. Now, I don't want to know who it was. I couldn't care less who it was. It's not my business who it was. As far as I'm concerned it could have been the CIA or else your groceries being delivered.'

The poor lamb went on like this for ages. He was aching to know, positively eaten up with curiosity. In my role as Ms Mis-chief, of course, I just sat there with an innocent look on my face – & as you know, I'm pretty good at that. Eventually he ran out of possible identities for our little brother.

'Well, we're both adults,' he ended incontrovertibly & opaquely. 'Have you heard of Brill?'

The name of a place? Something for cleaning saucepans? I said I hadn't.

'I can't say I'm surprised,' said Gerry loftily. 'No doubt in Voynovia you have a nationally famous balalaika player or

131

something. Brill is one of the most famous pop stars in the West. His real name, actually, is Nanty Riah, but most people don't know that. I wasn't going to tell you any of this, of course, but I'm afraid you're rather forcing my hand. Well, that's who my guest was the other night. An international celebrity. And I'm not telling you this for the sake of boasting – I'm hardly a pop fan myself. He was here for professional rather than social reasons. I was supposed to be writing his life story. I say "supposed" because it's no longer going to happen. And it's no longer going to happen because your helicopter visitor has driven him away.'

'He's frightened of helicopters?' I asked.

'Not as such, probably. No, he's convinced your helicopter was a UFO. UFO? You understand, from space? Like a flying saucer? Martians?'

'We call them CSU,' I said weakly.

'Well, Brill's got a thing about them. Rightly or wrongly, he's convinced your visitor was from outer space.'

I couldn't help myself, Mari, I simply howled with laughter. The idea of our little Uki dropping in from Alpha Centauri . . . Half an hour earlier Gerry might have looked like a cock on its dunghill but by now I'm afraid he resembled the way our hens used to look when they'd got at those rotten plums in the lower orchard – you remember how alcoholic the fallers used to get lying in the sun? He was woozy with Fernet & indignation. My laughter goaded a sudden squawk out of him.

'Marta! It's all very well your laughing but that's my livelihood we're talking about. You know: money? Earning a living? You might be able to live on a shoestring and faff around all day with your song-thingies but we ordinary folk have to work. I don't wish to come all heavy but the fact is this visitor of yours – whose existence you so deny in the face of witnesses – has done me out of a job. Not to get all pompous about it, here in Western Europe we might consider that worth a legal enquiry with a view to compensation for loss of earnings.'

He raised his hand as if to forestall a protest I was not about to make & then tried to perch himself on the arm of the sofa, I suppose with the idea of adopting an informal posture more suited to a change of conversational tack. Unfortunately, what with all the Fernet he misjudged it. His hip skidded off & he collapsed onto the sofa & went 'Ooh!' Then he began scrabbling urgently beneath him, his face very red, & came up with that antique mahogany metronome of mine that Father gave me when I went off to Moscow. I must have dumped it there off the table when the keyboard & computer arrived & some sheets had fallen over it. I was wondering where it had got to. These new keyboards turn out to have built-in electronic metronomes that go clack-clack-clack at any speed you like & I suppose pretty mechanical metronomes like mine are now antiques & obsolete. Still, I've got a soft spot for Father's & evidently Gerry had, too. I'm afraid I collapsed again.

'That's a bloody dangerous thing to keep on a sofa,' he said, grimacing & in obvious discomfort.

I pulled myself together & hastily plied him with more Fernet 'to take the pain away', as we say to children, & because he had slopped what remained of his glassful all over his shirt. I even offered to 'rub the place better' & his face was a picture.

'Poor Gerry,' I said, trying to sound contrite. 'I'm really very sorry. But I'm grateful to you for finding it. It's a genuine Maelzel from Vienna; 1817, I believe.'

'Well, I do hope I haven't damaged it,' he said, heavily ironic & still very tensed about the thighs.

'I've been thinking, Gerry. Maybe a fence isn't a bad idea after all. I tell you what: if you'd like to do some research and find out roughly how much it's going to cost I shall be happy to go halves with you. After all, we're friends as well as neighbours.'

At this he perked up. 'Really? You're sure?' Clearly he'd been expecting bitter resistance & was surprised by my sudden capitulation. To be frank, Mari, I'd suddenly realized how inconvenient it would be to let a neighbour stew to the point where he starts wanting to sue me for damage to his livelihood, to say nothing of his bottom. As our family history brilliantly shows, it pays to know when to be emollient as well as tough. So there we left it.

Gerry went off again, walking stiffly, to get estimates for the fence while I made myself some coffee to recover from his visit.

Darling Marja, I shall keep you posted on this ludicrous saga. Meanwhile I was relieved to hear you were so firm with Timi. Well done. He's not someone you should be emollient with. The news that he's spending August in America is even better. He's sure to meet someone he fancies more than you. Well, you know what I mean! This boy Mekmek sounds like a good ally for you. Just don't spoil him too much too quickly. But who am I to advise you? I'm hardly a brilliant example of a successful romantic.

Your loving sister
Marta

24

Very early one morning Filippo Pacini calls for me as arranged. Somehow I squeeze myself into his red Pantera. It's like getting into a canoe. It's such a *filmic* car, wonderfully dated, one feels one ought to be Sophia Loren. I should be wearing a sleeveless dress with long white gloves and a picture hat and present a spectacle of helpless chic, letting the equally filmic Filippo hand me in with maximum male gallantry, with me in giggly mode sitting down with a bump and a little feminine squeak. Or else I should be wearing a severe dark suit and get briskly in unaided, with the air of someone equally used to slipping behind the steering wheel. Fat chance. And anyway, I doubt Sophia Loren was brought up on a diet of *kasha* and *shonka*.

'My father's flying up from Rome,' says Filippo as he blasts round the steep hairpin in Casoli. I have a fleeting impression of a war memorial with bronze figures caught in the act of hurling grenades, though I suppose they might be Casoli's traffic safety officers reduced to apparent slow motion by the speed of our passing. I snatch a glance at this heir to the

Pacini fortune. Not at all like Cary Grant, as it happens; more like a very young Gregory Peck. I can bear that.

We are on our way to the main set of *Arrazzato*, whose construction is apparently almost complete. The same could be said of my score. In a sudden burst of inspiration I have put a lot down on paper very fast and can now relax a bit. My computer skills have also come on this last month, thanks to my sweet geek Simone who is patience itself. I don't for the life of me understand how any of it works, but by dint of writing myself copious memos and sheets of instructions I can do what I need, including e-mailing Pacini *père* bits of my score as sound files. He does seem very pleased so far, which is the main thing. He keeps on saying this film is going to be his masterpiece, but then this is an industry where egos seldom take a back seat. At least I can claim its score is also my masterpiece to date, being much better than *Vauli Mitronovsk* and really quite catchy. I've got a tango tune that Prokoviev would be proud of: apparent shmaltz but with something very putrid underneath. Pacini claims he's haunted by it and already it has become the sound of his film (and this before the screenplay has even been finalized, apparently).

Before we reach Pisorno Studios Filippo stops at a bar for coffee, which is just what I need at this hour. There are very few people about. The holidaymakers must all still be in their hotels among the dusty pines, sleepily tackling breakfast and nursing yesterday's sunburn. He helps me out of his car with a graciousness that makes me feel sorry for him that I'm not Sophia Loren, merely a dumpy East European with a gift for tunes. I do like Italian mannerliness. I'm afraid Voynovian manners are a little rough and ready. Pretty rough and eternally ready; which is why Father automatically suspects ulterior motives when men here are just being polite. It's an awful thing to think about one's own parent, but he more and more strikes me as a barbarian, a thought that never occurred to me until I came here.

'You're very silent,' Filippo says. 'I'm sorry it's so early.' He dabs fastidiously at his lips with a paper napkin. 'But it gets so hot later on.'

'I was just wondering whether Sasi will be waiting for us.'

'La signora Vlas has not been invited. Your Italian is so good these days we decided we wouldn't be needing her services. Were we right?'

'So far as I'm concerned.' This is excellent news. My compatriot and I were not destined for close friendship. The mock-refined vowel sounds of her Bunki accent are enough to spoil anybody's day. Nor am I grand enough for her, not by several orders of social magnitude.

No sooner have I re-inserted myself into the Panther than we are turning in at the familiar gates of the fascist villa. Or rather, completely *un*familiar. Our tyres ping and crunch up a gravel drive between neatly trimmed oleanders and the car stops in front of a dazzling white house. There is a balustraded verandah shaded by a striped awning that gives a view of rich lawns ending in glimpses of the sea between a pair of cypresses. The parking space behind the house is full of vans with muscular young men in jeans and T-shirts unloading film equipment. Aluminium boxes with handles are stacked in heaps.

'But . . .' I begin foolishly.

'It's not the same house,' he explains. 'That's next door and we haven't touched it. This villa's identical because Pisorno Studi deliberately built them as a matched pair. My father has decided he now wants a pre-war flashback, so we've restored this one and left the other. Then and now, you see.'

'Incredible. Was this house in as bad condition as the other?'

'No, luckily. There was a caretaker living here until recently. He was supposed to keep an eye on all these villas but it was obviously impossible and he was too old anyway. We've spent the last month making this place look new. Wonderful what a coat of paint will do. It's all a bit *finto*, though; one oughtn't to look too closely. Inside, we've only restored the room with the verandah for internal shooting. The rest of the house is pretty tatty but it'll do temporarily for our production offices. The real money went on landscaping. Can you believe the lawn was laid only fifteen days ago? And that left-hand cypress down there towards the sea? I think it's plastic or something. The one on the right's genuine but my father wanted two of them. Something about the fascist bourgeois ideal of symmetry. What do I know? I was born in nineteen eighty. The umbrella pines are original. All these oleanders are new. Well, they're transplants, of course, and as this is exactly the wrong time of year for transplanting things we're giving them intensive care until the flashback's in the can. There's a squad of gardeners here practically mainlining the shrubs with fertilizer or adrenaline or whatever it is you do to keep them alive for a week or two. After that they're on their own.' A blue and white helicopter clatters into view. 'That'll be Papa now.'

The helicopter banks and settles behind the house and presently the great Piero appears. His checked shirt and Stetson consort oddly with the reading spectacles dangling on his shirtfront from a cord. I now realize something about him reminds me of John Huston in *Chinatown*: just a faint flash of the reptilian patriarch, though nothing like as old and craggy. He comes to a halt in front of me and crinkles his eyes.

'Behold, Filo,' he says. 'This is the person about to make cine history. The lady composer of a master score. My God, how long we've waited for this!'

He slips an arm warmly about my shoulders and I smell an agreeable scent like old libraries. I'm grateful that last night I skipped Mili's goose grease and her statutory two hundred strokes of the brush. No amount of folk specifics can ever change my hair's colour from its undistinguished mouse but no one could deny it's looking lustrous without – I hope – giving off that faint barnyard smell I have always associated with childhood and which is so characteristic of provincial

137

Voyde girls. Despite myself I glow a little beneath his praise while giving a deprecatory shake of my head.

'Better wait until it's all done before you become extravagant,' I tell him.

'I have one hundred per cent confidence. Two hundred. Before you began, let's say I was eighty per cent confident. But now – it's magnificent. That tango of yours is lethal. Talk about hooks! I'm driving my poor wife nuts with it. She says I hum it in my sleep and now she's talking openly about divorce. Anyway, how do you think this place is looking? Don't you expect to see Il Duce and la Clara having breakfast on that verandah? And then down to the beach where Mussolini will indulge the photographers with a bare-chested run and Petacci will stand with her dimpled knees, gazing out to sea? Come, I must show you the beach and what we've done there.'

He leads the way across the lawn, the rest of us falling in with him obediently. I notice our party has been unobtrusively joined by a man and a woman with clipboards and alert expressions. They had better not miss anything the great director says.

'Has Filo mentioned this flashback idea of mine? He has? Our storyline has become still richer. I wanted to bring in some real fascist background, you see, because I don't think Italian cinema has reminded us enough of that extraordinary period, that strange mix of cultural aerobics and disease. You're going to say *The Garden of the Finzi-Continis*, and I'm going to reply that the film wasn't really about fascism, it was about an aristocratic family retreating from political reality behind the walls of their estate. A rather hackneyed theme, though always one that gives plenty of opportunity for a nostalgic wallow. The exact nature of the external threat scarcely matters; pretty much anything would have done, from typhoid to totalitarianism. I want that authentic fascist righteousness on its own, unopposed. I want the bourgeois values, the revival of Latin, the purging of foreign phrases from the language, the *telefoni bianchi* of it all.'

'So how will it fit into your story?'

'OK. Lando's father who owns the trawler fleet? It was his grandparents who owned this villa. They were thoroughgoing fascists, believed in it utterly. Lando's father has inherited the house – that's what we see next door, derelict – and Lando realizes it's the ideal place for his Green drop-out commune. He's a blank about Mussolini and the fascist period, of course. No one of his generation knows a thing about all that, or gives a toss.'

'Your idea being?'

'My idea being that of establishing some punchy parallels. I want to show that, contrary to what you might think, there is a deeply bourgeois streak in Green idealism. I also want to show that it takes very little pressure to tip that into fanaticism, whereupon certain behaviours become remarkably fascist. An old theme, you're thinking. Obviously I don't want to be polemical. I shall simply let it emerge by means of the metaphor of this villa's decay: that something of the political stupidity and rankness of 1938 was somehow built into its fabric where it has lingered and re-surfaces in 2003 to corrupt Lando's idealism.'

'I see. And the erotic, er, excesses?'

He gives me a shrewd sidelong glance. 'Those, my dear, are what happen when people lose their sense of purpose. I imagine that was the point of Pasolini's *Salò*, only he became sidetracked by his own pathology. As a result the film itself is quite unwatchably disgusting and tells us little about fascism and entirely too much about Pasolini's fantasies. I can assure you *Arrazzato* will be on quite a different level.'

Truthfully, I'm a little surprised by Pacini's simplistic reading of history, human nature, sexuality, whatever. It reminds me of the sweeping wisdom of our Voyde schoolteachers telling us about the inherent contradictions of capitalism, how it went against man's natural socialism and therefore could only ever be imposed under duress. The events of 1989 quickly revealed this as dire nonsense even if we hadn't already known. But when that happened and Voynovia was left without the purposefulness that Soviet ideology had presumably given us, did widespread fucking and abominable debauchery break out on all sides? Sadly, no. For a day or two we held tipsy street parties and sang old national folk songs with tears streaming down our faces. Then we grimly set about trying not to starve.

But here we are at the sea which lies seductively, twinkling and dimpling like a courtesan welcoming all comers.

25

As I already know, this coast is a fairly continuous stretch of sandy beach, arbitrarily divided in the summer season by the differently coloured umbrellas and low plastic fences of various resorts and hotels. Looking up the coast towards Viareggio I can see the nearest gaudy beach furniture about half a kilometre away beyond a corroded fence. This stretches down the beach into the sea and effectively excludes curious holidaymakers from the derelict lots of Pisorno Studios. Southwards, the beach soon thins and frays and ends abruptly in the container terminals, fuel jetties and gantries of Livorno's industrial port which, owing to their size, loom startlingly close.

The part of the beach on which our party is standing is a scene of some activity. To our right a bulldozer is heaping rocks and sand to form a low arm running down towards the tide line. Nearby, a shed-like building has been constructed of cement blocks to which a couple of men are applying a rough coat of plaster. Up on its rafters two more men are cobbling together a crude tiled roof.

'OK, so this is where some of the beach stuff will be shot but we have other locations lined up.'

Pacini is clearly in his element, dressing nature to look like a set that resembles nature. I am irresistibly reminded of Potemkin villages.

'That bulldozer is making one arm of a cove,' he explains. 'Just a low spit of land with scrub and a couple of pine trees. That way we won't be able to see all those beach umbrellas up the coast. This building's going to be an old fisherman's house. We'll age it, patch up some holes in the roof with rubbish, hang some sun-bleached shutters askew, that sort of thing. That will take care of our north-facing shots. The south-facing stuff will be exactly what we can see now: the industrial skyline of today's Livorno. Very stark, very *now* as it contrasts with that holiday blue Mediterranean. I like the shape of those cranes and ship hoists. I also love the effects of oil on water. I want occasional rainbow sheen as well as that blunted leaden look, so we'll arrange some small offshore spills. Nothing polluting, of course. Just light oil that will evaporate within hours.'

I suddenly feel all this is none of my business. The Potemkin beach, the messing about with history, this mapping of periods onto compass points: it's all a bit trivial. The only thing that really counts for me in a film is its psychological plausibility. I have never yet been convinced by ultra-realistic sets and an implausible storyline. But occasionally the reverse has been true, and one has willingly overlooked polystyrene rocks or a faint vapour-trail briefly crossing one corner of a Renaissance sky. Pacini meanwhile has wandered over and is giving instructions to the builders. He makes emphatic gestures. The men are sullen, their faces closed. For the first time a doubt is beginning to appear in my mind like the tiny smudge of smoke on the horizon that heralds a huge bulk carrier invisible just beyond. Of course I am still excited about working for Piero Pacini; but now that I have written most of the score and am drawing a salary as one of the team, the original thrill has slightly dulled. One's career serendipitously moves up several notches and with almost sinister alacrity one adjusts to it. How long before I start demanding a red Pantera of my own and a toy-boy to drive around in it?

The inner smudge of smoke is what the great Pacini has left in the wake of his new plot outline. I note that his political explanation referred exclusively to this historical flashback of his. Nothing, presumably, is to be changed in the contemporary scenes of the rest of the script as he gave it me six weeks ago. I suppose everything is in the filming and the sound effects and the score; but debauchery on the page could all too easily translate into outtakes from *Salò* on the screen. When Pacini has finished with the builders I put this point to him as we stroll back towards the villa.

'I quite understand your fears, *cara*,' he replies. 'You must have confidence. You've seen my other work. Has it ever yet struck you as vulgar or pathological?'

'*Nero's Birthday* treads a pretty thin line in places.' This is dishonest of me. I have never seen *Nero's Birthday*. I am extrapolating from my *dudi* neighbour's enthusiasm and from what a shocked Professor Varelius of Voynograd University apparently told Father about the film.

'It's the line's thinness in which the true art lies,' Pacini assures me. 'Even the Vatican City gave *Nero* an R rating.'

'R?'

'*Ragazzi*. Suitable for boys accompanied by a priest.'

'And *Mille Piselli*?'

'That we filmed almost entirely *in* the Vatican.'

The real truth? The real truth is that I have never yet seen a single one of Piero Pacini's films. Not one. He was just this amazingly famous name, this internationally renowned director who praised my score for *Vauli M*. How else was a starstruck Voyde composer supposed to react? Catapulted into Pacini's glittering circle, I affected a nonchalant sophistication so as not to seem the country hick out of touch with the latest products of the Western art world. I never deliberately pretended to know his work. Familiarity was simply assumed and suddenly it was too late to rectify things. If one was caught up in the great Pacini's entourage how could one be anything other than a groupie? Well, I'm not about to confess now. By the time *Arrazzato* is firmly on my CV nobody need ever know.

'But I have to be absolutely clear about the meaning you're attaching to the debauchery that overtakes your commune,' I tell him as he stops to pat the plastic cypress tree.

'It's brilliant,' he is saying. 'There's this company in Rome that will make you any tree you want. You suddenly need a giant redwood for your set, they'll do you one. But not cheaply. For *Brame discrete* I needed a hundred cherry trees in bloom. We were shooting in June. Imagine trying to find a cherry orchard blossoming in June. But this company came up with a hundred fibreglass cherry trees so damned realistic they even fooled the bees. I'm sorry, you were saying? *Meaning*? You want to know the meaning? The psychology of the breakup in *Arrazzato*?'

'Please.'

'Nihilism,' says Pacini fiercely. 'The meaning is nihilism. The dumb, druggy *nothingness* of the modern age. In *Salò* Pasolini was dressing up De Sade as fascism to give hard-core filth the gloss of intellectual respectability. In my view torture and shit-eating are fairly resistant to intellectual fig leaves. My film, by contrast, will show that the *only* way to counter the sheer vapidity of consumer preoccupations in a world where ideology is extinct is to adopt a principled stand. In this case, Green politics with specific targets: factory ships, dead dolphins, all that stuff. But when this principle, this political will, this *cause* if you like, becomes eroded from within by extraneous social tensions such as racism, everything collapses back into the jiggy gratifications of our time.'

This is the first time I have seen Piero anything other than suave and I suddenly find myself thinking that passion suits him better than being the urbane maestro does. It's surely how he must have been when he was starting out. Plain earnest.

'*Arrazzato* is about tension,' he goes on, 'the effort constantly required not to slump back into the baby-world of self-indulgence where the brain is permanently switched off and the appetites are permanently switched on . . . Have you

143

got it now?' He turns to me almost belligerently. 'It's bleak. It's unbelievably bleak. It will be my bleakest film to date. Over these last six weeks it has been defining itself ever more clearly in my mind and it's your music that has done much of the clarification, Marta.'

'It has?'

'You grasped more of what I was aiming at than I myself knew. That's what's so brilliant. You must have picked it up from the script when even the writers themselves hadn't got it clear despite the script conferences we've been having practically every day. You're a genius, *cara*.'

There really hasn't been enough flattery in my life, I think as we reach the white villa. But there has been quite a lot of pretentiousness recently. Pacini leads the way indoors and, tripping over cables, we enter the room with the verandah. It is empty but decorated.

'We're still waiting for the period furniture to arrive,' he explains. 'To say nothing of the white telephones.'

There are trompe l'oeil oval shields on the walls painted to look like rounded stone and inscribed with Latin mottoes such as ARX OMNIVM NATIONVM. The one on the wall opposite the balcony is a little larger than the others and surrounded by cherubs bearing it aloft in a swirl of ribbons and flowers. These disgusting creatures are not in the usual Renaissance *putti* mould with chubby limbs and fat cheeks. Somehow the painter has managed to endow them with a suggestion of incipient musculature like that of toddlers who have come under the ægis of a drill sergeant. The next step in their careers will involve their being fitted with tiny steel helmets. It is brilliantly sinister iconography. The era's motto is also there in Italian – DIO, PATRIA, FAMIGLIA: those three great intolerables. Pacini, meanwhile, has gone out onto the balcony and is leaning on the balustrade surveying his fake domain.

'But there's something else I've left out,' he says as I join him. His tone is heavy. 'I'm telling you this because you're one of us now and I should be sad indeed if you mentioned it to anybody else, especially *journalists*.' He hisses this word venomously and it is clear that the great Piero has had his run-ins with the press. 'Like any director in Italy these days – like practically any director outside Hollywood, come to that – I'm considerably dependent on American money and distribution, and Americans have ways of making their desires known. "All foreign films start under a handicap," they told me last year in LA with commendable frankness. "Like, they're foreign. Now your reputation precedes you, Mr Pasini" – they always call me "Pasini" – "but even so let's be realistic. You're never going to fill every last movie seat in Idaho. But the seats you do fill, we want them *damp*."'

Piero Pacini regards me bitterly.

'I imagine it's much the same everywhere these days,' I murmur sympathetically. I remember he had started out on the set of *A Fistful of Dollars*. 'But even if Italian cinema isn't what it was, directors like Sergio Leone still had to struggle for funding in their day, didn't they? And presumably there was money around then.'

'Yes, but even then it was beginning to dry up. Sergio became successful because he had the brilliance to put new life into a clapped-out genre. But now we're ruined. We've been ruined by the giant studios that only make films full of special effects for teenagers. There are no adults left in North America. Even Cinecittà is a shadow of what it was, selling off backlots and props like crazy. It's tragic. So when those bastards in LA said they wanted damp seats, some sort of orgy scene in *Arrazzato* became inevitable. Our task is to make it a meaningful orgy, OK? So now you know the deal.'

And all I can think amid these hard-luck stories of an industry's demise is the paramount importance of prolonging Father's ignorance of this project until it's safely too late. The very phrase 'a meaningful orgy' echoes in my head. I try to comfort myself with the reflection that any blame for a film's content can hardly attach to the person who wrote the soundtrack. Plenty of films are let down by lousy scores but nobody ever accuses the composer of having been complicit in the moral tone of the screenplay, do they?

The real problem Piero Pacini leaves me with is that, at least when it comes to social arguments, he seems not to be very intelligent. Can it be that the eminent director is a bit thick? He appears to think that when idealists collapse only nihilism remains. But just because a few members of a supposedly Green commune turn out also to be racist, drunk or lascivious, I should have thought it hardly invalidates environmentalist arguments against the damage done by commercial fishing. Oh well, that's showbiz. I'm far more convinced by the financial bind the man's in. That's an altogether better pretext for an orgy.

26

Between completing my score and trips down to the set I haven't seen anything of Gerry this last week. Seen, no; heard, definitely. From time to time I've been aware of noises off: truck engines, bangings, hammerings, and floating over all the hysterical falsetto arias that seem to accompany my eccentric neighbour's every endeavour. Since this voice of his is the one sound my life up in these hills and the film have in common, the two seem ever more associated. To that extent, though quite unknown to him, Gerry is already part of Pisorno Studios and *Arrazzato*.

It's curious how abstracted one can become. These last few days I must occasionally have glanced unseeingly out of the kitchen window; but not until a sudden burst of riveting am I now moved to look out and notice for the first time a large fence that has appeared surprisingly close to my house. At this moment Gerry's head and shoulders appear above the end panel. He is in his steel erector's kit: I recognize the yellow helmet. For some reason he is holding an obviously weighty machine gun in both hands. He reaches far over the top of the fence with it and turns it to take aim awkwardly at the wood on my side. Suddenly there is a distant sound of collapse and he lurches, hanging half over. His helmet falls off. Simultaneously the machine gun fires, rather to his surprise, I should say, and he drops it with a yell. It crashes to the ground, trailing behind it a cable. Meanwhile Gerry has become remarkably red in the face and is thrashing about as he hangs. I fling open the back door in alarm.

'Are you all right?' I ask with neighbourly concern. 'Can I help?'

'Oh, I shouldn't think so,' he says, struggling some more. There is banging on the far side of the fence as from a flailing boot. 'I, er, things are pretty much under control, thanks. I seem to have dropped the nail gun, though. Have it up in a jiffy.' He tugs one-handedly at the cable. The gun on the ground twitches. 'Better stand back, Marta,' he warns. 'It goes off very easily. *Incredibly* easily.'

'Why don't you just come over this side and fetch it? You look as though you need a rest, anyway. Come and have some delicacies from Voynovia.'

More banging. 'Most kind,' he gasps. He seems preoccupied and his face is congested with effort. I can't think why he goes on hanging over the fence until I realize he must have kicked his step ladder over and can't reach the ground. Really, he must be extraordinarily unfit if he can't lower himself back down. The fence is barely two metres high.

'Er, I'm sort of stuck, Marta. My boot won't, well, I *think* I might have shot myself in the foot.'

'In the foot, Gerry?'

'Damn silly thing.'

I walk around the end of the fence. There is a step ladder lying on its side on the grass and Gerry's left boot is indeed fixed to the panel halfway up.

'The bloody ladder slipped,' he explains muffledly from the other side. 'And these damned nail guns have hair triggers. Criminally dangerous. I shall most certainly have

147

something to say to the maggot-brained Japanese who made it.'

'But not until you've got down.' I examine his boot. 'You're very lucky, you know. I think all the nails went into the heel.'

'Well, can't you get something and lever it off? Look, go down to my toolbox – *toolbox*, for heaven's sake – and bring that wrecking bar. Oh God, that iron thing.'

Luckily he can't see me. I lean against the fence quite helplessly for a moment as he hangs above me, his meagre bum catching the morning sun as it glances through the trees. When I can speak I suggest it might be easier for the moment if I simply unlace his boot so he can slip out of it. This I do, raise the fallen steps, and he returns to earth leaving his boot nailed halfway up the fence. He fetches the bar and eventually, after much hefty levering, the boot is freed.

'Bloody thing,' Gerry says to no one in particular. 'Could happen to anybody, a thing like that.'

Once inside the kitchen I reach down the sacred bottle but this time he forestalls me firmly and calls for plain water.

'Thirsty work,' he says, draining a glass from the well that Signor Benedetti claims we share.

I sit him down and congratulate him on his work. Actually, the fence is quite hideous in its newness. The panels must have been painted in the factory with some sort of anti-rot treatment which has left them a chemical shade of green so unnatural it stands out like a turd in a teacup, as our huntsmen so graphically put it.

'How hard you've been working, Gerry, and all because of my helicopter.'

'Well, perhaps not entirely.' He is stuffing greedily from the plate of *mavlisi* I have given him, the last of the ones Ljuka brought me from home. I suppose you might say they are the Voynovian equivalent of florentines, although that scarcely does them justice. These are the very best, from Mrszowski's in Voynograd. He selects the one we call 'acorn': a pigeon's egg pickled in spearmint water, its base nestled in a delicate pastry cup, and pops it into his mouth whole.

'The only thing that surprises me, Gerry,' I say when I can regain his attention, 'is how very *close* your fence seems.'

'It's where the surveyor's pegs in the ground run, Marta. Feel free to go and check for yourself. The last thing I want to do is encroach on your property. Your house doesn't have much land this side, as far as I can see. It's all on the other side where you carry out your, um, aeronautical activities.'

I suppose he must be right. I'm afraid I wasn't paying much attention when Benedetti was explaining such things, partly because my Italian was more rudimentary then but mostly because I didn't really care. I loved the house and just wanted to get on with my work.

'Don't worry. It'll be reasonably aesthetic when I've finished, running artlessly through the trees. Now what I need to know is, should I put a door in the middle?'

'But of course, Gerry. We're neighbours. We need to have communication between us. Otherwise it will look as though we're quarantined from each other.'

'Mm. Well, no problem. They've got doors down at the yard. It just means a couple more posts. Simple job. I'd better be getting on with it. I couldn't have another glass of water, could I? Those little doughnut thingies pack quite a punch.'

'One day, Gerry, when we're both of us not so busy, I will explain to you the full theory of *mavlisi*. You are supposed to eat them in the proper order. Each kind has a special significance and represents a particular event in Voynovian history which all true patriots know. So when you eat them in the right way you are eating the story of our nation. It makes us feel so close. During the time of the Russians we could do that while sitting in cafés all over Voynovia and they never realized that each day we were making nationalist statements. They just saw little cakes and wolfed them down by the handful in any old order with vodka chasers. Ignorant pigs.'

'Absolutely,' says Gerry, collecting his yellow helmet and going to the door. 'Funny chap, your Russky. I'll be off, then.'

He is utterly preposterous. And yet, impossibly, there is something almost touching about him. How can this be? It's not the first time I have noticed it, while everything in me resists the very thought. He is so vulnerable, somehow, not to say fabulously incompetent. Who but Gerry in his bustling, DIY mode could have nailed himself to his own fence? And nor did I believe a word of all that nonsense he spun me some time ago about Ljuka having scared off his potential client. A try-on if ever I heard one. Obviously he and his one-night stand had fallen out, or it hadn't worked or something, and he decided to save face by blaming me. Well, of course, if he will go picking up bald strangers on the seafront in Viareggio at his age what does he expect? It's partly being able to see through him so easily that makes him touching. I wonder what he really did for a living before he moved here? I suppose he might have been writing people's life stories as he claims, though I wouldn't have said he had the necessary concentration to write a book. But here he is so obviously a gentleman of leisure just filling up his days with cookery and arias and bungled carpentry. A very nice life too, no doubt, but scarcely serious in any professional sense. That's a side of the West I'm still not used to: the idea of people just killing time yet comfortably managing to survive.

But if Gerry were only that I should merely despise him. I do despise him, of course, in a mild sort of way. Underneath, though, there's a bleakness, an abandonment. If he's at all close to Piero Pacini's notions of nihilism he oughtn't to be touching, either. To be made uncaring through injury – no, sad but not very attractive. So what is it about him?

Nothing important, anyway. And unquestionably none of my business. Piero's starting shooting next week and for reasons of his own wants me to be on hand. I can feel my career gathering steam. Sooner or later I shall need to think about the next job. I am *not* going back to Voynovia as a lady of leisure.

Gerald

27

This fence project has been keeping me pretty busy these last ten days or so and I haven't had time to brood much on Nanty Riah's aborted visit. However, if I'd hoped he was going to give up on me as I had on him I was mistaken. Frankie phoned to say he was still as keen as ever that I should write his autobiography for him. Apparently Nanty claimed I had 'the right vibes' as well as having come up with the perfect name for his re-vamped group.

'Huh. Did he tell you about the UFO he's convinced he saw here?'

'Oh yes. He says it's changed his life. He's thrilled to bits.'

'I suppose you know he's quite off his head, Frankie?'

'I take that for granted in celebrities. Interestingly so?'

'No, just the usual New Age drivel. Druids, karma, suffering beetroot, Men in Black. Alternative forms of stupidity. Hey, did you know he's bald?'

'*Brill* is?'

'Nanty is. Alopecia, he says. And there I was, congratulating him warmly on his bald wig at the airport. Honestly, Frankie, the whole thing could hardly have gone more wrong from start to finish.'

'That's not what he thinks. He's convinced you're the sort of person around whom things happen. Not only does he still want you to do the book, he has upped the ante to fifty thousand quid. Seventy-five if you can do it in six months.'

What is a poor author to say? I was simultaneously elated and depressed, a common enough state of mind these days when people are offered a great deal of money to do something repugnant. I pretended I needed a week to think about it, which might even make Nanty put the fee up still further.

On one of my daily trips down to builders' yards in Viareggio for fencing materials I investigated what the various fishing smacks were landing. In times of tribulation the kitchen is a great solace. Suddenly I was overcome with a yearning for that old classic,

Lampreys in Sherry
———◆———

Ingredients

1 kg live young lampreys (not over a foot long)
500 gm shallots
1 bottle –

but what's the use? They only had a hoary old monster well over a metre from sucker to tail, and dead at that. What I really wanted was live river lampreys such as had proved Henry I's undoing, although those might actually have been eels. The trick is to drown them in a good dry sherry. An oloroso will make a heavier, sweeter dish of the type favoured by TV chefs – need one say more? Not too much sympathy should be expended on the lampreys who suc-cumb in a manner to which countless humans aspire, from acute alcohol poisoning. Blissfully drunk, in other words. They then need to be kept in the sherry for twelve hours in a cool pantry so that the flavour of the liquor can perfuse their flesh from inside and out. But there were no river lampreys to be had in Viareggio so I was reduced to buying some small eels and a bottle of *vin' santo*.

Can I be bothered to tell you all about the sorrel, water-cress, tarragon, parsley, white nettle and rosemary necessary to the preparation of this zesty dish? And exactly what to do with the two eggs and celery stick? I don't believe I can; I'm too fussed about Nanty Riah. Although the act of making the dish is a perfect aide-oublier, giving instructions would be too much of a distraction at present . . . Oh, *and* the double cream. Not to mention the saffron. In due course I ate the eels beneath my ravaged vine, between whose poor naked stems I could see a million stars and not one single UFO.

It is very calming, this thinking about, inventing, preparing and eating food. Anything to do with food sets off reveries and memories and brilliant conceits while releasing floods of endorphins to take away pain. Sometimes I lie in bed and cheer myself up by gloating over the culinary challenges faced and overcome in the heroic cuisine of yesteryear. Maj.- Gen. Sir Aubrey Lutterworth's *Elements of Raj Cookery* (1887) would surely be on every insomniac's bedside table were it not so rare. He is full of cunning ways with fruit bats, python etc. and his recipes breathe a manly simplicity. 'With a sharp *dhauji* remove the paws of a medium-sized panda. Discard the animal. Soak the paws overnight in a crock of fresh *tikkhu* juice. In the monsoon months it will be found expedient to mount a guard since the smell of *tikkhu* fermenting is irresistible to both upland tiger and bamboo wolf . . .' Written, of course, at a time when the earth was ours and the bounty thereof. Nowadays we have pizza; and just look at the state of things.

These days spent putting up my beechwood cordon sanitaire have been surprisingly Marta free. I expected her to be in and out constantly, chattering and offering me her usual libations of Fernet Branca, which I now believe may be piped into her house like natural gas as part of some EU scam for chronic alcoholics and designed to benefit the Milanese economy. However, I think she was out a good deal at first and then has kept more to herself than usual by being quiet. Heard, no; seen, definitely. The glimpses of her in her kitchen have been most peculiar. I can't think what has happened to her hair these days. It looks frizzled and greasy as though she had been frying it in Brylcreem. She's a very odd person indeed and I can't say she's exactly going out of her way to appease me for having driven my potential client away and threatened my livelihood. You might have thought that the odd complimentary comment on the absolute plumb verticality of my fence posts would be in order. She is not to know that my client is still keen to the tune of £75,000. However, little sign of her until the other morning.

I was getting along nicely putting up a new panel when I suddenly caught sight of her staring at me through her kitchen window. Actually, she gave me quite a fright. That mass of hair with the wet red mouth in the middle. I was so startled to find I was being spied on I inadvertently kicked over the steps on which I was imprudently balancing and would have had a nasty accident with the nail gun but for my foresight in wearing protective gear. By now I'm rather an experienced handyman and those thick-soled Doc Martens are worth their weight in foie gras.

The ensuing contretemps unfortunately brought Marta out, which in turn took me into her house where as usual she tried to get me drunk with Fernet Branca. When that failed she plied me with what she called 'delicacies': brightly coloured Voynovian objects that were delicate to the same extent that traffic cones are. There were awesome pellets like miniature doughnuts wrapped in candied angelica leaf and injected with sweet chili sauce. Others looked like testicles set in dough. I gathered these were pigeon's eggs and couldn't catch her name for them although the phrase that came to me immediately was Christ on a Tricycle. *Spearmint eggs?* Who but a Voynovian pastry-chef . . .? I can now appreciate that history has muffed the chance of a great culinary partnership by segregating Maj.-Gen. Sir Aubrey Lutterworth and Marta in different centuries. Their respective tastes for a gastronomy unfettered by suburban norms would surely have made for a memorable association. On the other hand I detect from his book that the Major-General was a man of limited patience and it is likely that sooner or later Marta would have succumbed to a well-wielded *dhauji*. His subsequent recipe would have immortalized her.

At least this damned fence is nearly finished. Let nobody think I enjoy this DIY caper. I do these jobs because I can't afford – financially and aesthetically – not to. This Berlin Wall of mine snakes artistically among the trees for forty metres or so, broken only by a latched door with a heavy bolt on my side: a necessary Checkpoint Charlie for neutral commerce between us. By visibly marking the boundary it makes my property look bigger while adding to my sense of security. An additional advantage is that it may muffle some of the noise Marta makes with her pianos and keyboards and sound systems. The trouble with all this electronic gear is that it allows ('empowers' or 'enables', in the jargon of the times) the grossly untalented to pretend to be better than they are. Fire up the right program and even a cat strolling over the keyboard can sound like Scarlatti. The wonder is that despite this, Marta's stuff still sounds awful.

The new fence does add slightly to a mystery, which is that of her comings and goings. Like most mature Englishmen of a certain class I have not the faintest interest in my neighbour's doings provided they don't disturb me. Even before the fence went up, once the trees were in full leaf I could no longer glimpse her ratty old car because her access to the road runs mainly behind her house. But now that I come to think about it I have the impression of hearing sporty car noises from time to time over the last two months which might have some connection with subsequent long spells of silence over at her hovel. Maybe the humble charcoal burner's son has won the lottery and traded in his mule for an Alfa-Romeo? Of course I am not in the least inquisitive, but I will admit to the faintest curiosity as to who she is with and what they get up to.

And now this morning's bombshell. I had made a point of being down bright and early at the builders' yard on the outskirts of Viareggio for when they opened at eight a.m. I needed a couple of kilos more nails and another twenty litres of wood preservative that would enable me to finish the fence today. Driving back along the Camaiore road I stopped for the lights at the Capezzano junction and blow me if, waiting on the other side, there wasn't a flamboyantly scarlet open-top sports car of exotic design with Marta's unmistakable tangle of greasy ringlets bursting up in the passenger seat like tumbleweed. At that moment the lights changed, and to prove this wasn't an optical illusion she waved a bangled forearm at me as we passed while her merry scream *Gerree!* pierced the blare of exhaust. As I drove on, febrilely examining the after-image on my retinas of this unexpected vision, it was the driver who monopolized my attention. Who was *he*? A very young man indeed, of remarkable dash and hand-someness. Really extraordinarily good looking, now that I came to consider it. A real case of Beauty and the Beast. I admit it doesn't reflect well on my customary generosity of spirit that all the way home I refused to feel at all enchanted by the idea that they might be lovers. It would be at once inconceivable and deeply, deeply unjust.

28

As I keep saying, Marta's life is her own. We're both grown-ups and what she gets up to is none of my business. On the other hand, that's easier to say than to act on. All my life I've been interested in things that are none of my business, as well as bored by all the supposedly important things the good citizen ought to know (football scores, the name of the current Home Secretary, what 'DNA' stands for, where Voynovia is). None of my interests adds up to anything as dignified as knowledge, if only because in a world where knowledge is an infinite regression you may as well resign yourself to dilettantism. So I know lots of jolly recipes and spoof arias and can change a tap washer without either wringing my hands or ringing a plumber.

But the things that really interest me are other lives and *gossip*. I find the doings of my fellow humans irresistible. I suppose that's why I've always been able to manage even the least promising of literary hack work (Luc Bailly, Per Snoilsson). It's the mortal contingency that fascinates: the real deal beneath the public exterior. It's the only way I know to write the world – or scribe my globe, if I want an anagram of Lyme Regis Cobb. The thoroughly indecent bleak detail I collect along the way makes it diverting. The day I discovered about Luc's enemas (*Uphill all the Way*) was joyous and set me off on those idle speculations with which the civilized can so pleasurably fill their time. Such as why Christopher Columbus is known in Spanish as Cristóforo Colón, a name I'd encountered constantly in that gap year of mine in Latin America. Since to English speakers his name suggests the lower intestine, I was obliged to wonder about a port city in Panama being called Colón until further research revealed that when it was founded in 1850 it had been named Aspinwall after an American railway magnate. So which address would you prefer? One also wonders if, other things being equal, there might have arisen a therapeutic pastime known as Columbic irrigation. In any case I shall remember the erstwhile city of Aspinwall to my dying day; but until someone can associate a 'blind carbon copy field' with anything more interesting than computers I shall never remember or care what it is, regardless of the number of times it is explained to me.

The question of which Greek god is currently driving my frumpish neighbour about in a scarlet wingèd chariot is therefore of maximum fascination. That he has weak eyesight seems unlikely; it's not the sort of car the partially sighted drive. My next thought is that he and the pilot of the helicopter might be one and the same. In one respect Nanty was right: I never did get a clear impression of Marta's visitor's features that fateful night. Generically, he had looked in much the same mould as this dashing chauffeur of hers. Surely she can't possibly be on intimate terms with *two* such handsome boys, both manifestly younger than herself? Is there no justice? What was that frightful, though somehow unforgettable, expression she used? 'Close muscle'. I badly want to know which muscle, and how close. In short, I need to get to *el cólon* of all this.

Unfortunately it begins to look as though I may have to keep my curiosity on ice for a bit. Scenting dosh, Frankie has rung to ask whether I can meet Nanty again at his request, this time in Munich. Freewayz is shortly to give its last concert there before being born again as Alien Pie: an exercise in re-branding whose breathless news is already filling the teen mags. Frankie has just speedmailed me the latest issue of *Heart Beat*. Its PaceMakers column, which in the trade has far more authority than a *Times* leader, opens:

> Salutations, sistas! Jeez! Have I got secrets for you this month! This sizzlin' selection of celeb stories starts with a scoop fit to give all you Freewayz fans the big boo-hoo! The boys are re-naming your fave group! *Whaaaat?!?* Ooh, that wailin' is agony! But dry your tears, sistas, all is not lost. It's all 'cos of what happened to that gorgeous boy Brill the other day in Tuscany, Italy. Come closer, gang: right now this is the sizzlingest news in pop! Would you believe *UFOs* . . . ?

After yards more discursive nonsense in the same vein the column is artlessly signed 'Kelly' in blue felt tip pen in the handwriting of a girl of eleven and embellished with drawings of hearts. I immediately picture a steely harridan of forty wearing a suit. She is at her desk in a publisher's office knee deep in samples of the teen cosmetics that manufacturers shower copiously on such offices in the hope of keeping their products Where It's At. Twenty years ago she would have had a fag hanging out of the side of her mouth and one eye screwed up against the smoke as she pounded out deathless copy for her little sistahood on an IBM golfball machine. These days both her eyes are wide open but the pupils are shrunk to pinheads.

Flicking through the rest of *Heart Beat* I can see we are in a world where spellcheckers are switched permanently off. But really, it's pretty harmless stuff. Most of the fanzine consists of ads for clothes, shoes, CD players, cosmetics and all the other products so vital to a painless passage through this vale of tears. The rest is just pictures of celebrities like Brill and his group, together with interviews.

KELLY: So the UFO has changed your life. But will it change the group's music?

BRILL: It's definitely a weird vibe for us. But the way things are happening we've all gotta be more aware of what's going down out there. Remember: they're probably listening.

KELLY: Scary! Maybe they're even reading this issue of *Heart Beat*!

BRILL: You can joke, Kel, but it's really, really possible. Nah, our music won't change, 'cept it'll go on getting better, maybe a little funkier. Just that each time we perform, the boys and me'll be like, wow, those guys out there could be listening too. It gives me gooseflesh just to think. I mean, exciting or what!

KELLY: So you'll also be aiming at those supercool teen aliens?

BRILL: Gotcha!

KELLY: But the new name, Alien Pie? Why that particularly?

BRILL: Like it's pie in the sky? Gotta get your finger in it, right? Out there where it's at?

I hadn't expected public acknowledgement for his casual theft of my title for a private recipe I haven't yet perfected, so I can't say I'm disappointed. I'm more intrigued by flicking through *Heart Beat*. It's all on such a simple, guileless level it makes the contrast with the multimillion dollar business it serves all the more vivid. I like the huge, cynical gulf between this month's eager little adolescent faces and last year's identical but vanished teen celebs who never made it despite wearing Skechers Sport trainers and distressed jeans by Ralph Lauren. What went wrong? Should they have worn Lugz slip-ons and jeans by Fubu instead? They will never know, poor darlings, having been overtaken by oblivion. Come to that, I like the huge, cynical gulf between Brill in his blond wig (and surprising baby-faced good looks) and the hairless Nanty Riah talking confidently on his mobile about offshore negotiables. In fact, just give me a decent cynical gulf and my interest always begins to quicken. Suddenly I think Nanty's autobiography might after all yield some quite interesting stuff even apart from the orgies. The precise problem with Per Snoilsson was there was no gulf whatever, cynical or otherwise, between what he did and how he was presented. What you saw was, all too depressingly, what you got: a nasty dim bloke who made a rich living driving in circles. By contrast Nanty/Brill operates on several levels at once.

For a couple of days I drift about the house in relaxed fashion, tidying up and mentally clearing the decks before embarking on this new project. Despite initial misgivings I have managed to talk myself round. Normally there's nothing I so much enjoy as sidestepping a challenge but in this case my interest is just about piqued enough. Will it really be possible to extract anything as consistent as a worldview from Brill's fried little brain? If he does want to follow in Paul McCartney's footsteps and in twenty years' time turn into Sir Antony Riah he'll certainly need all the high seriousness I can invent for him. Some decent songs would help, too. A pity we can't enlist Marta's help here; but from what I've heard her 'songings' would put him out of business inside a week.

Now, what clothes to take to Munich? Laid-back elegance is the note to strike, with the emphasis on laid-back. I must finally resist my natural inclination to dress up the more my client dresses down. In the past it has always been enough to know a client will be wearing nylon sportswear that hisses when he sits to make me reach for a severe black linen suit from Agnès B. with a reproachful tie by Ermenegildo Zegna. It was this outfit that cowed Luc Bailly's manager into paying over the odds for my outline treatment of *Downhill all the Way*. He could see at once he was not dealing with some casual hack but with a businesslike man of letters: a misjudgement I'm happy to say cost him dear.

But having already met Nanty and secured generous terms for the next six months' work I don't have to play that game. The Homo Erectus jeans will do very well: I'm really rather pleased with them. Their cut emphasizes a feature of which I'm discreetly proud . . . Is 'proud' too vain a word for someone of my age to use about his own body? I suppose it is; but I can't help noticing that when I compare my derrière with that of certain of my contemporaries – who shall remain nameless until they do something to deserve naming – it still has pleasingly rounded and youthful contours.

How self-assertive I feel today! If I'm a bit high it's surely justified. A very respectable income now looks assured for the forthcoming financial year – something that we *auteurs* can never take for granted, living as we permanently do on the edge of a financial precipice in whose depths it is all too easy to visualize a gyre of vultures funnelling down to peck over our poor remains. Just as cheering is that I shall be briefly going away and leaving this house newly secluded from my irksome neighbour by forty metres of stout beechwood fencing. I feel sorry for Marta, of course, corralled in her alcoholic gloom with her electronic plinkings and plonkings, but no one is exempt from the crumblings of life's cookies. It is sad she should not have a marketable talent but there are other ways to be happy. One of them might very well be driving around with gigolos in red sports cars. I do hope so, for her sake. If I cared about casual sex I've no doubt the circles in which I shall shortly be moving could provide it in abundance. That's presumably what happens to those little teen faces that fail to cut the musical mustard.

29

At last I am in a position to set down the recipe for Alien Pie.

Have you ever embarked on something that looked completely straightforward but which has turned out to be bafflingly technical? For instance, I was completely flummoxed some time ago in a dentist's waiting room when trying to kill time with the crossword in the current number of *JAPEDA*, the *Journal of the American Pedophilia Association* – a scholarly magazine I had not encountered before. The trouble with these academic journals is that even their crosswords tend to be slanted towards their respective disciplines, with the result that what looks like an ordinary puzzle turns out to have highly specialized clues. I suppose this is what university professors like in their hours of relaxation. Personally, I would have thought a complete break with 'shop' might be preferable. I laboured in vain for half an hour, although it did occur to me later that Americans may spell 'pyjamas' with an 'a' in place of our 'y'.

This same principle sometimes holds good for recipes, and what may look like a familiar set of easy-to-follow instructions for preparing a dish in an averagely equipped kitchen turns out to be the blueprint for a procedure that would tax an industrial chemist. Unfortunately this could be the case here. Alien Pie, unlike all my other recipes, may be better treated by the non-specialist cook as a theoretical text, more of a thought experiment than an actual dish. This is a pity because, although to prepare the dish adequately requires a week (a month if you include smoking the cats), it will open up a universe of taste you never dreamed existed. It is partly for this reason its name is so appropriate.

However, as we already know, this is also a commemorative dish: the direct outcome of what Nanty Riah and I were eating that fateful night of the helicopter and our subsequent conversation. As I mentioned before, at least three of the ingredients must be cat, beetroot and potatoes. Now, any cook knows that a subtle and delicate meat like cat will not easily blend with the stolid, Calvinist flavours of root crops. Had I not spent years trying like an alchemist to achieve this magical fusion I would not be able to give this recipe. But six months ago I triumphed unexpectedly with oyster and turnip profiteroles – creations light as butterflies whose gauzy wings waft you the merest ghosts of disembodied flavours. Who until then could have imagined the spirit of the oyster bed and the spirit of the turnip field tiptoeing out to meet clandestinely by night in a frivol of choux pastry? It required the invention of a process I have modestly named 'sampering'. Sampering is somewhat analogous to the technique of enfleurage with which essential oils are extracted from flowers by aromatherapists (New Age charlatans who always come up smelling of roses). Sampering involves using fat to leach out delicate flavours. It is quite unnecessary to do it at midnight by the light of the full moon where seven ley-lines meet. I also doubt if it helps to be a virgin, whatever that is. All you need is a proper old-fashioned larder: a cool place where the French kept the *lardier* or bacon tub, since lard is what sampering requires.

Might I just mention in passing that lard also forms the basis of a stupendously successful weight-loss diet I pioneered for a women's magazine, now sadly defunct? It was called the LFM diet after its three ingredients: lard, Fernet and multivitamins. Half a bottle of Fernet Branca a day, plus a single multivitamin pill and *all the lard you can eat*. Just that! And the weight, ladies, *rolls* off. Hard to believe? Try it for yourself in the privacy of your home. But do be sensible and remember, as when starting any new diet, not to consult a member of the medical profession. For obvious reasons doctors are dead against your becoming healthy. Older readers will probably remember that the LFM diet became famous mainly because if you followed it faithfully you always lost weight but never suffered hunger pangs. Indeed, the only disadvantage that occurred in a small minority of cases was grease stains on the underwear. Otherwise it was wholly free of side effects. In view of her new romantic status it might be neighbourly of me, before I go, to introduce Marta to the LFM diet. All part of the Samper service.

All right, then,

Alien Pie

◆

Ingredients

1 kg smoked cat, off the bone
500 gm baby beet
1 tbs puréed prunes
50 gm kibbled peanuts
Nasturtium leaves
250 gm green bacon
250 gm lard
300 gm flour
Pepper
1 single drop household paraffin
500 gm old potatoes
500 gm rhubarb
4 pomegranates
1 baby hawksbill turtle
Fresh ginger
1 buzzard feather
Fernet Branca
White wine
Salt

◆

As I hinted earlier, securing and preparing the correct ingredients can be quite time-consuming. Alien Pie is as good a test as I know of *punctuality*: that innate sense of timing without which no one ever becomes a cook worthy of the name. The best commercially available smoked cat comes from just inside Italy, up by the Swiss border near Solda (or Sulden, if you're feeling Germanic). It is purveyed by the Ammering family in the little village of Migg and they run an efficient mail-order service. Those high cantons of the Alps long ago developed ways of preserving meat against the long, cold winters when communities might be isolated by snow for months on end. Some uplanders in Switzerland still eat dog, but sadly this noble tradition has lately been reduced to a hole-and-corner ritual like early Christians celebrating communion underground. It is even unclear how much longer the Ammerings can remain in business. Last year's production was interrupted by a dastardly attack made on their smokery by members of QI, the *Quadrupedifili d'Italia*. I am determined this distinctive taste be not lost to gastronomy and Claudio Ammering has now agreed to pass on to me his family's secret in order to keep the art alive. It ought to be something one can easily learn. Cats are plentiful enough, God knows. According to the Mammal Society in the UK alone they kill 300,000 birds every two days. If nature can be so unashamedly red in tooth and claw even when obese with Whiskas, no ethical cook should hesitate to redress the balance in the birds' favour. Cats are skinned and paunched like hares; it is the smoking process I have yet to learn.

Meanwhile, the baby beet should be lightly boiled and, when quite cool, thinly sliced and laid on a tray of cold lard before being covered with more shavings of lard topped off with a bread board on which is a brick. This is sampering. Over a period of ten days in the coolest place available short of the fridge, precious flavour leaches out of the beet into the lard. The pomegranate rinds, cut into thin julienne strips, should likewise be sampered.

Now the busy cook can relax and take himself down to the local fishing port for the turtle. These creatures are not as readily available as they used to be, apparently, and now only turn up from time to time as by-catch in fishermen's nets. If spotted they should be snapped up at once, killed by cutting the throat, bagged and popped into the freezer. For Alien Pie no more than 500 gm of turtle meat is required. The flesh of even baby turtles can be tough, so marinade it first in white wine, sliced fresh ginger and crushed nasturtium leaves.

The great day arrives when these carefully assembled ingredients can be translated lovingly into a rare repast. Prepare yourself. Rise early. Think pure thoughts. Ensure your neighbour – who these days looks more and more as though she has taken to sampering her hair – is safely battened away in her frowsty gloom behind the fence. Put on a clean apron. Choose an aria worthy of the dish, for the chef who cooks without a song on his lips cannot hope to infuse the right carefree improvisatory note into his art. Today the future looks as bright as the Tuscan sunlight striking mottles from the cliff face visible beyond the kitchen window. I break into 'Nuoce gravamente alla salute', Orazio's light-hearted warning to his friend and rival in love Ovidio that to fall in love will be the death of him. As indeed it proves to be in Act 3 when Orazio drowns him in a vat of cyanide: a perfect example of overkill and one unrivalled until the morbid excess of the much later opera *Rasputin*. I sometimes think *I Froci di Firenze* has to be my all-time favourite opera to cook by. Today I seem in fine form, melodramatically inspired, carolling away as with my terrible swift sword I chop the washed rhubarb stalks into one-inch lengths before subjecting the defenceless peanuts to the hammer blows of fate.

Soon the bacon and the crushed (but not ground) peanuts are frying in a generous lump of lard from the sampered beet and pomegranates. They are joined in our best iron casserole by the pussy fumé, the tortue marinadée and the rhubarb choppée. The puréed prunes should be thinned with a glass of Fernet and added to the pot. Then the pomegranate rinds and the beet are retrieved from the sampering. You will notice how pale the beet have become, the rich flush of their childhood having transferred itself to the lard over the preceding days. They can now be discarded, having served their purpose. The pomegranate rinds, though, are added, together with the peeled and diced potatoes. A tad dry, you feel? A glass of the marinade will rectify that; but remember there is a lot of moisture locked up in the turtle meat and the rhubarb. In my view pies should not be awash in that all-purpose brown soup the British call gravy. With a meat as delicate as cat we are aiming at a casket of disarming savours rather than a rugged stew a-swill beneath an iron roof of pastry. Add a pinch or two of salt and pepper and then – supremest master-stroke in all modern cuisine – the single drop of paraffin (or kerosene as the Americans call it).

You blench? Just a bit leery, are we? But listen: I have discovered that this single drop transforms the dish from merely very interesting into an unblushing classic. In such a tiny quantity paraffin is completely harmless, if that's what's worrying you. Nor can you taste it as such, any more than you taste the chocolate in that Mexican classic, rabbit in chocolate. It simply becomes something else, something inimitably itself. It is, well, *alien*, like the hint of industrial processes somewhere in the background of Knize Ten eau de cologne. Just be courageous! *Coraggio!* as I sing in the character of Orazio (who is trying to steel himself to cut out the heart of his poisoned friend and turn it into a paperweight by marmelizing). Add that drop, stir everything together, cover the pot and cook for two hours in a low oven (170°C).

In the meantime you can sift the flour into a bowl and work in 100 gm of the bright pink lard from the sampered beet and 100 gm of the faint pink lard from the sampered pomegranate rinds. You will need to add just enough Fernet to make it all cling together in a ball that can be briefly kneaded and rolled out into a half-inch-thick sheet of the oddest pastry you ever did see. Frankly, it looks like pink marzipan, for all the world like something that might be stockpiled by a Battenberg cake factory. Put it hastily into the fridge for half an hour. Then transfer the contents of the casserole (resist the urge to taste it but admire that deep smoky, plummy, geological smell like processes taking place deep inside a star) to a large, round, ovenproof dish. Lay a strip of the pastry on the pie dish's moistened rim; place a tall cake ring in the centre of the dish with a saucer laid upside down on top and carefully drape the pastry over all, sealing it well around the edges. The shape should resemble a UFO; it is very much up to the cook's individual ingenuity to add verisimilitude. I use small embedded olives for a ring of portholes. Then back into the oven with it for another forty minutes at 190 °C until it is the dark pinkish-brown of an unknown alloy heated to glowing by entry into a planet's upper atmosphere.

Beyond this point we enter the realm of the sacramental, and words all but fail me. All I can say is that Alien Pie, hot from the oven and with a jaunty buzzard feather stuck in the top, should be eaten on a terrace overlooking a distant ocean above which the remnants of sunset brood like old wounds seeping through a field dressing. It is one of those experiences poised exquisitely between sorrow and oblivion.

30

No matter how dubious the enterprise on which you're embarked, you can't beat the red-carpet treatment. I fizzed across the Alps from Pisa and was met at Munich airport by a Bavarian fixer with a turd-coloured Mercedes limo. Thereafter I was wafted to a hotel. Asked to guess, I might have imagined the Kempinski Four Seasons or the Bayerischer Hof would be adequate lodging for a ghost writer. To my surprise and pleasure we drove through the old city on the inner ring road straight towards the Hofbräuhaus, by which time I realized Nanty's minions had booked me into the Hotel Rafael.

My suite would have made the Centre Court at Wimbledon look poky. And until the words 'by their fruits ye shall know them' popped into my head it hadn't occurred to me that St Matthew had divided his time between being an Apostle and being a researcher for the *Guide Michelin*, for his observation is that of a seasoned traveller. Whereas in most hotels the complimentary fruit basket contains the bananas, oranges, apples and flavour-free grapes recently relieved from a long spell of duty on the dessert trolley in the restaurant downstairs, that of the Hotel Rafael was full of rambutans, mangoes, passion fruit, guavas, soursops, pomeloes and the fabled Nepalese persimmon.

In an envelope propped on my pillow in a nest of Mozartkugeln was a note from Nanty and a ticket for next evening's farewell Freewayz gig in the Olympiahalle. The note suggested we meet on the hotel roof after dinner for a swim. In due course I ate in the restaurant, one of those meals one only ever eats in a first-class hotel when someone else is footing the bill. There was a little too much of everything and I had the unsettling feeling that it was improper to read and eat at the same time. As a matter of fact, reading a book over a solitary evening meal in a foreign restaurant is normally one of my greatest pleasures, following the particular enjoyment of choosing a meal from a menu in a language I can't understand. Not knowing what I shall shortly be eating is just as exciting as not knowing what I shall be reading in half a chapter's time. The most extraordinary things arrive at the table, like the 'gourmet' dish I didn't realize I had ordered in Romania and which seemed to consist of tubing and flames, a sort of urinary tract flambé. It was full of Georgian brandy and rather good. I also well remember a meal in Dakar last year (Per Snoilsson was awarding prizes in the Paris–Dakar rally) which began with fig blancmange, went on to a soup that tasted agreeably of roast bricks, and ended with a deep-fried camel harness that was unaccountably delicious. You never can tell. Adventure – that's what I crave; and the older I get the fewer the lines I draw.

This dinner, though, was a little too perfect, too comprehensible (menu in English, English-speaking waiters), and it was plain that the Hotel Rafael's guests didn't much like surprises. There were also too many men with starched shirtfronts hanging about, waiting to scurry at my behest. No sooner had I become engrossed in chapter 2 than I could feel their accusing eyes on me and would look up guiltily as though I were deeply insulting the chef by not giving his creations my fullest attention. The result was that I couldn't really enjoy either book or meal. After the joys of Alien Pie (half of which was waiting for me in a fridge up a mountainside three hundred miles away) there was something depressingly *ordinary* about this five-star meal.

I always think rooftop swimming pools have a cachet all their own. For one thing, they represent a rigid digit waved gaily in the face of all human intuition and convention. The abominable folk wisdom of the human race just *knows* that pools of water form in holes in the ground. Nonsense, says technology, and promptly builds them in mid-air above historic city centres. This architectural chutzpah pays off by providing a genuinely new kind of experience – in this case lying afloat high above Munich's Altstadt on a hot summer's night. Each time I belched, a faint cloud of white wine and *Spätzle* drifted aromatically away. I decided I loved Bavaria. My only worry concerned my rented swimming trunks. These were made of an over-elasticated material and clenched me in a manner that did nothing for my profile, as I had observed with a pang in a mirror by the changing rooms. Somehow they made my derrière vanish almost entirely. A cruel illusion, and I –

'Gerry, hi there! You made it!'

A small Olympic swimmer surfaced next to me complete with racing cap and almond-lensed goggles.

'Nanty,' I gasped, spluttering. 'Good to see you. Wow – dig the racing cap.'

'It's getting old, that joke,' he said, briefly dipping his face beneath the surface and enabling me to view his clearly naked scalp. Oh God, not again. He came up with a smirk. 'Dig the trunks.'

'This underwater lighting produces some very odd distortions,' I told him earnestly.

'What you don't see is what you get,' he said, and laughed.

Was there just a smidgin of cruelty here or was he just trying to be witty, a job far better left to Samper? 'You sound like an AIDS awareness poster.'

'I was quoting. It's the title of one of our biggest hits. You really, really don't know anything about the biz, do you? It's great. It's like coming across an undiscovered tribe. Come and meet the boys.'

I had already noticed a group of likely lads sitting with some girls in one corner at a table covered in costly bottles. From a distance they looked reasonably harmless. Not actually cute, perhaps, but at least professionally winsome, like the Osmonds as I could dimly remember them from my infancy. I could tell that alcohol was rapidly eroding this patina to expose a solid stratum of brattishness. Now and then a raucous, champagne-fuelled laugh went ricocheting round the pool, for the rich we have always with us. (You're beginning to wonder about my easy lapses into Biblical knowledge? Wonder no more. My wicked stepmother Laura – she of the spotted bottom and frizzy hair – belongs to an evangelical sect and I grew up to scriptural quotations.) I hauled myself out, bathrobed myself securely and followed Nanty. He introduced me to Sput, Zig, Johnny and Petey. Sput had touched up his acne with dabs of Zitaway, nearly invisible to all but Samper's practised eye. Petey was trying to grow a moustache and wore the same sloppy expression as the others, which I recognized easily as that of people whose facial muscles are becoming temporarily paralysed by alcohol.

'Petey's our bass player, best in the biz. Zig's keyboards, Sput's drums. Johnny and me just fill in. Okay, the girls. This is Mel, Moonshine, Lissa, er, Beate? And Lisbeth?'

These last two, who looked young enough to be at home doing their homework, were clearly local girls signed on for the occasion. I filed them all away as best I could as I stood dripping beside the table. So this was a boy band off duty? True, once I'd troubled to see beyond the slightly ageing effects of drunkenness I could appreciate they were all quite young. None of them struck me as outstandingly good-looking but that was probably quite deliberate. It was the boy-next-door looks that had the widest appeal. Even so, we were a long way from Sunnydale. The ghost of Fothermuckers was beginning to materialize, with its hint of pubic lice and promise of blowing chunks into hotel swimming pools. Petey's tattooed arm thrust an open bottle of champagne at me. I noticed that it was by no means The Champagne Top Drivers Squirt, being a vintage effort by the widow Clicquot. Nothing but the best for these lads. Well, I was an old hand at this when-in-Rome lark. We Sampers are veritable chameleons. I took a respectable swig from the bottle. Then another.

The evening became increasingly blurred. I remembered bottles smashing. I remembered many more arriving at the table together with more girls and people I took to be groupies and road managers or something. A good deal of skinny dipping took place. I remembered squeezing Mel's behind experimentally, and then my own surreptitiously, to reassure myself that it was merely a matter of my swimming costume. And I remembered Mel giggling as Nanty came over and said, 'I see you've met the wife.'

'You're not *married*?'

'Why not? Sure, not where the fans are concerned, we're not. But in the real world yeah, Mel and me've been together six years now. She's my guru.'

'Golly, not the vegan queen?'

'Oh bollocks!' said Mel, maybe cheerfully, and pushed me backwards into the pool clutching a champagne bottle.

It all went on a long time, I think. Once the skinny dipping had begun most of the hotel's other guests willingly abandoned the pool to Freewayz and their entourage so the general boisterousness and noise were largely contained on the rooftop. Some meaty young men in jeans hovered in the background trying not to look like bouncers. At one point one of them rescued either Lisbeth or Beate from a watery grave. The Hotel Rafael was on top of it all, clearly used to these celebrity goings-on. As Nanty observed, when you've had Mick Jagger and the Stones staying many times, to say nothing of Rod Stewart, you learn to roll with the punches. In my function as fact-gatherer I strolled about, now admiring Munich's skyline (particularly the Olympic Tower, which more or less marked the site of next evening's gig) or else the Roman bathtime cavortings with what I hoped was the benign half-smile of an older brother. I'm afraid I became what Nanty had called 'totally stocious'.

Some time in the small hours I drifted down to my suite on a cloud and found Mel in my bed, fast asleep.

Marta

31

Dearest Marja

Your call the other evening was a lovely surprise. As I told you, from time to time I'd been looking up from work thinking 'Why don't they ever ring me? Why does it always have to be me that takes the initiative?' but I wasn't including you in that, my love, just the men, just our brother and father . . . Of course you were right – it's partly Voynovian males being Voynovian males & this image they have of the phone only being good for barking orders down. Any other use such as long gossipy calls keeping in touch with family & friends is strictly for women. Inevitably Pacini's film makes it easy to visualize: a young woman in a silk nightdress – probably a countess – curled up on her vast double bed amid rumpled pillows in mid-morning (read: after a night of passion), gossiping to her cronies about her husband's impotence & her latest lover's performance, the fingers of her hand sunk deep in the crisp white curls of a toy poodle . . . A dated male fantasy, Der Rosenkavalier meets telefoni bianchi. I bet that's still Father's image & it could even be Ljuka's as well. Incredible.

But I think the real reason they won't call me is more awkward. Because I've gone abroad they imagine it's me who's rejected them so it must be up to me to get in touch & reassure them I still love them. A girl's job. Something like that, do you reckon? And that in turn covers up for Father's phobia of telephones & especially of calling abroad & perhaps getting the wrong number or someone who doesn't speak Voysk or even – my God! – somebody who doesn't know who he is. Honestly, it's so damned feeble!

Anyway, thanks to your last call (& far from taking it on a poodle-strewn bed I was in the kitchen mending that lovely little metronome Father gave me for the Conservatory and which Gerry had drunkenly sat on, knocking off one of the tiny marquetry panels from the tip of the case) I can quite see this news about the date for Voynovia's joining the EU will have given Father more urgent things to worry about than daughters who defect abroad to write pornographic movies. I think you're right. Parts of the EU are vaguely law-abiding, others more patchily so, but all are bureaucratically self-pleased. Either way it will inevitably mean the clan's old high-handedness having to be moderated to some degree. Perhaps this seems more obvious to someone living abroad? Maybe Father will have to retire to somewhere like Marbella? Or rather no, not there. Apparently it's full of Russian mafiosi, half of them ex-KGB officers whom Father no doubt knew in the OKU.

These are things I can't say to you over the phone, my dear, you know why. I also like writing these letters to you. In a funny sort of way I feel closer to you when writing than I do talking on the phone – explain that if you can: definitely uncontessa-ish. (Incidentally, I was a bit surprised the other night to hear you say my voice sounded 'slurred'. I most certainly was not drunk. I think there's something the matter with this line up here in the mountains. I've noticed it before.) In any case, the important thing is my premonitions grow stronger that something's going to happen – or at least going to change – & I really wish you'd come here. You could use this house as a base for as long as you wanted – you absolutely would not be in my way or 'disturbing' my work as you sweetly put it. It's so lovely here, relaxed & civilized. Listen to me Mari: I truly think you'll have to make a break sooner rather than later. I increasingly feel we two daughters must make our own way in the world, otherwise we will always be compromised.

Are you shocked? I mean, by a sort of distance you can feel opening up between me & the family? I am. I admit it. I feel I've changed quite a lot since coming out here, & entirely for the better. Who knows where this 'career' of mine will lead, if anywhere? But it's making me feel truly independent for the first time – I never did in Moscow – or at least the mistress of my own fate. It's exhilarating. Dear Mari, you're so talented I just know you'll have no problems here. That gift of yours for languages means you can head in practically any direction. It's so enviable, & never a day goes by as I struggle with Italian or English when I'm not jealous of you & your facility. Really, my only fluent language is music. I think my Italian probably is becoming fairly reasonable now altho' I catch myself in the most awful lapses. The other day I heard myself ask Pacini 'Cos' hai fattato?' I mean, can you imagine, after all those conversation sessions with la Santoliquido in Voynograd – the poor thing would have a fit. It's pure baby-talk: 'What have you didded?' No wonder he laughed & laid his hand rather intensely on my arm. He must have thought I was ironizing our intimacy (which of course exists only at the professional level of getting his film successfully into the can, but he's galant). And as for my English, I'm afraid I probably sound like a dudi, altho' it's true I have no idea if Gerry himself sounds like one. I'm just assuming, which I probably shouldn't.

Great excitement here a few days ago. Pacini decided he wanted to shoot my house for a scene in the film involving a fisherman and his wife. He saw the place some time ago & thought it just right in its unreconstructed, time-warped squalor (like its inhabitant). At the time I said Why not? without really thinking. But really, filming's no joke. Had I known how much time it would involve (3 days!), not to mention invasion & the turning upside down of all one's private stuff, I would have told Piero to go off and build a set. Anyway, it's over now. For a while, though, there was endless noise & bustle outside as they were setting up establishing shots of the exterior – you wouldn't believe the cranes & dollies & lights & cables & clutter & technicians wandering about with a sandwich in one hand and a screwdriver in the other looking for something to screw. Mercifully Gerry turned out to be away & has been for almost a week now so far as I can tell. I don't know why I've got an uneasy feeling about him, & his absence makes me wonder if he really mightn't be seeing lawyers. Did I tell you he's claiming Uki's helicopter scared off his alleged celebrity client? He sort of implied he might have to 'consider' legal action. Silly pompous man – the fuss he makes over trivia. But I guess that comes with the type. Plus, of course, Gerry's real problem is he's bored (& drunk

& lonely) & it's only the bored who have the time & energy to
waste dreaming up vengeful legal actions that couldn't possibly
succeed. All the same, as I say, I'm uneasy but quite glad he wasn't
around this week. For one thing, I shouldn't have been able to keep
him away from the house. The great Piero Pacini alone would have
been enough to guarantee Gerry's hanging around, probably with
supplies of bizarre snacks from his kitchen to excuse his presence.
But add to that filming & muscular young technicians wandering
around without their shirts on . . . Surely irresistible to the Gerrys
of this world.

Incidentally, you said on the phone I was 'set up now'; but listen –
even if the film turns out a huge success there's no guarantee
Pacini will use me again & anyway, how many films does a director
of his age make? I'll need regular commercial work, TV at least, &
the trouble is no one wants to commission original scores these
days because they cost. To be boastful for a moment, I agree I could
become a pretty decent composer. But whether I shall get the
chance is another matter. Up to me, I guess. But either way I'm a
long way from being 'set up', alas.

Enough. All my love to you, the family & darling Mili – & tell
her I'm brushing my hair nightly with her lovely grease. And
please consider seriously coming to join me here. (But no need yet
to broach the subject openly with Father or even Uki!)

Your loving sister
Marta

32

Why did I bang on to my wretched kid sister about my career
prospects being less rosy than she might imagine, stuck as she
is in a feudal time-warp forty kilometres outside Voynograd?
I'm now sorry I did – not just because it's my problem and I
don't need to saddle her with it but because the real reason is
even less cheerful and I couldn't bring myself to tell her.

The fact is, the filming at my house showed Pacini in a wholly different light, one very much less urbane and *galant*. It wasn't that he was actually impolite, merely autocratic and ruthless. The first I knew was when he rang me the previous day to say there was some snag or other and he was having to re-schedule things at a moment's notice so as not to have to pay the crews for hanging around doing nothing. Would it be all right if they came and shot the scene at my house straight away? Frankly, with all these plot wrinkles he kept adding I was no longer clear how this scene fitted into the film. I assumed the fisherman was one of the locals whom the young Greens were trying to entice to their commune to teach them how to fish using traditional eco-friendly methods. My house was supposed to be where he lived in poverty some-where near the beach, the only one of his peers to have clung on to the old way of life. Or something like that. Since I had written enough music to go round I'm afraid I was rather let-ting the great director get on with his film in his own fashion without trying to understand it all. No doubt it would all come right in the cutting room. On the phone Pacini was apologetic and I was eager to accommodate him – why not? So I told him to come up the next morning and do it. They arrived at seven and the first thing that happened was that Piero took one look at Gerry's new fence and threw a fit.

'For God's sake! Who put that monstrosity there?'

I explained I had an eccentric English neighbour with para-noid friends.

'Well, it'll have to come down,' he said, in what I soon came to recognize as his maestro's voice. 'I need lots of wild footage of the exterior and as I told you earlier, what I really love about this place of yours is its not having been messed about with or brought up to date. That fence just *reeks* of *bricolage* and garden centres. We'll probably find there are gnomes behind it. It'll have to go. From almost any angle I'm going to be getting at least some of it in the frame. The place is ruined.'

I felt a bit hurt by his tone. It was almost as if he were blaming me.

'It wasn't my idea,' I protested, adding pacifically, 'but I'm sure if you ask Gerry nicely and supply the men to take it down and put it back up again it can all be amicably resolved. Shall I go and find him?'

But when I went over I realized at once Gerry was away. The windows were shuttered and his car was gone from the shed among the trees where he keeps it. I went back to Pacini and told him. Instead of saying phlegmatically, '*Che peccato*, we'll just have to come back when he gets home', he simply began giving orders to his men to start taking the fence down at once.

'Please, Piero, you mustn't do that,' I said, laying a restraining hand on his arm. 'You can't just tear down somebody's new fence without asking them.'

He patted my hand, presumably intending to convey reassurance but implying more of an admonition to just keep quiet and stay out of it. 'Don't worry,' he said. 'We're not going to *tear* it down, as you put it. We're not going to break anything. We'll simply remove it intact, do the exterior shots, and then put it back up again exactly as it is now. This English neighbour of yours will never know the difference, I promise. But each day we delay means going further over budget. He might be away for months.'

Faced with this cold, directorly determination there was nothing I could do short of making a scene – the very last thing I either wanted or needed with Piero Pacini of all people. So, thinking darkly of my future career, I went inside to begin purging my house of obviously jarring artefacts like the computer, music keyboard and sound system. Pacini helped by indicating the camera angles he was going to need. I was nevertheless surprised by just how much furniture had to be hidden or shifted before he was satisfied. And all the time there came suggestive sounds from outside and glimpses through the window of poor Gerry's fence being forcefully dealt with. There were some loud splintering noises which did not at all imply intactness. There were also some blasphemies new to me – the men were all-too-clearly native Tuscans – the gist being that the Madonna was unpopular for having yielded her virginity to a series of farmyard animals and the absent Gerry for having used a nail gun instead of an ordinary hammer. By the time I could bring myself to go out and look properly the deed was done and the fence unquestionably down. In fact, it looked down in a manner that surely precluded a quick resurrection. Yet it was generally agreed that the fault was Gerry's for having fired so many wire nails into the panels. As for the posts, they had simply been yanked out of the ground with ropes attached to the hydraulic platform used for low aerial shots. They came up with an ungainly clump of concrete at one end leaving ragged holes that even now were being expertly camouflaged with earth and turves. An hour later, with the immense splintery stack of panels piled safely out of sight behind some bushes, one would never have guessed there had been a fence there. I was aware of a distinct pang of pity for Gerry and all the work – not to mention near self-crucifixion – he had put into it.

'First-rate kindling,' a technician nodded towards the bushes, possibly hoping that I might look on the bright side. 'No problems getting your fire lit this winter. Can't survive up here in wintertime without nice big fires. Besides, a fire is company. We all need something to keep us warm,' and he leered a little.

The rest of the day was taken up with exterior shots from every conceivable angle and at every conceivable height. Then they were repeated when the sun had moved. By evening Pacini was mellower and drank a glass or two of Fernet Branca with me as his crew packed up.

'Very satisfactory,' he said. 'We've got all the establishing shots we need. Tomorrow we'll make a start inside. I'll be bringing the actors, the fisherman and his wife. I would be grateful, my dear, if you would sleep in that box-room of yours? Or at any rate not in the bedroom. The set dressers have almost finished up there.'

That sounded ominous. During the day I had been rootless and intimidated in my own home, jostled by strangers squeezing past me in the passage and clumping up and down the stairs carrying mysterious bundles. I had spent much of the time standing listlessly outside, now here and now there, permanently in somebody's way. More than once it struck me I would do better to clear out altogether for the day and simply give them the run of the place. But stupidly I felt duty bound to hang around. By the end of the day I couldn't think where the hours had gone, but they had, and their unaccountable passing had left me exhausted and headachy. God only knew what these people had done to my poor home in the interim.

Accordingly I went upstairs prepared to be surprised but not horrified. During the course of the day my bedroom, probably like its owner, had aged seventy years. My magnificent peasant-chic *matrimoniale* bedstead which Pacini had admired so much was still there, but my bedding had been replaced with a mattress that looked, smelled and felt like an immense burlap sack stuffed with seaweed. The window panes had been removed and chunks of plaster knocked artlessly out of the wall here and there. Black cobwebs now billowed slowly among the beams in the breeze from the glassless window. Surely I had never let them get quite so numerous? On closer inspection these, too, seemed to be props, probably squirted out of an aerosol can. All my nice rugs had been removed and replaced by a ragged straw mat. The rest of the floor had reverted to bare cracked bricks. I should have said the stripped and hollow room was uninhabitable except by teenaged hippies or a hibernating bear down from our high forests of Vilpi.

'Don't worry, Marta dear,' said Pacini as I came back downstairs looking, I should imagine, like a householder in time of war who has just discovered what it means to have her home forcibly requisitioned for the billeting of troops while being expected to smile patriotically. 'It's only for a day or two. We'll be out by Friday. Just you wait, it'll all be put back exactly as it was.'

The only possible advantage I could see in all this was that I might get a little housework done for free. As they removed their cobwebs they would, willy-nilly, remove mine too. Otherwise it was pretty much intolerable. After the convoy's exhausts had died away down the hill I found some bread and *shonka* and made a listless dinner. That night I slept fitfully on the kitchen sofa next to a large pile of smelly netting. Why a fisherman, no matter how poor, would need to keep nets in his kitchen was not clear to me, along with much else. The only thing that did become clear around three a.m. was that I was much less keen to imagine a future writing film scores.

It was this thought, in fact, that kept me awake until dawn broke and the chasms of dark air that filled the precipices outside were stealthily replaced by solutions of pearl. Goddamn it. I climbed stiffly off the sofa, picked my way around the reeking heap of nets and made a brew of coffee strong enough to stop a Bunki wrestler's heart. I had become acquainted with the flaw in that popular notion of 'the big break'. My big break had come when Pacini saw *Vauli Mitronovsk*, and it had led me here among the Apuan Alps with my own bedroom out of bounds to me and being obliged to sleep in a kitchen that was more like the hold of a trawler. And after it was all over, then what? Big breaks needed to keep on breaking if one were to make a sensible career. I decided I would have to become entrepreneurial after all. For as long as I was able to keep Pacini's company I ought somehow to capitalize on it. I supposed that if *Arrazzato* went platinum my name would have some currency in the film world, especially if it won an Oscar or two. Failing that (and far more likely) it would have a *succès d'estime* and film buffs would discuss it knowledgeably and show it at Piero Pacini festivals. But that wouldn't do me any good at all.

The coffee pot was empty and so was my mug. I was standing outside in the early cool, my heart pounding in my ears. Evidently it was stronger than the average Bunki wrestler's. It may also have helped that the coffee had been liberally *corretto* with Fernet Branca. I was watching a pair of buzzards with their two young crank themselves into the rising thermals, envying them their brief lot of graceful aerobatics and snacks of carrion. And then, from far below on the Casoli road, the growing sound of a convoy of van engines.

33

The second day's filming was much like the first; the third even more so. Pacini brought with him a muscular man of about thirty who looked as though he might drive lorries for a living, and a girl of about eighteen who might have hitched lifts in them. These were Franco the fisherman and his young wife. In the hours it took to make them up and dress them for the part the film unit busied itself setting up equipment in my bedroom and making sure the lighting was right. Meanwhile Pacini continuously played a CD of the music I had written for the film.

'Atmosphere,' he said. 'It's vital. I can't work without music and it's such a brilliant score, Marta dear. Each time I play it I can actually see the different scenes we have to shoot, and in complete detail. You know, this is the best score of all my films. Truly. Now I have to make the images we capture on film reflect what I see in my head and what I know in my heart.' He laid a hand somewhere over his oesophagus. 'But your music is wonderful. Hear that technician whistling? He's already hooked without realizing it. You're a genius.'

It was impossible not to be mollified by all this praise, of course, as Pacini doubtless intended. He knew I'd been upset by the murder of Gerry's fence and the upheavals in my house. Even so, I did think his response was genuine. Music clearly did mean a lot to him (and I'm quite able to spot the bogus enthusiasts who plainly can't tell one note from another).

Today I wished him *buon lavoro* and took myself firmly outside among the trees with a chair and a book. It was strange looking up at my own bedroom window in broad daylight and seeing the actinic white glare inside and the occasional dark shapes of people moving about. It was as though they were filming scenes that had been censored from my own life before I was allowed to live through them. They were secret episodes and would always remain hidden from me, viewable only by strangers.

Towards midday there came a familiar burping of exhaust and Filippo arrived amid a shower of gravel in his sleek scarlet beast. He hadn't come up the previous day and I was suddenly pleased to see him. From the car's cramped interior he extricated a wicker hamper. A trestle table was set among the trees, a cloth was laid and on it a superb buffet lunch spread with chilled bottles standing in coolers. I still couldn't gauge how much of this was part of Pacini's appeasement offensive and how much simply the way he normally worked. In any case I was not about to complain, especially when I could see food of a more plebeian nature being served to the crew from the back of a white van. The two actors appeared and stood about in silence eating pasta off plastic plates. The girl taking the part of Barbara, whom careful makeup had rendered positively dewy, was wearing a coarse shift. Her supposed husband had blotched cotton trousers rolled to the knee and a ragged jerkin beneath which his torso was bare. His skin was now several shades darker, having acquired a deepwater tan in my kitchen. His tousled hair also showed blond highlights as if bleached by sun and salt spray. To my eyes the pair of them looked profoundly fake, which was something I had noticed on the set of *Vauli M*. It was a problem I'd always

189

had with film and the theatre. Deep down, I knew I didn't quite believe in them. One never hears music as an approximation of ideal sounds that composers have heard in their heads, whereas visual re-creations of imaginary dramas so often have something slightly wrong with them. This is especially true of historical scenes. I remembered watching the actors in *Vauli M.* off the set and eating in the commissary. Ostensibly it was a canteen full of eighteenth-century people, but they were too obviously twentieth-century people in eighteenth-century costume. They held themselves wrongly, their gestures were wrong, they ate wrongly, and when they got up at the end they walked wrongly. How did one know? One just *knew*. No doubt eighteenth-century actors had been just as wrong when trying to act Shakespeare's characters of two centuries earlier. I found myself wondering exactly how salt-stained and piscatorial Pacini would expect the part of Franco to be acted.

He, Filippo and I finished our marvellous cold lunch (the cold roast aubergine anointed with oil and garlic and pesto was particularly divine) and they went straight back indoors to work. I picked up someone's copy of the shooting script and tried to identify the scene they were filming. There was a page whose numbering showed it had been inserted after the version I had worked from. It looked like a possible candidate:

Interior/bedroom. Night.

FRANCO (*enters*): Oh God, Barbara. What sort of a living is this? Another lousy catch. Those factory ships will be the death of us.

BARB: You are right, my darling. The politicians – bah! – they are against us too. What do they care for us little folk?

FRANCO: Little folk maybe, but not as powerless as they like to think.

BARB: My love, the sea teaches us not to give up. Like a woman, she is full of secrets.

FRANCO: And as with women, a man despairs of ever learning them.

BARB: Come here and see if I have any secrets from you.

FRANCO: Darling, did I not promise you an eel tonight, a big eel? At least I can give you that.

BARB: Oh Franco.

Mercifully, a blue line was scored through this piece of dialogue but I couldn't discover what, if anything, had replaced it. Did I really want to know, I wondered. That single glimpse was enough to remind me how truly dreadful most scripts were, even those of Piero Pacini films. Nor did I wish to remember that my career was probably riding on the success of *Arrazzato*. I tried to go upstairs to ask the great director if I might squeeze into a corner of my bedroom and watch the scene being shot but I was stopped by a burly boy in rank jeans. He was sitting on the stairs with cables running past him reading a Mickey Mouse magazine, *Topolino, Rodent Adventurer*. From beyond him the music I had written for an amorous beach scene could be heard playing behind a closed door.

'You can't go up. Sorry, miss.'

'This *is* my house.'

'I know,' said the boy uncomfortably, 'but the maestro said not. There's no room. Really. They're packed in there like sardines as it is. Hot as hell. We're much better off out here.'

So I retreated and went back outside to my book and what was left in one of the bottles standing in its sweating cooler. The next time I glanced up I could see the bedroom window had been replaced and blacked out, presumably for a night scene. But I couldn't concentrate. A vision of Father appeared to me demanding to know exactly what was being filmed in my bedroom, and I couldn't answer. 'It's pornography!'

asserted this menacing wraith. 'What did you think, you stupid girl? That a daughter of mine should allow such a thing *in her very bedroom*! The disgrace!'

No. No. It was nothing like that at all. I reminded myself that the character of Franco the fisherman was one of quiet nobility, in tune with oceanic mysteries and full of respect for the sea, that unpredictable but bounteous cradle of all life. Ironically, he and his young wife represented exactly the clean-limbed, sunburned tradition of outdoor labour that Italian fascism had once venerated and elevated as an ideal. No white telephones in his hovel, though, just the warmth of a good wife and well-earned rest after honest toil. It was enough to make you sick, but it was not the same nausea as the big eel scenario would have provoked.

And so I sat and wondered, rueful about my suspicions, amazed that they might be measuring a gulf that really did lie between my high hopes of a career and whatever was going on in my bedroom. The shooting must have gone well, at any rate, because by five o'clock they had finished and were packing up. The two actors borrowed my bathroom to shed their war paint and had soon gone off down the hill in one of the cars. From all over the house came sounds of furniture being moved back, of order being restored. Two men staggered out with the burlap mattress, another two with the fishing net.

Pacini and Filippo joined me at the table for a celebratory glass. I thought the great director looked tired, but when I said as much he denied it and said how well the sessions had gone.

'You must see some of the rushes. I'll have a selection transferred onto disc for you. After all, it is your home. And I do apologize once again for all the upheaval,' he added. Evidently his old *galanterie* had returned, refreshed from its short holiday. 'You've been wonderfully patient and understanding, Marta. Now, unfortunately Filippo and I have to be in Rome tonight. In an hour's time, actually. We've asked to be picked up here. I think we'll be away three or four days.

Bankers. You wouldn't believe the money problems that go with making a film, my dear. Quite horrendous. So might Filippo leave that slightly absurd car of his here until he can collect it?'

'You do go on, Dad,' said his son patiently.

'It runs on testosterone, you know, not *benzina*,' continued Pacini senior unabashed.

'It's wonderfully fast,' I interjected lamely. 'Anyway, forgive my asking, but what about the house? I mean, all those chunks of plaster knocked out of my bedroom wall, the cobwebs, and my God, the *fence*? I'd completely forgotten. What about Gerry's fence?'

'The boys have promised to leave the place as tidy as they can, if you wouldn't mind roughing it a bit for just one more night? I knew you'd understand, a *persona squisita* like your-self. Then I've told them to come back tomorrow morning first thing and get everything straightened out, including that fence.'

'Well,' I said doubtfully. 'OK. It's just that Gerry might –' but at that moment with a sudden blast of sound the blue and white helicopter I'd once seen bring Piero to Pisorno Studios appeared around a shoulder of the mountain, reared back like a fiercely reined horse and dropped lightly into the paddock behind my house.

After it had taken off again and whirled away down the valley I sneaked a glance around my ravaged home. Although it would take some days to get it back to the comfortable squalor that suited me, I could live with how it was. At least my bed had been restored, although the room smelt like underneath a pier at low tide. The men, who clearly had no intention of doing any more work that day, began to drift away in their vans, the one I'd taken to be their foreman reassuring me that he would return next morning.

'With enough men, I hope?'

'*Si, si*, plenty of men,' he said, and winked. But the wink was the least part of my unease.

34

It was a relief to take possession of my own house again, even if the place retained an unsettling sense of alien occupation. In that respect it reminded me a little of Voynograd after the Russians had finally left. The bathroom in particular looked like a crime scene, dabbled all over with suggestive reddish-brown smears and runnels. It was probably too much to expect actors to have any manners that weren't called for in a script so I set about clearing up.

To my surprise a van did arrive next morning with the foreman and three helpers who beneath my proprietorial eye began filling the holes they had artistically hacked in my bedroom wall. As well as a bag of plaster they had brought an immense industrial vacuum cleaner whose blustery howl filled the upper floor of the house as it sucked up cobwebs both real and fake. After a couple of hours' work the house was, frankly, cleaner than it had ever been since my occupancy began, but I was not about to say so. Instead I made them all coffee and asked them now, please, to address their energies to getting the fence back up.

'Remember what the maestro promised,' I urged. '"The Englishman will never know the difference." His very words.'

'It's always rash to make promises that conflict with the laws of physics,' observed the foreman, clearly wasted in this job. Presently I could see him and his helpers trying to batter the concrete lumps off the ends of the posts. After much labour they did get the worst off one and, going apprehensively outside, I could see that the wood was bristling with nails. The foreman threw down his hammer disgustedly.

'The bastard's shot these posts full of nails, see, to give something for the cement to key on to. This'll take us a month. There are twenty-one of the things.'

'Then you'd better send somebody off to get some new posts.'

'I don't have any authorization to spend *money*.'

'I will worry about authorization, you just get the posts. Get them on the Pisorno Studios account, whatever, I don't care. Just get them. And hurry.'

Managing to look both surly and startled the foreman whirled crossly away in his van, leaving two of his mates picking over the heap of discarded fence panels. Whether my new-found imperiousness came from anxiety lest Gerry should return suddenly or else from the simple fact of being my father's daughter, I couldn't have said. I discovered I was no longer thinking of Gerry as a ludicrous foreign *dudi* but more as an ally from the good old neighbourly days of barely a week ago, a fellow victim of the Pacini machine. According to tradition one of our national heroes, a Voyde high-school student who had lain down in the path of the Soviet tanks in '67, had had to be rolled up like pastry before he would fit into his coffin. Before my time, of course. I was beginning to suspect that a similar fate awaited anyone rash enough to stand in Pacini's way when he was making one of his films. It was a case of force majeure. Still, life is unfair and I was pretty sure that Gerry would blame me. My memories of dear Pavel Taneyev at Moscow Conservatory were hardly reassuring. Bitchiness is to *dudis* as mewing is to cats.

From their appearance Gerry's precious fence panels could themselves have been victims of a Soviet tank. When hauled upright they sagged wearily like boiled parallelograms, their ends ragged with white splinters. The men set about them listlessly with carpenter's tools, trying to put some backbone into them. I left them to it and retired indoors with my forebodings.

These were faithfully borne out within the hour. The foreman returned and announced that the posts would have to be delivered by lorry. But an even more basic problem remained, which was where to plant them when they did arrive. The holes in the ground had been so effectively camouflaged for the filming there was no longer any trace of where the fence had run. Did I know where my boundary was? Of course I didn't, I told the foreman.

It was then that I sent the men away and wrote a sharp e-mail to Piero Pacini. By now, though, I had little hope it would have any effect, still less in the time required. My job as the film's composer was largely finished. I had even been paid for much of it. I no longer had any leverage. Well, was it not for depressed, reflective moments like this that Fernet Branca had been invented? Luckily I was not like poor Gerry, who plainly took refuge in the familiar green bottle to an alarming extent. But whereas he was predominantly inter-ested in the drink's considerable alcoholic content, it was purely for the herbs that I sipped the infrequent glass. All that wormwood and gentian and quinine and rue became the essence of bitterness that now complemented my own. There was something soothing about it. We don't understand the mysterious properties of herbs like these. They have curative powers and can lift the spirits, like the 'monk's myrrh' the huntsmen back home put in their *galasiya*. Now that really *is* bitter. But it must have something else because they say only last year a man of ninety-seven became a father under its influence, a story that made me wonder if the mother had herself been entirely sober. I'm ashamed to say I found myself giggling a bit when idly wondering what effect *galasiya* might have on Gerry.

Gerald

35

There's nothing like coming home after a successful trip. Just watching Pisa airport dwindle in one's rearview mirror is fillip enough. Even if one has flown from Munich on an airline less plebeian than Ryanair, one has still been subjected to the same humiliating rituals, streamed and searched and processed before being herded through hideously carpeted corridors in the company of coarse, summer-clad travellers with bouncing body parts.

Cheerfully I set the nose of my trusty Toyota towards the mountains and reflect that Munich was an odd experience. I can't pretend I greatly enjoyed Freewayz' last concert in the Olympiahalle. Never having been to a boy-band gig, I suppose I'd been bracing myself for sheer aural assault. I need not have worried, though. The teen screams were louder than the music, which was anodyne stuff indeed. Just occasionally Nanty's words rose above his juvenile audience's ecstasy – '. . . missin' you . . . kissin' you . . .' – but that was it. I'd hardly been expecting Rossini but I must say I was astonished by the lack of even a slightly memorable tune. It was obviously not about music, though; it was about celebrity, which requires no talent of any kind. Sheer boredom soon obliged me to begin the long, painful process of worming my way towards the nearest exit. Through throngs of throbbing teenagers I caught glimpses of a tall saturnine man who looked for all the world like Christopher Lee playing Count Dracula. He was wearing a first-aid uniform with red-cross armbands: not the most reassuring first sight for a teenaged girl coming round from a fainting fit but as a landmark he was wonderful. I kept heading towards him across a heaving floor slippery with hormones. Once I had reached him I could afford to catch my breath and glance back across the immense arena to the stage where Nanty in his teen-dream livery as Brill was wailing and prancing most professionally, tossing his blond mane. It was amazing: in his wig and war paint he managed to look about fifteen. I suddenly saw how his public mistook him for one of them. Zig, Sput, Petey and Johnny were variously whacking and strumming. For all I knew their drum kit was a cardboard mock-up and their guitars strung with twine. It seemed to this cynic that the whole thing might well be mimed, the boys cavorting silently before a billion-watt barrage of pre-pubescent girl power, mouthing into dead mikes. But it looked good and was wildly popular, no question.

Once outside the hall I found the incessant screaming had left me slightly deaf – and that after a mere three numbers. Still, I had done my duty and seen the boys in action. I – but you're much more curious about the naughty scene in my bedroom in the Hotel Rafael, I can tell. You mean when I came down from the roof in the small hours and found Nanty's alleged wife Mel asleep in my bed? Well, I too am curious. The fact is, I have no further memory of anything until we both awoke at ten o'clock the next morning with headaches intense enough to take precedence over all enquiry. How had she got into my room? Had I lent her my key? Did Nanty mind? Had he even arranged it? Who knew?

But I have long learned not to ask these sorts of question. Being Luc Bailly's amanuensis taught me much about the etiquette of waking beneath a heap of partygoers on a floor in Klosters. That, of course, is how I can vouch for those famous twenty-five centimetres which for a while constituted a sort of informal Swiss national monument. I would have made all this clear earlier but I didn't think you were quite ready for it. Although I occasionally make a fuss about the tedium of my profession I have to admit that ghost writing does introduce one to sights one might otherwise not see.

Motorway exit coming up, Gerry, if you wouldn't mind *concentrating* this time . . . Excellent. The familiar peaks of

Monte Prana and Monte Matanna are now squarely in my windscreen.

Nanty stayed on in Munich for a couple of days after the concert and I was at last able to find out more about the sort of book he wanted. Old Frankie hadn't been far wrong: it's McCartney's Syndrome all right. The man's already rotten with loot and fame but he wants much, much more. He wants serious respect for his art, his opinions, his *philosophy*. Here I'm afraid my incredulity must have been showing because Nanty felt obliged to explain. Really, it's so awful it's touching. 'Philosophy' to him is not the late Mr Hegel writing his runaway bestseller *The Phenomenology of Mind* and pronouncing 'He who is not a father is not a man' (*he* never partied in Klosters). To Nanty, as to most businessmen, 'philosophy' is something that companies have as part of their public image. It's full of aims and goals and overviews, with a few tear-off calendar mottoes thrown in for added depth. To dignify a commonplace like 'The customer is always right' or 'We aspire to be always at the cutting edge of innovative design' with the name of philosophy is a bit like . . . no, it's *exactly* like calling Freewayz' noise music.

Why should I be at all touched by this and not driven into a downward depressive spiral from which there is little hope of rescue? – and here I snatch a glance at the seat beside me where fresh supplies of Fernet nestle clinkingly in their carrier bag. I'm not sure 'touched' is the right word. 'Intrigued' would be better. I'm intrigued as a writer by the extraordinary composite figure of Nanty-Brill, the bald boy who is half cynic and half mystic, half beady businessman and half rock orgiast, four halves that make him two people. When he started talking about boy bands as an enterprise he unconsciously lapsed into business-speak and sounded like one of those men in suits who can be overheard in bars talking about horses for courses and things going belly up or pear-shaped. I remembered the tales I'd heard about this same pin-striped side of Mick Jagger, who would discuss investments with his

Swiss bankers in a way that coexisted quaintly with the Stones rebel, the police busts, the minor drug charges and the jail sentences quashed because he'd been with the Queen of England's sister at the time. But there, that's showbiz: lots of noisy show tacked on to even more steely business.

On the other hand Nanty's brief outline of a Harpenden childhood *had* quite touched me. It turned out that he and I had something in common after all. His mother had also died when he was young and he had similarly acquired a step-mother whom he disliked on sight. Unlike mine, his had tried to seduce him when he was thirteen, causing him to run away from home for six months and ever afterwards to refer to her as his 'shtupmother'. Why had he ever gone home? Because of Julie his younger sister, who had Down's syndrome and of whom he was extremely fond.

'No matter what happens, Julie'll never want for anything,' Nanty had told me with the fierce satisfaction of someone who has at last done something unquestionably right. 'I've made sure she's got more than enough of everything.'

'Including three copies of chromosome 21,' I didn't say. That famous Samper *delicatezza*. But it was splendid news. A Down's sister, a dead mother, alopecia at the age of twenty and a Druidical beating-up at the University of Hampton: Nanty's life had been scarred to exactly the right degree for a pop biographer. He was such a refreshing contrast to those one-dimensional runners, skiers and racing drivers I was used to. With skilful manipulation on my part (such as play-ing down the New Age tomfoolery and the UFOs) Nanty's character could acquire real gravitas. He had explained to me that he saw this book as merely one part, although a vital one, of his life's campaign. I told him it was time to start work on the other parts as well. He needed some influential friends in the world of the serious arts whom he could wow by flying them to louche parties in his private jet or woo with tickets to Glyndebourne. He also should be known to be working on a weighty large-scale project of his own. What did he fancy?

Painting? Sculpture? Architecture? Music? Or there were always prestige projects of national significance, like Sam Wanamaker's replica of Shakespeare's Globe Theatre in oak and thatch. He thought for a moment.

'Stonehenge!' he cried. 'That's it! Re-create it as it originally was, with all those earthworks and stuff and twice the size, like you can see from the air. But – and get this, Gerry – align it to coincide with the heavens as they are now. The stars have shifted,' he explained vaguely. 'Bring it up to date and teach people how to use it as an observatory.'

'Mm. That sort of thing. And don't forget film. Remember David Bowie in *The Man Who Fell to Earth*. You might even turn out to be rather a good actor, Nanty. A heavyweight director could improve your standing no end.'

'Yeah, so he could. I've often thought I'd like to do a film . . . Or perhaps something musical? You know, *big*.'

'*Missa Harpendensis*? Double choir, organ, orchestra, rock group, electronics. Or how about *An AIDS Requiem*? Same instruments but with bongos. The African dimension, you know.'

'Yeah, that's got legs. Or . . . or maybe something more *democratic*. How about somewhere ordinary folk can have a real laugh? A humungous amusement zone in Hyde Park, sort of thing.'

'You could call it Funfair for the Common Man.'

'Right, and the band could do the music for it.'

I looked at him regretfully. 'Nanty, I have to tell you that if your Freewayz gig was representative you're badly in need of creative talent, musically speaking. Your aim is to become lovable, don't forget. You need to be enshrined in the nation's heart. You won't do that with Alien Pie numbers, not if they're like the ones I heard in Munich.'

'The kids go for it,' he said defensively.

'Sure, and it's brilliant in its way, Nanty, don't get me wrong.' Ghost applying butter. 'But for you to become establishment the same kids'll have to go on going for it when they're forty. Classics are what you're aiming to record. Stuff that'll be coming out of the loudspeakers in Harrods' lifts in twenty years' time. And for that, Nanty, you need a real composer. Even McCartney did his *Liverpool Oratorio* thing with Carl Davis.'

By the time he had jetted off somewhere in his private Gulf-stream he was in excited mood, looking forward to Alien Pie's launch and pleased that the first steps were being taken to orchestrate his future. Now as I drive up through Casoli I'm also quite cheered by this challenging and fabulously well-paid project which will keep me nicely occupied for the next six months. Thanks to our conversations in Munich, not only am I reconciled to doing his book but I now have more than enough background info on him for an outline treatment. That's always a good start.

Now then, enough of the humdrum. What treat shall I contrive for myself tonight in honour of my homecoming? Just a wee snacklet to take out onto the terrace with a celebratory cold beer. After which, of course, the uneaten half of the cold alien pie waiting in the fridge followed by an experiment I put in the freezer weeks ago and still haven't tried: liver sorbet. When I come to write (or ghost-write?) my own auto-biography – and I rather fancy *Under a Tuscan's Son* as a title, don't you? – I shall stress and re-stress the huge importance of novelty. I simply can't resist trying new things, and neither should you. Right this moment I can feel a theory trying to emerge that concerns the culinary possibilities of combinations of foods that are euphonious. If they sound good together they may turn out to *be* good together. This has a mediaeval ring to it, something like Paracelsus's 'doctrine of signatures' for matching ailment with cure. On the plane just now I was toying with the idea of Poodles in Noodles. Who knows, its consonance may be more promising than the actuality and I'll have to consult a Filipino friend of mine about it first. The same goes for Pekes in Leeks. Meanwhile I'm a little surprised that grand old campaigner Maj.-Gen.

Sir Aubrey Lutterworth never came up with Savage and Cabbage, although he did invent a most nutritious Moth Broth that ought to be commercially exploited by some enterprising outfit – presumably the Covent Garden Soup Company. There are plenty of other things to try: Horse Sauce, Bustard in Custard and – most hopeful of all – Parrots 'n' Carrots. And while we're on the subject of how food sounds, even dear old double entendre might serve to inspire an unusual dish or two. There would be a certain ice-breaking quality about a majestic head waiter bending behind a matronly diner and intoning 'I can recommend the Dill Dough, madam. It comes with our Thrush Marmalade. Very warming on a night like this.'

And now at last the familiar bend, the familiar crags aglow with Tuscan summer sun, my familiar roof poking between the trees . . . but . . . But something's wrong. What on earth's that damned great heap of firewood doing there? And where . . . *Sacred sperm banks!* She's actually done it! The fat bat's torn down my beautiful fence! Can you *believe* this? I brake violently, leap from the car and go over to kick incredulously at the pile of splintered beech that was so recently a necessary bulwark against neighbourliness, to say nothing of a work of art in its own right. So OK. Fine. If that's the way she wants it. This time she really has gone too far. No more Mr Nice Guy. It's a long worm that has no turning but this worm has definitely turned. Marta's about to find out that Samper's way with euroslag vandals is pretty damned harsh. I shall enjoy this. Hate is a many-splendour'd thing.

36

But as I march across to Marta's sty prepared to do battle I catch sight of the scarlet sports car discreetly tucked around the side among the trees. Oho, I think, that's awkward. The last thing one wants when reading the riot act to a neighbour is for her young and probably muscular boyfriend to be present. Still, a glance across at the twenty piled corpses of my lovely and expensive beechwood panels is enough to remind me that life in this idyllic mountain eyrie is now seriously threatened and something unpleasantly firm is going to have to be said. Accordingly I give her back door a good pounding.

She flings it open and reveals the usual squalid scene within. 'Oh Gerree!' she cries, 'you are home! How happy to see you,' and before I can recoil she gives me a hug. I can feel her bangles pressing into the small of my back. Trashy stuff. Pure Benares. 'Where are you went?'

'Munich,' I say briefly. 'Now, as regards –'

'Munich very interesting, Gerree. We have in Voynovia town is call Mjonkus. Is same name like Monaco also. It means –'

'Fence,' I say sternly. 'Right now, everything to me means "fence". What happened to it? Go on, tell me there's been a hurricane.'

'Oh the fence, Gerree. Is most saddest,' and blow me if her eyes aren't watering a little, although since she is thrusting a conciliatory glass of Fernet at me I have a shrewd idea about the likely wellsprings of her emotion. 'Sitting please.' And now the unscrupulous witch is pressing on me a chocolate kiss from a box of Perugina *Baci*.

Well, a Samper is not to be caught the same way twice so this time I feel around carefully beneath me before sitting down on her sofa. You wouldn't believe how invasive the tip of a metronome can be.

'What happens, Gerree: you know I am making music for film? So Piero Pacini he come one day here and say "I want to filming here but fence no good for filming so please take down now." I say is not possible. I say is asking Gerree first because he make fence. Is his fence. But Signor Pacini is not hear me and is order to his men, "Take down this fence" and promise put up fence after filming. And after filming . . .'

It has happened before. There is something about Marta's pidgin explanations that make my attention wander even though it's a story of some consequence for me. I'm afraid things that are important to know need to be particularly well phrased to get my attention. I am also wondering where lover-boy is hiding. Probably sprawled across the bed upstairs, equally poleaxed by the effort of penetrating Marta's tangled syntax.

'I see,' I say at length. 'Let's just get this straight, shall we? You are making a film with a world-famous film director. A few days ago he demolished my fence to improve the shot and now has failed to put it back up again. Have I got that right?'

Marta is nodding so violently she splashes her dress with Fernet. 'Exact!' she exclaims behind the threshing hair. What *does* she do to it to get it in that state? Anoint it with goose grease? 'Oh, Gerree, I really so sorry. I am e-mail to Signor Pacini. He will come and fix. He promise me.'

'You think Piero Pacini is going to come and re-erect my fence, Marta? The genius who made *Mille Piselli* and *Nero's Birthday* is, of course, also a partner in that well-known firm of landscape gardeners Visconti, Bertolucci & Pacini SpA: "We Give It Our Best Shot".'

'He promise,' she repeats sadly and a tear rolls down beside her nose. Good old Fernet, I think. In another moment she's going to start one of those scenes protesting her innocence, full of Slavic keening and hair-tearing. Hysteria is to girls as barking is to dogs, take Samper's word for it. To head her off I try a new tack.

'I see you've got a new car. Congratulations.'

She looks blank.

'The red one,' I prompt.

'Ah yes. Ah no. That is of Filippo, the son of Signor Pacini.'

'He's here now?' I glance at the ceiling.

'No, is in Rome. They come back soon.'

'That's good. We can discuss the little matter of legal action.'

But I admit this does make me think a bit. A hi-glam car like that is just what one would expect an Italian film director's son to drive. Or, come to that, the leader of a boy band. Can it be possible I've been doing her an injustice all this time and she's not quite the drunken fantasist I've been taking her for? Can my imagined charcoal-burner's son actually be Filippo Pacini? But then I have another glance around and note the loudspeaker half buried beneath an avalanche of limp sheets and the electronic keyboard with a three-quarters empty bottle of Fernet Branca leaning back against the music stand like a drunk against a lamp post. Be honest, Samper: is this the workshop of a fellow professional? If we flick open Occam's razor and give it a good whetting, would it not pare away the probability of her story to nothing? For hardly the first time in Marta's presence I am seized with a weariness that saps my resolve to confront her. It even makes my knees limp, as I discover when I put down my glass and get to my feet. To hell with her. Do I really care what the truth is? (As the late, great Pontius Pilate might have said, thinking of a quiet beer on his terrace well away from his wife wittering on about her nightmares.)

Marta is now unsteadily on her own feet. She ferrets beneath the ambient laundry and emerges with a slip of paper. It is, incredibly, a cheque made out in euros for a sum of money representing exactly half what I'd told her the fence cost. I can feel the last of my righteous anger shrivel.

'You see, I promise, Gerree,' she says, kissing me with tears in her eyes before I can get out of the door.

It's so bloody unfair, I think as I walk over to my house. The woman blames a famous film director for the destruction of my fence and now she pays me her own share of its cost so the fence is no longer mine but *ours*. Yet the damned thing's still down and all my labour wasted, and where's the justice in that? I linger mournfully by the heap of shattered panels and cement-caked posts. It's too bad. How like Marta to muddy the water with her blarney and cheques – not to mention her Fernet and chocs.

The next morning I am down in Camaiore buying stationery when I catch sight of a vaguely familiar figure. Of all people it is the egregious Benedetti, the weaselly house agent who lied to me about my neighbour. A sprauncy little turd in a dove-grey suit, he is trotting along looking executive and carrying one of those fetishistic Italian briefcases made of cassowary leather or albatross skin, complete with gold fittings and monogram. I hail him squarely in the middle of the pedestrian thoroughfare.

'*Ingegnere! Buon giorno.*' He stops and pretends to be flipping through the dogeared Filofax that passes for his mind. 'Gerald Samper,' I help him out. 'The Englishman who bought the house up at Le Roccie.' His eyes flicker sideways. I'd never buy a used car from this man, I think to myself in amazement. How come I bought a used house from him?

'Signor Samper!' he exclaims, recovering. 'What an unexpected delight to see you. And looking so well, too. *Sempre in forma.* Your wife too is well?'

'I have no wife.'

'Ah, wise, wise man. Blessed bachelordom! I always say it's the sign of a superior sensibility, that's what I always say. I also say "*Donne e motori: gioia e dolore*", but I'm inclined to change that to "*sempre dolore.*" Haha.'

'You always did have a way with words, *ingegnere.* Like when you told me my neighbour's house up at Le Roccie was lived in for one month of the year by a mouse-quiet foreigner. Your exact phrase, I remember.'

'Ah, that memory of yours, Signor Samper. It is a jewel. And now –' Benedetti glances at a preposterous watch that will tell him the time in Vancouver when he is a hundred metres under water '– I'm afraid I'm already late for my appointment. Mustn't keep the Chief of Police waiting.'

'Policemen are famously never on time,' I say, taking a tiny but significant step to one side to block his escape. 'This won't take long, Benedetti. I just want to know why you misrepresented the situation to me.' Better not use a word as blunt as 'lied' at this stage.

'Misrepresented, *signore*? Oh, I trust not. The lady in question –'

'You know her, then? Marta?'

'Only most vaguely. But I was assured she is scarcely ever there. She is of Russian origin, I think.'

'I wouldn't tell her that if I were you. She has rather strong views on Russia. All I know is she's not at all quiet and mouselike. In fact, and between ourselves, over the last three months she has proved to be a damned nuisance in all sorts of ways. Being visited by helicopters is one of them.'

'Helicopters?' The weasel perks up.

'Helicopters. Blew my pergola to shreds. Is that how you define a quiet neighbour?'

'Not,' he begins cautiously, 'as such, perhaps. Not altogether.'

'Well, I'm none too happy about it. To be honest, I'm beginning to feel you sold me that house under false pretences. I explained to you several times that being a writer I need extreme quiet for my work. But a neighbour who plays weird music at all hours and has visitors who drop by in helicopters hardly fits your description of her.'

'*O Dio.*' Benedetti makes a pout with his lips to indicate deep concern. 'What can she be up to?'

'Who knows?' I ask rhetorically, suddenly finding the pent-up frustrations of the last few months venting themselves with agreeable passion. This fence business has definitely been the last straw. 'Who knows? *Che ne so io?* What do I care if she's an East European call girl? The point is you promised me peace and quiet and I have neither.'

'Maybe there is an element of exaggeration . . .?' he begins, but catches my eye. He shifts his briefcase to his left hand and with the right takes out a crisply laundered handkerchief with which he carefully mops his receding forehead. Hair weaving, I note with satisfaction. And it's all very well to moan about women but someone irons your shirts and handkerchiefs beautifully and I bet it's not you.

'Allow me to observe, *ingegnere*, that in future you could be a lot more scrupulous about what you say when trying to induce someone to buy one of your houses. Especially a foreigner. We may be a minority but I think you will find that as a community we are not entirely without significance. Word gets around,' I add meaningfully.

Benedetti draws himself up, plump weasel provoked. 'I sell all my houses in the best of faith, Signor Samper. Unfortunately I cannot be held responsible for my buyers' eventual lack of breeding. I don't believe I gave you a written guarantee of your prospective neighbour's hermit-like qualities?'

'True,' I concede, beginning to enjoy this sword-crossing as Camaiore's citizens eddy around us with curious glances. 'But you did give me verbal assurances whose validity a gentleman like yourself will readily recognize as scarcely less binding. At this late stage, though, I can't see how reparations can easily be made, can you? Things are as they regrettably are. I merely thought I would inform you that Le Roccie is very far from being the nexus of bucolic harmony you painted it to me last year. Well, as I say, word has a habit of getting around. And now I believe I'm delaying you.'

We take formal leave of one another and Benedetti scurries off, plying his handkerchief once more. I take myself into a handy bar for a well-deserved mid-morning reward. I haven't enjoyed myself so much in ages. Being able to dump on the weasel has been a pleasure I hadn't anticipated when I drove down this morning. It won't have done him any harm at all to feel the edge of the Samper tongue and it has done the Samper spirits a power of good. I can return home *purged*.

37

A couple of days now go by most agreeably. I make good progress with roughing out the outline of Nanty's book. Left in peace by myself I always work well. This was, after all, the whole point of choosing to come and live up here among the crags and gulfs. How was I to have known that the casual lie of a greedy house agent would have put me at the mercy of an eccentric floozy like Marta?

The floozy, however, is unusually quiet. By positioning myself at the extreme corner of an upstairs window I've been able to catch a glimpse of crimson between the trees surrounding her house, meaning the mysterious sports car is still there. So who really is the owner? This, like many other questions about Marta, is unanswerable and hence rapidly becoming a bore. Just as long as I'm left to get on with earning a living she can do what she likes. It might even turn out to be her own car, an unlikely example of impulse buying that makes me wonder whether she mightn't be well off after all. In that case one is certainly allowed to speculate about the source of her wealth. The East European provenance, the black helicopter: it isn't difficult to drift off into tabloid day-dreams of those mafias allegedly always busy smuggling drugs or plutonium or illegal immigrants. Now I come to think of it there are also those unsavoury rackets one associates with governments in the Balkans, wherever the Balkans are. Isn't there supposed to be a trade in indentured prostitutes being infiltrated into the EU? One never pays quite enough attention to these stories. They seem a permanent part of existence and doubtless always have been. I think one or two of the girls – and maybe even some of the boys – who filled out Luc's heaps on the floor in Klosters were rumoured to be from Zagreb or Sarajevo. Somewhere like that. Is that Poland? It sounds sort of Polish to me. I ought to buy an atlas but I'm loath to lose my illusions.

Still, the idea of old Marta being involved in anything like that is too absurd. She's far too drunken and slatternly to be a ruthless madam even if Le Roccie were the ideal site for a bawdy-house. And as for her being on the game herself . . . But I have no wish to be ungallant, still less downright cruel.

In the evening I toy with a little creation of mine while sitting out beneath my pergola. There is no denying it: summer is over the hump. The days are marginally less stifling now, the evenings appreciably cooler. In another week or two I shall have to wear a cardigan as I sit out and watch the sun languorously extinguishing itself in the sea somewhere behind Sardinia. Already one can begin looking forward to lighting the first fires of autumn when the fragrant woodsmoke rises from hissing hearths to drift slantingly through the baring branches outside. I am at peace. The distant ocean is at peace. The surrounding cliffs and forests are at peace. Far away down there among that coastal sprawl of lights people are doing frightful things to each other as usual, often casually but sometimes with such berserk attention to detail I can only assume it has been genetically coded by evolution as necessary for the race's survival. Down there is the world as run by a handful of corporations, an army of lawyers and millions of religious zealots. It is not a place that has a niche for Gerald Samper. Up here, thank goodness, I needn't pretend to be a member of the human race at all and can remain minimally contaminated by its germy lies. (Yes! You recognized it! Another anagram of Lyme Regis.) I can enjoy my cold trifle of sweetbreads – tripe and blueberries were made for each other – and a glass or three of Barolo while thinking peacefully anarchic thoughts.

You may be wondering, impertinently, why I have no wife, or at least no partner. Please feel free to keep right on wondering. Your impertinence is your own affair. About *my* affairs – and there have been many – I can but make the obvious point that marriage has nothing to do with sex. Of course not: it's a social pact entered into by two people who miraculously find they can bear each other's company at breakfast over an indefinite period. Personally, I have never met anyone who fits that description and doubt I ever shall. Besides, wives are famously and massively expensive. Even that witty old fag-hag Jane Austen started one of her incomparable novels – was it *Donna*? – with the telling sentence 'It is a truth universally acknowledged, that a good man in possession of a wife must be in want of a tidy fortune.' And there you have it, memorably expressed. So far as I'm concerned the whole marriage business is not something to lose sleep over. All I require is regular work, occasional louche gossip, Rossini and a well-supplied kitchen. And after many years, when the pleasure quotient has sunk irretrievably low, one can follow the sun's example in the sea somewhere behind Sardinia.

In the morning I breakfast on the terrace bright and early. The sun rising behind our mountains throws their chain of shadows far below almost to the coast. I enjoy watching this dark blotch shrink back from Viareggio towards the foothills, allowing the fresh day's sunlight to wink once more on the greenhouse roofs. When the penumbra has retreated across Camaiore's football stadium I shall know it is time for me to start my own day's work on the story of Nanty Riah's life. When we parted at Munich airport he had rather shamefacedly thrust a fat envelope into my hands.

'Dunno if your bloke ever mentioned it,' he said, 'but I sort of once began, you know, putting some stuff together about my life. It's no good, of course, I can't write for nuts. A professional like yourself, well, I guess it'll give you a laugh. But who knows, for Chrissake, you might find *something* to help you.'

His self-deprecations had been reassuring. It was still hard to believe this suddenly shy, hairless man of almost thirty-one was the same person as the triumphant teenager I had watched whip thousands of adoring fans into screaming hysteria only a couple of nights previously. A streak of modesty was probably the one thing that, if he were ever to transcend his status as a mere celebrity, was crucial. It was certainly a great recommendation to his biographer because it made him likeable. Once back home and able to read through his scattered notes and scribbles I liked him even more. Nanty was quite correct: he was no writer. But he was frank and seemed not to care what impression he made. His papers included a poem addressed to his afflicted sister Julie. As poetry it was toe-curling. As a revelation of love and protectiveness, though, it was wholly convincing, and to such an extent that for once I shall resist the temptation to quote an extract. Well, maybe I might later. It all depends on how Nanty behaves himself.

I am becoming aware that a familiar *whup-whup* sound is growing in volume somewhere below me. I glance over the tops of my basil plants that fragrantly edge the verandah and finally spot the helicopter. It is difficult to see at first because it is rising steadily, head on, bringing with it a pungent sense of déjà vu. Surely not *again*? And me with my pergola's vines as painstakingly re-woven as that weasel Benedetti's thinning hair. In amazement I watch its approach and am soon able to see it is not the same sinister black craft that so terrified Nanty some weeks ago. It is painted blue and white and has reassuringly civilian contours rather than those of an attack gunship. What is more it is evidently not going to overfly my pergola, for it banks a hundred metres away to make a circle around my house. Inside the bulbous canopy I can see three figures. I follow the glittering arc of the tail rotor behind the trees. This is unbelievable: another airborne visitor for my neighbour. Who *is* this bloody Marta woman? Implausible alternatives race through my mind. She is Mother Teresa's illegitimate daughter, paid handsomely by the Sisters of Charity to keep out of the public eye. She is the last living member of Voynovia's deposed and exiled royal family, awaiting the call by her loyal citizenry to return and rule again from her shattered palace. She is . . . But this time, goddamn it, I'm going to find out. What do you mean, none of my business? The suspense is affecting my entire life. Even as the helicopter settles invisibly but very audibly in Marta's paddock I am on the way over to her house.

The question is, do I need an excuse? Surely a helicopter landing eighty yards away is unusual enough to give the average householder a reason for being inquisitive? What role should I play, though: eager young planespotter or irate literary gent whose peace and quiet has once again been disturbed? Fortunately the matter is taken out of my hands. By the time I arrive Marta and two strangers are standing beside the red sports car in conversation. The younger man, though, is not quite a stranger. I recognize him at once as the handsome boy I saw driving her on the Viareggio road in this very car. And handsome he most certainly is. Many, many plainer boys than he have snorted a line of coke in Klosters and taken their clothes off presuming they look as rosy to others as their private world now does to them.

Marta spots my tentative approach and calls me over.

38

'Gerree! This you meet *il maestro* Piero Pacini. And this his son Filippo.'

You could knock me down with a buzzard feather. There is now no doubt about it: I recognize those world-weary and distinguished features from a thousand press photographs. Here before me on Marta's patch is the genius who gave us *Nero's Birthday*. Numbly I extend a hand.

'*Piacere. Piacere.*'

'And this gentleman,' Marta goes on to explain in serviceable Italian, 'is Mr Samper, my English neighbour. Mr Samper, alas, is not very pleased with us because we took down his fence the other day. In fact, he was talking of legal action the last time we met.' She smiles sweetly at me.

Bitch! I never said anything about – oh well, maybe I might have dropped a rhetorical sort of hint, but only as a gesture to indicate how peeved I was. I hardly expected her to pass it on to Piero Pacini himself, for heaven's sake, if only because I never really believed her story of knowing this celebrated man. I naturally assumed she'd had the fence destroyed for her own arcane reasons. And anyway, *can* this be Marta speaking such fluent Italian?

'Well,' I begin with what I hope is a disarmingly humorous note of protest in my voice, 'I think the lady's exaggerating slightly –' but at that moment the helicopter pilot guns his engine and the thing rises from the paddock in the background, tilts nose down for forward speed and clatters away with a battering of echoes thrown back from the cliff face. When we can hear ourselves think Marta has offered us all coffee. Most fervently I trust she has run out of those *mavlisi* things of hers. Somehow I can't see spearmint-flavoured pigeon's eggs striking her grandee visitors as a delicious new alternative to boring old florentines. We follow her into the house where Pacini and son seat themselves among the laundry with a courteous show of unconcern. The father opens a small leather grip. I notice he is wearing a silver Old Florence watch. None of your tacky Rolexes for a man of his distinction.

'Marta, *cara*, I've brought you a disc of the rushes we did here.' His hostess is banging away with tins and cupboards and percolators. When it comes to anything involving kitchens and cuisine she has the dexterity and unobtrusiveness of a stevedore. Already I am looking forward to inviting these people to my own house for some proper Samper hospitality. I fancy they will be well able to discern the difference. Pacini is meanwhile waving a DVD in Marta's direction. 'You have a DVD player, of course?'

'I'm afraid I don't, no,' she says. 'Nor a video machine. Not even a television. You know how backward I am, Piero. But it was a sweet thought.'

As you may imagine, my mind is turning over in high gear. By suppressing a mental choking reflex I can with effort swallow the idea that Marta is on chummy terms with debatably the world's greatest living film director, that footage has been shot in this very hovel, even that when she told me she was writing music for a film there might have been an element of truth in it. All this is amazing enough. Yet the real revelation is that she evidently speaks quite passable Italian. I'm absolutely certain she never used to. Somehow in the last few months she has managed to acquire a fluency that will make it possible to have an actual conversation with her in a language other than pidgin. The old bag has been playing that one pretty close to her ample chest, I think with resentment. All this time we could have been having civilized social relations. Or at least I would have been able to make my grievances unmistakably clear to her. But Piero Pacini is addressing me.

'I understand from Marta that it was you who put up that magnificent fence, Signor Samper? I most deeply regret my apparent vandalism in having it taken down. But you see, the scene in my new film depends so much on the view here. I shall of course put it back up at once to your specifications and reimburse you financially. If it's any consolation, it took my workmen no little labour to remove. The foreman told me that it was "a devil of a job because it had been put up by an expert". Those were his very words, weren't they, Filo?' He turns to his son.

'Perfectly correct, *papà*,' says this vision, flashing me a smile I want to lay away in lavender in a dark drawer for the rocky years ahead.

'*Ma scherza?*' I make a gesture of dismissal. 'You can't be serious. It is perhaps true that carpentry is something of a hobby of mine – just an amateur's *passatempo*, you understand. As for the fence itself, it's really of no importance. Marta and I had decided it would be a good thing to mark our properties' boundary, that's all.'

'It shall be restored this week,' the film director promised. 'You have Pacini's word. Now, as regards this legal action of yours, which I willingly concede you have every right to undertake: may I ask, sir, how far it has proceeded?'

'Oh, it hasn't,' I assure him. 'No, no. I'm afraid dear Marta has got hold of the wrong end of the stick. She sometimes does.'

Dear Marta gives me a look from behind her hair that I can't interpret before she is distracted by the *caffettiera*'s strident bubbling – to my ears one of the great civilized sounds, along with that of corks being withdrawn. Pacini meanwhile has produced from his bag a beautifully wrapped package tied with a springy yellow ribbon.

'A little nothing from Rome, Marta, for having looked after Filo's car for him.' He hands it to her. 'They ought to go well with your coffee.'

With her familiar piggy squeal of pleasure Marta tears the wrapping off an assortment of florentines from one of Rome's most exclusive *pasticcerie*. Saved by the bell. The dread spectre of *mavlisi* fades. We sip our coffee and sample the florentines which are exquisitely nutty and chocolatey. Little do these two goofs know what so nearly might have been.

'And could I ask, sir, what it is you do?' Pacini enquires.

'Gerry's a famous writer,' says Marta.

'Hardly famous,' I protest, 'but undeniably I write, yes.'

'Wonderful. And what sort of books?'

'Having been a journalist I've so far stuck to journalistic things. No blockbuster novels yet, I'm afraid. Recently I've been writing biographies of, well, sporting figures.'

'Lucrative?' Pacini asks keenly.

'Very,' I lie, equally so.

'And who are you currently writing about, if I might ask? Please don't feel you have to answer,' he adds. 'I quite understand the necessity for discretion.'

'No, it's no secret, just a departure from my norm. I've been approached by a pop star, of all people. We can't always choose exactly the client we would ideally like, can we? Actually, that's what I was doing in Munich last week while you were filming here. I went to see Freewayz' last public appearance.'

'What?' The gorgeous Filippo looks startled. 'Are they disbanding?'

'No, no,' I reassure him. 'They're merely re-branding themselves. From now on they'll be known as Alien Pie. Why, are you a fan?'

'Not so much of the group,' Filippo admits. 'It's just kid stuff, though they're pretty good. Better than those boy bands whose members are chosen by TV polls on the basis of what they look like rather than their talent. Freewayz has always been way ahead of Take That or Westlife. No, it's Brill himself I admire. There's some musical muscle under there somewhere, don't you think? He's much more than just a pretty face like Justin Timberlake or Aaron Carter or those other all-American kids.'

Aaron *Who*? This hunk's a lot better informed than I am. 'It's Brill I'm writing for,' I tell him, offhand purveyor of trade secrets.

'You're not! You actually know him?' Filippo suddenly looks still younger.

'Sure. As a matter of fact he's even been here. He was staying over in my house some weeks ago. Would you like to meet him? It could easily be arranged.'

I'm satisfied to note that throughout this exchange Marta has been looking at me in amazement. I can see her putting things together in her fuddled, Voynovian way. Was this pop star perhaps the client her helicopter had driven away? And is she not obliged to view her neighbour in a rather new light?

'It didn't take you long to find Filo's weakness,' Pacini is telling me with a father's indulgence. 'From now on he'll be eating out of your hand. Meanwhile, Signor Samper –'

'Gerry, please.'

'– Gerry, you might be interested to drop down to Pisorno Studi one day when you have a spare moment and watch us do some filming. Marta has written a completely brilliant score for my new film and most of the sets we'll be using are there. It's just down the coast. Filo often collects Marta in that absurd car of his. I'm sure if you didn't mind curling up in the back somehow he would happily bring you too. Failing that, there's always our helicopter. Filo can bring you in that. He's a fully qualified pilot, you know. They say he's a natural,' he adds fondly. 'And now, Marta, our thanks for the delicious coffee. Filo and I ought to be getting down to the studios. We've got a heavy shooting schedule as from tomorrow. Oh, and Gerry, how long was that fence of yours?'

'Forty metres. With a door in the middle. But –'

'I shall attend to it immediately. The men will be up within a day or two. You'll only have to show them where it runs and they'll do the rest. Come along, Filo.'

As the great man shakes my hand again I recognize his discreet, unusual cologne that somehow suggests damp prayer books. It really *is* Messe de Minuit. Etro and Old Florence! I wonder Marta's shack doesn't slump to the ground in the face of this sophistication. But it doesn't, and within minutes the Pacinis have roared off in the red car with Filippo at the wheel. I stare after them wondering who cuts the boy's hair. Someone in Rome, probably. There's no one around here, except maybe Severino in Pisa on a good day. Marta and I are left standing there listening to the Panther's exhaust burping its way down the curves below.

'Well!' I say at last. 'A morning of revelations.'

'Yes, Gerry. Not the least being that you speak such good Italian.'

'And the same for you, Marta. I at least have been living in Italy some time. From now on it seems we have a language in common. I wonder if we'll be the same people?'

'I do hope not,' she says, unfazed by my philosophical pleasantry. And with that familiar sinking feeling I glimpse the edges of a leer behind her dun curtain of hair, like one of those hunting spiders of dark design that lurk beneath leaf mould.

39

It is sometimes hard not to succumb to banality and reflect a little on life's ironies. Had I not deliberately bought this charming house on the lip of a precipice as a retreat from the world? Was the scenery not well stocked with sighing forests, mewing buzzards, the occasional clatter of rocks? Weren't the nearest shops two miles below in Casoli and wasn't that idle slob of a *postino* reluctant to bring me letters on his motor scooter all the way at road's end? In short, everything about living up here stands successfully in opposition to the turmoil of towns, office hours, parking spaces and the importunings of double-glazing salesmen.

And yet ever since I'd taken up residence and finally got the place looking as I wanted it (the mushroom and eau de Nil kitchen gives me frissons of pleasure still), my life up here had been nothing but punctuated uproar. An insane neighbour who looked like a bag lady, a daily stream of helicopters and sports cars: I might as well have gone to live in the short-term car park at Heathrow. Oh well, no one ever accused me of not being fair minded. Given that the uproar had occurred, I admit this latest development did offer interesting possibilities. As you will appreciate by now, Samper's ways are ways of wiliness and all his paths are peace, to improve a favourite saying of stepmother Laura's.

I spent the rest of the morning wandering from room to room addressing remarks variously to a sugar sifter, a patch of sunlight on the floor, a row of very unimaginative cookbooks and finally to Gazzbear. He was the only one who replied, responding to a probing thumb with his usual expression of wisdom. 'Piero *Pacini*?!' I kept exclaiming. '*Marta*?! A *film*?!' And each time Gazzbear made brief acknowledgement. After a meditative sandwich lunch (home made bread, pecorino cheese and a fabulous rhubarb & sardine chutney of my own – who else's? – devising), I had spotted the silver lining. I reflected on the curious coincidence that not so many weeks ago I had actually thought of Piero Pacini myself as a possible subject for a biography. At least, his was one of the names I had come up with as someone who could lift me out of my 'sporting heroes' rut and get my intellectual pleasure centres working again. That, of course, had been before Nanty Riah entered my life. I could now see it was altogether less of a coincidence that, when I had idly proposed Pacini's name to Marta as an example of the sort of subject I should ideally like, she pretended she'd barely heard of the man and then flattered me with all that stuff about how someone of my musical talents would be better off writing about a musician like that alleged pianist friend of hers, Pavel Taneyev. With calculated meanness she had obviously been trying to keep Pacini to herself, though for what purpose I could not imagine.

However, now that the truth was out and we had all been introduced to each other I could take steps to ensure there would be life after Brill, so far as my own career was concerned. It struck me that once I had finished helping Nanty get to Base Camp on his ascent of Parnassus, a biography of Piero Pacini would be the perfect next project. Certainly that would be the averagely smart thing to try for. The extra ingredient of Samper wiliness would surely guarantee it happened, but for the moment I had no idea how to bring it about. What I needed was leverage, and I could think of no suitable lever. I knew these Oscar-winning celebrities. One needed to persuade them that no extant biography did them justice, that everything written about them so far was pitifully inadequate, lightweight and sensational; that the story must be right for posterity's sake. Step one, therefore, would be to find out if there already was a Pacini biography. Step two was to rubbish it. Step three was to suggest the promising young author Gerald Samper as the ideal person to undertake *the* biography. This proposal would be made with bewitching modesty; the crucial lever would clinch the deal. Step four was to find that lever.

As always when faced with a puzzle I turned to cooking as therapy, flicking through that sadly unpublished compilation of culinary and even erotic wisdom, *The Boys' Reformatory Cookbook*. Budgies in Overcoats? Popular, of course, since children are unused to food that makes them laugh. Unfortunately I didn't have the ingredients to hand. Tripe & Meringue Pie? This was not an unqualified success when I invented it; afterwards I had learned either to leave all the sugar out of the meringue mix or else to cut it with a little Fernet Branca. If one is to reform boys one needs to begin with their expectations and modify those with a touch of sternness. Tripe & Meringue Pie is quite stern, especially in its Fernet version. At other times, of course, a little cajolery is helpful and one turns to something more seductive like Kidneys in Toffee. This bears no relation to that coarse concoction known as 'banoffee pie', as irresistible to popular taste as urban legends are to a journalist. 'Banoffee pie' was invented by a Sussex publican in the seventies, I think, and anyway the 'toffee' in it is – and I shudder to relate this – condensed milk boiled in the can until it becomes brown and rubbery. In my far more adventurous dish the kidneys provide the protein the boys need after an afternoon spent breaking rocks. Mere bananas and condensed milk never built muscles. And to answer a question from the Mirabelle in Curzon Street, the toffee in my dish is nearer to fudge.

I spent several happy hours emptying my mind of mundane affairs and filling it instead with dishes: dishes sublime, dishes disgusting; classics and near-misses and even (a gastronomic category I have myself invented) non-starters. I would rather experiment and fail than slavishly follow someone else's recipe and produce someone else's dish. And there, in that single sentence, you have the Samper philosophy of life. So what about Marta's cuisine? What about her admirably dire *shonka* and *mavlisi*, that *kasha* dumpling of hers with the gravitational field of a dead star? Don't those also qualify as essays in culinary imagination? Don't they speak eloquently of a cracked but original mind? No, I'm afraid not. Marta, like the food she serves, isn't cracked but merely foreign. Her food is traditional. That it tastes to you and me like a deliberate assault on our most intimate membranes is incidental. That is simply the way they are in Voynovia, a testament to historical harshness: generations of their peasant bodies being lashed by landowners and their various orifices scarified with red pepper.

The trouble with thinking about food, and especially with thinking about Marta's food, is that it left me nearly without an appetite. A snack, then. But what? My listless eye fell on the last recipe for the boys' reformatory and was immediately rekindled:

Lychees on Toast
———◆———

Ingredients

Lychees (tinned)
Olive oil
Peanut butter
Hard cheese
Toast
Anchovies
Tabasco sauce

◆

This was specifically designed to cheer them up after a hard day being reformed: a bedtime snack to tickle their palates and give them energy for whatever rigours lay ahead in the long hours of dormitory darkness. Do you remember, years ago, the slogan an advertising agency came up with to sell some massively calorific slop or other? It involved the concept of 'night starvation', a brilliant idea that suggested life-threatening affinities between a suburbanite's slumber and the months-long hibernation of a bear in its cave. 'Night starvation' implied a portly man retiring to bed and waking up eight hours later with the physique of a famine victim, a mere collection of bones and hanging skin barely able to totter down to breakfast. The underlying message was clear: each moment spent *not* putting something into your mouth is a step nearer starvation. Ah, spin! They were not about to say that each moment spent *not* putting something into your mouth is a step nearer to losing weight. Lychees on Toast was designed to render it unnecessary from the nutritional point of view for the boys to put anything in their mouths until breakfast next morning.

A simpler dish there never was. I planned it with institution cooks in mind in the hope that they, too, might have reformed since my day. The tinned lychees should be drained and their scented syrup put aside, possibly for my Quails in Sponge *bonne bouche*. The anchovies and peanut butter should be mashed together to a smooth consistency and enlivened with a few drops of Tabasco. Then the lychees should be gently, sympathetically stuffed with the compound and arranged in beguiling patterns on slices of lightly toasted bread that have been sprinkled with finely grated hard cheese or (better) spread sparingly with Gorgonzola. Drizzle olive oil over them and pop them under the grill. If the boys' reformation is still at an early stage a gram or two of a good proprietary benzodiazepine makes a sensible addition to the lychees' stuffing.

I had finished preparing several slices of this tempting snack and had just put them under the grill when, with the punctuality of the inevitable, the phone rang. It turned out to be Filippo Pacini, owner of the best haircut in Tuscany, the nicest profile, the most absurd car. I was at once all ears. He said that, quite independently of our 'fascinating' meeting at Marta's house that morning (*'affascinante'*, eh? Doubters of the Samper charisma please note), his father had been considering a small addition to the film. Towards the end of *Arrazzato* there was apparently a scene where some young members of a hippie commune or something go to town for a night out and then return to their beach, whereupon the film reaches its climax of dissent and mayhem. I hadn't the faintest idea what Filippo was talking about, I just liked listening to him saying it. It seemed that the hippies' night out on the town was supposed to provide an ironic contrast between their comfortable bourgeois roots and the radical discomforts of their beach-squatting Greenery, something I would scarcely have thought needed emphasis. But Piero Pacini had now decided to add a further twist by having them briefly attend some sort of pop concert. The idea of this was to show the brainless seduce-ability of modern youth. More specifically to the film, it would illustrate the ubiquitous siren song of postmodern capitalism undermining whatever idealism has been left in some young minds already worked on by insidious fascist influences. Crikey. At this moment my lychees burst quietly into flame beneath the grill and I had to dash over and extinguish them in the sink, where they floated on a series of charred rafts. Too sad.

'And?' I prompted, returning breathless and apologetic to the phone.

'And my father wonders whether your friend Brill would consent to have the band make a brief appearance in this scene. Well, to be honest, it was my suggestion that it might be Brill. You sort of put it into my head this morning. We'd been thinking of an Italian group but Alien Pie would be better. Just a guest appearance, you know. Of course they'll be booked up for months ahead but we thought there would be no harm in asking. We could make do with very few shots just so long as we get a good chunk of their soundtrack to lay underneath. What do you think, Gerry?'

Suddenly flattered to be 'Gerry' after all that respectful '*Lei*' stuff, I assured him I would put it to my friend Brill and sound him out. We ended the call with mutual expressions of goodwill, mine being more sincere than his, I suspect, but there we are. I was left feeling strangely excited in a kitchen it was hard to see across, thanks to the black fallout of my supper. In every other respect the lychee moment had passed, so I made myself more toast and spread it thickly with a terrine I'd long kept sealed in the larder and which seemed not to have suffered for it. I well remembered making it. Jack Russells are absolute buggers to bone, notoriously so, but yield a delicate, almost silky pâté that seems to welcome the careworn diner with both paws on the edge of the table, as it were. A scratch meal, but delicious. As I ate I mulled over the implications of Filippo's call. Might this not be the very lever I had been looking for? Being able to arrange the right band at short notice would surely put me in Pacini's debt and make it that much more likely he would agree to my becoming his biographer. For the moment I had to pigeonhole the disturbing incidental thought that to judge from the scene Filippo had just been sketching out *Arrazzato* sounded like being a real clunker. Could this be the man who brought us *Mille Piselli*? Green communes and politics in the twenty-first century, for pity's sake? What was he doing? Have faith, I told myself, removing lead shot from my mouth. One never gets them all out.

As for what would be in it for Nanty, that was easy. An appearance in a film by Piero Pacini would afford exactly the right association with high art he needed so badly to foster. I tried to phone him there and then but got only a recording of his voice suggesting in impeccable Califockney: 'Like, leave yer number an' that.'

The next day I went messing about on the internet and discovered there were dozens of academic studies of Pacini's work (*Visual Signsponge: The Derridean element in the post-structuralism of Piero Pacini's later films*) but only one biography, *Piero Pacini*, now seven years out of date. Good. That was step one completed. Step two was to get hold of a copy and be shocked by its triviality. Amazon.co.uk would no doubt provide me with one in due course. The Samper plan was whizzing along nicely. Full of energy I walked down to Casoli. Happening to be in the bar I asked for my mail which the indolent *postino* would have left in blithe expectation that the letters would sprout wings and complete the journey themselves. But there were no letters for me, only one for Marta. Feeling a sudden burst of neighbourliness for her, I walked back up the hill with it in the brilliant sunshine. I looked at the postmark and wondered who she knew in Venice; but these days I shouldn't have been surprised if it was the Doge himself. Once one was over the shock of discovering Marta to be well connected the possibilities were legion.

It turned out that I couldn't hand her the envelope with a graceful bow after all. She was out and her rat-coloured car gone. Her house, of course, was unlocked so I left the letter propped on the music stand of her electronic keyboard next to an almost full bottle of Fernet, the one place amid the kitchen's clutter where I could guarantee she would find it.

I spent the rest of the day working on a plan of campaign for Nanty by which he might achieve some street credibility in the thoroughfares of mainstream British culture. Nobody else would want such a thing, of course, a reflection that lent the whole project a somewhat surreal air. Then, taxed by what the Japanese call the *shokku* of the last few days, I went to bed early and fell instantly into hibernating bear mode. I awoke in darkness with a pang, not of night starvation but of fear. It took the usual blurred few seconds to focus on the sound that had woken me and to separate it from the remnants of a dream. There could be no doubt: in the night outside a helicopter was approaching. For the love of Pete, I thought, sinking back on the pillow and following its course in the dark with sightless eyes. As before, the machine missed my house by what sounded like inches and clattered and moaned to a standstill in Marta's field. Oho! I thought (though with a pang of a different sort). We can guess who *that* is, can't we? A little midnight visit from the boy racer, h'm? *How does she do it?* That's the question. What has Marta got that I – I mean, what has she *got*? Well, perhaps it isn't him after all. Maybe it's one of the Branca family whom she has urgently summoned from his bed in Milan with emergency supplies of Fernet. Voynovia's St Cecilia calls for refreshment in the small hours. I see it as an allegorical painting.

Marta

40

I'm assuming it was Gerry who delivered Marja's letter, given that our postman seldom calls. That was kind of him. I wouldn't have returned home so late had I not impulsively decided to stay down in Camaiore and have dinner after doing the shopping. I had gone to see that smarmy little house agent, Benedetti, to tell him he should ignore the letter of complaint about my neighbour I wrote to him, oh, weeks ago now, and which needless to say he has never even acknowledged. Once the sale is through they wash their hands of you. Anyway, he was out of his office and I certainly wasn't going to wait. Probably it doesn't matter now. It was just that after this surprise discovery that Gerry is perhaps serious after all, or at any rate interestingly connected, I felt I'd been a bit hasty and mean to complain about him to a maggot like Benedetti. From now on, thanks to the discovery that underneath that pose of inflexible Englishness Gerry actually speaks amazingly good Italian, if I have complaints I can make them directly to his face. Anyway, enough of him. Let's see what my darling sister has to say. Venice, *ek ni*? I smell drama.

Dearest Matti

Well, that's that: Mekmek & I have eloped! We just got the hell out. The fact is that since Timi got back from America he's been making a perfect pest of himself & I couldn't bear it any longer. I didn't ring you because I was scared you'd try to talk me out of it. Mekki's being just great. He's a computer programmer, did I say?

Heaps to tell you. I got away without telling a soul, not even poor Mili, & we flew direct from Voynograd to Vienna & then on to Venice. By the time you get this we'll probably be heading

*slowly in your direction. I expect Timi & Father will have set
Captain Panic on my trail but it'll be way too late. Once we were
in Venice I e-mailed Ljuka so he'd know I was safe. With any luck
he'll head Father off from drastic action.*

*Sorry, Matti, this is in haste. Will call in a day or 2 when we've
decided what to do. Making straight for you would be feeble as well
as being the first place they'll think to look so we'll probably linger,
either here or on the way. Venice is a first taste of real freedom at
last & boy does it feel gooood! I don't have to explain, do I?*

*Can't wait to see you. You'll know what to tell them when
they call. Oh, and you're going to love Mekki, I just know it.
He's cuddly & mmm!*

*Tons of love
Mari*

Well, I was right to smell drama. No doubt my phone has
been ringing these last several hours. Thank God I haven't
got one of those answering machines yet. So that's that. She's
made the break and we'll just have to see what happens.
Tonight's meal has left me very *mellowed* and much inclined
to go to bed, to be honest. Time enough to worry about Marja
tomorrow which, as we Voynovians so wisely say, is another
day. (I wonder if other nations have these devastating
insights?) I'm also beginning to wonder if that second bottle
of wine wasn't a mistake, especially with the Fernet over
coffee; but what the hell, it was just the once. I surely have a
long way to go before I risk becoming like Gerry, poor fellow.

I'm cleaning my teeth and trying to ignore that perennial
sneaky worry about exactly what my next job of work is to be.
Pacini hasn't so much as hinted what he intends doing after
Arrazzato's in the can and it's time I was thinking seriously
about the future and an income if I want to keep my independence. Nothing in the universe will make me run to Father
to ask him to bail me out, not now. (*What* an independent
tearaway this studious elder daughter has become!) I'm just
about to pour myself a tiny nightcap of Fernet when a familiar

sound begins to steal into the house. Of course! Dear Ljuka wouldn't wait for phones to be answered at a moment of family crisis, bless him. Action men *act*. His helicopter approaches and I'm ready outside the back door with a torch when he lands. Up here on the otherwise silent mountainside the noise seems cataclysmic and I'm briefly conscious that Gerry's complaint about disturbance was not unreasonable. Then my attention is distracted when I notice it's a different helicopter, but I'm quite sure the pilot's my baby brother and so it proves. We embrace beneath the still-whirling main rotor.

'Rather too much,' is his reply, half muffled as he eases his helmet off, to my anxious greeting 'What's new?' 'Marja's done a bunk – did you know? Much worse, though, is they've arrested Father.'

'*What?* Who? Why?'

'The police, apparently working with Europol. Panic called me in Trieste and warned me to lie low for a bit and certainly not to come home. It's politics, of course. Basically, our dear government will do absolutely anything to get the country into the EU at the next intake, whenever that is. Panic says the old alliances are far from reliable any longer. So the police rolled up without the usual courtesy warning and took Father off with them to headquarters. I can't imagine they'll hold him for long. Panic got the lawyers down there within the hour. But even so. Oh – and they impounded that black helicopter of ours, as well as the Cessna, so that's why I came in this.' Ljuka gives a backward jerk of his handsome head to indicate the machine in the paddock, now dark and without sign of life except for a faint ticking of cooling metal. 'It belongs to the company.'

My brother towers in the kitchen shedding his jacket. He catches sight of Marja's letter lying on the keyboard where I dropped it and picks it up. 'When did this arrive? Is she OK?'

'Read it,' I tell him. 'I was out earlier and she may have phoned. As far as I know they're somewhere between Venice and here. Have you met this Mekmek fellow? Is he all right? I mean, is he at least better than Timi?'

'Probably. She only told me about him the other day, cross-my-heart top secret, and I haven't been allowed to meet him yet. Computer geek, I think. That could be useful, in the circumstances.'

I make us coffee and Ljuka takes the torch and goes back out to fetch a small overnight bag from which he produces a bottle of *galasiya* from the estate – the real thing, ninety-two per cent proof. 'Luckily I had this in the Trieste office,' he says. 'Make the most of it. It looks as though you may have to do without food parcels from home for a bit.'

He sits on the sofa with his cup and leans back, eyes closed. I suddenly realize he's all in. For the first time I can remember, my little brother looks like a tired adult.

'How bad is it?' I ask. 'Really?'

'Pretty bad.'

'Are they after you?'

'Oh, probably. Possibly. I don't know. It's too early to tell whether they're trying to give Father a scare – or a warning, which amounts to the same thing – or if this really is it and from now on we're going to be chivvied and harried wherever we go. Arrested, released; arrested, released – you know. Much the same tactics as the Russians used, I gather. Only this will cover most of Europe. Raids on our offices, bank accounts frozen, our people picked up on trumped-up charges, our computers hacked into, electronic surveillance.' His voice dwindles as he takes a gulp of coffee.

'"Trumped-up", Uki? No – I'm a coward; I don't really want to know. That makes me a hypocrite, too, since we all know how this house was paid for, the car, my subsistence here until Pacini's cheques began coming in. But . . .'

'Better you don't know, Matti. If there are innocent parties in all this they're obviously you and Marja and we must keep it that way. Not that I think ignorance will be much defence if they're really determined.'

What a fool, I think, looking at him with such fondness it may not be that second bottle of wine that fills my eyes with tears and swells my heart with protectiveness. What a stupid boy and how predictable all this is. How predicted it *was*, given my last conversation with him in this very room a month or two ago.

'Stay here, Uki,' I tell him. 'You'll be safe here.'

He shakes his head with a smile. 'As safe as anywhere, that's true. Anyway, I'll gladly sleep the night here. I'm bushed.'

'Do we still have money?' Really I'm thinking of dumb practical details like being able to fill the helicopter's tanks.

'They can't possibly know all the accounts. They've been disguised and dispersed over years. Hell, Matti, you yourself have a dozen at least.'

'*I* have?'

'Of course you have. So has Marja. What do you think Father's been doing with his money all this time? He's been steadily salting away a good part of it for us children. "Family first", remember. What did you imagine?'

'You'll think me crazy,' I say humbly, 'but to tell the truth I've never really given it a thought. I've been too interested in, well, music I suppose. And wanting to make my own living.'

'Oh, Matti, you're hopeless. Small wonder Father despairs of you.'

'He does, does he?'

'Honestly, this misconception of Father is ridiculous. He loves you deeply. He loves all of us deeply. But you know his character, that generation. It's perfectly natural that sometimes he gets a bit exasperated by your, I don't know, other-worldliness or something.'

'Only I bet he doesn't use that word. I bet he says I'm *prikmul*.'

'It's true.' My brother smiles into his empty coffee cup. 'Other-worldly to the detriment of your family obligations. He says what other word can he use about a daughter who shows no inclination to settle down and get married and make a grandfather of him, as is his right. *Prikmul*. Says it all.'

'And do you think that too, Uki?'

'No. No, I know you better than Father does. I know you're not deliberately *prikmul*, Matti. I guess you're an artist, and that's that. God, I'm bushed,' he repeats.

Prikmul or not, I suddenly become concerned for my little brother and start throwing sheets over the sofa. 'I'll get you a pillow from upstairs.' But by the time I come down with it Ljuka is already asleep. There is a light sheen of sweat on his forehead. Although he has taken his jacket and trousers off and despite the altitude up here it is a warm Tuscan night in September. I leave him with the sloppy smile one bestows on sleeping babies and go up to my empty *letto matrimoniale* where I remember I never asked him whether Father already knows that his other daughter, too, has fled the coop. I'm smitten with a pang of guilty affection for this father who, all unbeknownst, has been making generous provision for me and whose empire may even now be starting to collapse around him. I stare sleeplessly up through the darkness past the invisible beams and through the stone roof, but without seeing the hard-eyed galaxies staring back. For the first time in a long while I realize I actively miss my mother.

The absolute uselessness of regret.

41

'How was the sofa?' I ask next morning as I make coffee and Ljuka begins to stir. 'No metronomes?'

'Huh?'

'That *dudi* neighbour I've told you about, Gerry? Sat himself down there some weeks ago right on top of a metronome Father gave me when I went to Moscow. It's quite a sharp little obelisk. From his expression I'd say he became intimate with at least ten centimetres of it. I was hoping you didn't have a similar mishap last night.'

'Really, Matti,' he says sleepily but still managing to sound shocked. I smile, knowing exactly what his problem is. Not only should a Voynovian elder sister not be coarse; she shouldn't make jokes that imply shared experience with a *dudi*, no matter how accidental or innocent. Ah me. Moscow Conservatory taught me a lot more than music. Pavel might have won the Tchaikovsky Prize that year but when he wasn't practising for six hours a day his thoughts weren't much on music. The parties we had in those little student flats were hardly in accordance with the public face of Soviet sexual morality. But then we were artists, and the Russians have always understood there can be no rule that has no exception. I believe that was just as true under the Soviets, if not more so. It may be heresy for a daughter of Voynovia to say so, but there's lots of good stuff in the Russians. Some of them.

'I've been misjudging Gerry rather,' I tell Ljuka, waiting to hand him a cup of coffee as he swings his feet to the floor and runs both hands through his enviable mane of hair. He has the smudged look of a suddenly woken child.

'Oh?' he says disinterestedly, sipping and shuddering. So I tell him of the recent revelations and at the mention of Luc Bailly, Per Snoilsson and Brill he perks up. 'He *knows* those people?'

'Apparently, yes. He's written books about them. Or is writing, in Brill's case. Of course, I was forgetting you're a motor racing fan.'

'Yes, well, Snoilsson's world famous, Matti. He's still Formula One champion. And just about everybody's heard of Freewayz and Brill. Their music's in every disco from Spitzbergen to Sydney, I'd think. Pretty crappy it is, too, but the kids go for it in a big way. Brill must be making a serious fortune. And this Gerry of yours has got his hooks into him? Smart guy.'

'I can't work out if he's smart or not but he's obviously much more professional than I've been giving him credit for. Plus he speaks fluent Italian. I've been underestimating him because he's such a queen. For all I know I'm wrong about that, too. Anyhow, he's been underestimating me as well, so I suppose it's mutual.'

'He'd better not have been disrespectful.'

My little brother, my champion. 'We're grown-ups, Uki,' I say. 'Right now, you and I have far more urgent things to worry about than Gerry. What are we going to do? How can we find out what's happening with Father? Can't you call Panic?'

'I'll do that right away.' He gets to his feet and struggles into his trousers. He still looks dazed and underslept but the coffee's beginning to work. He pulls the phone over, dials an interminable number and then turns round, flattening his hand over the mouthpiece, to say rather shockingly: 'Go away, Matti,' nodding his head towards the back door.

I understand and go out. The less I know the better. And it would be safer not to risk Panic overhearing my voice. We have to assume the line may be tapped at that end. Or even at this end. The long arm of Europol. It's depressing: too much like going back to an era I'd hoped had been left behind for ever. I wander apprehensively across the grass to the helicopter whose top surfaces, I notice, are shawled in dew. I've always liked these machines. I like the way they smell purposefully of kerosene. This one looks a lot tamer and more civilian than the last thing Ljuka turned up in. Still, the twin blades of its tail rotor are painted black with two yellow stripes across them, waspish colours implying that if you were thinking of making it your prey it might be safer not to. Flight; escape. I'm chiefly worried because I can't tell how worried I ought to be. I would have thought Father and Ljuka had long since made provision against this moment, would have all sorts of contingency plans. But there again, too much power for too long slows people down. It makes them cocksure and slack, which was part of what I was trying to tell Ljuka the last time he was here.

I go around and lean my head against the cold plastic of the window in the pilot's door and gaze in at the beautiful functionality of the instruments and levers and switches, all of which I've had explained to me. Flying these things is tricky. It's all a matter of co-ordination, with both hands doing things in two different planes and independently of the feet. In its way it's quite like playing the organ. It surely oughtn't to be any more difficult to fly one of these than it is to play a Bach trio sonata. Easier, actually, given the number of qualified helicopter pilots and the dearth of organists good enough to play the trio sonatas.

I'm just trying to remember where the ignition switch is when Ljuka himself comes out. His face is suddenly very adult indeed.

'They've kept him,' he says. 'I had to get it from Franek. Panic's gone. He got away in time. They're at the house and they've impounded all the papers they can find. Franek says he thinks it's co-ordinated and they've arrested people in Sarajevo, Pristina, Christ knows where. What are we going to do, Matti?'

'I was hoping you'd be able to tell me, Uki. What do I know about all this stuff? I shall be all right; it's you I'm worried about. They're probably looking for you. Where could you go?'

It's as if an old plan is coming back to him. 'Marseilles. I'll be fine once I'm on the ground there. I've got reliable friends. I guess after that North Africa and eventually the States. At least until the pressure's off and we know where we stand.'

'As long as it's not in a dock in The Hague.'

'Don't. Ah, *kakash*!'

I follow his gaze. A dark blue car plainly marked CARABINIERI in white capitals along the side is gliding quietly to a stop beside the house. Two uniformed men get out of the back, the senior greying handsomely and festooned in braid. Both wear pistols in polished holsters whose flaps they unbutton automatically as they walk towards us. It's true what they say in books: your knees really do feel weak suddenly.

'Can you get away if I distract them?' I say foolishly, my mind blank of heroic tactics.

'The machine's keys are in the kitchen,' Ljuka says briefly. And since that is that, we begin walking calmly to meet them.

It starts off very civilly. The senior of the two announces himself as *maresciallo* Sgrizzi. I introduce myself and my brother. We all shake hands. The policemen appraise the helicopter with interest and walk around it. I remind myself that the carabinieri are part of the Italian military and not strictly civilians at all.

'I assume you are the pilot?' Sgrizzi addresses Ljuka, whose Italian seems well up to simple question-and-answer stuff.

'I am.'

'And of course you have the necessary *documenti*?'

'In the house.' We go in and from his bag, rather to my surprise, Ljuka produces a sheaf of official-looking papers and licences covered in stamps which the *maresciallo* examines briefly but keenly. He then asks to see my own *permesso di soggiorno*, which by some miracle I remember is marking a page in Prokoviev's eighth sonata. He hands everything over to his subordinate with a nod. The younger man takes them outside to the car: standard practice familiar to any Italian motorist. He or the driver will get on their radio and check the details.

'Please forgive this intrusion,' Sgrizzi is addressing me, I presume as the lady of the house whose brother is about to be taken away in handcuffs. I interrupt graciously to offer him coffee which he politely refuses, a bad sign. 'I'm afraid my business is official.' Worse still. 'It is with you, *signora*, rather than with your brother. At present.'

Worst of all. I sit down. 'With me?' I repeat feebly.

'It is a delicate matter. You may wish your brother not to be present.'

'What on earth . . .? No, I don't want him to leave.'

'As you wish. I must tell you, *signora*, that a very serious charge appears to have been levelled against you and it is my duty this morning to question you about the matter with a view to appropriate action being taken.'

'Against *me*? "Appears"?'

The *maresciallo* looks at me a little sadly, I think, like an uncle disappointed in his niece. 'It has been suggested that you are actively engaged in prostitution.'

There is a long silence in which my blood abruptly stops circulating and jells to embalming fluid. I catch Ljuka's eye. He has understood, all right. His face is crimson and swelling. I shake my head urgently. The last thing we need is one of his explosions.

'Can we get this straight, *maresciallo*?' My tone is reasonable. 'You're saying you think I'm some sort of call girl?' At this point, mainly out of relief that this isn't about Ljuka, I'm afraid I begin to laugh.

'An allegation has been made to that effect,' he replies cautiously.

'Oh? And by whom, may I ask? This is incredible.'

'It is a serious matter, *signora*,' the *maresciallo* chides me. 'Unfortunately I am not yet at liberty to divulge the name of the person concerned. As I said, this is in the nature of a preliminary enquiry. But the allegation implied that not only may you yourself be engaged in this profession but that you might also be acting to procure others from Eastern Europe. Er, Voynovia, isn't it?'

At this moment the dam bursts and Ljuka submerges our polite exchange beneath a torrent of Voysk – mercifully. The tirade is aimed at Sgrizzi's honour, lineage, sexual practices and personal hygiene. Before long he will be challenging the *maresciallo* to a duel in the paddock, I realize with horror, but a noise from outside is becoming steadily more insistent above my kid brother's impassioned voice. Soon the sound of an approaching helicopter fills the room.

That does it, I think. These people are not fooling after all. The policemen outside have found out about Ljuka on their radio and have sent for reinforcements. And a glance at my brother's face shows he has reached exactly the same conclusion. I lay a restraining hand on his knee.

Gerald

42

I am making a leisurely breakfast, trying not to wonder if tarty Marty is having hers in bed with Filippo Pacini. 'A natural pilot,' his father called him. I'll say. To take the taste away I spread my toast from a carefully hoarded jar of my precious Log Jam. Not actually logs, of course, but oak twigs. I am probably the only person in the world who knows how to make oak twigs as soft as the slices of rind in Seville orange marmalade. They have a sumptuous aromatic flavour, faintly resinous like the waft from a closing cigar humidor. The secret – which has probably been lost since the Late Bronze Age – lies less in the cooking than in the steeping to break down the xylem fibres. That's the bit which feels so like a trade secret I'm not sure I shall ever pass the recipe on. To have discovered how to impart the scent of freshly sawn hardwood to a preserve is, if I may say so, a real feat. To have reduced a piece of oak to the luscious consistency of crystallized ginger is the mark of a gen– (but here the phone interrupts what is beginning to look like an uncanny prediction of posterity's judgement).

'Gerry? This is Nanty. Returning yer call?'

'Bit bright and early for you, isn't it?'

'Nah, it's only just after midnight. I'm in the States, aren't I?' Music in the background, voices, laughter. 'Mick says to come on round.'

'Where, exactly?' I ask with sarcasm that sinks and is lost in the night that lies between us.

'This pad in, er,' and the line scuffs and crackles as he turns to ask someone, 'Denver, I think. But it's easy to get to. Just ask the cab driver for Olympics subdivision and it's where that becomes Therapists' Village, actually right on the corner of Slam Dunk and Oedipus? You can't miss it.'

'Oh, *that* house. Funny, I'd always thought of it as being on Home Run and Penis Envy.'

It's going to be OK working with Nanty after all. We're just testing each other out, really, like potential lovers. Suddenly I suspect he no more believes in the death agonies of potatoes than I do. But UFOs? 'Listen,' I say. 'You know Piero Pacini? I remember you admiring *Nero's Birthday*. Get this: he wants you and the boys to do a short gig for a scene in his new film. I know you're all booked solid for the next twenty-eight years but we wondered if you could squeeze it in. It could be useful, Nanty. Give you some weight.'

'We're busy, Gerry, but we're not *that* busy. Pacini? Wow – tell him he's on. We'll find time, don't worry.'

'I'll have to check, but we may be talking about the next few weeks.'

'We'll work it in. Jeez, appearing in a Pacini film. Is this one anything like *Nero's Birthday*?'

'I don't know exactly. There's certainly a beach orgy.'

'Done a few of those, mate, but always in the market for more. Christ, Gerry, at this rate you'll have to become my manager. *Pacini*. How'd you do it?' A short pause and then, 'Gerry? Is that a chopper I can hear?'

Well, yes, incredibly it is. The familiar noise has been growing steadily louder these last twenty seconds. Now the thing passes smack over the house and I can see yellowing vine leaves raining down on the terrace outside. It may be too late in the season to matter but we're talking principle here. When I can hear myself speak I say: 'It's landed. Er, Nanty? What do you think a strong smell of ozone means?'

'*Ozone?* Are you kidding, man? Listen, Gerry, you've got to get the hell out of there, I mean like *now*!'

'I . . . Nanty, I think I may have left it too late. There's this huge shadow on the kitchen door and . . . Oh-my-God-it's . . . it's so *big* and incredibly *old*! No, no! Help! It's an alien paedophile! I'm underage, mister! I'm not even forty – *aaaargh . . .*!'

I break off and knock the receiver around a bit before replacing it. We're going to get on just fine. But this sodding helicopter business has reached the giddy limit. Le Roccie is turning into a veritable oil rig. I've been far too kind to Marta, just as I was infinitely too polite to Benedetti. Well, the Samper worm is about to turn. A stop has to be put to this. I wrench open the back door and set off through the trees with purposeful stride. As I approach her hovel the sound of raised voices comes from inside the kitchen. I catch glimpses of sunlight winking off metal and perspex over in the paddock. Suddenly I don't give a damn what I'm about to intrude on. I bang on the door and throw it open, at the last moment registering the carabinieri patrol car parked off to one side. Too late. I'm in.

The first person I notice is the gorgeous Filippo, standing by the back door looking incredulous. Marta is slumped on the sofa looking wronged. Beside her yet another handsome young man is looking murderous. There is something faintly familiar about him but my attention is distracted by the two carabinieri, obtrusive in full fig. Tableau.

'Oh hello, Gerry,' Marta says dully.

'Hello, Gerry,' Filippo echoes in an aside. Then, obviously resuming the sentence I had interrupted, he adds: 'It's utterly ludicrous. Preposterous.' This is addressed to the senior of the two officers who from his uniform must be at least a Field Marshal.

'I'm sorry to interrupt,' I say. 'I just came over to, well, I heard the helicopter and, you know, it came *slap over* my house.'

'This gentleman is my neighbour,' Marta explains to the policeman.

'*Piacere.*' We nod to each other and then he frowns for a moment and says, 'Mr Samper? Is that correct?'

'Um, yes. Yes, that's me.'

He looks me over as if measuring me for a shroud and then returns to Filippo. 'I'm sorry, sir. A serious allegation was made against this lady and we are duty bound to investigate, especially since she is an *estracomunitaria*. Voynovia is not yet a part of the EU. As you're surely aware, these activities of which our informant spoke are politically highly sensitive these days. The international trade in human lives is not something we can ignore.'

Filippo merely hands the officer his ID card. It is obviously he who has just arrived in the family chopper. 'My father is Piero Pacini.'

'*Il maestro* Pacini?' The two carabinieri examine the card and then glance at each other, clearly taken aback.

'Exactly. Check the helicopter's registration. I'm not trying to impress you but to tell you that this is a straightforward case of mistaken identity. Marta, the lady you're foully accusing, so far from being a common *lucciola* is an internationally distinguished composer who is writing the musical score for my father's latest film currently in production down at Pisorno Studi. I've just come straight from him to fetch Marta because he needs her on the set this morning. This is also something you can very easily check. In fact, *maresciallo*, I think you had better go away and do that before you make a serious mistake you will later regret.'

And all this time I'm standing here trying to get my head around this. I didn't at all like the way the *maresciallo* looked at me when I came in, and the bizarre conversation certainly indicates I'm an intruder. God knows what all this is about. I'm on the point of making an apology and drifting unobtrusively away when Filippo thinks of something else. I'm impressed by the way the boy handles these minions of the law. For a kid his age he's certainly got confidence. That's what comes of having a father who is world-renowned and a Cavaliere or a Commendatore or something. A good few zillions in the bank must help, too.

'It seems to me the very least you can do for Marta is to tell her exactly who laid these grotesque charges,' he is saying. 'She has a legal right to know that. Who made this *denuncia* against her? My father will need to know when he briefs our lawyer,' Filippo adds significantly.

For a moment it looks as though the *maresciallo* is about to cave in before this unexpected heavyweight attack. Apparently, though, he has a last little something tucked away, and when it comes his timing shows he has a streak of the thespian in him.

'Very well, *signore*,' he begins. 'I agree it is only fair and proper to identify this lady's accuser, although as I have said several times already this was not an official *denuncia* but a serious rumour that was brought to the attention of a senior officer of the Ufficio dei Stranieri at the Questura in Lucca. It was reported purely in the public interest by *ingegnere* Benedetti, an estate agent in Camaiore. As a matter of fact he was the gentleman who sold this and the neighbouring house to its present occupants.' He indicates Marta and myself and produces a notebook. Finding the right page he reads out: '*Ingegnere* Benedetti swore in deposition that his informant said: "What do I care if she's an East European call girl?".' He pauses before delivering the coup de grâce. 'His informant, of course, was Signor Samper here,' and he turns to me with a little flourish.

As a rule I hate to be literal, but when I say 'all eyes are on me' they really are, Marta's in particular. She is nodding to herself with a sad half-smile of bitter resignation. What with her hair the old frump looks like Mona Lisa being handed her first Senior Citizen's bus pass. I can see I need to put my case swiftly and well.

'The *ingegnere* is quite correct,' I tell the *maresciallo*. 'That is pretty much what I said to him – although since I believed it was a private conversation it never occurred to me he would be passing it on to his police cronies. If it had, I would have made myself clearer. We were having this private conversation because I felt that Marta's social life with visiting helicopters hardly fitted Benedetti's promise to me when I bought my house that my neighbour was a mousy recluse who would only be in residence one month of the year. My tone was one of protest and Benedetti himself said he wondered what Marta was up to. And then I said: "What do I care? What do I care if she's an East European call girl?" – something like that. Obviously it was a rhetorical gesture. I didn't mean she *was* a call girl, for heaven's sake. I meant I didn't care what she was, so long as life up here became a little quieter. And that's it. If Benedetti mistook a figure of speech for an informal *denuncia* he has only himself to blame for being both mean-spirited and abnormally stupid. I believe poor Marta will bear me out in this since her own dealings with the *ingegnere* have probably led her to a similar diagnosis. Frankly, the man's a cretin.'

A *cretino* sounds even better in Italian and I can see my nifty explanation has gone over well. Marta Lisa is looking as though the bus pass was a bureaucratic error and she can go back to being eternally thirty-three. The *maresciallo*, too, is looking relieved.

'So, Signor Samper, you expressly deny that you made any specific accusation regarding this lady's profession?'

'Of course I do. What's more, since that conversation with Benedetti I've learned that she is indeed the composer for *maestro* Pacini's latest film. Consequently the helicopter visits were a necessary part of her distinguished professional connection with the production. Once that became clear there was no further problem. As I've just said, I never made any charges so I can't withdraw them. My charge against *ingegnere* Benedetti still stands, of course.'

'Of being a cretin?'

'Exactly.'

'To take action on that, *signore*, lies beyond the scope of the carabinieri. But we shall certainly explain his mistake to him.'

'And caution him, I hope, against making malicious and actionable allegations in the future?'

Instead of replying, the *maresciallo* bows his head sadly and says to Marta, 'I am truly sorry, *signora*, to have troubled you over this matter. But I hope you understand that in the present political climate we could hardly take no action at all once we'd heard the allegation. At the very least we were bound to come up here and make enquiries. However –' and he shuts his notebook with a decisive snap that clearly implies the closing of the case against Marta.

Almost instantly she is transformed from crushed victim to gladhanding hostess. She bustles about the room with smeary glasses and a villainous-looking bottle.

'Gentlemen,' she says, sounding bizarrely like a CEO at a moment of boardroom triumph in a made-for-TV series about oil moguls. 'This calls for a drink. A very special drink from Voynovia.' The *maresciallo* and his colleague look apprehensive in the way Italians do when threatened with foreign food. 'Just an *amaro*. If you like Fernet you'll love our *galasiya*.'

'Well, just a small one, *signora*. We're really still on duty.'

I have the impression that under any other circumstances the *maresciallo* would have declined politely but firmly. However, surrounded by Piero Pacini affiliates and in the wake of what nearly proved a seriously bad career move on his part, he is in no position to refuse. The glasses of dense black liquid are passed around. It looks like sump oil.

'*Salute!*' everyone echoes and takes an obligatory quaff.

Holy bicycling Christ, I think as projectile tears leap from my eyes and splash into the glass. I dimly recall Marta having mentioned this stuff as being a more butch version of Fernet Branca made by huntsmen or something. Actually tasting this distillation of gall and lighter fuel simply confirms what I've long known, that Voynovians lack an essential element of human physiology. A central nervous system, possibly. Through dancing lenses of tears I can see the *maresciallo* has been equally hard hit but is bearing up with noble shreds of dignity.

'*Madonna puttana della Madonna, ma quanti gradi ha?*' he rasps at last, his vocal cords evidently cauterized.

'Ninety-two, I believe,' says Marta brightly, examining the bottle. 'But they seldom put it on the label. Everyone in

Voynovia knows *galasiya*. In our language it means "mother's milk".'

Score one for Voynovia. Filippo is clearly beyond speech and I deduce that the handsome saturnine ruffian next to Marta must be Voynovian since he is smacking his lips judiciously as though he'd just taken a mouthful of Château Yquem. The *maresciallo*'s sidekick, I notice, is looking thoughtfully at his empty glass and shaking his head with an incredulous smile. A serious drinker. When his commanding officer has recovered enough to walk, the two men take their leave. Hands are shaken all round. I notice the *maresciallo* pause by Marta's mysterious companion and croak something like 'I shouldn't delay too long, *signore*,' before they go out, replacing their caps. Watching through the window I'm touched to see the second carabiniere solicitously take his senior comrade's elbow well before he finishes his totter to the car. All very mystifying, but the interlude has taught me one thing: that in a world containing *galasiya* the brothers Branca must look to their laurels.

Yet now the police have gone the atmosphere in the room scarcely lightens. Marta and her young visitor still look strained, while Filippo has recovered enough to be contemptuous.

'It's disgraceful, the way these *vagabondi* harass law-abiding citizens,' he fumes, suddenly sounding elderly. The experience of *galasiya* is curiously ageing. 'I'm mortified you should have been put through this, Marta. Also you, Gerry. A frivolous misunderstanding that could have been cleared up with a phone call. It's no way for artists from other countries to be treated. I'll have my father lodge a formal complaint. We'll get that *maresciallo* busted down a rank or two before we finish.'

'Oh no, Filippo, don't do that,' Marta urges with what I assume is a mixture of relief and tender-heartedness brought on by *galasiya*. 'Far better not. No, really, I shall be most upset. No harm's been done and they've gone away. Please do nothing.' But underneath I detect something like genuine fear. I suppose if you're an immigrant from one of those vague ex-Soviet countries the last thing you need is police attention.

Filippo is shaking his head dubiously. 'If you insist,' he says. 'But I still think it would be better. Anyway, Dad sent me up here to ask if you and Gerry would like to come down to the set today and watch the shooting. He didn't actually say he needs you urgently, Marta; that was for the benefit of the police. But if you'd like to come?' He glances awkwardly at the dark young man beside her.

'I'm sorry, how very rude of me,' Marta says. 'I'd forgotten you'd not been introduced. This is my brother Ljuka.' We all shake hands. 'I believe, Gerry, it was your pop-music friend who mistook Ljuka for an alien some weeks ago.'

Ah, *that's* why he looks vaguely familiar. When I picture him in flying kit as Barbie's better half, Ken, I can see it exactly. Well, well. The unwitting cause of a boy band's re-branding. He looks as though he could be deliciously mean but at the moment he seems more uneasy. Marta and he launch into urgent conversation in a language that sounds like sand being poured onto a kettledrum. Filippo and I gravitate together as sole representatives of the known world.

'Speaking personally,' I say, 'I'd be delighted to come. Would that really be all right?'

'Sure it would. We can go at once.'

'And I can tell your father that Brill and the boys will be happy to do a gig for the film. In fact, they're dead keen.'

'That's great news. Dad'll be pleased about that. Me, too. To tell you the truth, that part of the film probably could do with a bit of a lift.'

From outside at that moment there comes the sound of airhorns and a wheeze of hydraulics. An enormous lorry has arrived full of timber and men. At long last they have come to put the fence back up. Marta already seems to know the fore-man so she and Filippo make arrangements until the foreman sensibly remembers to ask where it should go. Having spent so long putting up the original masterpiece I know exactly where the boundary runs and the line is quickly marked again with orange tape. Meanwhile the men have begun to unload the truck.

'I think we might get away now,' Filippo says as Marta joins us. She and her brother have been deep in discussion while I was re-establishing our boundary.

'I hope you don't mind, Filippo, but Ljuka and I have decided we should stay here. Our kid sister's on her way from Venice and we're waiting for her either to call or to arrive. Will your father mind if I don't come down today?'

'Of course not, Marta.'

'Then please offer him my thanks and apologies. Family matters, you know.'

'Perfectly understood.'

Better and better. I shall have Filippo Pacini all to myself while Marta and her dangerous brother can slump in a huddle of Slavic gloom and *galasiya*. I hardly expect much in the way of gratitude but it may occur to Marta that it was Samper who just saved her from a future of treadmills, mailbag-sewing and assisted showers with lesbian skinheads. After a few more minutes' delay to allow me to nip home, slip into my Homo Erectus jeans and shut the front door, I find myself sitting beside Filippo in his pretty blue and white helicopter. He presses a button, the turbine at our backs whines into life and the rotor blades overhead cast shadows across the canopy that slowly chase each other, scamper, flicker and finally blur out of existence. Best move I ever made, coming to live up here at Le Roccie, I think happily as the ground tilts and we hang nose down over an abyss of air.

Marta

43

The silence that falls after Filippo and Gerry's departure only intensifies my anxiety. So long as there was a Pacini in the room I felt nothing too terrible could happen, not even if Gerry was also there with his brainless capacity for putting his foot in it. Ironic how little they know about me and the sour forces that really shape my life. Now I'm left with Ljuka, quite alone and with the urgent sense that the world beyond these mountains is plotting our downfall. The carabinieri's visit was a horrid near miss – at least, I think it was. It rather depends on the force of that *maresciallo*'s parting shot to Ljuka.

'That was close,' he now says. 'I didn't like that a bit. I'm afraid they're on to us, Matti.'

'*Us?*' I hear myself say, somewhat bitterly. 'I'm just a composer, Uki. All I've done these last few months is write music, hardly a reason to call the police out. If it hadn't been for that muttonheaded *dudi* gossip Gerry they wouldn't have come to see me at all. Thank God Filippo happened to drop in when he did. No, Uki, there's no *us* about it. What do you think was behind what the *maresciallo* said to you about not hanging around?'

'Maybe his colleagues heard something when they radioed in. They'll have matched the chopper's registration to our company in Trieste. Whether that name has become part of a Europe-wide alert yet I doubt, but it's safer to assume it has. I think those carabinieri are dozy locals, while the *maresciallo* is an old jerk so terrified of this Pacini big cheese he'd do any-thing to avoid confrontation. I know the type: fawning, indolent and nearing retirement. I think they really did come up here to question you but unexpectedly found hints that they might be on the edge of something much bigger which the *maresciallo* can pretend not to know about, so he went away. He doesn't want paperwork, he doesn't want enquiries, which is what would happen if they'd been proper cops. He just wants us to vanish and leave him in peace. That's why he as good as told me to go away fast, because the next lot they send up will be for real.'

'You keep saying "we", Uki.' A surge of very un-familial resentment heaves itself into my words, a sense of injustice that all my efforts to make my own way are about to be tainted with my brother's asinine behaviour, his pig-headed refusal to break with a sordid career all too obviously doomed to a violent end. The recalcitrant *stupidity* of Voyde males with their primitive notions of masculinity brings tears helplessly to my eyes. 'Let's be plain about this. Our father is a racketeer and you're involved up to the hilt. People-smuggling, prostitutes, drugs, who knows? In Gerry's own words, what do I care? But you're in it up to your neck, you stupid idiot. Everything I was trying to warn you about last time you were here. And did you take a blind bit of notice? Of course you didn't. You're a Voyde: balls galore but not a bit of brain and less moral sense than an earwig.'

Ljuka is white with anger and I imagine I have gone too far – far enough, in fact, for him to overcome his equally fatuous Voynovian code of chivalry and strike his elder sister. But he manages not to. Instead he says:

'Well, listen to Miss Goody Two Shoes. I stand here being accused of involvement in organized crime by someone engaged in making porno movies. Terrific. This must be a definition of hypocrisy I missed in the dictionary.'

This time I can't help it and am overwhelmed by tears. A long moment passes, frozen by these angry words, before the air between us melts and my brother comes over, sits beside me on the sofa and puts his arm around me.

'Oh Uki,' I say when my sobs ease, 'I didn't know. Not really.'

'Sure you knew,' he says, but quite gently. 'You knew Pacini's reputation. When Father found out he went ballistic. And maybe my Italian's not up to much but it's good enough to discover for myself what *Arrazzato* means. I'm not blaming you, Matti. You saw Pacini's name as a passport to better things. In your position I'd have done exactly the same. Get established and move on. Of course – why not? But for the purposes of this conversation we'd probably best skip the moral judgements. Right now we ought to be making plans. We really do have to get out of here.'

I look around at my house, at the kitchen, at my beloved Petrof piano. Through the window come the confused, sporadic shouts and banging and grunts associated with men putting up a fence. It sounds purposeful and domestic. For the first time I notice the leaves on some of the trees are just beginning to turn. Autumn. I sigh. 'You go, Uki. I'll stay.'

'Don't be silly, Matti. The next time they come they'll take you in regardless. You're my sister; you have the family name. They'll be rounding us all up.'

'Maybe. But anyway, someone's got to stay here and wait for Marja. What happens when she arrives?'

'God almighty, I keep forgetting she's not at home. Damn her – why did she have to do this schoolgirl eloping lark at exactly the wrong moment?'

'It's not her fault it's the wrong moment,' I say hotly. 'She, too, has a life to lead. I agree, though, it's hardly conven–'

But at this instant the telephone rings and, blessed relief, it's Marja herself cheerfully announcing that she and Mekmek are at Viareggio station. I glance up and see Ljuka urgently mouthing 'Taxi'. I nod and tell her to get a taxi here. Although she has the postal address of the house I give her some simple instructions to relay to the driver, tell her to hurry, and ring off without mentioning her brother's presence. I'm becoming paranoid about telephones, evidently. While we're waiting for them to arrive I ask: 'And what then?'

'We all go,' Ljuka says decisively. Now he's out of the messy emotional stuff and back into Action Man mode he sounds self-assured again. 'Thank God we had big tanks fitted. Four of us –' he looks into the middle distance while calculating and murmurs, 'just about. Yes, what we'll do is use the mountains to get good and low before we cross the coast north of Viareggio. With any luck we won't be noticed because I doubt they're co-ordinated enough to bother. I mean, there's no war on and we're not suspected terrorists. We're just ordinary civilians they might like to question in connection with some arrests made by the police a thousand kilometres away in Voynovia. Hey, this is Italy. They're laid-back, these guys. So we fly across the Gulf of Genova and, depending on fuel, hit the other side as close to the French border as we can get. We ditch the chopper somewhere not too inhabited up in the hills and get ourselves to Menton where we rent a car using my US passport and drive to Marseilles. Once we're there, we're safe, as I told you. I've got friends.'

'It sounds hare-brained, Uki. Like a James Bond film. And what about this boyfriend of Marja's, Mekmek?'

'He comes too. At least, as far as the French border. After that it's up to him. Don't worry, Matti, it's not at all like James Bond. We're in the EU so frontiers aren't what they were. Things are fabulously lax. We'll just drift over to France to avoid getting picked up by officious Italians, that's all. God, I could very easily murder that *dudi* of yours. But for him . . .' Ljuka lets the thought trail bitterly away.

'Gerry didn't mean it. He was just cross with me for the disturbances, a large part of which was you flying right over his house at midnight, let's not forget. He wasn't to know that Benedetti would run to some police chief he wanted to butter up and spread imaginary rumours about me. And remember, it was Gerry owning up that made the carabinieri go away again.'

'Rubbish. It was that obsequious old *maresciallo*'s fear of pissing off your famous director. Anyway, he's still a little *dudi* and I'd still like to break his neck.'

'Well, you'll never have to see him again.'

Shortly after this Marja and Mekmek arrive. A good deal of embracing goes on, none of which includes Mekmek, who stands on the outskirts of this family reunion looking on with a bewildered smile. I confess he's hardly my idea of yummy. From the ecstatic description in her letter Marja had prepared me for something eager and boyish and her own age. Instead Mekmek is a bland, blobbish, thirtyish sort of creature with slightly receding sandy hair. His pale eyes somehow betray that they have never gazed on a horizon wider than that framed by a computer monitor. He must either be phenomenally kind or else a really demon lover. Still, I've long given up trying to match people I know with the partners they wind up with. I'm so naïve I very often don't even get the gender right.

Then in a surreal flurry in which I feel scarcely present I have to run upstairs, grab a few precious things and stuff them into a bag. Ljuka shouts up, 'Keep it light! Make it quick!' in a brittle, commanding voice which only makes me panic and scurry about in indecision, grabbing pointless things at random. What am I doing? Why am I allowing myself to be bullied into abandoning my own home? I can't quite believe I shan't return so when it's time to go I deliberately don't lock the house. Pacini's workmen are still busy, making swift progress with the fence. We go out of the back, climb into the helicopter and take off. It is the least real thing I have ever done. Yet again I am in stupid tears. Below, my little house rears as though suddenly mounted on a wall: its lovely grey stone roof shines and so does the bright line of fresh wooden fence posts dotted beyond through the trees. This whole thing is absurd, *disloyal*. And one disloyalty prompts another: Damn my bloody father.

Gerald

44

The short flight down to Pisorno Studios with Filippo Pacini is exhilarating. The noise makes conversation difficult so I become lost in my own world, watching the approach of the matte blue carpet that is this morning's Mediterranean on which breezes have left random marks like hoovering and assorted tiny craft are affixed with dabs of white glue. The tinted canopy overhead makes the sky look much darker than it is, strengthening the impression that we are approaching the earth not from Le Roccie but from outer space. Stranger still to look up at the whizzing blades that keep us aloft and realize they are revolving around a single axle at whose centre is an imaginary shaft thinner than a barely-turning needle. We are literally pinned to the sky by twirling molecules.

Don't worry – I'm given to these nervous fugues of fancy when in the air, even more so when flying Ryanair. I'm not, however, nervous at heart. On the contrary, I am filled with a sublime fatalism brought on by being in Filippo's hands. If we do crash I couldn't have wished to be flown into the ground by a handsomer pilot. This is oddly consoling. But we don't crash, and come swinging in over the pines and the barely breaking waves that mark the Tuscan coast just north of Livorno, whose urban sprawl and industrial docks suddenly look very modern. As we sink below the treeline in the grounds of a gleaming white fascist villa, however, the twenty-first century vanishes from view and we settle in the nineteen thirties with a gentle bump. The helicopter has turned out to be a time machine. Certainly I feel about fourteen as I hop to the ground and thank Filippo.

'Any time,' he says, and I may well hold him to it. 'Come on. Papa said he's doing beach shoots all today and some of tonight. The forecasters say it'll get cloudy in a couple of days' time so we've got to take advantage of this weather for continuity. Unfortunately, summer's over.'

We walk through dusty oleanders down towards two tall cypress trees that seem to mark the end of the garden proper. Beyond, a sandy track leads through evergreen scrub to the shore. Unexpectedly, the beach is contained within a small cove that has obviously been constructed on what is otherwise a long, straight coast. There is a dilapidated low house with a sun-bleached dinghy propped upright against it. Heaps of nets, lengths of frayed rope and orange plastic fishing floats are scattered artistically about. A small tractor hitched to what looks like a steel mat is parked to one side. A generator thuds somewhere in the background. Black cables converge on the doorway of the house whose roof, I notice, is patched with scraps of sheet tin and plastic. The interior is lit brighter than the sunlight outside, to judge from the glimpses visible between the heads and bodies of cameramen, technicians and grips clustered around the entrance.

But what really grabs my attention is the music. It is not very loud but extremely clear, giving the impression of large speakers with the gain level turned low. I recognize it at once as the same incompetent squalling idiot going '*Uffa . . . buffa . . .*' that Marta was playing when I went over to remonstrate on the morning after Nanty's UFO. But that's not why it sounds familiar; it sounded familiar the first time, too. At that moment there comes the sensation of at last dumping a nameless heavy load, and I can hear what it really is. It gives me the same visceral shock as passing the window of one of those electronics shops on Tottenham Court Road and catching sight of a pervert slouching across the screen of the TV monitor displayed inside. This low-life, a worn looking creature of the streets, stops, backs up, shakes his head, finally sticks his tongue out, and yes! recognizes his image. *That is you.* That is your alter ego who lives in a CCTV world parallel to your own and lampoons the real you with pixel accuracy.

Here on the beach of Pisorno Studios I am listening to a parody of my own singing. I now know what it sounds like to stand outside Samper's house and hear him cheerfully at work in the kitchen. I can almost see some fabulous dish taking shape beneath my hands – as it might be Stuffed Udder with Butterscotch Sauce – while my spirits soar with an extemporization from Act 2 of *La Tranca Vispa*. Now it sinks in: the music score of *Arrazzato* is basically one long mockery of Gerald Samper, friendly neighbour, jobbing wordsmith and culinary genius.

My first reaction is almost my last, such is the rush of dizzying rage. Out of it emerges one clear thought: this time Marta has *really* gone too far. This time the adipose hairy hag will pay. After all I've done for her: putting up fences, supplying her Fernet habit, freeing her from the clutches of the police. And how does she thank me? My peace is shattered, my life disrupted, my clients frightened away, my fences torn down and now my private voice is travestied and about to be exposed to the mockery of film audiences across the world. Right – go for it! (I tell myself in a steely inner voice that makes me tremble slightly, at least partly with pleasure). Go for it! Sue the bollocks off them! Pacini'll be good for a decent sum. Marta too, with her shady mafia connections, whatever they are. I'll reduce her to a sebaceous husk, a grovelling puddle of grease and hair. I'll sue her to her last emetic inch of communist sausage. I'll sue her out of that bloody hovel and then I'll bulldoze it and the entire neighbour problem will be solved at a stroke. I'll –

Hang on.

Just hang on a moment.

Cool it, Samper. Is this not the very lever I need to ensure that Pacini consents to make me his latest and best biographer? Wouldn't the heavy threat of legal action also be quite a nifty way of wringing out of him the sort of frank details he might otherwise withhold but which will practically guarantee newspaper serialization and an eager readership? Maybe after all, righteous petulance – no matter how excusable and enjoyable

– is not the most canny way of ensuring Samper's future.

So with massive patience I bide my time, like a great heap of damp grass cuttings not visibly steaming except that inside it is already hot and turning yellow as it prepares to burst into flame at the least expected moment. Meanwhile the scene they are shooting is finished, Pacini appears in – I kid you not – a green eyeshade, catches sight of us and waves in a preoccupied fashion as he gives orders and directions with sweeps of his hands.

'We'll catch him at lunch,' Filippo says. 'Another hour if this goes OK.'

The grips and technicians vacate the house and retreat to where we're standing. The tractor starts up and drags the mat over the sand in front of the house, obliterating the marks and footprints before men turn hoses on it, the nozzles screwed down to a fine spray, wetting the sand to flatness. Soon it looks just as though the tide had recently gone out and inside the house a yawning motley of hippie boys and girls are finally getting up for lunch as they stagger sleepily to the door and gaze blearily out, presumably contemplating another day of clean Green living. I can't imagine what this film's about. It looks dire. Clapperboards snap, cameras roll, Pacini waves them all back inside again several times until he gets what he wants. He checks the rushes on a tiny monitor, approves what he sees, makes satisfied lunch-break gestures with both arms, shouts 'Two o'clock!'

I fall in with Filippo and his father as we walk back towards the house. Filippo explains the earlier dramatic events in Marta's house in indignant tones as I coolly plot and scheme and wait for the *moment juste* to lob my little bomb.

'Thank God you were there, Gerry,' Pacini says at one point.

'Thank God Filippo was,' I echo piously. 'With either one of us alone it mightn't have worked. But both of us together were too much for the *maresciallo*.'

'I shall settle *his* hash shortly, believe me,' says the great director.

'That's just what Marta doesn't want you to do,' I tell him. 'Things are maybe not quite so simple.' And on this enigmatic note we arrive at the villa and find our way into a splendid spacious morning room with a terrace. The décor is quite marvellous: Latin mottoes and tough little cherubs who would clearly give you a good kicking if you so much as patted them on the head. A huge table is laid with buffet dishes from which we begin spearing and spooning liberal portions of this and that before seating ourselves with a large glass of white wine apiece. Be honest, who would live in England?

'I'm afraid the food isn't right for the room,' Pacini observes. 'Your politically correct fascist went in for simple, traditional dishes like *pastasciutta* with plain tomato sauce. You almost never saw people eating in those *telefoni bianchi* films they shot in this very house. They could be seen sipping an occasional glass of wine or fruit juice, a cup of tea or coffee, that's about all. There was a manic cult of fitness at the time, everyone cycling and running and hiking like crazy. Just to be fat was quite suspicious. Mussolini and the *gerarchi* were always being filmed stripped to the waist and pounding along a beach. A strange period. There are several things about it I don't dislike,' Pacini adds. 'Modest amounts of simple food and plenty of exercise sound rather sensible to me.'

I'm taken up with an interior vision of 10 Downing Street stripped for action with a succession of doughy ministers sprinting across the PM's office. I see power-dressing women teetering on high heels, ricking an ankle, collapsing asprawl on the burgundy carpet, State papers scattered from an outflung hand. I see a puce-faced Chancellor of the Exchequer jogging on the spot before the desk, hairy breasts bouncing beneath his Savile Row jacket, trousers inching their way downwards over a white jelly bottom too restless to hold them up. I see a rabbit nose nodding frantically inside voluminous boxer shorts dotted with little space rockets. The lecture on the fiscal implications of the Third Way goes on and on . . . I see all this and think Bring back fascism!

This puts me squarely into the mood to make my play.

'You were talking about Marta just now,' I say to Pacini.

'Brilliant lady, isn't she? The more I hear her music the more I feel inspired.'

'Me too. I'm inspired to sue her.'

Pacini laughs, probably reckoning he has misheard this foreigner. *You wish*.

'To sue her,' I repeat with as much bell-like clarity as one can manage around a mouthful of cold seafood salad. His smile fades a little.

'*Sue?*'

'Sue. I don't suppose you realize it, but that score of hers for your film contains a deliberate pastiche of my singing. Not only is it theft of my intellectual property but defamatory, calculated to make me a laughing-stock.'

Immediately I can tell by his expression he knows it's true. Filippo does, too. There is a difficult silence.

'Surely not,' Pacini says without conviction.

'Your doubts can be easily settled. I have only to bring over some friends of mine from England who will testify to my habit of singing as I work. All you'd have to do is play them those bits of Marta's score. They would identify it at once. The resemblance is beyond question. Indeed, a former friend of mine named Dennis once made a tape recording of me without my knowledge which you can bet he has kept.'

Pacini has stopped eating and now replaces his plate on the table. I know exactly what's going on behind that noble, Oscared brow as if it were made of glass and I could see for myself the glittering fizz of electrical activity. Marta is taken to court on such a charge and what happens to *Arrazzato* without the music? What of his own part in this? This is the moment to start drawing the outlines of an escape route for him.

'I'm really sorry about this, Piero. I know it has absolutely nothing to do with you. Even I only realized what was happening when I heard the music out there on the beach an hour ago. I didn't at first recognize myself – one doesn't. But once I had, it was unmistakable. Pretty wounding, too, I may say. I'm still upset about it. I hadn't expected this – what can one call it? "Betrayal" sounds too self-dramatizing and "malicious" too intentional. But I definitely think Marta has taken a terrible liberty.'

Having thus adroitly inserted the cat into the midst of the pigeons I leave them to it. Father and son engage in a flurry of alarmed exchanges out of which fly words like 'plagiarism' and 'pasquinade'. I go back to my seafood salad. Since we're on the subject I might point out that Cat among Pigeons is a great Samper dish, one of a series in which I was inspired by English figures of speech. The two different meats, feline and avian, happen to go extraordinarily well together. Pigs in Clover are excellent, too, when rationalized as loin chops done in a bed of clover so that a succulent sweetness pervades the pork. More exquisite still is Dog-in-the-Manger, when interpreted as a version of haybox cookery. I once released the smiling ghost from a neighbour's snarling dachshund by means of a dough-sealed Le Creuset casserole packed away piping hot in hay for eighteen hours. It was this dish that made me speculate that Aesop, too, may have been an experimental cook at heart and I'm planning a cookbook in his honour, provisionally entitled *Aesop's Foibles*. I can't wait to try Fox and Grapes. I know it will be sensational. But Pacini is addressing me.

'This is disastrous,' he is saying. 'Can I ask what your intentions are?'

'I've certainly no wish to cause unnecessary trouble and disruption,' I lie virtuously. 'The more I think about it, the more convinced I am that Marta didn't act with genuine malice. It seems to me we all of us have to give some thought to our respective futures: she, me, even such a distinguished person as yourself.'

'I've got there,' says Pacini with a touch of sourness. 'How much?' I think he looks relieved at being able to see, amid my froth of delicacy, the gleaming heads of brass tacks.

I make an effort to look horrified. 'I hope you don't think I'd stoop to blackmail?' I cry. 'What a dreadful idea.' I take a large gulp of wine to emphasize how badly I need a restorative after such a thought.

Pacini may be a smooth number but he doesn't need things spelt out. 'Have you ever thought of writing a film?' he asks ingenuously.

'Often, now you mention it. Though not long ago I happened to read a biography of you and ever since then I've been thinking more about that, to tell the truth. If you don't mind my saying, the book hardly does you justice.'

'No. My family would certainly agree. Especially Filo here. He didn't recognize his father at all. I'm quite sure you could do better, Gerry.'

'Immodestly, I think so too.'

'I'll have a contract drawn up right now. I can't possibly go on working on *Arrazzato* with the constant threat of legal action hanging over the production.'

'As I said, my quarrel is with Marta and not with you.'

'But nor could I hire your valuable talents if I believed you still had an outstanding dispute with my composer. I may as well tell you, Gerry, that although she doesn't yet know it I fully intend using Marta again.'

'I'm glad to hear it. Obviously if she and I are to be colleagues at some time in the future I would make quite sure that any little misunderstandings were behind us. Really, I'm well on the way to forgiving her right now.'

'Excellent. After all, don't forget this film might easily make your voice famous, even a potential source of income, like the gentleman who did the whistling for Morricone's spaghetti western scores.'

'Or Florence Foster Jenkins massacring the Queen of the Night's big aria? Terrific.'

Pacini nods unhappily, takes out his mobile phone, punches a number, gets to his feet and goes out onto the balcony, speaking rapidly. Filippo smiles another of those collectable smiles.

'I think you're a generous person, Gerry. My father's very grateful, you know. This could have been a crisis for us.'

'Nonsense, just a passing awkwardness. These things happen.' I glance up at the wall above his head and catch the eye of a fascist *putto* who I swear winks at me as his little rosebud mouth lisps the words 'Kick ass!'

'The lawyer will be here in an hour with a draft agreement,' Pacini announces as he comes back in, tucking his *telefonino* away. 'Filo, will you please go and tell Mario to have everything ready for two-thirty on the dot instead of two? We can delay the shooting schedule long enough to settle this.'

And so it was. Within fifty minutes I had signed a document agreeing that Piero Pacini would assign me exclusive rights to a biography with an option on writing a script for a forthcoming film as yet untitled, this agreement to be dependent on the complete renunciation of any legal action intended or actual in connection with the musical score of *Arrazzato* and its composer. (Or many florid paragraphs to that effect.) In short, Samper has won. Thank you, Marta, you malevolent old baggage. Things have turned out quite well for me despite the worst you could do. But golly, what a day! It started with me being grilled by a *maresciallo* of the carabinieri and has now turned into something of a triumph. A good example, though I say so myself, of the advantages of preserving a cool head and a firm purpose.

What I don't know, of course, is how this day is going to end.

45

With the agreement signed I feel more relaxed about things and am determined to enjoy myself. I mosey around the villa, eye the kitchens and the cellar, wander through the grounds and watch some more shooting on the beach. The film remains a complete enigma to me. Putting these few scenes together with what little I have gleaned from Marta and Pacini I can't begin to work out what it's about, nor how it might be 'lifted' by Nanty's guest spot with Alien Pie. But there, I'm not a famous director, just his future biographer.

Whether or not Pacini and his crew know where they're going with *Arrazzato* they certainly set about it with terrific enthusiasm and conviction, which is very Italian of them. This prompts me to rueful reflection of how very un-English enthusiasm and conviction are: possibly the two things most notably absent from my own poor land, utterly lost as it has been these last fifty years. We've had our day and simply can't think how to enjoy the evening . . . Ah! You can't beat home thoughts from abroad, especially not after a good lunch by the ageless Mediterranean. Take heart, Samper (I tell myself sternly). Don't get feebly Carlylean; make me laugh instead. *Cheer me, slobby git!* The past is but an anagram: only rearrange it. How? Experiment, how else? Do something new with dull old ingredients.

For example, Stuffed Udder might equally well be Stuffed Adder: the good cook is as flexible as his raw materials are available. My udder recipe is basically something I borrowed during that Per Snoilsson trip to Senegal I mentioned earlier. There, it is de rigueur for First Communion, when they use camel. The Samper version uses cow with – as Nanty might say in business-speak – bells and whistles. The butterscotch sauce is its crowning glory. It's all a matter of being on the qui-vive for amusing possibilities, for making interesting tracks that cross the well-beaten paths of stuffy cuisine at right angles.

Towards seven o'clock Pacini asks if I would like to stay to watch them do a night shoot. He explains they're going to film the scene where the Albanian fisherman is rounded on and attacked by the Green commune. The principled youngsters have become wildly racist as the result of fascist contamination by the genius loci, by the strident anti-immigrant propaganda of the downmarket Italian media, and by the dumbing effects of going to a deafening Alien Pie gig. It all sounds like stupendous tosh to me but Filippo says it could be interesting and besides, he can't anyway fly me back until the shoot's over. I therefore agree, and later find myself peaceably watching the sunset on the beach with a muscular technician named Baldo who has sprained his wrist and has been given time off. We share a bottle of Fernet Branca – oddly enough – that he has liberated from somewhere. As it grows dark I find my natural British reserve becoming seriously compromised. I feel the urge to bestow on the deepening twilight, the lilting sea and Livorno's distant floodlit docks Sergio's lovely farewell to Marilena from the end of Act 1 of *I Testimoni di Genova*. The wicked Arabian magician Tazio, who lusts after Marilena himself, has told Sergio that the only way to be certain her love for him was predestined is to go to the Great Pyramid of Giza and take the measurements of the burial chamber, all of which are a sure prediction of the future. Reluctant but tragically dim, Sergio buys an expensive tape measure and sets sail for Cairo, though not before he has given Marilena his portrait. From the deck of the departing ship he sings his celebrated warning against loving a portrait more than its subject: 'Le immagini sono a puro scopo illustrativo'.

When I finish this moving aria Baldo wipes his eyes on his sleeve and becomes most flattering. He says I must have a truly wonderful musical ear because I'm able to produce such a hilarious pastiche of the score of *Arrazzato*: an astonishing feat for someone who has only been on the set for a day. Others, too, have heard it and run up to collapse around us on the sand, rolling and laughing. The trouble is, when people are practically overcome with mirth, slapping you on the back and saying what a dazzling send-up it is, you have little option but to agree, no matter that the fervour of your own performance has brought tears to your eyes. It turns out that young Filippo Pacini is one of those who has overheard my performance. Although it's now too dark to see much of his expression I gather from the way he's nodding his head that he realizes I really did have Marta over a barrel, as the saying is. There can be no further question where her inspiration came from, fraudulent old toper and plagiarist that she is.

But Filippo has been sent by his father to reclaim my admirers. They are needed to ready the sets for the sequence about to be shot. The Fernet seems to have melted away so I also get to my feet and wander across to the fake cove, although not with much hope of diversion. I'm assuming that night filming is going to be remarkably like filming by day, only darker. Pacini, who in deference to the night is now wearing his eyeshade backwards on his head, gesticulates at the centre of a group that includes a swarthy fellow wearing cut-offs, flip-flops and a threadbare T-shirt. He, I take it, is the Albanian: an illegal immigrant who began by teaching the eager Green communards how to fish by handlining but who is now about to fall victim to their racist ire. My muscular new friend Baldo, whose sprained wrist is most affectingly strapped up in dramatic swathes of pink plaster, informs me that the script calls for the Albanian to arrive running along the beach, looking over his shoulder at his invisible but audible pursuers. He stops and does a stag-at-bay in front of his house before making to escape inland towards the villa, but lights and voices appear from this direction, too. He dashes down to the water where his boat is drawn up, obviously hoping to push off and get away to sea, but the boat is stove in. Now in a panic, he runs into the house and emerges with an armful of distress flares, races to the very end of the artificial promontory and begins setting them off in desperate profusion. This is heavily ironic because it's all too late, nobody is going to respond in time, the State is anyway seen to be indifferent and incompetent (cutaway of local coastguards sprawled in their offices, drinking wine and commenting languidly on the money people spend nowadays on firework displays).

Eventually the Albanian is cornered by his pursuers at the end of the spit, ritually hacked to death and his torso raped for no obvious reason other than that of cinematography. There follows a general orgy to be backed by Alien Pie's soundtrack and intercut with Mussolini-era newsreel footage. The girls are driven to erotic frenzy by the violence, using rockets in a most improper fashion (see the film's title). A dead seagull is found and spitted on someone's erect cock, its wings held out on either side to simulate flying.

Well, *really*. You might think Albanians get quite enough of this sort of primitive violence in their own country, with their blood feuds and whatnot. And anyway, you don't have to kill illegal immigrants. Why not punish them instead by taking them on compulsory tours of the Uffizi, obliging them to attend interminable courses on the iconography of Renaissance art, making their *permessi di soggiorno* contingent on a thoughtful essay about the Etruscans? Pretty soon there would be hardly any illegal immigrants in Italy. They would all have stampeded elsewhere, principally to Britain where there isn't enough culture left to constitute a threat to them.

But as for the great Piero Pacini, what can he be up to? I'm beginning to wonder if I want to write this fellow's biography after all. It will obviously involve wading through some pretty murky depths, very different from the skittering shallows in which my sporting heroes posture and prance. Indeed, short of having been Pasolini's psychiatrist I can hardly imagine more specialized employment. Oh, well. Samper will find a way; he always does.

I'll say one thing for Pacini: he knows his job and likes to get a move on. I gather he prefers to get as much as he can in a single take. Marta's score starts up, a sort of sinister tango. The chased and bayed Albanian sprints about on the sand, looking over one shoulder, cameras tight on his terrified face, other cameras panning over the scene. The whole area is lit with great floods covered in a sort of pink cheesecloth which, together with the right filters on the camera lenses, apparently gives the effect of moonlight. Eventually, after much to-ing and fro-ing, the moment arrives for the scene with the distress flares. For this Pacini will need close-ups of fingers fumbling with a cheap disposable lighter, the thin T-shirt trembling to his thudding heart and gasping breaths, the fuse igniting, then pull back for the fiery whoosh of the rocket and its burst of starshells against the night sky. A large polythene bin is carried into the fisherman's dilapidated house. The bin is covered with stencils saying 'Explosives', 'Danger' and so on, as well as being criss-crossed with adhesive red and yellow warning tape. I'm glad to say they're being careful, keeping their store of flares safely under cover and removing only enough for each shot. Before sending up the first flare Pacini makes what are obviously pre-arranged calls on his mobile phone, presumably to the local police and coastguards, warning them that whatever they may shortly see is a false alarm: genuine filming of fake distress.

There is no question, these rockets are terrific. They scoot up with blazing orange trails and burst silently into brilliant red flares that sink slowly earthwards on little parachutes, winking out before they reach the ground. But try as he may, Pacini can't seem to get exactly the shot he wants of the Albanian's face when he lights the fuse. The rockets go up and the flares come down and soon everyone loses interest in them and concentrates instead on the Albanian. Between shots he is instructed to run on the spot so as to be suitably breathless while Pacini towers over him giving him instructions in a gravelly voice. The man nods, the lighter flicks, the rocket goes up, the flares come down and still it's not right.

It is after one of these failures I notice something mildly interesting. I've been spending much of the time watching the display instead of the actor because the flares against the night sky produce an agreeably psychedelic effect that may well have something to do with Fernet Branca. Indeed, the gorgeous red hanging in the night sky for thirty seconds is a good deal more interesting than the Albanian, a dull-looking fellow who has anyway turned out to be Moroccan. I've been watching the moment when each flare goes out and noticing that often there is still a spark left glowing dully as it drifts the last fifty metres to earth. Some fizz into the sea, most vanish into the night. But I'm watching one that has landed on the roof of the fisherman's house and suddenly glows a little brighter. That's interesting, I think: that's not what you'd expect with tiles. I suppose it must have landed on one of those sheets of plastic that have been so stylishly deployed to cover holes in the roof and simulate threadbare poverty. In which case, surely it could melt its way through and even perhaps fall into –

Retrospectively, I deduce this is my last constructive thought for several minutes. According to next day's newspapers the explosion is well audible in Viareggio and the ensuing pyrotechnic display visible from Massa, some say La Spezia. Like everyone else within a hundred metres of the house I'm knocked flat on the sand amid a total confusion of orange roaring. The sky is a burst kaleidoscope of whizzing red lights. My ears are made of felt and packed with wool. Slowly, slowly the thought 'Samper has survived' assembles itself like an unlikely word in the hands of a Scrabble player. I drag myself upright and find I'm naked from the waist up. Disaster. That was a very nice Cerruti shirt I'd slipped on in honour of Filippo this morning – I *think* it was this morning but things aren't functioning properly, time included.

The scene is lit by fire, most of it from the summer-dried undergrowth fringing the beach. The house itself is now roofless, its empty doorframe and window embrasures flickering with flames within. It looks as though we've been saved by superior bricklaying: the stout, low walls are mainly intact, suggesting most of the blast went straight up. People are everywhere struggling to their feet. The Madonna is ritually invoked; the Moroccan actor is appealing to – or maybe thanking – Allah. Somebody finds a mobile phone lying uninjured on the sand and has the presence of mind to call for ambulances and fire engines. There seem to be remarkably few serious injuries. Among the worst is Pacini himself, the back of whose head and shoulders are badly burned, his hair crisp and the remains of his plastic eyeshade welded to it. Filippo is kneeling beside him, tears streaming down his face and glinting in the firelight.

'Are you hurt?' I ask solicitously, but he just shakes his head.

Soon most people have recovered enough to busy themselves with meaningless tasks such as stamping out embers that are harmlessly burning out in the sand and exchanging hysterical jokes when they meet. The first emergency vehicle to arrive is actually a police helicopter. It is quickly joined by a cacophony of fire engines and ambulances and the scene becomes still more frenetic and dishevelled. People in uniform sprint about, shouting. A stretcher appears, Pacini is loaded into the helicopter with Filippo in attendance and they disappear upwards into the night. So much for my lift home.

As I'm sure this whole narrative has testified from the start, there is something in the Samper character that makes him shy away from fuss and drama. Having survived, I discover that all I really want is to trot away up the beach into the sheltering darkness and leave the arena to those whose profession it is to enjoy such things. There's another good reason, too, which is that by some bizarre fluke Pacini's sound system is still working and from behind the livid scene of disaster rises the awful travesty of my own voice going 'Uffa . . . buffa . . .' in a demented falsetto. Accordingly, I sidle over towards the bogus promontory, scramble up and over it, and slip away along the line of surf in the direction of Viareggio. For some reason my teeth won't stop chattering. I have a brisk wash in the sea before resuming my walk. The eminently sane, salt taste restores my senses more than a little. When I turn back to the scene I've just left – which despite the fire brigade is still considerably ablaze – it's just in time to see an extraordinary thing. The two tall cypress trees are standing up to their knees in incandescent scrub and brushwood. One is just beginning to catch fire, the flames running up it like a bright liquid under pressure. The other, though, simply begins to – and I can scarcely believe what I'm seeing – to *bend* very slowly from the waist, as if it were an elderly butler greeting a monarch. As I watch, the bend accelerates into a grovel and the cypress wilts like a dildo in a smithy, its crest coming to

282

rest on the ground. Curious, I think as I trudge woozily away up the beach with my ears singing. Most curious.

46

By the time I was out of bed next day and vaguely dressed it was noon and I was hungry. I put together a sturdy luncheon which I ate on the terrace. Today the distant ocean was as flat and polished as waxed linoleum, impeccably laid and tacked neatly along the edge of Tuscany. With binoculars I tried to pick out the site of Pisorno Studios among the stain of pines down towards Livorno, but without success. It was too far away, the place itself too small. I suppose I'd thought a lingering wisp of smoke might still mark the spot, but there was nothing.

I dipped a chunk of pecorino into honey and chewed luxuriously. Samper had made it home alive, that was the main thing. Last night I had gone on trudging up the beach, shirtless and dazed, until I came to a resort that was still open, despite summer season being over. It had one of those interchangeable marine-themed names that even in my confused condition made me ponder the mentality of both proprietors and their guests. There were still some lights and activity in the gardens of Blue Sea, Golden Sands, The Captain's Compass or whichever it was, where a few late diners had probably been further delayed by rushing out to the beach halfway through their meal to gaze at the spectacle and excitement down the coast. Now that there were no further explosions and fireworks they had gone back to their coffees and brandies. I sidled in through the gate and found – the luck of the Sampers! – a white unlined mess jacket, presumably belonging to a waiter, thrown over a chair. I appropriated it and walked shamelessly up the sandy track to the road. This was deserted except for the guests' parked cars and some *fin de saison* moths trying to mate with a street lamp. The waiter's pockets were empty except for an unopened condom and a tin bottle opener but I found enough euros in my trousers for some phone calls. It took an hour to get a taxi and the driver needed a good deal of persuading to take me all the way into the hills above Camaiore. Actually, I had to promise him the emergency hundred-euro note I knew I had at home in the fridge. And so to bed, a bit trembly and still faintly deaf.

After lunch I thought I ought to tell Marta about last night's fiasco if she hadn't already heard. True, I was definitely still sore about the unscrupulous way she had lampooned me. She had clearly thought long and worked hard to achieve that odious degree of musical realism, and she was not going to be able to wriggle out of it by pretending it was just a little affectionate private joke she'd impulsively worked into her score. Not a chance. Still, Samper's way is subtle and his memory for slights legendary. He can bide his time. For the moment it would cost me nothing to play the good neighbour so I headed across to her hovel. The replacement fence was up, although to my practised eye there were plentiful signs of sloppiness and haste. In order to do the whole job in a day they would have had to use quick-setting concrete to sink the posts. Still, they had at least remembered to put a door in the middle so I went through to find the house unlocked as usual and a total absence of the hairy hag herself. In some way I couldn't quite define, the place felt as though she had simply abandoned it rather than that her sister had finally arrived and they had just popped out to do some shopping for the weekend. I felt the coffee pot on the stove. Stone cold. Having come this far I thought the obligations of the good neighbour had to outweigh the diffidence of the trespasser so I ventured upstairs, preceded by loud cries of 'Marta?', to make sure she wasn't in bed dying of alcohol poisoning. But the upstairs was empty, too. God, what a mess: the bed strewn with hairbrushes and incredible stout knickers. I hurried downstairs and out.

It was the same the next day, and the day after that. As the immediacy of the drama at Pisorno Studios faded and the singing in my ears died away I began bit by bit to resume a normal life. I again took up my outline of Nanty's story. The world retreated and went back to lying at my feet as I sat on the terrace. This was, I kept telling myself, my house as I'd always imagined it: silent, neighbourless, and not a helicopter within miles. The leaves slowly changing colour, autumn evenings drawing in, my next six months' work assured and overpaid: these were the mellow reflections that accompanied my jottings. My more distant future was nothing like so clear. To my own amazement I soon discovered that in the limited time I had spent with Piero Pacini and his charming son I had never even thought to acquire so much as a phone number for either of them. Consequently I had no easy way of finding out how the great director was, whether he was recovering or what. However, the back pocket of my tragically scorched Homo Erectus jeans yielded a damp and creased copy of the agreement I'd signed with him. The headed paper of course had the lawyer's address and number but for some reason I put it aside. If Pacini didn't make it there wouldn't be a book, obviously; but in my present strange mood it didn't seem to matter very much. I wondered what would happen to his unfinished masterpiece, how much of it was already shot and safely in the can. To be honest, I could hardly imagine it was worth finishing a film that suggested a pornographic remake of *Zabriskie Point*.

The days passed, work proceeded. I rang Nanty and left messages outlining what had happened to Pacini and telling him not to hold his breath where a guest appearance in *Arrazzato* was concerned. I cooked and sang and scribbled as usual. Yet all the while there was something missing. I remembered a story I'd heard about Carl Philipp Emanuel, Bach's eldest son, who as a boy had occasionally taken revenge on his father by practising the harpsichord at night in the room directly beneath his parents' bedroom, winding up to a terrific cadence and stopping suddenly without playing the final chord. Invariably his father was forced to come clumping sleepily downstairs in order to play it. Probably apocryphal; but that's how I felt, without being quite able to say what might do for the lost chord. I kept finding myself glancing towards the distant door in the fence which I'd propped open with a log. When upstairs I would go to the window and wonder if I ought to do anything about her house. Absolutely none of my business, of course. Still, the place was unlocked and she'd left a lot of stuff lying about: her Soviet-bloc piano, for instance; her computer and keyboard; even an unopened case of Fernet Branca hidden away beneath the stone sink. Not that I was remotely nosy but one didn't wish to attract thieves up here at Le Roccie, and squatters least of all.

Well, it was very nice at last to be free of a troublesome neighbour, I thought as I busied myself with my own affairs, such as baking an exquisite sponge cake topped with a mortadella icing to kill for. Still, the belated idea did occur to me that Marta could have been exactly the right person to advise or even partner Nanty on his project for a serious large-scale piece of music. She might even need the work. I still favoured my vulgar idea of an AIDS Requiem. Definitely headline-grabbing stuff for the leader of a boy band who needed to start being thought of as an artist in his own right. Good and solemn with lashings of tear-stained social conscience. I was relying on old Marta to come up with some appropriate wordless keening to set the tone. I had to hand it to her: the old bat certainly had a knack. That corrupt little tango of hers I'd heard on the beach that night kept coming back to me even now.

And then quite suddenly she herself was back. I happened to be passing the window upstairs with a pair of binoculars when I caught sight of an unmistakable figure hanging out her laughably misnamed smalls on a washing line among the trees. The Iron Curtain's Mrs Tiggy-Winkle, although she was actually wearing her voluminous beige shift that for some reason put me in mind of a Bedouin traffic warden. I could barely contain myself for half an hour before drifting ever so casually across.

Marta

47

I couldn't bear it – that's the truth of the matter. It grew on me all the way to France and as far as a farmhouse thirty kilometres to the west of Marseilles. The others seemed to enjoy the adventure, which went impeccably according to Ljuka's plan. We helicoptered, landed, walked, caught a bus, hung around sinister bars. But the longer it dragged on the more I told myself I was not cut out to be a fugitive. The farmhouse, which belonged to some desperado friend of Ljuka's who might have been an Algerian prizefighter, was semi-derelict and reminded me fondly of my own house far away in Italy. I still couldn't believe I had actually walked out and abandoned my beloved Petrof, to whom I yearned to return and make amends by playing my way back into his affections. First he had been usurped by a soulless electronic keyboard and now he had been orphaned in a moment of shameful panic. I made a promise to him and myself that when I got home I would write him my best-ever song.

So the long and the short of it is that I've deserted my own family instead. I've left my darling brother and sister and her dreary boyfriend, wishing them Godspeed and all the rest of it. Feeling grown-up and apart, I said that no matter what anybody else had done, I was definitely not guilty of anything worthy of criminal charges and police pursuit. I was therefore going home to Italy. At that point there were tears galore but my mind was made up. It was only slightly dampening that Marja and Mekmek decided to throw their lot in with Ljuka. She had anyway burned her boats by eloping and would have to live with that however things turned out. It also looked as though none of us would be able to return to Voynovia for the foreseeable future so I guess it made more sense to throw her lot in with her little brother and go adventuring with him. He looked so alert and dashing and super-competent that I felt instinctively that Marja would be safe, that they would all fall on their feet somewhere. They had the ebullient flexibility of young people without careers. Beside them I felt old. Ljuka agreed that perhaps it was for the best if I went back. At least they'd know where I was and I could act as a contact and clearing house for information about the doings and whereabouts of our newly scattered clan. Tearfully we took our leave.

All this took several days, but now I'm home I can't imagine how I ever allowed myself to be stampeded into leaving in the first place. All those helicopters and sensational phone calls about arrests and visits from the carabinieri – I suppose I temporarily lost my head. So now I bustle happily about, setting things to rights, apologizing to Petrof with a reassuring arpeggio, rinsing the dried dregs of *galasiya* out of glasses, washing some underwear. I have the feeling that something nameless and awful has happened recently – something like death or surgery – but that with every hour it is receding further into the past.

But what I really needed to make me feel I'd come home is the sight of Gerry, *dudi* as ever, trotting through the door in the new fence. Do I quite wish a few more days had gone by before I was strong enough to deal with this? Too bad; here he is. And incredibly, as he prances in, smiling, I actually feel pleased to see him. It shows how much he has become a part of the place, if not of my life. Almost beyond belief, though, is the way he comes straight up and gives me a sisterly hug. Well! He's never risked being *that* demonstrative before! What can have come over him? Drink or news, I suspect. Probably both.

'Ooh, I'm *so* glad you're back, Marta,' he cries.

'Sweet of you, Gerry,' I say cautiously. I was right about the drink, anyway.

'No, you see, your house, you know,' he babbles. 'I was frightfully worried. The place all unlocked and you vanished.

I hope you don't mind but I'm afraid I came in to check if you were dead.'

'Most kind of you.'

'Well, I can see you're not and I'm terribly glad about that. No, look, have you heard? Did you hear about your friend Piero Pacini? You haven't? Oh, good –'

And he launches into the most dramatic story imaginable about how the whole set of *Arrazzato* as well as Piero himself was blown up by a spent rocket falling into a dump of flares. I can't quite follow some of it but he does make it riotously funny even though poor Piero is burned and the film has been badly put back or even ruined and my future with it.

'And, Marta dearest, you're such a wicked old thing and I'm *not at all* best pleased with you.'

'With me, Gerry?' I'm perplexed.

'Well, let's just say with whoever wrote a painstaking pastiche of my singing for *Arrazzato*'s musical score.'

'Oh,' I hear myself say guiltily. 'Oh, that.'

'Yes, that. It was too naughty of you, Marta.'

Beneath the flippancy he is so obviously hurt that I fill with contrition.

'I'm sorry, Gerry,' I say and take his hand. 'Truly I am. It was wrong of me. I never meant it to be hurtful, you know. You've no idea what an inspiration it was – what a gift, hearing you singing away like that. It was so *right* for the film. You were too perfect to ignore.'

'I was?' He perks up, vain creature. 'Well, I guess if it was useful to you . . . Yes, yes, I suppose if it worked . . . Piero thinks it's completely wonderful, you know. He thinks you're a fabulous composer and he wants to work with you again, did you know?'

'He really does? Honestly?' This certainly is good news and my spirits do a little internal dance.

'If he survives, of course,' Gerry characteristically adds. My spirits stop in mid-dance. 'If he doesn't, we're both out of a job. But look, there's always Plan B to fall back on. You remember my pop-musician client, Nanty Riah? The world-famous Brill who so impresses your friend Filippo? Well, he's in the market for some professional musical help and he's got oodles of dosh and I'm going to bring you two together the next time he's over here. Call me matchmaker *extraordinaire*,' he says expansively.

I suddenly feel a little overcome. Genuine remorse for having hurt this occasionally sweet ninny and now equally genuine gratitude for his soliciting on behalf of my probably faltering career. Evidently Gerry fears I might suddenly become gooey because he springs to his feet and says:

'Never mind about poor singed Piero. Time enough to find out about him tomorrow. You're back and I'm unblown-up so let's celebrate. What other excuse do we need?'

And until that moment I promise I hadn't realized that today, yes, the last day of September, is my birthday, which seems like an excuse in itself. When I tell him Gerry gives a little scream and tells me not to go away for ten minutes and he'll be right back. When he does return he's carrying a bottle of champagne and a plate with a cake on it.

'You see? I've baked just the thing for a present. Fresh sponge. Smell that.'

The cake has icing of a strange Spam colour. In its centre he has traced a large letter M in bright red wet icing.

'Bit fresh, that,' he says apologetically. 'I've only just done it. I didn't have enough left over to write "Marta".'

I'm afraid this time I do weep a little as I reach for his hand and squeeze it. He looks so touching standing there with his cake. How can I be angry with him for virtually shopping me to the police? And how can I not be slightly anxious about what might be in the cake? Gerry's cooking is, I have to say, an acquired taste.

Gerald

48

Poot

Poot

T. S. Eliot, casting around for onomatopoeic words to suggest what the thunder said, came up with *Datta, Dayadhvam* and *Damyata*, three Indian Test cricketers of the early nineteen twenties. When it comes to verbal equivalents for my own personal thunder, I can only produce

Poot

and a bit later

Pheeee . . . truff-*wuff*

Consciousness begins to coagulate gently around the notion *I am*. Opening my eyes is not yet an option so I assume I'm once again lying on the ground outside my own front door, helplessly venting gas after many hours' oblivion beneath the stars. Well, well, Samper. Stocious again. When I do get an eye open I see roses. That can't be right, but I don't really care.

Blutter

This time I open both eyes and notice the roses are painted on some sort of pale green surface. More, I find I am not on the ground at all but lying on a bed looking up at its headboard. Curious. Slowly I roll over and find beside me a dead camel.

Strange. That beige colour . . . *No!* My God, that's . . . that's *Marta* lying right next to me, blinking at the ceiling. The Bedouin traffic warden herself. This is her *bed*.

'You woke me up,' she says.

'I didn't speak,' I croak.

'Quite.'

Oh my God. We *can't* have . . . No, impossible. Unthinkable. No, no, no. Please God, *no*. 'That's the very last time I drink *galasiya*,' I promise, rolling away and falling painfully to the brick floor where I find an empty black bottle.

It's all right, Samper. Don't panic. All you need do is get yourself home, take lots of Alka-Seltzers, put on a pair of dark glasses and sit quietly under your pergola for the next few years. Then everything will get back to normal.